MISS BUSBY I... ...LONGATES

A
VERY
ELEGANT
MURDER

KAREN BAUGH MENUHIN
& ZOE MARKHAM

*For Heidi, for teaching me
not to walk over three drains xx*

CHAPTER 1

November 2nd, 1923

'Inspector McKay! What a lovely surprise.' Miss Busby smiled at the handsome Scot on her doorstep. Dressed in his customary sombre grey suit, his red hair and green eyes brought a warm flash of colour to the cold autumn morning.

'Good morning, Miss Busby,' he said, in his usual austere manner.

A horrible thought crossed Miss Busby's mind and she raised a hand to the pearls gracing her lilac twinset in alarm. 'I do hope there's nothing wrong?' she asked, thinking how unusual it was for the inspector to call unannounced, and so early to boot.

'No,' he was quick to reassure her. 'But I would like a wee word, if you've time?'

'Of course, do come in.' Smiling in relief, Miss Busby stepped aside and ushered him into the cottage. She had been up early that morning and the fire in the sitting room was cheerily ablaze, the room bright and cosy with her reading lamp lit beside her favourite armchair. She bade the inspector sit in the chair beside hers, as she moved her library book to the small end table where an empty coffee cup sat.

On the rug beside the fire Barnaby, her scruffy Jack Russell, wiry-haired, white with black and tan patches, opened one brown eye and offered their visitor a disdainful look. The inspector returned it in kind.

No barking this time, at least, Miss Busby thought. They were almost becoming friends.

'Would you like some tea, or coffee, Inspector?' she asked.

'No, thank you. I just met Lucy for breakfast at Brown's Café in Oxford. We had sufficient.'

'Oh! How is Lucy?' Miss Busby sat beside him, smoothing her dark woollen skirt neatly in place.

'Very well,' he replied, a smile momentarily lifting his stern face.

Miss Busby beamed, her blue eyes alight with warmth. Lucy Lannister, and her father Sir Richard Lannister, were dear friends of hers. The inspector had recently taken Lucy to Scotland to meet his family, and tongues had been wagging ever since regarding the prospect of an engagement on the horizon.

Miss Busby blinked. Was this what the young Scot had come to announce? Although surely Lucy would have come with him if that were the case. She peered closely at him in curiosity. He shifted uncomfortably in his chair.

Miss Busby, a veteran of the schoolroom for many years, sat patiently, eyebrows slightly lifted, and waited for him to come out with whatever was on his mind.

'I wonder if I might ask a rather…unorthodox… favour,' he opened cautiously.

Intrigued, Miss Busby sat forward and gave a small nod of encouragement.

'Are you familiar with Hamnett Hall Hotel?' he asked.

Miss Busby thought for a moment. 'Out Cheltenham way?'

He nodded. 'Quinton village, just the other side.'

'I've never had the pleasure of staying there, but I've driven past it several times with Adeline. A beautiful building in such elegant surroundings. There's a lake, I believe?'

He nodded again. 'The owner, Mrs Olivia Fortescue, died of a heart attack two nights ago at the hotel's annual Halloween Ball.'

'Oh.' Miss Busby was rather taken aback by the blunt delivery. 'What a shame.' She bowed her head a little in respect, before looking back at the inspector with a quizzical expression.

'Yes,' he murmured. 'But also rather convenient.'

Miss Busby tilted her head to the side. 'Not for Mrs Fortescue, I shouldn't imagine.'

'No,' he conceded, cheeks flushing slightly before his face hardened once more. 'But according to the hotel manager, she held a private dinner earlier that evening with several close friends and family, and was due to make an announcement the following morning regarding the heir to the hotel.'

Miss Busby felt a quick spark of suspicion ignite. Convenient indeed. But, as she reminded herself, leaping to conclusions rarely ended well. And she was hardly in possession of all the facts.

'How odd,' she remarked. 'Perhaps the lady was aware of a health issue, and was simply trying to ensure all her affairs were in order?'

The inspector shook his head. 'The doctor who attended, Dr Woods, had been her physician for years. He said she was in excellent health.'

Curiouser and curiouser, thought Miss Busby.

'With no children of her own, there was some debate over who would be chosen to inherit,' the inspector continued.

'Ah.' Miss Busby sat back in her chair. 'Did she not leave a will?'

'She was reportedly in the process of writing it prior to the announcement,' he replied, one fiery brow arched in evident suspicion.

'And has a copy been found?'

'It has not.'

'Oh dear.' Miss Busby clasped her hands in her lap. 'And so you suspect foul play.'

'I do,' he confirmed. 'The woman was in good health, and was seen dancing enthusiastically at the ball.'

Miss Busby straightened her sleeves and took a moment to think, determined to remain objective. 'How old was Mrs Fortescue?' she asked.

'In her early seventies.'

She sighed. Her own range. 'It pains me to say it, Inspector, but perhaps enthusiastic dancing straight after dinner at that age could be considered quite capable of bringing on a heart attack?'

The inspector looked into the flickering flames of the fire for a moment. 'Aye,' he finally conceded, 'that's what the doctor said. But not once in all the years he'd seen her prior, had he noted anything to indicate a weakness of the heart.'

'I believe that's often how these things happen,' Miss Busby said softly. 'A blessing, perhaps, in its own way. Are you sure I can't offer you tea or coffee?'

'Yes, quite sure.' He looked down at his watch. 'I'm due in Oxford at 11 and don't have much time.'

Miss Busby raised an expectant brow.

The inspector took a breath. 'You said you haven't had the pleasure of staying at Hamnett Hall Hotel. Would you like to?'

'I would like a great many things, Inspector,' she replied carefully.

He ran a swift hand through his dark red hair and tried again. 'As a favour to me, Miss Busby, would you consider staying there for a few days? We're waiting for the post-mortem, but there's a backlog just now. All the flu that's so prevalent. Given Mrs Fortescue's age and the implication of natural causes, she must wait her turn.'

'I… why on earth would you want me to do that?' Miss Busby asked, confusion creasing her brow.

'I'm leading another investigation in Cowley,' he explained. 'And given the circumstances, there's nothing I can do at Hamnett Hall until we receive the results of the post-mortem. If something suspicious shows up, as I'm convinced it will, I can take action. Until then, my hands are tied.'

'But what can I possibly do there that you can't?' she pressed.

'You can watch the guests for me.'

'All of them? There must have been hordes at the ball!'

'Just the seven who attended the private dinner. The hotel closes for the winter on the 7th of November, and doesn't re-open until Christmas. I'm afraid if the Post Mortem drags on too long, I may lose my suspects.'

'But you don't know whether they are suspects,' she pointed out.

'I'd rather not take the risk.'

Miss Busby rose to her feet and took a log from the basket by the fire, adding it to the flames with the aid of a good prod from the poker to ensure it caught. 'I'm afraid I need another coffee,' she said. 'You'd better come through to the kitchen.'

Barnaby followed instantly, suspecting there would be biscuits involved. Miss Busby passed the tin containing his treats to the inspector, before busying herself with the range and the coffee pot. She usually only had one cup of coffee a day, but today, she felt, was to be an exception.

'The hotel must have been full for the ball. Presumably any one of the attendees could have been responsible,' she said, leaning over to open the window and let Pud, her ginger Tom, in. He'd appeared the moment he heard voices.

'Does the cat have biscuits, too?' the inspector asked, both animals now sitting expectantly at his feet.

'He does not. He can have a little milk, though.' She passed him the jug and indicated a small saucer on the side as she set the water to boil.

'The hotel manager confirmed that Mrs Fortescue didn't eat or drink anything during the course of the ball,' the inspector said, straightening up as Pud lapped contentedly. 'If anyone were to have given her something that would bring on heart-attack-like symptoms, they would have had to do so at the dinner.'

Miss Busby nodded thoughtfully. It made sense. 'And if they were all close acquaintances, I suppose one of them would have been the heir about to be named.'

'Aye, and any of the rest might have been none too happy about it,' he added.

'Well, surely you have a list of the names of those present?'

'Of course.' The inspector reached inside his jacket and pulled out a sheet of paper covered in small, neat handwriting. 'Sergeant Miller made a note of those present, along with their circumstances.'

'Then once you have the results, and if your suspicions are confirmed, you'll be able to swoop in and put matters right. I can't see what I could possibly achieve in the meantime that would be of any help.'

The inspector gave a wry smile. 'I'm sure I don't need to remind you of your track record. You have a rare way with people, Miss Busby. They confide in you in a manner they never would with me.'

Miss Busby felt her cheeks flush. She had rather reluctantly been involved in solving a number of murders since the inspector had come to Oxford, and thought it had been a source of irritation to the Scot. 'Well… I had a great deal of help,' she pointed out. 'And no one likes talking to the police. Besides, you were never far behind.'

The kettle began to whistle.

Miss Busby poured the water onto the pot, the rich, warm smell of coffee quickly filling the small space. She took a seat at the scrubbed pine kitchen table. The inspector set the sheet of paper down in front of her.

'I'm sure I needn't remind you that this is confidential,' he warned in stern tone, 'but if you were to require company in the form of, say, Mrs Adeline Fanshawe, the two of you could perhaps peruse the list en route to the hotel, before making your own discreet observations in situ?'

Miss Busby's eyes widened. It wasn't often she heard the words 'Adeline' and 'discreet' in the same sentence. 'You want me to take Adeline?' she queried. The inspector and her forthright friend hadn't always seen eye to eye, to say the least.

'I suspect Mrs Fanshawe would prove something of a distraction,' he explained with a tight smile. 'Enabling you to focus your attention more carefully on observing the suspects.'

'If, indeed, they are—'

'Aye.' He waved a dismissive hand.

Miss Busby poured her coffee, dropped in a cube of sugar and added a generous dash of milk before stirring thoughtfully.

'You've always been rather forthright in your opinion of "civilians" getting involved in police matters in the past,' she reminded him.

The inspector gave a rare chuckle. 'I may have been, yes. But even I learn from my mistakes, Miss Busby. You've been a help to me, and I'm asking for more of that help now. It's selfish of me, perhaps, and you're more than entitled to say no. But… should you have a few days to spare, Oxford Station will gladly foot the bill for your stay at Hamnett Hall.'

Miss Busby's mind raced. The inspector had never asked her for help. Quite the reverse – she and Adeline had frequently had to creep around so as not to tread on his toes. But he is asking now, and surely I can't refuse? she thought.

He reached into his inside pocket once more, pulling out a small photograph which he passed to her. It was of a mature lady with white hair and bright, lively eyes not dissimilar to her own.

'Mrs Fortescue,' he said gently.

The woman's face was creased into a merry smile, round cheeks, kindness and a zest for life clear in her expression. The image was somehow captivating. She looked the sort who could be a friend, and Miss Busby instantly understood the inspector's concerns.

What if it was me, she found herself thinking. Who would be my advocate, I wonder, if I were ever in such a situation? Adeline, of course, wouldn't hesitate.

Noting the inspector giving a worried glance to his watch once more, Miss Busby handed back the photograph.

'I haven't had a night away in longer than I care to remember,' she said. 'I will walk you to your car, Inspector, and we can agree the arrangements.'

CHAPTER 2

When Sir Richard Lannister pulled up at Lavender Cottage an hour or so later to collect Miss Busby for their weekly trip to Lily's Tea Rooms, he was surprised to hear she'd telephoned Adeline to ask her to join them.

'There's something I'd like to talk to both of you about,' she explained as he drove them through Bloxford's narrow lanes – the bordering hedges awash with red hawthorn and holly berries bright in the cold sunshine – and towards Little Minton.

'Should I be nervous?' Richard asked with a smile. He was wearing a smart navy blazer with dark, impeccably creased trousers, a crisp white shirt, and a navy and yellow patterned tie. Although retired, he still dressed every day as if he were en route to the newsroom. Miss Busby always thought it made him look rather dashing.

'Oh, I shouldn't think so,' she mused, but wouldn't say any more until Adeline was with them.

As they came into Little Minton, the gleaming lamps of Lily's Tea Rooms shone invitingly through the large bow window at the front, and Richard was pleased to find space to park right outside. Although his arthritis had improved somewhat over the late summer, the cold was starting to leave its mark; the shorter the walk, the better.

Maggie Trounce, the waitress, smart as always in her black and white uniform, showed them to their usual table in the window, where they ordered a pot of tea and a large mixed platter of sandwiches.

'No Barnaby today?' Maggie asked, as she set an extra place for Adeline.

'No, I left him to keep the cat company,' Miss Busby explained, just as the sight of Adeline's distinctive white Rolls Royce appeared at the top of the road. Purring down the High Street, it came to an abrupt halt mere inches from the back of Richard's black Austin Twenty, causing him a momentary twinge of alarm.

'I'll be back in just a tick,' Maggie said.

'Isabelle!' Adeline entered with a wave and a smile. Dressed in a maroon frock under a mink-trimmed tan coat and a string of fat pearls, she looked elegant and striking as she strode into the room. 'And Richard.' She held out a hand, which he pecked gallantly. 'Now, what's this all about?' she asked as she sat and looked at them both expectantly.

'No good asking me!' Richard said. 'Isabelle?'

And so Miss Busby recounted the details of the inspector's visit, and his offer, as Adeline's eyes widened in surprise throughout.

'He wants us to observe each of the seven guests who attended the private dinner, to see if any of them are uneasy, or seem unnaturally relieved, that sort of thing,' she concluded, recalling his parting remarks to her as he'd rushed off back to Oxford. 'We are to keep an eye and an ear out for any hint of motive, or anything at all that points to Olivia's death not being of natural causes.'

'Are we indeed?' Adeline asked, one eyebrow raised.

'If we agree to help, of course,' Miss Busby qualified.

'And he asked for me specifically?' Adeline narrowed her eyes.

'He did,' Miss Busby said gravely.

'Well, it is about time we were properly appreciated, I should say!' she suddenly beamed, then had another thought. 'But Hamnett Hall is terribly expensive, will he really pay, do you think?'

'Yes, or the police station will, I suppose. What do you think?' Miss Busby looked from Adeline to Richard. 'Should we go?'

'I'm not sure it's a good idea,' Richard said. 'It may be dangerous, Isabelle. Have you looked at the notes Sergeant Miller took?' Richard seemed less swayed by the thought of the all-expenses-paid holiday.

'I only glanced down at the names,' Miss Busby said, reaching into her bag to retrieve the sheet of paper. 'I thought we could read them together.'

'Here we go then.' Maggie arrived with the tea and sandwiches, distracting them as she bustled about with pretty cups and plates, and stacks of salmon, ham, cheese, and cucumber sandwiches. They busied themselves with the generous fare, only returning to the matter at hand when plates were empty and a refill for the pot was called for.

'If someone murdered the poor lady, they won't take kindly to you turning up and nosing about, Isabelle,' Richard continued in a cautious tone.

'We don't nose about,' Adeline objected. 'We simply observe. And besides, it's more likely than not Mrs Fortescue simply overdid the dancing. But under what guise would we check in here?' she asked, the glint of excitement taking hold in her eyes.

Miss Busby and Inspector McKay had discussed this en route to his car. 'He thinks one of us ought to pretend we knew Olivia, if only very loosely. That would let us talk to the others about her more freely.'

'I'll do it!' Adeline instantly volunteered. 'What sort of woman was she? I shall need to concoct a credible tale.'

Miss Busby returned her attention to the sheet of paper, placing it on the table between them. Adeline swept it up and read aloud, 'Mrs Olivia Fort—'

'Shh, quietly, Adeline,' Miss Busby cautioned.

Adeline looked around. The tables nearest them were empty, but several couples on the edges of the tea room had looked over at her pronouncement. She cleared her throat, lowered her volume, and continued, 'Mrs Olivia Fortescue. Displaced Hungarian aristocracy. Worked as a chambermaid at Hamnett Hall before marrying the owner. Inherited the hotel outright upon his death.'

She set the paper down thoughtfully. 'Well, I can't imagine how I would find a link between myself and a chambermaid,' she said.

'Yes, it might be tricky,' Miss Busby agreed. 'Unless we say we stayed there several years ago? And perhaps knew the woman from her earlier role?'

'They'll keep records,' Adeline warned.

'Yes but I doubt they'll go trawling through them,' Miss Busby pointed out.

Richard set his cup on the table and made a faintly disapproving noise. 'I think you should be rather more careful ,' he warned. 'Any connection to the woman might put you in the frame yourselves. You ought to see who you're dealing with, at least.' He took up the paper. 'Let's see… Arthur Fortescue,' he read, 'the late Mr Fortescue's nephew. Ah, an inheritance candidate, I'm sure.'

Miss Busby nodded. 'Olivia had no children of her own to consider.'

'Next is Miss Clara Harrowby,' Richard continued, 'orphaned daughter of Kitty and Harold Harrowby, the former housekeeper and groom at the hotel. Taken under Olivia's wing upon her parents' demise. Interesting.'

'Perhaps considered a child of her own in all but name,' Miss Busby mused. 'There could have been conflict between the two.'

'But why kill Olivia, and not simply bump off the cuckoo?' Adeline pointed out. Then, the hunt clearly on as far as she was concerned, she asked eagerly, 'Who's next?'

'Mr Ludlow, Olivia's solicitor,' Richard supplied.

'Odd,' Miss Busby mused, 'that he should be included in the gathering.'

'He must have been helping her with the will,' Adeline said excitedly. 'We ought to start with him!'

'Next are two old friends of Olivia's,' Richard read on. 'Lady Flora, and Major Gresham.'

'A Lady and a Major? Neither likely to need the money from bumping her off, then,' Adeline dismissed them with a wave. 'Next?'

'The hotel manager, another Hungarian by the looks of the name. Mr Lázár.'

'He must have been the one to tell the inspector about Olivia not eating or drinking anything at the ball,' Miss Busby noted.

'Thereby putting himself in the frame as one of the seven at dinner,' Richard observed

'Could be a double bluff,' Adeline suggested. 'Covering his tracks. His job would have been at risk if the heir didn't approve of him. One to watch. Who's the last?'

'Sir Gregory Penn,' Richard read. 'An old friend of the family who resides at the hotel permanently.'

'Sitting tenant.' Adeline thought for a moment. 'Also at risk if the heir isn't a fan. Although he may be well-off enough not to worry either way. Hamnett Hall isn't cheap! Well, they don't sound too formidable a bunch,' she concluded.

'No, I suppose not,' Richard admitted.

'And it's not as if we'll be taking statements or making an arrest,' Miss Busby added, seeing the concern in his eyes all the same. 'We'll only be watching them until the inspector receives the results of the post-mortem. Then, if need be, we'll tell him everything we've noticed, and we'll be home in no time.'

Richard took her hand in his and smiled, his deep blue eyes alight with warmth. 'Of course. Silly of me to worry. Alistair McKay would never put you in danger, and Lord knows you deserve a treat. But you will telephone me, won't you?'

'Every evening, if you'd like me to,' Miss Busby replied with a smile of her own.

Adeline gave what sounded like a very quiet *tsk*. Miss Busby knew her friend was fiercely independent and would hold little truck with her checking in with Richard. But Richard was her friend too, so she would just have to put up with it.

'When did you say the place closes?' Adeline asked.

'November the 7th,' Miss Busby said.

'Well then, there's no time to lose. We ought to go today! I'll go and pack, and then collect you from Lavender Cottage Isabelle. How soon can you be ready?'

'In no time at all,' Miss Busby replied with a smile. She had packed a small suitcase as soon as the inspector had left. She had also included a few other items – a magnifying glass, a lady's magazine to read (and hide behind) as well as a notebook and pen.

'Then I shall head off. Thank you for lunch, Richard,' she added graciously, before disappearing with a swish of her elegant coat.

'The woman is always such a whirlwind,' Richard said, indicating to Maggie to bring the bill. 'But I'm glad you're both happy. It seems you have quite an adventure ahead!'

'It does rather, doesn't it?' she agreed, picking up her handbag, ready to leave. 'I'm rather excited to go. There are said to be some lovely walks around the grounds, with a very pretty lake. Barnaby will be in seventh heaven.'

Miss Busby waved goodbye to Maggie as they left the cafe.

'You're taking the dog?' he asked in surprise.

'Of course. I can't leave him on his own. He's not as independent as Pud.'

'He could have come and stayed with me. Should I take Pud?' Richard asked, holding the car door open for her.

'Oh, I never thought of that,' she said, sliding into the leather passenger seat. 'I telephoned Enid before I left. She's going to keep him at Spring Meadows for a few days. Dennis is going to drop him off with the afternoon post. Pud will adore it, there'll be so much fuss on offer. But perhaps you'll take my spare key, in case of anything amiss?'

'Of course,' Richard said as he turned the wheel to head away up the High Street. 'So…you'd already decided you'd be going before you spoke to us, then?' he asked.

Miss Busby cleared her throat and smiled as she looked out of the window. Perhaps she was rather more independent than Adeline had given her credit for.

CHAPTER 3

Barnaby sat in the back of the Rolls on his tartan blanket, sandwiched between Miss Busby's small suitcase and Adeline's larger, and smarter, one. Miss Busby had telephoned ahead to the hotel once she'd returned to Lavender Cottage, and booked them adjoining rooms.

'The receptionist sounded nervous,' she told Adeline, as they swerved around an oblivious pheasant and headed for the main road. 'She said she wasn't sure about new bookings "under the circumstances", and would have to check with the manager.'

'The Hungarian chap,' Adeline said, nodding sagely. 'It'll be his job to keep everything running smoothly until the legalities are all settled. Without a will, I expect everything will be up in the air for a while. But it's no good them turning everyone away in the meantime.'

'Yes, well, he must have agreed as she soon called back to confirm the booking.'

'I should imagine most guests left the morning after

the ball. The death will have cast a pall over the place,' Adeline said.

Miss Busby nodded as she gazed out of the window. The leaves of the trees lining the road and dotting the passing fields were taking on autumn shades of deep oranges, reds, and yellows, in colourful contrast to the dark green surrounding them. It was a striking enough canvas to forgive the sharpening chill in the air ten times over.

'I suppose McKay is banking on all seven of the others staying put?' Adeline continued.

'Yes,' she agreed, returning her attention to the road ahead. 'They're all connected to Olivia, and he's quite sure they'll remain for the funeral, at least.'

'Even if only to keep up appearances,' Adeline added darkly.

Miss Busby sighed. It was rather sad that both Adeline and the inspector immediately assumed the worst of people, but she could understand why. Her time spent helping the inspector over the past year had certainly highlighted the darker side of human nature. But there had been bright flashes of love, kindness, and compassion to boot. She resolved to keep an open mind once they arrived at the hotel, if only to counterbalance an avid Adeline on the prowl.

'Are you really going to telephone Richard every evening?' Adeline asked, eyes narrowing as she looked across at her.

'Yes, because he would like me to. I would do the same for you if you asked,' she pointed out.

Adeline harrumphed. 'You know, there are rumours of more than one engagement on the horizon…' she teased.

'Started by whom, I wonder?' Miss Busby riposted, one silver brow arched.

Adeline turned her attention back to the road just in time to take the left turn for Cheltenham. The road led them down into the valley and carried them from the bright autumn sunshine into a deepening hazy mist. 'Well, the two of you are certainly close, and he clearly cares for you. You could do an awful lot worse, you know,' she added, surprisingly gently.

Miss Busby gave a sad smile. 'I've told you before, Adeline, I could never do that to Randolf.'

'He has been gone an awfully long time, Isabelle. And he would want you to be happy.'

Caught rather by surprise, Miss Busby swallowed back a sudden lump in her throat.

'I keep thinking about Olivia,' Adeline went on. 'Having a heart attack whilst dancing. Any of us could be taken at any moment, Isabelle. We really ought to dance while we can.'

Miss Busby thought to mention that dancing may well have been the cause of Olivia's demise, but decided against it. Adeline was being kind and thoughtful and she loved her for it.

'I am happy. I'm extremely fortunate to have wonderful friends around me, and I thank the Lord every day for my good fortune.' She reached a hand to Adeline's, and squeezed briefly, before letting go and clearing her throat. 'But now we really ought to decide on our plan of attack. What are we going to say when we arrive – did we know Olivia? Or not?'

'I've been thinking about that,' Adeline said, speeding up to overtake an omnibus struggling with the incline. Miss Busby gripped the bottom of her seat as they swung around it at speed. 'And I think I ought to say I have a friend in Cheltenham I often visit – we are visiting her now, in fact, and staying at the hotel to make things easier on her. I shall mention that I encountered Mrs Fortescue in town from time to time and exchanged pleasantries. The woman must have done her shopping there, and it will be almost impossible to disprove.'

'That would have been a passing acquaintance at best,' Miss Busby pointed out.

'Yes, but that's all we'll need, and it keeps us safer from suspicion if anyone were to find out we were lying.'

Miss Busby glanced to Adeline with a look of respect.

'This isn't my first investigation you know,' Adeline said with a mischievous smile.

'Indeed. Oh, there's the sign for Quinton Village, look,' Miss Busby pointed as they sped past it.

'No matter.' Adeline powered on until the road widened before jabbing at the brakes, then swinging the car around in a generous arc. 'We'll get it this time.'

'Oh do slow down a little Adeline,' Miss Busby pleaded as they turned off for the village. 'I haven't been this way for a while, and with all this mist...I can't remember exactly–'

'There it is,' Adeline interrupted as the grandeur of Hamnett Hall Hotel emerged dramatically from the haze on a rise before them. 'You can't miss it!'

'Season of mists and mellow fruitfulness,' Miss Busby said, momentarily lost in the idyllic view.

'Yeats?' Adeline asked.

'Keats.'

'Ah, I always get the two muddled.'

A long, winding drive led up to the elegant, ivy-covered building dominating the surrounding land-scape. Impeccably manicured grounds sprawled into the distance beyond. To the right of the lane, a small street with a few little shops, including a baker, Post Office, and a chemist, stood quietly in the mist, a row of pretty thatched cottages sitting just behind, and a small public house on the corner.

Adeline steered them left, and Barnaby sprung up in the back, front paws on the window to look out at the delights awaiting him.

'Barnaby come off there,' Adeline admonished, before offering a consolatory, 'You'll be out exploring in no time. We all shall!'

As they purred up the drive, gravel crunching beneath the tyres, Miss Busby found she didn't share the same enthusiasm as either her friend or her dog. It must be the weather, she thought. It made the place look rather foreboding. And not in the least bit mellow.

They were met in the hotel courtyard by a young porter, his plain country face betraying a nervous air.

He fidgeted with the sleeves of his smart blue coat as he waited for Adeline to park. She made several attempts to fit in between the two other automobiles present, before simply disembarking and handing the young man the keys. His nerves appeared to dissipate immediately, and his eyes lit up in anticipation.

'I shall check it carefully for scratches,' Adeline warned, as Miss Busby let Barnaby out of the back.

'Miss Busby and Mrs Fanshawe is it?' the lad asked. 'I'll park it proper after I take yer bags up. Annie's making up Rooms 10 and 11 on the first floor. There's a lift,' he added, looking to Miss Busby. 'It's 'fer the suitcases really, but y'can come up with me if y'like.'

She straightened. 'That won't be necessary, thank you.'

Adeline made a brave attempt to mask a laugh.

'Well, I'm Jimmy. Just ask 'fer me if there's anything you need bringin' up or down. I'm 'ere to 'elp!'

'Thank you,' Miss Busby said with a smile. 'I think I ought to let my dog have a walk first before going inside.'

'He's lively, in't he?' Jimmy said, watching Barnaby dart through a beautifully planted flowerbed full of lavender and roses, his nose to the soil. 'I can watch him for you, miss, and bring him up with the cases after, if y'like.'

'That would be kind, thank you,' Adeline answered for her. 'Come along, Isabelle, let's go inside and out of this damp.'

'It'll be bright again in the morning, miss, you'll see,' Jimmy promised cheerfully. 'Gets like this in the afternoons sometimes down this way, but it don't stay like it 'fer long.'

Miss Busby smiled and reached into the pocket of her skirt, passing the young man a shortbread biscuit. 'His name is Barnaby, and he'll follow you if he knows you have one of these,' she explained.

'I always say you ought to dress younger, Isabelle,' Adeline said as they made their way through the glass front doors. 'It would take years off you, then young porters won't assume you need to use the lift.'

'I am perfectly happy with my wardrobe,' Miss Busby admonished. She was wearing her favourite fawn jacket with a matching skirt and cream blouse. 'I was just a little stiff from sitting in the car for an hour, that's all!'

A polished reception desk stood in the foyer, which was large and imposing with a distinctly grand feel. The walls were papered in heavy red and gold patterns, and the fixtures and fittings gleamed with gilding and beeswax. There was a log fire burning in the hearth of the reception area just beyond the desk, with several comfortable looking armchairs set in front of it. A large oak staircase wound upwards on the right and two heavy doors led off the foyer, one of which was opened by a short, older man in a dark suit.

'Miss Busby and Mrs Fanshawe?' he asked.

Miss Busby nodded.

'I am Lázár, the manager here. Your rooms are not yet made ready. Annie should have explained. The booking was made late, and so there will be a slight delay. If you will wait in the lounge, I will come when preparations are completed,' he said, a slight Eastern European accent giving his words a rather abrupt tone. He added more warmly, 'You will find tea and coffee, to your preference.'

'Nothing stronger, to drive out the chill?' Adeline asked hopefully.

'Of course, should you wish,' he said, with a nod.

'Is Annie the receptionist I spoke to on the telephone?' Miss Busby asked.

A flash of irritation shone in the man's dark eyes. 'Annie is the maid. She should not have answered.' A look of sadness suddenly softened his stern exterior. 'But she is only trying to help. We are at sevens and sixes. The owner of our hotel has passed away.'

'Oh, I am sorry to hear that,' Miss Busby said, just as Adeline flung a hand up to her mouth.

'Not Mrs Fortescue?' she gasped, taking a step back.

Lázár looked at her in surprise. 'You were acquainted?'

'Yes indeed. Well, in passing,' she added, at a slight nudge from Miss Busby. 'I met her in town on several occasions, and found her most charming.'

He nodded. 'It was most sudden. A heart attack. We can hardly believe she is gone.'

'What will happen to–' Adeline began, before a mud-covered Barnaby pitter-pattered across the black and white ceramic tiles.

'Sorry, miss,' a breathless Jimmy called, hot on his heels. 'He found the lake and got reet dirty. I'll take him through to the scullery an' get him all cleaned up fer you.

He's fast, in't he?' he said, scooping the muddy dog up in his arms. 'Sorry, sir,' he muttered to the manager, 'I'll mop that mud right up,' he promised, before hurrying off.

Lázár shot his departing figure an exasperated look. 'Sevens and sixes,' he sighed. 'It cannot be helped. If you will follow me, please?' He strode to the door opposite and opened it for the ladies. 'The lounge may be found in this way.'

They followed down a thickly carpeted corridor with several paintings of the hotel, gardens and surrounding countryside lining the walls. He opened another door off to the left and ushered them into a large room furnished with small round tables surrounded by more cushioned armchairs and sofas upholstered in a deep maroon. There were standing lamps in the corners as well as a glittering chandelier overhead. Tea and coffee urns were set at either end of a gleaming mahogany bar, where an elegant young woman dressed all in black was pouring a large glass from a bottle of red wine.

Adeline gave the place an appreciative look, as Miss Busby noticed four other guests seated on sofas in front of the blazing fire.

'Please, you may freely serve yourself of tea or coffee.' Lázár said as he glanced at the young lady. The young lady gave him the scantest of nods in return, and he added, 'or choose as you wish from the bar. I will return when your rooms are ready.' He gave a bow then turned smartly about and left.

Adeline was preoccupied with the other people in the room. 'Look, Isabelle,' she whispered, taking them in. 'Shall we guess which ones they are?'

CHAPTER 4

'Let's get our drinks, and then we'll see,' Miss Busby said, crossing the room and offering the young woman a gracious smile. 'May I have a small sweet sherry, please?' she asked.

Close up she noticed that the woman's grey-blue eyes were red-rimmed, as if she'd been crying, and for a moment she thought they flashed angrily at her.

'We shouldn't be open,' she said, flicking her long blonde hair back from her forehead as she looked from Miss Busby to the group in the corner. 'I think it's disrespectful.' She took a sip of the wine she'd just poured.

'Oh,' said Miss Busby, taken aback by the young lady's tone. 'I'm afraid we—'

'You only booked this afternoon,' she continued, looking Miss Busby up and down. 'You've come to gawp, I suppose?'

'We most certainly have not,' Adeline objected sternly, joining her. 'I am visiting a friend in Cheltenham and made a late booking as she is feeling too unwell for overnight guests. And I will have a sherry, please.'

'There's no need to be so rude, Clara. Ladies, I'd be very happy to serve your drinks,' a young man with a rather dishevelled but rakishly handsome appearance called from the corner. He rose from his seat, then thrust a hand to his head almost instantly, wincing as if in pain.

Clara gave a snort of derision, turning towards the array of bottles behind the bar. 'I'm perfectly capable, Arthur. I wouldn't want to disturb your hangover.'

Miss Busby could almost hear Adeline's brain whirring. Clara and Arthur – the two youngsters from the list, and the most obvious choices for the inheritance. They did indeed seem to be at odds.

The young man sat back down with a huff.

'Look,' Clara said sulkily, banging a sherry bottle onto the bar, 'it's been a terrible couple of days and I don't know why Lázár is still taking in guests. But I'm sorry, it's not your fault. I didn't mean to be rude.'

Miss Busby noticed the expensive jewellery adorning her neck and wrist.

Adeline asked, 'Are you Clara Harrowby?'

'Yes,' she said in surprise. 'How did you know?'

'I am Mrs Adeline Fanshawe. I was acquainted with Mrs Fortescue,' she said. 'She often mentioned you.'

'Did she?' Clara's eyes widened. 'What did she say?'

Miss Busby turned to Adeline with a quizzical look.

'It was such an awful shock,' Adeline adeptly sidestepped the question, 'hearing of her passing just now. I had no idea.' She added a sniffle for verisimilitude.

'Oh, you poor thing.' Clara's entire demeanour

softened instantly. 'You ought to come and meet the others. It was a dreadful shock to us too; we're all in the same boat.' Abandoning the sherry bottle, she came out from behind the bar and took Adeline's arm, leading her over to the fireplace. Miss Busby, rather bemused, followed suit.

'This is Mrs Fanshawe,' Clara announced, pointing Adeline at an armchair. 'She was a friend of Olivia's, and has only just heard the news.'

Miss Busby cleared her throat.

'Oh, and this is…' Clara continued, uncertainly.

'Miss Isabelle Busby,' Miss Busby supplied.

'Did you know Olivia too?' a frail, elderly lady who seemed to have almost been swallowed up by the sofa asked. She, too, was dressed all in black, with a matching bonnet covering all but a few determined wisps of thin white hair. Pale pink lipstick was poorly applied to lips that creased upwards into a welcoming smile.

'I'm afraid I didn't have the pleasure,' Miss Busby replied, taking the armchair beside Adeline. 'I am simply accompanying my friend, Mrs Fanshawe.'

'This is Lady Flora Benbow,' Clara supplied.

The old lady smiled sadly. 'I prefer Flora, dear. I never was one to stand on ceremony.'

Miss Busby liked her immediately.

'Olivia was a dear friend of mine,' Flora went on, reaching into the depths of her handbag and withdrawing a handkerchief. 'I don't know what I shall do without her.'

Clara stepped across to place a comforting hand on the old woman's shoulder. 'And this is Major Gresham,' she continued, indicating the distinguished gentleman sitting ramrod straight next to Flora. Dressed in a smart but rather worn navy blazer, with perfectly pressed grey trousers and a pale blue shirt, he sported a striped regimental tie. He looked to be in his seventies and took both newcomers in with intelligent grey eyes. He nodded politely to each in turn but remained silent.

'And I am Sir Gregory Penn,' a slightly younger gentleman spoke. Tall and distinguished-looking, in a dapper navy suit, with dark hair greying at the temples, his brown eyes alight with curiosity as he looked up at them. He rose from the second sofa. 'And I must confess, I do stand on ceremony. After all, one must use everything at one's disposal, mustn't one?'

He bowed to both ladies. Miss Busby noted that his eyes lingered rather longer in Adeline's direction.

'Have you stayed here before?' he asked Adeline with a disarming smile.

'No, I usually stay with friends in town,' she explained, a slight flush rising in her cheeks.

'Ah. Thought I would've remembered you otherwise! I pop down quite often. Used to be good pals with Olivia's late husband. Capital chap. Is that your Rolls outside?'

'It is,' Adeline said with a gracious nod.

'Fine machine!' he pronounced, giving Adeline another smile before sitting back down. 'Very fine indeed!'

Miss Busby noticed Major Gresham shoot him a look of disapproval.

'And I'm Arthur Fortescue,' the handsome young man said quietly from beside Sir Gregory. 'Olivia Fortescue was my aunt.' He spoke with a refined accent. His charcoal grey suit indicated he had an excellent tailor, as well as complementing his light-grey eyes beautifully.

'She wasn't really,' Clara was quick to correct. 'She married your uncle.'

'Yes, that's generally how it works, old girl,' he sighed with exasperation, rubbing his temples once more.

'And how did you all know poor Olivia?' Adeline asked.

'She was my dearest friend.' Flora was the first to answer. 'She allowed Major Gresham and I to make Hamnett Hall our home. She wouldn't hear of taking a penny from us, would she Major?' She turned to her neighbour who nodded a gruff assent. 'And of course she never charged you either, did she Gregory?' She turned sharp eyes to him.

Miss Busby noted the lack of the title 'Sir' with interest.

'She greatly valued our companionship,' Gregory replied easily. 'You can't put a price on that.'

Flora looked about to reply, when the door to the lounge swung open and a tired-looking man in a crisp navy suit entered. He looked at the newcomers with surprise.

'And here's Mr Ludlow,' Clara supplied. 'He's Olivia's solicitor. He's dealing with…well… there are the usual legal matters to resolve, of course. Although things are rather complicated, given the circumstances.'

'Good afternoon,' Ludlow said, with a raised eyebrow as Clara introduced them. 'I'm surprised Lázár took a booking. Where is he, anyway? He's not at reception. I need to talk to him.'

'I don't know,' Clara said, 'but he'll be back as soon as the ladies' bedrooms are ready.'

The man sighed, and slumped down into the last remaining armchair, hugging a worn leather briefcase in his lap. Miss Busby thought he might at least have offered the seat to Clara.

'And so you are all staying at the hotel until these… legal matters… are resolved?' Adeline asked.

The solicitor's weary eyes darkened as he shot Adeline a suspicious look.

'It must have been such a terrible loss for you all,' Miss Busby jumped in. 'Was there no warning at all of poor Mrs Fortescue's condition?'

'No,' Clara said, tugging at the long sleeves of her black dress. 'One minute she was dancing, and the next–'

'Oh, don't, Clara dear,' Flora interjected, her voice cracking with emotion. 'It's too awful.'

Clara nodded sadly. 'It was terrible, but she always appreciated a grand exit. I suppose she would've rather enjoyed the drama of it all. I mean, not that she'd have wanted to die, of course. But if one has to…'

'At least it was all over quickly,' Arthur said, closing his eyes. 'Aunt Olivia wouldn't have wanted to linger on with a bad heart, drama or no drama.'

Major Gresham's eyes flashed angrily between the two

youngsters. Miss Busby watched him with interest; he hadn't yet said a word but there seemed to be something brimming beneath the surface of his stiff exterior.

'I'm sure, all things considered,' Ludlow said, his voice heavy with an edge, 'Mrs Fortescue would have much preferred to live long enough to finish what she had started.'

Miss Busby's head shot up with interest, just as the lounge door opened once again, and a now damp and rather fluffy Barnaby flew into the room.

'Who's this now?' Sir Gregory asked, eyebrows raised.

'This is Barnaby. My Jack Russell,' Miss Busby said.

'Oh, isn't he adorable!' Flora gushed, as Barnaby went straight to her. She bent to stroke him softly. 'Such an intelligent breed.'

'Mischievous little blighters,' Sir Gregory muttered.

'Yes,' Flora agreed. 'Mischief takes a great deal of intelligence, you know.'

Miss Busby smiled.

'Your rooms are ready, ladies.' Lázár's clipped tones sounded from the doorway, making her jump. He must have come in behind the dog and not been noticed in the commotion. 'Would you like to please, follow me?'

'I never did get my sherry,' Adeline huffed as she rose to her feet.

'What's that? Sherry? I should be delighted to buy you one, dear lady,' Sir Gregory offered gallantly, shooting to his feet.

Flora arched a brow. 'Goodness me, I don't know that I've ever seen you buy a drink, Gregory.'

He turned to her with a rather strained smile. 'Now, Flora, you are very upset. I quite understand. Perhaps I can bring you a drink as well?'

'No, thank you. Having observed young Arthur's suffering this afternoon, I should rather not.'

Arthur offered a wry smile.

'Very well. Mrs Fanshawe, are you game?' Sir Gregory asked. 'I should be delighted to see you up to your room once you're suitably fortified.'

Adeline shot an enquiring look at Miss Busby, who gave a little shrug.

'How kind, Sir Gregory,' she smiled and sat down again.

'Come along Barnaby,' Miss Busby called with a sigh. 'Lovely to meet you all,' she called to the others, turning to find them all preoccupied with Adeline, who was now the centre of attention. She watched her friend for a moment, realising that the inspector had known exactly what he was doing in suggesting she invite her.

'Mrs Fortescue seems to have been very well-loved,' Miss Busby said to Lázár as they made their way up the grand staircase. Barnaby scurried on ahead with his nose to the thick carpet.

'She will be greatly missed,' Lázár said, then fell silent once more.

Before Miss Busby could think of another way to try and get him talking, they reached the first-floor landing. A young maid in a simple black and white uniform, dark hair pinned neatly back beneath a starched white cap, was wheeling a cart of cleaning items down the corridor towards them. She stopped in delight at the sight of the dog.

'Well now, you're a handsome chap!' she said, bending to ruffle his ears.

Lázár cleared his throat loudly and she quickly straightened, not meeting their eyes as she scurried past.

'Is that Annie?' Miss Busby hazarded a guess.

'Yes. She is not meaning to be rude, but is too busy to loiter.'

'I take it you're rather short of staff?' she asked. It was odd that Clara had been behind the bar.

'We did not expect new guests after what has happened,' he explained as they made their way down the corridor. 'Most of the staff I let go early for their holidays. Just a few remain. But, we will manage.' He stopped outside Room 10 and swung the door open to reveal a large, elegant space, sparkling clean and polished, with a four-poster bed, fireside chairs, a merry fire burning in the grate, and mullioned windows overlooking the gardens.

'Oh!' Miss Busby exclaimed, 'this is delightful! Thank you.'

He handed her two keys and unlocked the connecting door to Adeline's room. 'Dinner is served at seven, if you would care to join.'

'Might we take a light supper in our rooms?' Miss Busby asked, thinking some time alone to talk to Adeline might be useful. 'I'm rather tired from the drive,' she added in explanation.

He nodded. 'As you wish. I will have Jimmy bring you something.'

'And is there a telephone I might use?' she asked as he turned to leave.

'To the rear in the foyer, there is a cubby designed for guests to make their calls.'

She nodded gratefully as he bowed and closed the door behind him. Turning to the little terrier with a smile, she said, 'Well, Barnaby, I suppose we ought to unpack.'

Her modest suitcase had been left at the end of the bed. She took her nightclothes from it to place on the pillow, secreted her magnifying glass and notebook in the desk drawer, and hung a change of clothes in the wardrobe. She removed two magazines along with her library book, and put them on the nightstand. Placing her few toiletries by the sink, she took a moment to look across the grounds, still swathed in a light haze. Such a beautiful place, she thought, but what on earth had gone on here? The group of guests in the lounge seemed ill-matched, and the hotel almost a ghost ship sailing in the mist. She gave a little shiver, despite the fire.

Lying on the bed, barely disturbing the red and gold damask cover, Miss Busby closed her eyes for a while. She was rather wearied, but it was all just a little too intriguing for sleep. It wasn't long before she was back on her feet to make her way downstairs to telephone Richard.

'Hallo! How was the drive?' he called cheerily, some-how instantly making her feel better.

'Fine,' she said. 'Rather rapid, as always.'

Richard chuckled down the line. 'What's the place like?'

'It's beautiful. But rather sombre, currently.'

'And the suspects?'

'Hm,' she replied. 'Yes.'

'Ah, can't talk?'

'Not at present.' Miss Busby smiled at Richard's understanding. Lázár was behind the reception desk and she didn't dare say anything she wouldn't want overheard.

'Well, I'd better leave you to it then. Do be careful, though, Isabelle, won't you?'

'I will,' she assured him. Then after a moment's thought, added, 'Would you mind telephoning Spring Meadows to check on Pud?'

'Ha, I'm a step ahead of you for once!' he announced proudly. 'I rang a little while ago. Matron reported that Pud's charmed everyone and is absolutely adoring all the attention – just as you said he would.'

As Miss Busby was replacing the receiver, Adeline emerged from the corridor to the lounge on Sir Gregory's arm. Her smile was quite dazzling as she caught sight of her friend.

'Isabelle, perfect timing,' she said, then turned to Sir Gregory. 'I shall be quite alright from here,'

'Very good! Off to settle in! I look forward to seeing you anon, dear lady.' He spotted the manager at the reception desk. 'Lázár, there you are. Ludlow wants a word. We're gathered in the lounge,' he called, before striding back through the door and down the corridor, a jaunty spring in his step.

CHAPTER 5

Adeline was delighted with their rooms, but even more delighted with all she'd learned from sharing a drink with Sir Gregory.

'Just the one drink?' Miss Busby asked, glancing at her friend's glowing cheeks and bright eyes as she helped her unpack.

'Well, a couple,' she admitted. 'But Clara was rather stingy with the measures so it comes to much the same thing.' She put down the dress she'd just taken out of her case and turned excitedly. 'Oh, let's leave this, Isabelle. There are more important matters at hand! I have found out where Olivia's rooms are; up on the next floor, and the access staircase is right at the end of this corridor! We ought to take a look!'

'Surely they'll be locked?'

'No, that's the thing: Sir Gregory said the key was lost a couple of weeks ago.'

A spark ignited in Miss Busby's brain. 'Interesting...'

'Yes, I thought that, but Sir Gregory said she hardly

ever bothered to lock up anyway, so it wasn't much of an issue.'

'What if we're seen?' Miss Busby worried.

'By whom? They're down to a skeleton staff, and besides, the others all have rooms on the ground floor. Come on, Isabelle, while we have the chance.'

Leaving Barnaby sleeping off his lake-side adventure by the fire, Adeline led the way to the end of the corridor where a heavy set of double doors led to another staircase. 'Through here,' she stage-whispered, holding the door for Miss Busby.

'Olivia must have been fit for her age, to manage these stairs every day,' Miss Busby remarked as they climbed.

'Yes, not the mark of a woman with a weak heart,' Adeline observed.

'Unless she used the goods lift, of course.'

'We'll have to ask Jimmy. Ah, here we are.' A wide landing spread out before them, a heavy oak door opposite.

'Should we knock?' Miss Busby whispered.

'The woman's dead, Isabelle,' Adeline tutted. Crossing to the door, she turned the handle and slowly pushed it open. 'Living room,' she called over her shoulder. 'Come on.'

The room was clean and tidy, plainly decorated, with bookshelves against one wall, a pale green damask sofa and two armchairs against the other, and a large desk under the window. A typewriter sat atop the desk, with paper, ink, blotting paper and all the usuals arranged neatly around it.

'All her books are in English,' Adeline remarked, glancing at the shelves.

'Bobby Miller's notes said she was "displaced Hungarian aristocracy,"' Miss Busby recalled. 'If she took up work as a chambermaid, she must have fled the country without a thing to her name.'

'Imagine,' Adeline said, pushing open the door to her bedroom. 'Coming from wealth and status, to find yourself with nothing.'

'And then working your way right back up again,' Miss Busby said, entering the room behind Adeline.

'Hardly working,' Adeline objected. 'She married into it.'

'But if she hadn't taken the job, she would never have met the man to marry him,' Miss Busby pointed out.

'Well, now, this is a bit more like it,' Adeline said, walking further into the room rather than conceding the point.

The bedroom was more cluttered and personal than the living room, the walls papered in flamboyant pink, a dressing table groaning under the weight of an assortment of exotic-looking perfume bottles, and lots of watercolour paintings hanging on the walls. Miss Busby crossed to look at them – all of the hotel, grounds, and the interior from various aspects and in various seasons. An ottoman sat at the foot of the bed, with blankets and shawls piled high, and on the night table stood a pile of papers and a small pair of half-moon spectacles, which Miss Busby thought rather poignant.

'Invoices and suchlike for the hotel,' Adeline said, taking a few pages off the top. 'She must have been hands-on.'

'A businesswoman,' Miss Busby said sagely.

'Not if she let three of her friends stay here for nothing,' Adeline pointed out, crossing to the dressing table. 'Do you smell lavender? It must be this talc.' She pointed to an intricate porcelain dish in the style of Meissen. Its shallow centre covered with a layer of white powder, a glass jar appearing to contain the same sat beside it, along with a pink powder puff.

Miss Busby went over to investigate. 'It is. What a pretty dish, I've never seen one quite like it.' The creamy white porcelain was decorated with hand-painted roses, peonies and delicate violets.

'Quite exotic, these foreigners. Well,' Adeline said, looking around with a slightly disappointed air. 'Ought we to look in the drawers, do you think? And the bathroom?' she added, pushing open the final door and peering through.

'I think that would be a step too far,' Miss Busby said firmly. 'Besides, if her rooms have been unlocked, anyone and everyone could have been through them before us. Let's go back, Jimmy is bringing us some supper at seven.'

'We're not dining with the others?' Adeline asked in surprise.

'I think it's best if we keep to ourselves tonight. We can try and get each of them on their own tomorrow.'

'Good idea,' Adeline said as the pair made their way quietly back to their rooms.

Miss Busby opened the door to find Barnaby still asleep beside the fire. She added a small log from the wicker basket on the hearth, watching the flames for a moment while Adeline finished her unpacking in the adjoining room.

'What do you make of young Arthur's drinking?' Adeline called through.

'Perhaps it's his way of dealing with the grief,' Miss Busby suggested.

'Sir Gregory doesn't think so. He suspects the young-ster is simply enjoying running up a bar tab he'll never have to pay.'

Miss Busby thought that a bit rich, given that the man didn't pay for his stays at the hotel. Or his drinks, according to Flora.

'Nice chap, Sir Gregory,' Adeline went on. 'Rather dashing, wouldn't you say?'

'Mm,' she replied noncommittally.

A knock sounded at the door. Barnaby emitted a low growl.

'Come in,' Miss Busby called.

Jimmy poked his head in. 'Mr Lázár said I was to bring you some supper, miss. I didn't know what ye'd like so I brought a bit of everything.' With that, he wheeled in a gilded trolley filled with plates of miniature pork pies, scotch eggs, sandwiches, a large pot of tea and several cream cakes.

Barnaby sprung to his feet and sniffed the air. Adeline came through to investigate, and they thanked the young man.

'Y'can just push the trolley outside, after you're done,' he said. 'G'night!'

'Oh, Jimmy?' Miss Busby called as he turned to leave.

'Yes, miss?'

'How did Mrs Fortescue manage with the stairs to her rooms?'

'Oh, she always said they did her the power of good. Kept her fit, like. Mind you,' he added, suddenly whisking off his smart porter's cap and holding it in both hands, 'she took the lift up a few times in the last week or so. Anyhow, I'll be back up for the trolley later, then. G'night!'

'That's interesting,' Miss Busby said, as she passed Adeline a pretty china plate.

'Yes, perhaps she was feeling unwell recently, and simply didn't mention it to the others,' Adeline suggested, helping herself to the goodies.

Miss Busby thought she noticed a hint of disappointment in her tone. She poured them both tea, and they sat in the wing chairs beside the fire, eating and contemplating quietly. Before long, another knock broke into their thoughts.

'Come in,' Miss Busby called again, looking up in surprise as Lady Flora appeared.

'I hope you don't mind the interruption, but young Jimmy said you wouldn't be joining us for dinner, and

I had saved a little something for your dog,' Flora said, holding out what appeared to be an entire chicken breast. Barnaby immediately left his post at the trolley, his tail wagging excitedly.

'Goodness, how kind!' Miss Busby said.

'Here, take my chair,' Adeline added, getting up and seating herself at the desk so the older lady could make herself comfortable.

'Thank you. The stairs do tire me, rather. But there's so much food left over from the ball, after it came to such an abrupt halt,' Flora explained as she sat down, 'And it's a shame to waste any of it.' She passed the chicken to Miss Busby, who cut it into small pieces and placed it on a napkin for Barnaby.

'Olivia loved dogs,' Flora went on, watching him gleefully tuck in. 'She always wanted a pack of them; sighthounds were her favourite, but they require so much walking.'

'Barnaby came to me purely by accident,' Miss Busby explained. 'And he's quite happy with the odd circuit of the village green. Oh, I'd offer you tea, but I'm afraid there are only two cups.'

'Shall I go and ask Jimmy for more?' Adeline suggested.

'Oh, I never drink tea this close to my bedtime, thank you. Olivia and I would sometimes share a sherry at this time, though…' she added wistfully.

'I shall go and ask Jimmy for three glasses!' Adeline volunteered again immediately, rising to her feet and heading for the door.

'You must miss your friend dreadfully,' Miss Busby said as Adeline bustled out.

Flora nodded, her eyes downcast. 'She was such a dear soul, so kind; a little too kind for her own good, perhaps. It wasn't difficult to take advantage, you see, given her nature. She was such a generous benefactor to us all…' Her voice faltered and she withdrew her handkerchief again.

'Was there anyone in particular who may have taken advantage?' Miss Busby pressed gently.

Flora sniffled. 'I suppose we all did, to a certain extent. Such a ragtag bunch! And Olivia took such wonderful care of us. I only wish we'd been able to repay her kindness.'

'I'm sure you did,' Miss Busby assured her. 'Each in your own way.'

Flora's expression darkened for a second. 'Most of us tried our best, although not all friends and family are created equal. But you are very kind to say so,' she added, dabbing at her eyes and smiling bravely.

'I wish I'd met her,' Miss Busby said. 'She sounds a remarkable woman. Adeline was so surprised that she'd succumbed to her heart after seeming in such good health,' she added, feeling a twinge of discomfort at the deception.

'Well,' Flora said, putting her handkerchief away and taking a breath. 'That's the thing. Olivia had been feeling rather dizzy of late. Not enough to bother the doctor, but now that I think of it, I do recall a couple of occasions when she had to sit down and get her bearings, which wasn't like her at all. Perhaps that was the start of it. Oh!' she said, her eyes widening. 'I should have made her bother the doctor, shouldn't I? Perhaps if he'd known, he could have helped her.'

'You mustn't think like that,' Miss Busby was quick to comfort her. 'It could have been anything at all. Especially at our age.'

'Here we are,' Adeline proclaimed as she flung open the door. Jimmy followed with a tray holding a bottle and three glasses. 'Whatever's the matter?' she asked, noticing Flora's distress. 'Thank you, young man, I'll pour,' she said, taking the tray and dismissing Jimmy.

Flora took several small, fortifying sips as Miss Busby brought Adeline up to date.

'You couldn't possibly have known,' Adeline assured her. 'And how fortunate Mrs Fortescue was to have such a considerate friend,' she added kindly.

'Olivia was the most considerate friend a person could have,' Flora replied with a smile. 'Her little family. That's how she thought of us.'

'Us?' Adeline asked.

'Myself, Major Gresham, and Clara. And Sir Gregory. She adored Hamnett Hall, and loved us enough to allow us to make it our home alongside her.'

'It's a beautiful hotel,' Miss Busby said. 'She must have been incredibly proud to run it.'

'And accomplished, too,' Adeline added, passing a glass to Miss Busby before taking up her own. 'One must need a certain flair for business to run a place like this.'

Miss Busby blinked. Adeline didn't look at her.

'Oh, it was so much more than a business,' Flora said. 'Olivia fell in love with the house and grounds the moment she first came to work here. Mr Fortescue was the businessman. He would never have approved of her allowing us all to stay here for free.'

Adeline shot Miss Busby a brief look of triumph.

'Really?' Miss Busby asked, leaning forward with interest.

'Henry wasn't a cruel man, simply a practical one,' Flora was quick to qualify. 'His older brother inherited the majority of the family fortune when their parents died. Henry really only got the scraps left over, but he knuckled down and worked hard to build his own wealth by establishing Hamnett Hall. He saw it purely in terms of profit and loss, whereas to Olivia it was simply home.'

'How did Henry die?' Adeline asked.

'A heart attack,' Flora answered mournfully. 'Olivia always thought it was from the stresses and strains of running the place.'

Adeline's eyes widened as she looked to Miss Busby, who could almost hear her friend immediately developing theories of a double murder. Although, she considered, perhaps someone had seen an opportunity to duplicate the previous owner's demise...

'Do you think Olivia was under similar pressure?' Miss Busby asked.

Flora considered for a moment. 'Well... she had her moments. It's not an easy business to be in. But for the most part I'd say she couldn't have been happier. She missed her husband, of course, but she had her friends and her home. She was mostly relaxed and at peace, I would say.'

'But what about this business with the will,' Adeline asked, then added. 'It was mentioned to me in the lounge, and I must say it does seem odd that she hadn't written one sooner. Could she have been concerned over naming her heir?'

'Oh, Olivia never considered herself a likely candidate for dying,' Flora replied with a wry smile. 'I suppose none of us do, really. She never thought a will was needed.'

'Then what changed her mind?' Miss Busby asked.

'Mr Ludlow, I suppose. They had several rather long chats recently. And it did make sense. It's always better to be prepared. But I don't think she was concerned,' Flora considered. 'If anything, she seemed rather excited. As I said, she adored Hamnett Hall, and was keen to see it pass into the hands of someone she trusted to run the place in a similar vein. She called the hotel her 'life's work'. And even with a few of us staying here for no charge, it did awfully well financially. Olivia never wanted for anything.'

'Is that what Mr Ludlow was referring to, I wonder?' Miss Busby asked. 'When he said it was a shame she didn't live to finish what she started?'

Flora looked surprised. 'Oh. Yes, I should imagine so.'

'And did you have any idea who she might have chosen?' Adeline asked.

Flora shook her head. 'She was always so full of surprises none of us could guess. Clara is young and full of energy. Headstrong. I think Olivia saw glimpses of herself in the girl, and she was unendingly fond of her. But she hadn't proven herself to be reliable – quite the reverse, in fact. And Arthur is family, of course, but…'

'What?' Adeline asked, eyes shining.

'I find it hard to imagine she would have left the place to him,' Flora confessed.

'Why?' Adeline asked eagerly. 'Because of his drinking?'

Flora thought for a moment, seeming to choose her words carefully. 'Not just the drinking, there were… other considerations.'

'Did he gamble?' Adeline asked. 'The two go together so often,' she added knowingly. 'And of course you're quite close to the racecourse here.'

Flora laughed. 'Nothing quite so exciting, I'm afraid. Although he did lose a few bets of sorts on the stock market, I believe. No, Olivia thought him rather hopeless,' she explained. 'Not that it was his fault, it was all down to his parents. Arthur never had the chance to stand on his own two feet.' She sighed, looking down at her watch. 'Goodness, I only came up to give your little dog a treat. It is past my bedtime. Thank you,' she said, nodding to each of them, 'for your company and your kindness. It has been a tonic as much as the sherry,' she said, placing her empty glass back on the tray. 'Goodnight!'

Miss Busby saw her to the door, before closing it behind her, her head spinning.

'Well!' Adeline exclaimed. 'It does seem there may be more to this than meets the eye after all!'

'Perhaps,' Miss Busby conceded, stifling a yawn. 'But I'm rather tired too. Shall we come back to it fresh in the morning?'

Adeline deflated a little, but conceded defeat. 'That sherry was rather stronger than I thought, and I shouldn't mind an early night myself.'

Miss Busby suspected it was more to do with the drinks she'd enjoyed earlier with Sir Gregory, but nodded all the same and wished her goodnight. Looking to the empty seat at the desk, she decided she ought to take a moment with her notebook and jot down all they'd learned while it was fresh in her mind.

Once finished, and just as she was about to get into her nightclothes, Barnaby nudged her leg with his nose and gave her a meaningful look; she realised he'd need a last outing before bed. 'Come along, then,' she said, reaching for her jacket and his leash, as she had no desire to chase him around the lake in the dark. Leaving the room quietly, in case Adeline was already asleep, movement caught her eye to the far left of the corridor. She glanced around to catch sight of a dark-clad figure disappearing through the double doors to the stairs leading up to Olivia's rooms.

Looking from the expectant dog to the softly closing doors, she hesitated. Adeline would follow without thought, but what possible reason could she give for being there if she were seen? Barnaby gave a soft whine, and made the decision for her. They walked downstairs together, and made a quick turn of the courtyard, the sky clear and bright with stars, the bite of frost in the air, until Barnaby's business was completed.

Back in the comfortable warmth of her room, and finally abed with the door firmly locked, Miss Busby closed her eyes and pondered the strange group they'd encountered. Sir Gregory appeared to be the only relaxed member, seemingly without a care, whilst the Major hadn't said a word. He hadn't seemed to approve of Arthur or Clara, though, and neither Clara, Flora, or indeed Olivia, if Flora was to be believed, seemed to approve of Arthur. The solicitor, Mr Ludlow, had seemed suspicious of their presence, and Miss Busby found she was now feeling equally suspicious thinking of the figure in the corridor.

Just as her eyes were finally dropping, she thought she heard faint footsteps in the corridor outside. Was it the black-clad figure returning? As the little dog snored softly beside her on the bed, she wondered fretfully if their story of a late booking and a passing acquaintance with Mrs Fortescue hadn't been quite as convincing as they'd hoped.

CHAPTER 6

Miss Busby, Adeline, and Barnaby descended the stairs the following morning and were greeted by the young maid, Annie, at the reception desk.

'Lázár said I'm to show you through,' she said, bobbing a quick curtsey before leading them to the dining room at the far end of the corridor. South-facing, the room was brightly lit by crisp morning sunshine and offered a picturesque view over the grounds and the lake in the distance. Square tables were covered with smart linen cloths, neatly laid with silverware, napkins and delicate china cups.

'Or there's the conservatory, if you prefer,' she added, nodding to a glass door open at the rear of the room. 'Only it can take a while to warm up in the mornings.'

'This will suffice, thank you,' Adeline said, not being at all fond of a chill.

Only two of the tables were occupied. Major Gresham and Flora were seated at one, talking quietly over coffee. Flora looked up and gave the pair a smile as they walked in. The Major offered only a sombre nod. Sir Gregory Penn sat alone at the other end of the room, an empty plate and cup before him as he read a crisply folded newspaper. He rose to his feet when he spotted them.

'Mrs Fanshawe, good morning!' he called eagerly. 'Would you care to join me? Shall I fetch more chairs?'

Adeline stood a little straighter, her red dress set off by a snug fitting black cardigan emphasising her comfortable but elegant figure. Heels added to her height, her perfectly coiffed hair gleamed and new lipstick in a daring shade shone as her lips twitched upwards.

Miss Busby looked down at her own russet twinset with matching wool skirt, and felt rather dull in comparison. Practical, she thought determinedly, not dull.

'We shouldn't like to hold you up, Sir Gregory,' she said, with a pointed look at his empty plate.

He took the rebuff gallantly. 'Oh. Well, perhaps a walk later this morning?' he suggested. 'The grounds are delightful when the sun is shining!'

'Lovely,' Adeline agreed with a smile.

'Then I shall look forward to seeing you anon!' he called, snapping his heels together smartly and offering a deep bow before leaving the room. Miss Busby smiled, suspecting he'd hung back, hoping to see Adeline.

'This one alright for you?' Annie asked, leading them to a table set for two. She glanced down at Barnaby and frowned.

'Perfectly,' Miss Busby said, setting down her bag. 'He will sit under my chair. He doesn't need one of his own.'

The young maid gave a giggle. 'I was just thinking what he might like to eat, miss,' she said. 'I can ask Cook what there is. Is there anything he doesn't like?'

'Vegetables,' Miss Busby said, her eyes shining with mischief.

'Oh, me too!' Annie bent to give him a stroke. 'I'll find you something nice,' she told him as she ruffled his ears. 'And the buffet is all laid out, miss.' She straightened and pointed to where lidded silver tureens shone. 'There's orange juice in the jug and coffee in the pot, but if you'd prefer tea I can make fresh.'

'Tea would be perfect, thank you,' Miss Busby said, as Adeline strode to the buffet with purpose.

Plates and cups filled, and a fresh pot of tea on the table, the pair sat and looked out over the grounds, the delicious smells of breakfast swirling around them

'No sign of the youngsters,' Adeline pointed out, attacking her kedgeree with gusto.

'I suspect they keep rather later hours than we do,' Miss Busby said, trying some of the scrambled eggs and finding them delicious.

Annie soon returned with a bowl of flaked haddock for Barnaby, and a dish of water to go with it.

'I wonder if you might ask Jimmy to walk him for me after breakfast?' Miss Busby asked, as a plan for the morning began to formulate.

'I will, miss,' Annie replied then left the three of them to enjoy their breakfast.

'Well,' Adeline said, setting her cutlery down on her

empty plate with a contented sigh. 'What's our plan of attack?'

'I think we ought to track down Mr Lázár and have a quiet word.'

'And find out what the solicitor wanted to talk to him about yesterday?' Adeline asked.

'Partly, but I was thinking more about his relationship with Olivia.'

'Isabelle!' Adeline's eyebrows shot up. 'Surely you don't think—'

'Not in that respect,' Miss Busby chided swiftly. 'But he seemed genuinely upset regarding her passing. And Flora told us the hotel was Olivia's life work; as such, her professional relationship with her manager must have been a close one. And as a fellow countryman, too.'

Adeline blinked. 'You think she may have been planning to leave the hotel to her manager?'

Miss Busby furrowed her brow; she hadn't been thinking anything of the sort, but filed the notion away to consider later. 'I was simply thinking he may be able to offer some insight into her situation,' she clarified. 'And that talking to him would be the most logical place to start.' She wiped her mouth delicately with a napkin, as the door to the breakfast room flew open and the affable young porter strode cheerfully in. Barnaby went to greet him, and Miss Busby and Adeline rose to their feet in turn.

'Annie says you'd like me 'ter walk him, miss?' Jimmy said.

'That would be very kind.' Miss Busby passed him another napkin, this one wrapped around a rasher of bacon. 'Should you need to persuade him to return to you,' she explained. 'And I wonder if you might show us to Lázár's office en route?'

'On what, miss?' he asked, looking confused.

'On the way.'

'Oh, yes miss!' He nodded, looking down at the little terrier with a smile as he crammed the napkin into the pocket of his button-up blue jacket.

They passed the reception desk and crossed into the opposite corridor, then through the door bearing the words 'Staff Only.' The floors here were stone-flagged, and no paintings adorned the walls, but everything was clean and fresh. They stopped at the first door on the right. Jimmy rapped lightly and the manager's sombre voice called out, 'Yes?'

As Jimmy pushed the door open, Miss Busby caught sight of the manager sitting perfectly upright at his desk. He wore the same dark suit as yesterday, his hands folded in his lap, his eyes troubled. Arthur Fortescue turned to look up from the seat opposite in surprise.

'Miss Busby and Mrs Fanshawe to see you, sir,' Jimmy announced smartly, before trotting off with the dog at his heels.

Both men rose politely to their feet, as Miss Busby stepped in with a smile.

'I do hope we're not interrupting,' she said.

'Not at all,' Arthur replied, 'we'd just finished. Is

everything alright?' he added, looking between the two women. His eyes shone with curiosity and, Miss Busby thought, a soupcon of suspicion.

'Yes, how may I assist?' Lázár asked, a smile fixed on his face although his own eyes remained wary.

'Sticky lock,' Adeline said, shimmying into the room with purpose. 'The door to my room is a devil to open.'

'Ah, right. I'll leave you to it,' Arthur said, nodding to Lázár before making his exit.

The office was small and spartan but smelled pleasantly of beeswax polish. The window was open a crack to let just enough crisp morning air in to be pleasant. A single painting of the front of the hotel hung above the desk, and one hard-backed chair sat opposite. The fireplace was laid but unlit, and a typewriter and several neat piles of paper took up much of the desk space between them.

'I am sorry to hear this,' Lázár said. 'Our handyman is not present currently, but I will be pleased to–'

'That's quite alright, I'm sure we'll manage,' Miss Busby said, with a grateful smile towards Adeline for her quick thinking. 'But whilst we're here, I wonder if we might talk to you about Olivia Fortescue?'

The manager remained perfectly still, regarding them both in turn with the same cautious expression. 'How would this be?' he asked, tone polite but guarded.

'In regard to her rather conveniently timed death.' Adeline took charge. 'We are no strangers to such things, Mr Lázár. Miss Busby has investigated similar circumstances in the past, and indeed been instrumental in solving several murders—'

'Adeline!' Miss Busby interrupted, turning to her friend with wide eyes.

'— and I am concerned that my acquaintance, Mrs Fortescue, may have been vulnerable to attack, given the imminent naming of an heir in her will,' Adeline finished, unrepentant. 'I'm sorry, Isabelle, but I see no reason for pussyfooting around,' she added.

Miss Busby blinked, momentarily lost for words.

Lázár remained stock still for several moments, before a small sigh slumped his shoulders. He indicated that the ladies should sit, which they duly did.

'I really must apologise,' Miss Busby said, recovering herself. 'My friend can be rather forthright, but I assure you we only mean to help.'

Lázár sat back down and sighed more heavily this time. 'I understand. And I must be honest to inform you that I did not believe you arrived here at this time only by chance.'

Adeline raised triumphant brows in Miss Busby's direction.

'But, if I may ask,' he said, turning a curious gaze on Miss Busby, 'how is it that such a lady could become involved with such a terrible thing as murder?'

'Oh, I'm afraid that's rather a long story,' Miss Busby explained. 'But a dear friend of mine is a police inspector, and when he heard what happened here he was….rather concerned.'

Lázár nodded sadly. 'I am concerned also,' he confessed. 'Olivia was strong and in good health. It is strange she should suffer such a devastating attack, without warning. But the police, they have talked with the doctor, and are satisfied with his opinion.' He gave a helpless shrug, his dark eyes filled with dejection.

'Not entirely satisfied,' Adeline pointed out. 'Which is why we are here, to investigate further. Our friend, Inspector McKay, is convinced—'

'A post-mortem will be carried out,' Miss Busby cut in, 'regardless of the doctor's opinion. It is standard procedure, and will serve to put everyone's mind at rest. But I'm afraid these things take time. The inspector suggested that while they await the results, we might come here and talk to people, and perhaps find out a little more about Olivia Fortescue.'

'But she was also a friend to you, yes?' he asked, looking at Adeline.

Adeline's cheeks reddened. 'Acquaintance,' she murmured.

Lázár's eyes narrowed slightly.

'Adeline, perhaps you could take notes,' Miss Busby said, keen to occupy her friend whilst she encouraged the man to talk. 'Here you are.' She reached into her bag for her notebook and a pencil, which she passed to Adeline, who was looking none too pleased at the delegation. 'Please do be assured, Mr Lázár,' Miss Busby continued, 'that everything you tell us will be treated in the strictest confidence.'

He thought for a moment. 'And you work with the police inspector, yes? This… McKay?' he asked carefully.

'We…have his ear,' Miss Busby hedged.

'He relies on us,' Adeline insisted.

'We really do only want to help,' Miss Busby reiterated. 'We spoke to your other guests last evening, and Olivia sounds as though she was a remarkable woman. It's rare to find someone who cares so deeply and so unselfishly for her friends.'

He looked at Miss Busby, eyes widening, before a genuine smile crossed his thin lips. 'Unselfish, yes. That is the most perfect word for Miss Olivia. And from someone who has never met her…' He tilted his head thoughtfully. 'Most astute. Very well,' he nodded, 'I will tell you what you need to know. For Miss Olivia, God rest her soul.'

'Thank you,' Miss Busby said, offering a warm smile. The man was clearly concerned, and he was right to be wary in the first instance. It was impossible not to warm to him, even though his manner was rather stern. He is suffering, she thought, taking in his pallor and the shadows under his eyes. And his caution speaks volumes of his loyalty to his late employer.

'What did that solicitor want to talk to you about yesterday?' Adeline jumped in. 'Ludlow, isn't it? I thought he seemed rather agitated.'

The manager's eyebrows rose in surprise. 'Mr Ludlow is a most respected professional. He worked also for the late Mr Henry Fortescue. He wondered again if I had thought of any place other than her safe where Miss Olivia would keep such an important document as her will. I have not. She was never one to hide a thing. It was not in her nature.'

'You've all looked for the will, I imagine?' Miss Busby asked.

He nodded. 'Mr Ludlow himself has searched Miss Olivia's rooms with my permission. As have Miss Clara Harrowby and Mr Arthur Fortescue.'

Miss Busby gave Adeline's foot a slight nudge with her own, and flicked her eyes to the notebook. Adeline took the hint and wrote down the names of those who'd been through Olivia's rooms.

'And were you and Olivia acquainted in Hungary, Mr Lázár?' Miss Busby changed tack.

'Just Lázár, please,' he insisted. 'It is what most people call me. My Christian name is hard for you to pronounce. And yes, of course. But I knew her then as Kisasszony Olivia.'

Adeline snapped the lead of the pencil against the page in surprise. 'I beg your pardon?' she demanded, as Miss Busby's eyebrows shot up.

'Kisasszony. It means "Miss", as you would say in English,' he explained.

'Does it really!' Adeline said archly. 'Well, perhaps we might stick to the English version.'

'Why is this?' Lázár enquired politely.

Miss Busby wasn't fooled. 'I suspect you know very well why.'

Adeline narrowed her eyes as she realised Lázár's tease.

'I must apologise, madam. I see you have understood.' Lázár deferred with a gentle smile. 'Kisasszony is indeed as I say. Miss Olivia and I discovered that it has a sound rather shocking in your language and it was sometimes a little joke we played.'

'Humph,' Adeline snorted.

'Perhaps we could continue,' Miss Busby suggested. She found another pencil in her bag for Adeline and exchanged it for the broken one.

CHAPTER 7

'As you wish.' Lázár nodded. I worked many years for Miss Olivia's father. He had a large estate on the outskirts of Budapest, and was a wealthy man. A good man, also. Clever, and kind. Miss Olivia was his everything. His wife has died birthing her, and he worked always to give her the very best. A good education, to make her clever just like him, and his kindness she learned at his knee. He said she was to be a strong woman and to stand always on her own two feet, always to make him proud.'

'How lovely,' Miss Busby said, thinking fondly of her own father for a moment. An education, and the independence it offered, was a great gift indeed, and one not all fathers considered their daughters equipped for.

'But then he was struck down by typhus, and died so fast. No one could have imagined. He was still a young man, and strong. It was a bite from ticks, or fleas from the livestock. He was a man who, how do you say? Get his hands dirty?'

Miss Busby nodded.

'Always he would check on all aspects of the estate, and the animals were without exception,' he continued, turning his head for a moment to gaze out of the window. 'Miss Olivia, she was heartbroken, of course. Her world dissolved. Then even more so when the lawyers came and her home was passed to her older cousin.'

'She didn't expect to inherit, surely?' Adeline asked, wide-eyed.

Miss Busby glanced across at the almost blank page of her notebook and sighed. Adeline had become caught up in the story.

Lázár shook his head sadly. 'She knew the law, of course, but had always thought she would be settled with a family of her own by the time it was to be a concern. With her father's untimely passing, she was unprepared. And when her cousin and his wife arrived, Miss Olivia was no longer welcome.'

'They surely didn't throw her out?' Adeline leaned forward, aghast.

Lázár nodded.

'But why?' Miss Busby asked. 'She was still family.'

'And it was her home,' Adeline added.

'The new master's wife, she was jealous of Miss Olivia,' Lázár explained. 'She was not clever, this woman, and Miss Olivia made her seem even less so, although never with intention. The two of them, they begin on the wrong foot. And the new master, he gives his young wife whatever she wants, the moment she asks.'

'Ah. I suppose she was very beautiful?' Adeline asked, a cynical brow raised.

He nodded. 'Most striking indeed.'

'Always the way,' Adeline muttered.

'And so, suddenly,' Lázár continued, 'we have nowhere to go.'

'The woman got rid of the servants as well?' Adeline asked, eyes alight with indignation.

Lázár shook his head. 'No, she keeps the servants, although she added also some of her own. But I did not wish to stay. I preferred to follow Miss Olivia. She had nothing, and no one to help, if I did not.'

'Good Lord,' Adeline breathed. 'You gave up your position, and your home, your family, to follow her?'

'All but my family. I lost them many years prior. My parents died when I was very young,' he explained.

Miss Busby looked at the man opposite with growing respect. She had recognised his loyalty, but couldn't have guessed at the depths to which it ran.

'Where did you go?' Adeline asked, all pretence of notetaking forgotten. 'I should imagine tongues must have been set wagging viciously at the pair of you leaving together.'

Lázár's eyes flashed at the implication.

'That is,' Adeline went on, rather more carefully, 'if Olivia was of old-fashioned aristocratic stock, any form of close association with a servant would surely be frowned upon.'

'In her circles, yes,' Lázár conceded, 'but she was

leaving those circles behind. And with them, all their prejudices also.'

He raised his chin and held Adeline's gaze. She gave him a small nod of approval.

'Miss Olivia did not wish to remain in Hungary,' he went on. 'The new mistress would make trouble for her, she suspected. And memories of her father were so strong, and so sad. When she was sent from her home the one thing she managed to take was her passport, held within her purse. I had some savings from my work, and so I obtained one also. Together we worked our way for passage to England. It was slow, and the work was hard, but Miss Olivia was determined and never once did she think of giving up.'

'But why England?' Miss Busby asked, fascinated. 'It's such a long way to travel, under the circumstances.'

Lázár smiled. 'Miss Olivia read very many books, and all her favourites took place in England. Heathcliff's Yorkshire moors, Rochester's Thornfield Hall, and the estates of Mr Bingley and the Bennett sisters. For her, a country full of such stories had a great pull.'

'And did she speak English?' Miss Busby asked.

'No. Neither one of us did. But Miss Olivia learned. The words came easily and fast, another sign, she said, that her choice was the right one. And she helped me learn also, so as we arrived here, we were able to find work.'

'And that was when she took up a position here as chambermaid?' Miss Busby pressed.

'No. First came a time of struggle. I worked as stable-hand, waiter, porter, to support her.'

Adeline cleared her throat. 'And did you…the two of you…were you…' She shifted slightly in her chair, and took a breath. Miss Busby had an inkling of where her friend was about to go, and quickly stepped in.

'You still maintained a professional relationship, even though you both were on much more of an equal footing in England?' she asked delicately.

Lázár drew himself up proudly. 'I have served ever since I can remember; it is what I was raised to do. Miss Olivia, though, she had to learn a whole new way of being. It was hard for her, but she…how do you say? Rolled up her cuffs and–'

'Sleeves,' Adeline interjected.

Lázár nodded. 'Sleeves, thank you, and she began to work too. First as kitchen maid, then seamstress, then for a little time as maid to an elderly lady who found her accent charming.' He smiled. 'Miss Olivia was charming, always, and made friends wherever we went. We came together to Cheltenham as I was offered good work with the racing horses. Miss Olivia had a golden reference from the elderly lady, and was then able to take the position as chambermaid here at the hotel.'

'Where she caught the eye of Mr Fortescue,' Adeline prompted.

'Yes. Always she is very beautiful, but Mr Fortescue recognised also her intelligence, and kindness. Over time he learned her history, and they grew close. Miss

Olivia had good English by then, but she is Hungarian at heart, and it was important to her that people she was close to understand this. Mr Fortescue was so enamoured of her, he learned some Hungarian words, and this delighted her. Although others working at the hotel, they resented Miss Olivia for his attention.'

Miss Busby nodded sadly, having suspected as much.

'After some time, Mr Fortescue proposed marriage, and Miss Olivia accepted,' he continued.

'Did she love him?' Adeline asked, a little bluntly in Miss Busby's opinion.

'Whoever would marry without love?' Lázár countered, his grey eyebrows raised.

'Plenty of people,' Adeline pointed out, 'if it meant elevation from maid to mistress of an estate.'

Lázár considered this for a moment. 'Love, I think, can take many forms. Perhaps there is love to be found in safety and security, just as much as in other things. And Miss Olivia truly loved the hotel. It was a magical place to her. Like in one of her stories, she said to me. A magical place that felt like home.'

'And so she took you on as manager?' Miss Busby asked, keen to move the story along.

'No. I kept to my work with the racing horses. I had been promoted to managing the accounts of the owners, and our lives became separate for a while. Although we would meet to drink coffee occasionally, and we each knew where the other could be found if there was a need.

But Mr Fortescue, he was…perhaps…a little possessive of his new Mrs Fortescue.'

'As is often the way with newlyweds,' Adeline said sagely.

Lázár nodded. 'I did not become manager until after he passed away. It was easier for Miss Olivia if there was a man seen to be running the business. Although, always, she truly ran the place. The hotel was like a child to her, and I was perhaps a teacher, overseeing some of its education, but it remained hers to raise as she saw fit.' He paused for a moment, raising a hand to his forehead, before saying softly, 'She truly loved Hamnett Hall with all of her heart.'

'A heart that failed her at the Halloween Ball,' Miss Busby replied, equally softly.

Lázár, stalwart until this point, lowered his head into both hands. 'Such a tragedy,' he murmured from behind closed fingers. 'She was so happy at dinner, excited to reveal to us who would inherit the hotel. She said it was to be a great surprise, and much cause for celebration.' He looked up. 'She was more alive than ever in that moment. It is impossible to think how soon she was taken from us.'

'And did you have any idea who it would be?' Adeline pressed, picking up her pencil once more. 'The heir?'

'I did not,' Lázár said. 'But now I cannot help but wonder if someone knew…' He turned to look out over the lawn. The sunlight caught the white in his grey hair and made his skin look paler than ever. Miss Busby found herself thinking sadly that if anyone were at risk of a heart attack it would be him; he looked as if the weight of the world hung on his narrow shoulders.

'Miss Olivia,' he continued, turning back to the pair, 'was an intelligent and cautious woman. She knew to take care of herself. She had her plan for the hotel, and would never have risked—'

A dull thud from outside the office door caused him to stop. Adeline, quick as a flash, dashed from her seat to pull the door open, revealing Annie, face flushing bright red, standing awkwardly just outside.

'What are you doing there?' Adeline demanded. 'Were you eavesdropping?'

'No, m-miss,' the young maid stuttered. 'I… I was just going to knock for Mr Lázár, only I heard voices and didn't want to disturb anyone. Then I dropped the carpet sweeper as I turned to go back,' she said, bending to pick up the item concerned. 'I'm ever so sorry. I'll finish clearing the breakfast room and come back later,' she said quickly, before scurrying off through the doors.

Adeline scowled after her.

Lázár had stood up, but now bowed. 'If you'll forgive, I must return to my work. There is much to do before the hotel closes. If I can be of further assistance,' he said, looking between them, 'you may find me. But, please,' he added, looking now to Miss Busby, 'be careful. Friends may begin to take on the shape of enemies in the light of such uncertainty.'

Miss Busby thanked him, and a thought occurred to

her. 'I wonder if you might be kind enough not to mention to any of the others that we are…acquainted…with the police?' she asked, thinking it would probably make them reluctant to speak openly if they knew. Although Adeline had proved the opposite in her impromptu earlier confession.

'Of course.' He nodded solemnly. 'I would not put you in danger.'

Miss Busby felt disquiet descend once more as she walked back to reception with Adeline, who handed her the notebook and pencil. Miss Busby glanced at the near blank page with disapproval before putting it back in her bag.

The look wasn't lost on Adeline. 'I'm sorry, Isabelle,' she said, flushing slightly, 'but there was a lot to take in.'

'There was,' Miss Busby agreed. 'Which was why taking notes was important.' She stopped by the fire in the hall. It was freshly lit, with several large logs burning brightly. She gazed into the flames for a moment. 'Lázár thought Olivia was perfectly healthy, so she couldn't have mentioned any dizzy spells.'

'I suppose Flora would have been much more of a confidante,' Adeline said, 'being a close female friend. Olivia would have talked to her of aging and aches and pains and suchlike.' She waved the issue aside in favour of more compelling matters. 'Why would Olivia's choice of heir been "a great surprise" to them all? I expect she had decided to spurn the obvious choice,' she went on, giving Miss Busby no pause to answer. 'Her own experience in losing her home in Hungary may have had a bearing on her decision, don't you think?' she added. 'She'd had a terrible experience of her own, having been made homeless by a male heir, and may have decided not to leave the place to Arthur, who would surely have been the expected choice.'

'It sounded as if her experience was more to do with the heir's wife,' Miss Busby reminded her.

'Well, perhaps Arthur has plans to marry,' Adeline said, refusing to give up, and gathering pace as the idea took hold. 'We must find out! He may have fallen in with someone Olivia thought unsuitable, and that's why she changed her plans! And what was he talking to Lázár about in there, do you think?'

'Hallo there!' Both women turned as Sir Gregory emerged from the opposite corridor. Smartly dressed in a linen jacket complete with red bow tie, crisp tan trousers and shirt, and a pipe sticking jauntily out of his top pocket, he bowed to both. 'Is it time for our walk, dear lady?' he addressed Adeline, then realised his slight. 'Or dear ladies, I should say!' he added gallantly. 'The more the merrier!'

'Thank you, but I think I shall go to my room,' Miss Busby said. 'Do enjoy the grounds, Adeline. And if you see Jimmy, perhaps you could ask him to return Barnaby? He ought to come in and warm up.'

'Would you rather I stayed with you?' Adeline asked, turning to her, clearly torn between investigating her newfound theory and walking out with her eager suitor.

'Of course not,' she replied, dropping her voice to a whisper to add, 'Perhaps you can find out more about the others, while I add to our notes.'

Adeline's eyes shone with excitement as she nodded, then went to take Sir Gregory's arm. He began chatting eagerly to her straight away. Miss Busby noted that the man offered a stark contrast to Lázár: he truly didn't seem to have a care in the world.

Of course, he's titled and most likely wealthy, she thought, which would make all the difference. Although Flora had mentioned that he too, stayed as Olivia's guest free of charge, so perhaps the title didn't quite tell the whole story. Still, he certainly didn't behave like a man who had just lost a dear and generous friend.

As she turned to make her way up the stairs, Clara Harrowby was just beginning to descend them, and the young woman stopped as she saw her.

'Good morning,' Miss Busby called brightly.

'Hello,' Clara said, seeming rather flustered. Her cheeks were rosy red, as if she'd been for a brisk walk, but she was dressed in a smart tan overcoat as if she were just leaving.

'I'm afraid you've missed breakfast,' Miss Busby said, stepping down to avoid any possible misfortune from crossing on the stairs. It had been one of Randolf's great superstitions, and although she'd mocked him for it, she'd observed the ritual since his passing.

'Thanks,' Clara said, making her way slowly down. Miss Busby thought she saw a rather strange shape under the overcoat, before the girl turned her body and ran lightly down the remaining stairs. 'I'm off into town. I'll get something while I'm out. Bye, then.' And she hurried through the front doors.

Miss Busby sighed as she climbed the treads and thought of all they'd learned that morning. It seemed that the more pages of the mystery they tentatively turned, the more complicated everything appeared. The sound of a motorcar starting up rang out in the stillness of the morning. Someone here knows the truth, Miss Busby reminded herself. And we shall get to it in the end.

CHAPTER 8

Barnaby made straight across the lawn for the lake, his paws leaving frosty indents in his wake. Picking their way more carefully along the smartly raked gravel path that encircled it, Miss Busby and Adeline followed.

'I don't see why we couldn't have discussed this in your room, Isabelle,' Adeline grumbled. 'I've already had a long walk with Sir Gregory.'

'Because I want to know what he told you about the others, and we don't know who might be listening behind doors,' Miss Busby explained, thinking not only of the flushed young maid earlier, but also the dark figure of the previous night. Adeline had been in such a rush to get downstairs for lunch when she'd returned from her walk with the man in question that they hadn't had time to discuss anything, and with Flora having insisted they join her at her table, they'd had no time to talk alone since.

Miss Busby had hoped to ask Flora about Arthur's possible marriage prospects, but the young man himself had been seated at the next table. Flora had seemed vague and distracted, too; a far cry from the previous evening. She'd complained of a poor night's sleep, and had eaten her soup unbearably slowly. Adeline, in the meantime, managed both a steak and kidney pudding and a treacle sponge and custard.

Clara Harrowby had returned and taken lunch at her own table, but there had been no sign of Major Gresham or Sir Gregory.

'I suppose it was quite a heavy lunch. We'll do well to walk it off,' Adeline conceded, striding out with renewed purpose.

They soon reached the lake and stopped to admire the crystal-clear water. Well-maintained and free of all the usual autumn debris, Miss Busby spotted several marsh marigolds and water violets, thinking they would look beautiful when the spring brought its magic.

A wooden bench was set a little way ahead, sheltered from the wind by an acer tree, its leaves a vibrant mix of red and orange in the autumn sun.

'Let's sit and catch our breath a minute,' Miss Busby suggested, pointing ahead. 'You can tell me everything Sir Gregory said.'

'Good idea.' Adeline settled on the bench, pulling her cardigan a little tighter around her. 'Arthur Fortescue,' she announced, 'is a ne'er do well who has taken to drinking more than is good for him for. Sir Gregory said he can't imagine any marriage prospects on the horizon, as what young lady worth her salt would consider him a catch? The young gentleman has squandered one inheritance already, there's little chance he'd do any better with another.'

Miss Busby set her bag down between her feet. 'He's really quite a handsome young fellow,' she noted. 'And seems personable enough. And, of course, if he is in line for all this…' she added, glancing back towards the grandeur of the hotel.

'*If*, indeed,' Adeline said. 'But of course, no one knows… And he may seem alright, until you scratch the surface. Sir Gregory said Clara is hardly any better,' she went on, 'being the flighty, socialite sort. Apparently she's been milking her parents' death and sponging off poor Olivia for years.'

Miss Busby's heart sank to think of such a kind and hardworking woman being taken advantage of.

'And he says Flora is losing her marbles,' Adeline added for good measure. 'Apparently she has been growing increasingly discombobulated and frequently comes out with all manner of things she shouldn't.'

'Hmm,' Miss Busby considered. 'I wonder if that might be because Flora pointed out that he, too, benefitted from Olivia's financial support?'

Adeline bristled. 'I am only telling you what he said, Isabelle. It makes no odds to me either way. I was detecting. Did you put your notebook back in your bag? You ought to write this down.'

Miss Busby reached down to extract it and cast an eye over what she'd already written. 'Flora told us there were three guests indebted to Olivia for free bed and board: Herself, Major Gresham, and Sir Gregory.'

'Now we can add Clara,' Adeline said. 'And Arthur. If he is as inept at this stock market business as Flora suggested, he'll no doubt be in debt to boot. I can't imagine he's been paying his way.'

'Would family be expected to pay, I wonder?' Miss Busby's pencil hovered over the page. 'Flora said Olivia thought of them all as her "little family."'

Adeline thought for a moment. 'Not all,' she said. 'I don't recall her including Arthur.'

Miss Busby cast her mind back. 'You're right, but she did include Clara. How odd, not to mention Arthur, with him the only true family among them.' She made a note in the margin, before asking, 'What did Sir Gregory say about the Major?'

'That he's a terrible bore, always blathering on about the war and blaming it for everything. And whilst he may have more marbles than Flora, Sir Gregory doesn't quite think he's playing with a full set.'

Miss Busby blinked. 'That's not a very gentlemanly thing to say.'

'Sir Gregory speaks his mind.' Adeline shrugged. 'There is something to be said for honesty, Isabelle. Apparently the Major is destitute and wallows constantly in the unfairness of it all.'

Miss Busby looked out over the lake and thought for a moment. 'Olivia certainly seems to have been a most generous benefactor. I can't imagine any of them wanting her dead,' she went on, 'as they'd all lose out as a result. But if any one of them were afraid the named heir wouldn't offer them such continued generosity…'

'It may have been in their interest to prevent the revelation,' Adeline concluded darkly. 'The question is, with Olivia dead and her intended heir unrevealed, what happens now?'

'I should think, as the only next of kin, the hotel will go to Arthur,' Miss Busby said. 'But as we've already considered, Clara may have a case to contest his claim, having been under Olivia's wing for many years. And the law is rather more equitable regarding women now than it was at the time Olivia lost her home,' she added.

'But that sort of legal process could take years,' Adeline said.

Miss Busby nodded. 'And in the meantime, they all seem to be onto rather a good thing.'

The pair looked up as a red kite let out a sharp cry above them, effortlessly circling the lake.

'I do hope he's interested in the trout rather than Barnaby,' Miss Busby said with a worried glance towards the little terrier.

'He can hold his own,' Adeline said. 'Now, what do you think about Lázár?' she asked. 'Olivia, to whom all seem to be indebted, must have herself felt indebted to the man. I don't think it beyond the realms of possibility that she may have been intending to leave the hotel to him. Or indeed, that he would have been expecting her to do so. He may have felt betrayed if she had chosen someone who hadn't given up so much for her, and had, in fact, done little but take from her.'

'Perhaps, although his position as manager would have repaid a good deal of that debt, I'm sure. And he supported her entirely out of choice, don't forget.'

'We only have his word for that,' Adeline countered. 'For all we know, he could have been in trouble in Hungary, and Olivia's flight provided a convenient escape.'

'Adeline,' Miss Busby chided. 'We mustn't get carried away with ifs and buts; it would never end. We can only work with what we are told. And from what Lázár said, he was managing perfectly well before Olivia offered him the post.'

'A post he didn't earn until Olivia's husband was out of the picture,' Adeline reminded her. 'He had to continue working with the racehorse crowd until then.'

'Surely you're not suggesting Lázár killed Henry Fortescue?' Miss Busby asked, eyebrows raised. 'You might as well put forth that Sir Gregory killed him to ensure his free visits.'

'What? Why?' Adeline asked, her own brows shooting heavenwards.

'Well, Flora did say Henry Fortescue would never have approved of Olivia allowing her friends to stay at the hotel free of charge.'

Adeline harrumphed. 'Don't be silly, Isabelle. Would you suggest the same of Flora?'

Miss Busby smiled wryly and shook her head.

'I'm simply trying to keep an open mind,' Adeline sniffed.

'I did think it slightly odd that Olivia and Lázár went their separate ways after her marriage,' Miss Busby admitted, looking down at her notes.

'Yes, although I suppose it's only natural,' Adeline reasoned. 'And when Henry Fortescue did die, it sounded as if Lázár helped Olivia as much as she did him.'

Miss Busby nodded.

'I still find that solicitor chap shifty,' Adeline went on. 'If he was the one to persuade Olivia to write the will in the first place, he might have taken against Arthur for some reason. Him squandering his parents' inheritance, perhaps. What if in those long chats with Olivia that Flora mentioned, he'd been trying to persuade her to leave it all to someone else?'

'Really Adeline…' Miss Busby tried to rein her in. 'As her solicitor his only job was to see her wishes carried out, not impose his own.'

'It wouldn't have taken that long if he were just doing as she asked,' Adeline objected. 'And Lázár was very quick to defend him, too.' She warmed to her theme. 'The pair of them may have been in league! Lázár let him into Olivia's rooms to search for the will – Isabelle, what if he found it, and got rid of it?'

Miss Busby shivered as the wind picked up. 'Let's not get carried away,' she cautioned, putting her notebook back and rising to her feet. 'And we mustn't forget, the poor woman could still have died from natural causes.'

'But that doesn't explain the missing will. Surely it would have been locked in the safe,' Adeline reasoned, standing. 'Unless one of them removed it.'

'You suspect there's a safecracker among the group?' Miss Busby asked with a smile.

'Lázár may have had the code,' Adeline pointed out. 'And any of the others may have seen Olivia open the safe and noted the process.'

'Yes, I suppose you're right. We ought to speak to the rest of them as soon as possible. Then we can pass on what we've learned to the inspector, and make our way home.'

Adeline blinked in surprise. 'But Isabelle, it's beautiful here, why the rush to go back?'

'It's lovely, but we must have a good reason to be here, and there doesn't seem to be any real indication of murder,' Miss Busby said. 'Let's get a tot of something warming from the lounge. Clouds are gathering and a cosy fire will be just the thing. Come on, Barnaby,' she called, setting off at a brisk trot.

CHAPTER 9

Lázár was behind the bar, making a note of which bottles needed replenishing. The Major was the room's only other occupant, sitting in an armchair by the fire. Dressed in the same blazer and tie as yesterday, he was staring morosely into the flames. Miss Busby noted a coffee cup on the table beside him.

'May we have two coffees, please?' she asked Lázár.

'And could you make them Irish?' Adeline added.

Miss Busby looked at the clock over the bar, then to her friend, a single brow arched.

'A tot of something warming, you said,' Adeline reminded her. 'We don't want to risk a chill.'

Lázár smiled. 'Please, sit. I will bring them. Only very gently Irish?' He added quietly to Miss Busby.

'Yes, please.' Smiling in turn, she crossed to the fireplace.

'Good afternoon, Major,' she said, startling the man from his reverie. 'May we join you?'

After the briefest of pauses, he nodded to the chairs beside him.

Adeline, noting that his cup was empty, asked if he'd like another.

He nodded, raising a hand towards Lázár.

Miss Busby settled into the comfortable armchair, enjoying the warmth from the fire. Adeline sat on the other side of her.

'Handsome little dog,' the Major said, as the terrier lay down by the hearth and rested his chin on his front paws.

'We've just been out walking him,' Miss Busby said. 'The lake is beautiful. I can see why Olivia loved her hotel so much.'

Now that she was closer to him, she noticed that the collar of his shirt was frayed, and his shoes, though highly polished, could do with reheeling.

'Saw you out there with Gregory Penn this morning,' he said, looking to Adeline with disapproval. 'You ought to be careful.'

'Why?' Adeline asked, blinking in surprise.

'The man's an incorrigible flirt. That's why he comes here. His place in Scotland is halfway up a mountain and utterly remote. No ladies to chase. Makes the trek down when he feels like hunting.'

Adeline's cheeks reddened.

Miss Busby threw her a sympathetic look. 'That's a very long way to travel. Surely there are hotels nearer that would suffice?'

'Not with free bed and board,' he huffed. 'Or a resident wealthy widow to stalk.'

Adeline's shoulders drooped.

'Dear me. Well, thank you for the warning,' Miss Busby said.

He nodded.

'I did wonder, Adeline,' she added quietly, reaching to give her friend's hand a squeeze.

'Shrewd!' The Major's eyes brightened with interest as he looked at Miss Busby, his lips drawing up into the first smile they'd seen from him. 'Not many people sniff him out for what he is.'

'If he's so awful, why did Olivia let him stay?' Adeline huffed.

The smile faded. Lázár brought their coffees on a tray.

'Waifs and strays,' the Major said once the manager had returned to the bar. 'Olivia couldn't resist them. Look at Clara. And Flora. And me, I suppose.' He fell silent and blew on his coffee.

'Sir Gregory is hardly a waif, with a title and a home in Scotland,' Adeline pointed out, recovering herself.

'Oh, he's wealthy enough,' the Major conceded, 'but miserly as they come. Never parts with a farthing unless he has to. And even then...'

'But...' Adeline struggled to understand.

'Olivia was generous to a fault. She had nothing, you know, at one point. Changes a person,' the Major explained. 'She fell for Gregory Penn's nonsense about his money being tied up in the estate, and never charged him a bean when he stayed. He fawned over her endlessly in return.'

'Did they get along well?' Miss Busby asked.

'Well enough, I suppose,' he huffed. 'She found him charming. Gallant Sir Gregory, she called him. Foppish fraud, more like.'

Adeline bristled. 'Well, really. He comes across very well. Lovely manners. Well presented.'

The Major shot her a glare. 'If you can't see past a smart suit and an oily smile, there's no hope for you.'

Adeline was momentarily rendered speechless.

'And was it…just…friendship, between them?' Miss Busby pressed, as delicately as she could manage, keen to avoid an explosive retaliation from her wounded friend.

'Of course it was! Olivia was far too clever to truly fall for his nonsense.' He shot another meaningful look at Adeline. 'Although she enjoyed the attention, I should say,' he conceded. 'Penn certainly did. And he made sure he got as much of it as he could from any other unattached lady in residence. Wouldn't have done that if he cared a fig for Olivia, would he? Besides, they'd known each other for years. Nothing ever came of it. They didn't have anything in common. Not like Olivia and me. I'd always rather hoped…' He blinked, looking startled, then cleared his throat. 'Ahem. Well. It's all academic now.'

Adeline, who'd taken several sips of her coffee and recovered somewhat, leaned forward. 'What is?'

'Well,' he straightened his shoulders, 'I had rather hoped that Olivia and I might one day enjoy a more formalised companionship. We rubbed along well; we had both taken terrible knocks in our time and it leaves a mark, you know. But,' he added dejectedly, 'I'm afraid she never felt quite the same way for me as I did for her. And when I broached the subject, she was adamant she would never marry again.'

Miss Busby nodded in understanding, thinking of her Randolf and once more feeling strangely connected to Olivia.

'But she offered you a place to live here with her,' Adeline said. 'So she must have been fond of you.'

'Oh, yes,' he replied, a hint of pride in his eyes. 'She took a keen interest in the war, and adored hearing about my time in the military. That's how we met. I was giving a talk in Cheltenham and she came along. I had a celebrated career, you see. Coldstream Guards – First Battalion,' he explained, smoothing down his regimental tie. 'Involved in a great many battles. Had good men with me, of course, but they'd all tell you I led with discipline and honour. We never lost a battle, you know. Not one. The men thought I was lucky, but it was hard work, meticulous planning, and valour. That's what gets you through.' He fell silent for a moment, his expression changing. 'Luck rather failed me when I returned home. Lost my wife. Bronchitis. Couldn't plan for that, and no one ever fought more valiantly than my poor Helena. The following day I received word from India that the tea plantation I'd invested in had folded. You couldn't have found a more solid prospect. I'd gone through the accounts in minute detail before investing my entire savings in the thing.' His eyes took on a haunted look as he stared out through the window. 'The war took more than men, let me tell you. Crops, shipping routes, and every damned penny I ever earned serving King and country. If you'll pardon my language,' he added, looking back to the pair of them. 'And with no way to recover my losses, here I am. Completely dependent on the kindness of others.' He sighed, picking up his coffee cup with a hand that showed a slight tremor.

'How terrible for you. But thank goodness for Olivia,' Miss Busby said.

'Yes,' he rallied. 'My luck held on that front, at least. Said I had a home here for life, if I needed it, and she was a woman of her word. And she knew I'd have done anything for her.' He stopped for a moment; his voice had wavered at the last, and he cleared his throat once more. 'I shall miss her dreadfully. Already do, in fact.' He turned his face aside. Miss Busby thought to offer him a handkerchief, but feared it might upset his sensibilities.

Lázár approached quietly, asking if anyone would like another drink. Heads shook in reply.

'Very good. Afternoon tea will be served shortly,' he announced, then turned and left the lounge.

'I lost my fiancé,' Miss Busby said softly. 'Many years ago now, but I remember it as if it were yesterday. You must think of the good times, and how fortunate you were to have enjoyed each other's friendship.'

'Olivia was my lifeline. After the war, it felt as if the world had become nothing but cruel, taunting me with disaster after disaster. She showed me kindness again, and I believe she loved me in her own way. I still can't believe she's gone. It was so sudden. So unexpected...' His voice tailed off.

'We'd heard she was in good health,' Adeline said, 'and, as you say, the attack seemed so sudden, it's hard not to wonder if–'

He looked up sharply. 'I know what you're implying, and I can assure you that, whatever happened to Olivia, I had no hand in it. I loved her dearly and would never have hurt her.'

'Well, of course not,' Adeline said, rearing back in her chair a little in surprise. I wasn't–'

'Everyone is thinking it,' he continued, his tone more sad than angry now. 'Of course they are. With the timing of it. Everyone is wondering if something was....done. We are not stupid. But who in their right mind would want to hurt her? She cared for us all.'

'Yes, of course. I really didn't mean...

'Are you sure you wouldn't like a small tot of something?' Adeline asked kindly.

'No, thank you.' He glanced over to the bar. 'I'm surprised there's anything left, the way Arthur goes at it.'

'We've heard he's a demon for the drink,' Adeline said, tone heavy now with shared disapproval. 'And not too clever with his finances, to boot.'

The Major gave a snort of derision. 'Messed about with the stock market, apparently. Seems he's as ineffective at that as he is everything else. Lost most of his inheritance that way after his parents died. All he's got left is the house, and that's beginning to crumble around him. That's why he's here sniffing around now. Wants to be first in line for Hamnett Hall.' He scowled. 'Won't get a look in, of course.'

'Won't he?' Miss Busby asked, leaning forward with interest.

A dark smile crossed the Major's features. 'Olivia was no fool. She made sure her husband left the place to her outright, meaning if he died first that young fool would have no claim to it.'

Miss Busby thought back to Olivia's own experience in Hungary, and exchanged a knowing glance with Adeline.

'But what will happen to the hotel, if the will isn't found?' Adeline asked.

'No good asking me,' he replied sadly. 'Arthur and Clara will fight over it, I expect. She's no better than he is. Charming, when it suits her. Not unlike Gregory Penn; the pair of them both play their cards boldly. Ask Ludlow, if you're that interested. I expect he'll be the only winner out of all this. Legal battles drag on forever and rack up immense costs. What little is left will probably pass to Arthur, in the end, and the whole business will have been for nothing. Olivia would be heartbroken. The hotel meant everything to her.'

'What will you do, Major? Where will you go?' Adeline pressed gently.

He sighed. 'I shall just have to wait and see. I doubt anything will happen quickly.'

'Unless the will is found,' Miss Busby said.

'Of course,' he replied, 'and I hope it is found, and soon. Olivia was in such high spirits over it. And I am quite sure she would have made provision for those of us she had always cared for.'

He looked aside, clearing his throat once more. 'Will you please excuse me?' he asked, rising to his feet. 'I would like to smarten myself up before tea.' Nodding politely to both, he hurried from the room; but not before Miss Busby noted that his eyes had begun to water.

'Well,' Adeline breathed. 'What do you make of all that?'

'*Curiouser and curiouser*,' Miss Busby said, exhaling slowly.

'I can't fathom how they all profess to have been so close to Olivia, and so indebted to her, yet not one of them knew who she was planning to leave her legacy to,' Adeline remarked.

'To whom,' Miss Busby muttered automatically, tapping a finger against her chin in thought. 'She had a manager who gave up everything to follow her to England, and two gentlemen here vying for her attention—'

'Although I can't imagine Sir Gregory was serious about her,' Adeline pointed out. 'As the Major said, it was just…his way.'

'Perhaps, but it should serve as a reminder that men aren't always what they seem, Adeline,' she sighed, before continuing, 'Olivia also had two youngsters to whom she stood in *loco parentis*. One of whom appears to owe her everything, and the other who seems to expect everything, regardless…'

'We ought to find out exactly what happened to Clara's parents,' Adeline suggested. 'Women, especially young women, aren't always what they seem either, Isabelle,' she cautioned. 'If both the girl's parents died whilst working at the hotel…'

'You think Clara may have been out for revenge?' Miss Busby raised a sceptical brow.

'I think we ought to check,' Adeline said firmly. 'We seem to be going around in circles, currently.'

'Oh, I don't know,' Miss Busby countered. 'We have uncovered unrequited love, a terminal flirt, manipulative minors, and evidently a good deal of tension between all concerned.'

'Sir Gregory isn't tense,' Adeline noted.

Miss Busby nodded. 'You're right. But I'd say he's the only one. You don't think he may have been rather more interested in Olivia than he let on?'

'I have absolutely no idea. If he was, he certainly wouldn't have mentioned it to me. Why do you ask?'

'The Major said they'd known each other for years, and that Olivia liked the attention. What if Sir Gregory had proposed marriage, and Olivia accepted, and that's why she refused the Major when he "broached the subject"?'

'Rather a large "what if",' Adeline pointed out. 'And I thought you were against ifs and buts in general?'

Miss Busby's cheeks flushed. 'Yes, fair point. It is easy to get carried away, isn't it?'

Adeline nodded gracefully. 'Well, surely they would simply have announced their engagement, if that were the case.'

'Unless Olivia didn't want to hurt the Major's feelings.'

'She would have had to, at some point.' Adeline shrugged. 'I'm not sure where you're going with this, Isabelle.'

'No. Neither am I.' Miss Busby sighed. Her head was spinning; she suspected the Irish coffee was to blame, even though Lázár had indeed been gentle with the whisky. 'The inspector said we must always consider motive, and two gentlemen vying for the attention of one lady is somewhat traditional in the motive stakes.'

'Not when it's the lady who's killed,' Adeline pointed out. 'Besides, I don't think she was particularly interested in either of them. It seems it was the hotel Olivia was in love with.'

'Perhaps someone was jealous of that, and wanted to see it pass from her hands?'

'I think you're trying too hard to make a motive fit the circumstances,' Adeline cautioned. 'It's not like you, Isabelle.'

'I think you might be right,' she admitted. 'I feel rather like the inspector, viewing everyone with suspicion and not trusting what I'm told.'

'Probably because you're becoming an old hand at detecting,' Adeline remarked cheerfully. 'And it makes sense, when you think of the people who've lied in our prior investigations. When it comes down to it, it's people in general who aren't always what they seem. Men or women. Young or old.'

'I suppose you're right,' Miss Busby hedged, not liking the idea.

'I expect you just need something to eat. I find that always helps me. I wonder when this afternoon tea is to be served?' Adeline asked, then turned the conversation to home and family, to divert her friend from darker thoughts.

The lounge slowly began to fill with the others, and soon enough Annie and Jimmy appeared pushing trolleys of sandwiches, cold cuts, and little delicate cakes, along with pots of tea. Sir Gregory reappeared, but after receiving a rather chilly glare from Adeline, he chose to sit with Clara. Arthur sat alone, as did the Major, who seemed rather embarrassed when he returned.

Flora, to Miss Busby's concern, wasn't present.

Barnaby soon cottoned on to the occasion, visiting each table in turn and receiving something from everyone except Clara, who stroked him instead, saying she didn't want to cause the dog to become fat.

'I ought to telephone Richard,' Miss Busby said. She hadn't felt very hungry, but had managed a couple of sandwiches to appease her friend. 'Finish your cake, Adeline,' she insisted. 'I'll see you upstairs.' She cast one last curious look at the Major before leaving the lounge. Something about his manner troubled her. Desperation, she knew from previous investigations, could make people do strange and occasionally terrible things, and love wasn't always as pure as one would believe.

As the operator connected her call to The Grange, she was cheered to hear Richard's voice and told him that she thought they would be home soon.

CHAPTER 10

Miss Busby and Adeline lingered over breakfast, hoping to catch either Arthur or Clara to engage in conversation. They'd been unable to do so at dinner the previous evening, which had been a somewhat tense affair. Several eyes had been cast their way none-too-warmly, and Miss Busby was wondering if people were guessing at their reasons for remaining there.

Neither youngster had made an appearance this morning, and nor had Flora, which concerned Miss Busby.

'Is Lady Benbow alright?' she asked when Annie came to clear their plates.

'She hasn't been sleeping, miss,' she said, concern in her brown eyes. 'I've taken tea and crumpets to her room. She'll be along later.'

Miss Busby smiled, relieved. 'I know how that feels,' she told Adeline quietly as the young maid bustled back towards the kitchen. 'I didn't sleep well last night myself. Thoughts of motives and deceit were dancing in my mind until the small hours.'

'I slept like a log,' Adeline remarked, brushing crumbs from her ample chest. 'What's our next step?' she asked, as they left the breakfast room and walked into the reception area.

Before Miss Busby could admit that she wasn't entirely sure, the sound of tyres on gravel could be heard. They turned to see a gleaming silver motorcar draw up in front of the glass front doors.

'Who's this?' Adeline wondered aloud. 'Is that a Talbot? It's rather nice,' she added in envious tones.

Miss Busby watched with interest as a slim young woman dismounted from behind the wheel. Tall and elegantly clad in a long white coat, matching cloche hat, and leather driving gloves, she looked up at the hotel with a smile of approval. Jimmy instantly ran out from behind the desk, cramming his cap in place en route.

The pair exchanged a few words, then, dropping a set of car keys into Jimmy's hand, the woman walked towards the entrance. Adeline, never one to miss a trick, quickly smoothed down her cream silk blouse, straightened her long dark skirt, and stepped smartly forward to open the door for her. She could almost be mistaken for staff, Miss Busby thought, if it weren't for the heels and bright jewellery.

'Oh! Thank you,' the newcomer said. Her features were delicate and pretty, highlighted by deftly applied make up. She took her hat off to shake out a stylish blond bob, smiling and looking around with interest.

Barnaby gave her a cursory look before darting through the door to see what Jimmy was up to. The porter was struggling forward with three large suitcases.

'Mrs Olivia Fortescue?' the young lady said, looking to Miss Busby. 'Lydia Whitfield.' She held out a hand. 'So lovely to meet you at last!'

Miss Busby blinked. 'Oh, no, I am Miss Busby.'

'Gosh, I'm so sorry!' Lydia turned to Adeline instead, uncertainty flickering in her large, grey-blue eyes.

'And I am Mrs Adeline Fanshawe,' she said, just as Lázár emerged from the staff corridor.

'Good morning. May I help you?' he asked, looking curiously up at the young lady.

'Oh, yes! Good morning! Lydia Whitfield. I have a room booked.'

Jimmy struggled in with the suitcases precariously balanced.

'I am Lázár, the manager here, and I am afraid we have no record of a booking,' he said. 'Are you quite sure…?'

Lydia nodded. 'Quite sure! It's to be rather a long stay, over the winter break. Perhaps you'd check with Mrs Olivia Fortescue? She's expecting me.'

One of the suitcases fell to the floor.

'Sorry, miss,' Jimmy muttered, trying to pick it up, then dropping them all with a thud.

'That's alright,' she said, giving a light laugh. 'It's my own fault, I always pack far too much!' Looking back to Lázár, she noted his expression and her smile faltered. 'Is there a problem?'

'I am most sorry, Miss Whitfield, to have to tell you that Mrs Fortescue has passed away. We would have let you know, if we had a record of your booking.'

Lydia's hand flew to her mouth. 'Oh, my goodness! How absolutely dreadful. What happened?'

'Heart attack,' Adeline was quick to explain. 'Completely out of the blue. Tragic.'

'Poor Olivia. I'm so sorry. I had no idea, of course. We had plans to… Oh, I can hardly believe it.' Her eyes had widened in shock.

Lázár nodded. An awkward silence fell, into which Adeline offered, 'I arrived the day before yesterday to find myself in exactly the same position.'

Lydia looked to her. 'Really? Goodness. I'm so sorry, but I'm afraid I don't know quite what to do now…'

'Come through to the lounge and have a drink. It will bolster you up.' Adeline took command. 'That's what we did, isn't it Isabelle?'

'Yes,' Miss Busby said, watching the young woman with interest. 'Jimmy,' she called over her shoulder, 'do you mind if Barnaby stays with you? He'll have much more fun.'

'Course, miss,' Jimmy said, the suitcases finally balanced once more.

'But, shall I be able to stay?' Lydia looked back to Lázár, wringing her hands nervously in front of her. 'I don't think I could face driving all the way back to London, and Olivia has already made a payment… Oh, gosh, it's all so very…'

'I will have Annie to make up a room,' Lázár said, stepping behind the desk and making a note in the book. 'Please, do not worry. We are open for three days more, so you may rest and recover.'

'Oh, so kind, thank you! And yes,' she said, turning to Adeline, 'I think I would like to sit in the lounge for a moment. Gather myself together, that sort of thing.'

'We'll take you through. Come along.'

'Just let me remove my coat, first.' Lydia let the beautiful coat fall from her shoulders to reveal a very pretty pale pink dress in shimmering silk and a long string of pearls in the latest fashion. She turned to drape the coat over the suitcases still held in Jimmy's arms and followed the ladies out.

They all heard the thud as the young porter dropped the lot, but pretended not to notice.

Major Gresham was in his usual chair by the fire, his back to the door, newspaper in hand.

Lázár followed them into the lounge, explaining that tea and coffee had not yet been provided, with breakfast having only just been cleared away.

'I can make fresh,' he added.

'Yes, tea would be most welcome,' Miss Busby suggested before Adeline could get any ideas – it was barely ten after all. 'With plenty of sugar for the shock, Miss Whitfield?'

'Yes, thank you. And it's Lydia, please,' she insisted.

Lázár bowed and headed back towards reception.

The newspaper rustled and the Major turned at the

unfamiliar voice, gazing with open suspicion at the newcomer.

Miss Busby politely introduced the pair from a distance. 'Lydia, this is Major Gresham, a friend of Olivia,' she called. 'And Major, Miss Lydia Whitfield is…?'

'Oh, yes, I'd like to think I'm a friend, too,' she said, raising a hand to wave at the Major before Adeline steered her towards a table at the far end of the room.

'She has only just heard the news,' Miss Busby explained, before crossing the room and taking a seat in turn.

As the young woman removed her gloves, Miss Busby saw that her hands were trembling slightly. 'Would you like to sit closer to the fire?' she asked.

Lydia followed the direction of her gaze. 'Oh, no, thank you. It's just the…unexpectedness of it all. Actually, I think I might just… Is there a ladies lavatory?'

'In reception, to the right,' Miss Busby said.

Lydia smiled gratefully and went off in that direction.

'Well!' Adeline exclaimed. 'This may be the missing piece, Isabelle!'

'How so?' Miss Busby asked.

'Olivia made arrangements for the girl to stay without telling the staff, not even Lázár!' She dropped her voice to a whisper. 'She could be the intended heir!'

'It's possible, but I don't think it likely. She has rather expensive luggage, Adeline. Goyard, if my eyes didn't deceive me. Not to mention the motorcar.'

'What has that got to do with it?' Adeline asked, brow furrowed.

'Would someone who was used to such luxury dedicate themselves to the daily drudgery of running a hotel?'

'Why not? You oughtn't judge, Isabelle. Just because she enjoys the finer things in life doesn't mean she wouldn't roll up her sleeves and work. That may well be how she's able to enjoy such luxury in the first place.'

'Perhaps, but she's very young, Adeline. I suspect it's more a case of her parents, or grandparents, having rolled up their sleeves. And she seems nervous…' Miss Busby found herself thinking back to when she first met Lucy Lannister, and wondering for a moment if Lydia could be a newspaper reporter, here for the undercover scoop on a wealthy widow leaving no heir.

'She seems upset,' Adeline corrected. 'Isabelle, you really are every bit as suspicious as the infernal Scot these days.'

Miss Busby sighed. Adeline was right, she was viewing everyone with suspicion and it wasn't like her; the poor girl did seem genuinely shocked, after all. She wondered if it were as much because she didn't have her cosy cottage and her ginger tom to return to at the end of the day, as it was her repeated involvement in murders. No matter how duplicitous and deceitful the individuals in their other cases had been, there had always been a safe and comforting dose of normalcy before bed. And of course, she realised, this is the first time the inspector has ever asked me to investigate, and I don't want to let him down. It brought a new sort of pressure to proceedings.

Lázár returned with a tray of tea things, and Adeline busied herself stirring the pot.

'Should there be anything more, I will be in reception,' he said, before hurrying away, no doubt to alert Annie to prepare a room.

Lydia returned with an apologetic smile, and Miss Busby poured. Adeline dropped four sugar cubes into Lydia's cup. Then one more for good measure. 'You came from London, did you say?' she asked. 'How was the drive? I thought about a Talbot, but my husband loved the Rolls. I don't think I could ever part with it.'

'Oh, is that yours? It's very striking! I wouldn't part with my car either,' Lydia said. Miss Busby noted that she placed her hands in her lap, out of sight.

With her question unanswered, Adeline decided to take a more direct approach. 'Did you know Olivia Fortescue well?' she asked, taking a sip of her tea as if unconcerned about the answer.

'Not as well as I would've liked,' Lydia confessed. 'We'd planned to spend the next few weeks together, and I was so looking forward to finding out more about her.'

'Yes, you mentioned that Olivia had already made a payment?' Miss Busby pressed.

'Oh, yes, I… Well.' Lydia's eyes flicked to the door, before she turned and glanced briefly back towards the Major. 'I suppose there's no harm… if poor Olivia… Gosh, it's rather difficult. It was supposed to be a secret, you see.'

Adeline immediately straightened. 'You needn't worry,' she assured. 'Isabelle and I are the very souls of discretion.'

'You only arrived here recently, you said?' Lydia asked. Adeline nodded.

'Well, then I suppose… Oh, it will all come out anyway, I'm sure. I'm a writer, you see. I was engaged by Olivia to write her memoirs.'

Adeline's eyes grew almost as round as the saucer beneath her cup.

'Really? How interesting,' Miss Busby said, as a small tingle of satisfaction began in her chest and slowly spread outwards. *I was close*, she thought; *not a reporter, but a writer all the same.*

'Yes indeed,' Adeline added, leaning forward eagerly. 'We have only just learned of Olivia's remarkable life ourselves. I'm sure it would make fascinating reading.'

'Oh?' Lydia said, confusion crossing her delicate features. 'But I thought you were–?'

'Recent acquaintances,' Adeline cut in. 'Her time has been so cruelly cut short.'

Lydia nodded. 'I feel just the same. There was so much Olivia seemed to want to discuss. We talked briefly of the hardships she'd endured in coming to England and building a new life for herself. And she said that as her story was drawing towards its natural close, people were owed the truth of it.'

'Which people? What truth?' Adeline breathed.

'Well, that's what she was going to tell me,' Lydia said. 'We'd spoken on the phone several times, and corresponded briefly, but Olivia said she would only go into further detail in person.'

'It sounds as if she had something important to divulge,' Miss Busby remarked.

'Yes, I rather think she had,' Lydia replied. 'But she was so careful about it all. It felt like some kind of great–'

'Secret?' Adeline supplied, eyes shining with the intrigue of it all.

Lydia nodded, as Miss Busby's brain revved into high gear.

'Did anyone else know that Olivia had engaged your services?' Miss Busby asked.

Lydia shook her head. 'I don't think so. I assumed that's why she wanted me here when the hotel would be quiet, so we could talk privately. I was rather looking forward to it,' she confessed. 'Other people's secrets are always so interesting, aren't they?'

Adeline locked eyes with Miss Busby, who knew they were both thinking the same: Had someone killed Olivia to prevent her secret being revealed?

'And did Olivia give you any idea at all as to the nature of this secret?' Miss Busby asked, placing her cup back on its saucer.

'Not really.' Lydia smiled ruefully, taking a sip of her own tea before adding, 'She said once we'd done a few more interviews together, everything would fall into place. It didn't sound like the sort of thing you'd just come out with. But she did say she wanted to leave behind a true record of her life. She was rather adamant about it, actually.'

'And was there no one else Olivia suggested you might speak to–' Miss Busby began, before the door to the lounge flew open and Sir Gregory strode in. 'Whose is the Talbot outside?' he called. 'Absolute beauty of a motorcar!' He caught sight of the newcomer and immediately pulled his shoulders back. 'Hallo! I don't believe we've met.' Crossing the room to give a gentlemanly bow, he introduced himself. 'Sir Gregory Penn, at your service. Is the car yours?' he asked eagerly.

Lydia shifted a little uncomfortably in her seat, as Adeline's eyes narrowed dangerously.

'Erm, yes. Lydia Whitfield. Pleased to meet you.'

'Mrs?' Sir Gregory asked.

'Miss,' Adeline growled.

'Miss Whitfield, delighted to make your acquaintance! And may I say, you have excellent taste. Might we take a look at her, when you've time?'

'Well, really,' Adeline huffed, before the door swung open once again. The Major flung his newspaper down in annoyance at the constant disturbances.

'Miss Whitfield?' Annie came over. 'Your room's ready for you now. Number 12. You're upstairs, next to Miss Busby and Mrs Fanshawe. I can take you up, if you'd like?'

'Oh! Yes, thank you. So sorry,' Lydia said to Sir Gregory, looking anything but. 'Lovely to meet you, Miss Busby, Mrs Fanshawe.'

CHAPTER 11

Miss Busby nodded politely, as Adeline continued to look daggers at her now ex-suitor.

'See you anon!' Sir Gregory called after her, oblivious to the daggers. 'Lovely girl,' he said. 'Why is she here? Do you know? I didn't think we were expecting anyone else.'

'She is here on a matter concerning Olivia's secret,' Adeline announced, with a certain amount of relish.

Miss Busby winced. She would have preferred to keep it between them for the time being, but as Lydia had said, the news would spread soon enough. And she noted with interest that Sir Gregory's colour had faded. In fact, he'd gone rather pale.

'Secret? What secret?' he asked.

'Miss Whitfield had been engaged to write Olivia's memoirs,' Miss Busby explained, watching him closely.

His brow furrowed. 'I hardly think that likely. Olivia was an open book to her friends, but very private in all other respects. She wouldn't have wanted to publish details of her personal life for any Tom, Dick, or Harry to gossip about.'

'Worried you'll come out of it poorly, Penn?' the Major called out, rising to his feet.

Anger rose in Sir Gregory's voice. 'Don't be ridiculous. Olivia wouldn't have indulged anything of the sort, and you know it.'

'She was her own woman,' the Major said. 'Why shouldn't she tell her story, if that was her choice?' He nodded politely to the ladies and made his way stiffly to the door.

'Because… it's not… Bah,' Sir Gregory huffed. 'It's nothing to do with me either way. I can't see Olivia having agreed to it, that's all. Someone must have put her up to it. And I'm hardly the one who should be worried,' he muttered, glaring at the Major's retreating back.

'Come along, Isabelle.' Adeline made to follow the man out with a rather satisfied smile. 'We've a lot to discuss.'

'Do excuse us,' Miss Busby said to Sir Gregory.

They pushed the door open to reveal Lázár making a telephone call at the reception desk.

'Then I may please leave a message?' he asked into the mouthpiece. Looking up, he caught sight of the ladies, nodded, then turned his back to continue in a lower tone, 'Please ask him to come to Hamnett Hall at his most soonest convenience. Thank you.'

Putting the receiver down, he turned and gave them a rather strained smile.

'Lázár, do you think it odd,' Miss Busby asked softly, crossing to the desk, 'that Olivia didn't mention the young woman was coming to stay?'

'Miss Olivia had no obligation to tell me her plans,' he said, although his tone was rather defensive.

'But surely if the girl was to be a guest, the hotel manager ought to have known,' Adeline pointed out.

'I expect she would have told you,' Miss Busby said kindly, 'in good time.'

'Yes, it seems there was something she was going to tell *everyone*, in good time,' Adeline added.

'I've been meaning to ask,' Miss Busby cut her off swiftly, 'is the groundsman still at the hotel? Or was he one of the staff let go for the holiday?'

'Mr Wallace?' Lázár asked, looking to Miss Busby in surprise. 'He works only very few hours at this time of year. He was with us the day before the ball, but now won't return until the break. Is there a problem with the grounds?'

'Not at all,' Miss Busby assured him. 'They're immaculate.'

'Mr Wallace has been with us for many years. His father before him was groundskeeper under Mr Henry Fortescue.'

'And the cook?' Miss Busby asked. 'Has she worked here for a long time, too?' Miss Busby pressed.

'Many years, also. Miss Olivia engaged Mrs Burton herself. She was previously Cook at the Bell Hotel in Cheltenham. It was quite the coup when Miss Olivia enticed her away. Although,' he added, 'the lady is known to be of a temperamental sort.'

Jimmy pulled the front door open just as Miss Busby was about to ask more, and Barnaby trotted through.

Stopping to give his mistress a quick wag of his tail, he scurried intently up the stairs.

'He's been after the pheasants, miss, so he should be tired out 'fer you,' Jimmy said. 'Almost got one! Inches from his tail, he was.'

'Thank you.' Miss Busby smiled. 'Come on, Adeline, let's go up. He'll want a lie down.'

They followed the dog upstairs. Once safely behind the door of Miss Busby's room, Adeline burst into excited discussion.

'Now, Isabelle, we shall see who is the most unnerved by the arrival of Miss Whitfield!' she announced.

'Yes,' Miss Busby agreed as Barnaby jumped onto her bed, turned around three times then curled up with his nose under his tail. 'She already appears to have set the cat among the pigeons.'

She went to sit at the desk and picked up her pencil to add to her notes. Adeline crossed to the window and looked out.

'Why did you ask about the groundsman?' she asked.

'I worry we might be focussing too much on the guests,' Miss Busby explained. 'We oughtn't overlook any other possibilities. Speaking of which...' She put the pencil down. 'I've been thinking about what Lázár told us about her father's estate, and wondering if there may be a Hungarian connection.'

'How?' Adeline asked, turning to her in surprise.

'What if the cousin's wife heard of Olivia's subsequent success here, and felt...aggrieved?'

'Isabelle, that was decades ago,' Adeline objected. 'How would she have heard about Hamnett Hall? Or made the trek to exact revenge? And revenge for what, exactly?' she added. 'Olivia never did anything to her.'

'That didn't stop her putting the girl out of her home,' Miss Busby pointed out. 'But it does seem rather a remote chance,' she agreed with a sigh. 'There's the issue of the other servants being disgruntled at Mr Fortescue's interest in Olivia, too.'

Adeline tsked. 'Years ago, again!'

'They do say revenge is a dish best served cold. And some of them may still be local, and perhaps have connections to existing staff.'

'But how do you imagine they may have exacted this supposed revenge? If Olivia didn't eat or drink at the ball, whatever may have been done to the poor woman must have been done at the dinner. There were no visiting Hungarians, and no servants, current or otherwise, present.'

'Except Lázár.'

'He was there as a guest.' Adeline dismissed the point.

Miss Busby blinked. It wasn't like her not to jump on any suspicion aimed the manager's way. She waited a moment, but when nothing else was forthcoming added, 'And Cook provided the meal, of course. She would have been well placed to put something in Olivia's food.'

'Lázár said Olivia hired the woman herself. I can't imagine there being any resentment there.'

'No.' Miss Busby raised a weary hand to her temple.

If even Adeline couldn't see anything of concern, she felt she must be barking up the wrong tree. 'I expect you're right. We ought to check what they ate, though.'

'Very well, but are we agreed that our killer must be in the hotel?' Adeline pressed the advantage.

'It's very likely. But with none of them seeming to know who Olivia would have chosen as heir, I can't help thinking an outside influence may be at play.'

'We shall just have to keep a close eye on whoever seems the most concerned by the possible revelation of Olivia's secret,' Adeline said. 'That will lead us right to the killer, I am sure of it.'

'Hm,' said Miss Busby, 'secrets do tend to be difficult to unlock. That's if there even is one, of course.'

'Good Lord, Isabelle! Why on earth would Lydia have been invited to talk in person otherwise?' She shook her head, and tutted, before continuing, 'Now, the Major didn't seem perturbed in the least,' Adeline went on, 'but Sir Gregory's reaction was more telling.' His recent behaviour, it seemed, had painted him a far more likely suspect in her eyes than when he'd played the dashing suitor. 'And who do you imagine Lázár was telephoning earlier?' she went on, answering her own question before Miss Busby had a chance, 'That solicitor, Ludlow, mark my words. Didn't I say I thought the two of them might be in league?'

'But Lázár doesn't know why Lydia's here yet,' Miss Busby reminded her, back in the familiar position of having to defend the man. 'Besides, letting the family solicitor know that Olivia arranged a meeting with a stranger prior to her death is probably eminently sensible.'

Adeline *harumphed*. 'Well, perhaps, but matters are accelerating, Isabelle; we mustn't let them overtake us!'

'Nor should we rush headlong into any wild theories,' Miss Busby cautioned. 'And yes,' she added, 'I do appreciate I've possibly fallen into that trap myself. Let's ask Lydia to come to lunch with us when we go down to the dining room, then we can watch how the others react.'

'Good idea,' Adeline replied, mollified for the moment.

Dropping into the armchair beside the fire, she gazed into the bright embers and stretched out comfortably, before asking, 'What if she goes downstairs before us?'

'We'll hear her,' Miss Busby said.

'Yes, of course. I'll listen out for the door.' Adeline straightened in the chair with purpose.

Miss Busby continued her notes, adding new pages for the cook and the groundsman, in addition to Lydia. The clock ticked softly above the fireplace as Adeline's head began to nod forward, the excitement of the morning and the warmth of the fire combining to take their toll. Miss Busby kept a close eye on the time as she worked, and an ear open for the sound of footsteps outside. The moment noon struck, she gently roused her friend who, it turned out, had only been resting her eyes.

Deciding to leave Barnaby sleeping, they set out to knock on Lydia's door.

'Oh, thank goodness!' The young woman beamed as she saw them. 'I thought it might have been that man, wanting a look at my car.'

Miss Busby smiled sympathetically. 'We wondered if you would like to join us downstairs for lunch?'

'Yes please! I'm feeling rather peckish,' Lydia confessed, locking her door and following them down the corridor. 'I've been trying to think what to do. I've made a few notes already and I wondered about leaving them for Olivia's next of kin, but as I don't know what she wanted kept under wraps I'm rather torn…'

'Yes, it's a tricky situation,' Miss Busby agreed.

As they approached the staircase, raised voices could be heard in reception. Adeline, quick as a flash, held out an arm to stop the others long enough to hear someone complain angrily that, 'A memoir could potentially expose details that would complicate legal matters even further.'

Lydia's eyes widened and she brushed Adeline's arm aside, darting for the bannister rail to lean over and see who the voice belonged to.

'Ah.' Lázár looked up nervously from behind the desk 'This is the young lady now. Miss Whitfield, here is Mr Ludlow. He is Miss Olivia's solicitor.'

Lydia trotted briskly down the stairs with Miss Busby and a rather disgruntled Adeline in her wake.

Mr Ludlow, smartly attired in a crisp grey suit, looked as weary as he had the day they'd first encountered him, with dark circles under his eyes, but there was a hard edge to his voice now.

'What's all this about a memoir?' he demanded. 'Mrs Fortescue didn't mention anything of the sort to me.'

Lydia had approached him with a smile, but seemed taken aback by his tone, 'Didn't she? Well, I'm sure she had her reasons.'

'Be that as it may, you can't just turn up here and start rummaging about, you know,' Ludlow objected. 'It should have been run past me first, as Mrs Fortescue's legal advisor. It's not like her at all.' He shot Lydia a suspicious glare.

'I won't be rummaging about,' she replied, taking a step backwards. 'Olivia engaged my services, and work has already begun. Obviously, given the circumstances, I'm in rather a quandary. I shall have to talk to my editor.' She turned her back on the solicitor and smiled politely at the manager. 'Is lunch ready, Lázár?'

Adeline gave the young woman a look of approval.

Lázár nodded. 'Yes. Please, go through.'

The trio were the first into the dining room. Choosing a table with a clear view of the door, they took their seats.

'Mr Ludlow was awfully rude, wasn't he?' Lydia said.

Adeline nodded. 'I haven't trusted him from the off. And thick as thieves with Lázár, again,' she added, looking to Miss Busby.

'Olivia hadn't completed her will when she died,' Miss Busby explained to the writer. 'Nor can anyone find a draft of it. I think Mr Ludlow is struggling with matters of the estate.'

'Oh…' Lydia's eyes widened. 'Goodness. Yes, that must make things complicated,' she conceded. She thought for a moment, then added, 'but of course, given what Olivia talked about, it does rather make sense.'

'Does it?' Adeline prompted, as Annie came to take their order.

'There's glazed ham with peas and potatoes, or pea and ham soup,' the maid announced. 'Cook's running down the larder for the break,' she added apologetically.

'Glazed ham sounds lovely,' Miss Busby said, and both Lydia and Adeline chose the same. As Annie rushed off, the dining room door opened to reveal Lady Flora. She tottered in dressed in the same simple black dress as yesterday, but had paired it with a cheery yellow cardigan.

'Flora!' Miss Busby exclaimed. 'How lovely to see you! Would you like to sit with us?'

Blinking in the bright sunlight streaming through the windows, Flora's smile widened. 'I should be most happy to,' she agreed, as Lydia sprang up to pull out a chair for her.

'This is Lady Flora Benbow,' Miss Busby introduced. 'And this is Miss—'

'Oh, but I know who this is! The hotel is abuzz with talk! You are Miss Whitfield.' Flora extended a thin and wrinkled hand, which Lydia shook with a smile.

'Have I upset someone else?' Lydia asked. 'Perhaps I ought to have just kept the payment and driven straight home. But it didn't seem right somehow.'

'Oh, you mustn't worry about upsetting people.' Flora smiled. 'They're always upset about something. Gregory was haranguing poor Lázár in the lounge earlier, and

Major Gresham was haranguing Gregory in turn. Young Clara and I rather enjoyed watching them! Men can be so silly. I thought Arthur might say something to quieten them down, but he was in a mood of his own. Will you be able to complete the memoir?' Flora asked eagerly. 'Olivia led such an interesting life. An inspiring tale of hard work overcoming adversity. I should think it would do a lot of people good to read it!'

'I'm afraid we'd hardly got into the details at all,' Lydia explained.

'Oh, what a shame! But I was her closest friend. I could tell you what I know, if you'd like?' Flora's face was bright and animated, in complete contrast to how she'd appeared the last time they'd shared a meal.

'That's awfully kind of you,' Lydia replied. 'But I rather think there was something in particular Olivia wanted to touch on.'

'Ah, yes, the crux of the matter! I do believe there's talk of a secret!' Flora said. 'Gregory was grumbling over it. I was Olivia's confidante for so many years, there won't be anything she hasn't told me. What is it concerning?'

'That's the trouble,' Adeline jumped in. 'They hadn't got to that part.'

CHAPTER 12

The door swung open again, revealing Clara Harrowby. Still dressed in black, her dress was shorter today, her long blonde hair hanging loose on her shoulders as she approached their table. 'Miss Busby, I'm surprised to find you still here. How is your friend in Cheltenham, Mrs Fanshawe?'

'I… she's… much the same, thank you,' Adeline managed, recalling her initial excuse for coming to the hotel.

'And you must be Miss Whitfield,' Clara continued, smiling brightly at the young woman. 'How do you do?'

'Quite well, thank you,' Lydia replied with a nod.

'All this talk of memoirs has the hotel all agog. How exciting, to be a writer.'

Lydia nodded again, her manner rather guarded.

'Do you write many such books?' Clara went on, the wind dropping from her sails somewhat.

'Not too many, as yet.'

'Oh. Well, Olivia was a mother to me in all but name; if she wanted her story told, I should be only too happy to talk to you about her.'

'Thank you.' Lydia smiled, but made no further comment.

'It must be awful,' Adeline said, looking thoughtfully at Clara, 'losing two mothers.'

Clara nodded, her lips dropping, but she quickly compressed them.

'And so like Olivia to take you in,' Adeline pressed.

'Yes,' she said. 'My father was killed in the stables. Henry and Olivia kept a stallion, he was quite magnificent but utterly unpredictable. He was badly injured by a visiting mare one day and put in his stall. Daddy went in to put a salve on his leg, but the horse kicked out and hit him on the head. It killed him instantly. Mummy heard the commotion, and ran to help him, only…her heart was weak from where she'd had diphtheria as a child.' The girl's voice caught. 'Anyway, she didn't survive long after the shock of it all.'

'Oh, I'm so sorry,' Miss Busby said.

Clara looked down for a moment, composing herself. 'It was a long time ago,' she said. 'I had no one else, and Olivia was so upset that it was their animal who'd caused it.'

'She felt simply awful,' Flora added. 'I remember her crying for hours, the poor dear.'

'Yes, I cried for quite some time myself,' Clara added.

'Whatever did Mr and Mrs Fortescue want with a stallion?' Adeline asked.

'He was an ex-racehorse Lázár saved from being put down. Olivia took him in as a favour,' Clara said.

Adeline gave Miss Busby a look heavy with suggestion.

'She was like that, of course,' Clara sighed. 'Always wanting to save everyone. Daddy should have waited for the vet, and Mummy was always weak. It wasn't her fault,' she added softly. Then, straightening, she said, 'Do enjoy your lunch,' and crossed to a table in the other corner to keep her own company.

'Well now, everyone wants to talk to you, dear!' Flora said to Lydia. 'It must be so interesting, being a writer.' Her cheeks were flushed and her eyes shone. 'So many stories! Such possibilities! Tell me, do you ever write fiction?'

'I'm afraid not.' Lydia shook her head, her pretty face lighting with a smile.

They chatted amiably about books, and Flora ordered the soup. As they ate, Adeline told Lydia and Flora that she knew several writers: a newspaper reporter, a gossip columnist, and her most gentle of friends, Ezekiel Melnyk, who was a poet. 'Did Olivia discover you through one of your previously published books?' she asked Lydia.

'I imagine so,' Lydia replied vaguely. 'We never actually discussed it. I get lots of enquiries; so many people are keen to tell their stories.'

Miss Busby kept an ear on the conversation while watching the reactions of the others who came in for lunch. Major Gresham offered Lydia only a curt nod, whilst Sir Gregory was rather less polite, ignoring her completely and sitting alone at the table furthest from them. Arthur, upon opening the door and spotting Lydia, scowled, marring his handsome features. Thrusting his hands into his pockets, he crossed the room towards their table and rather abruptly said, 'So you're the writer, are you? My aunt didn't mention this memoir to me.'

Lydia blinked in surprise, before composing herself and answering, 'I am Lydia Whitfield, yes.' She gave a meaningful pause.

'Arthur Fortescue,' he grudgingly offered, before adding, 'You can't write the thing now of course, given Aunt Olivia's death, but Lázár tells me you're staying with us?' His look was accusing and cold. Miss Busby was surprised by the change in the young man.

'Yes, he was kind enough to offer me a room so I didn't have to make the long drive back,' Lydia said.

All four women looked at Arthur with a mix of astonishment and disapproval. His cheeks reddened.

'Oh. Well. Yes, of course.' He gave a quick bow of his head. 'Sorry if I… It's all been such a shock. Everyone is already fraught, and now… But of course, it's not your fault,' he stammered. 'Sorry,' he repeated, his voice gentler now.

'That's alright,' Lydia said. 'Family business can be so complicated, can't it? And really, it's quite common for my clients to keep my engagement private.'

'Is it?' Arthur asked, looking at the young writer curiously. She nodded. 'Well, I suppose that's alright then. It's just, it doesn't seem at all like her to do something like that.' He gave a slight shake of his head. 'Anyway, enjoy your lunch,' he offered politely, before turning on his heel and crossing to talk to Annie. After a brief chat with the young maid, he left the room.

'Such an awkward fellow,' Flora tutted, before proclaiming the soup delicious.

'Flora,' Miss Busby began, thinking it a good moment while she was so animated. 'The dinner you all had on the night of the Halloween ball, can you remember what Cook served?'

'Oh, now, let me think…' Flora wiped her mouth delicately with a napkin, then exclaimed, 'Lamb! Cook made a roast, with all the trimmings. Steaming bowls of vegetables, and a tureen of potatoes. A large bowl of mint sauce. The table was practically groaning! Far too much for me, of course. One's appetite declines with age, don't you find?'

Miss Busby nodded. 'I expect poor Olivia was the same?' she pressed.

'Oh, yes, Olivia ate like a bird, bless her dear heart. That's why Cook always laid everything out so people could help themselves to as much or as little as they liked.'

Adeline caught Miss Busby's eye. She looked rather pleased with herself. Miss Busby gave her a tiny nod. It did indeed seem unlikely the cook could possibly be to blame if the attendees all helped themselves to the same food

'I don't think she drank much that night, but usually enjoyed one, though,' Flora went on. 'And the odd sweet treat, too. Which reminds me, did Annie say anything about dessert?'

Adeline called the young maid over. Before she left, Miss Busby quietly enquired of her if Arthur would be taking any lunch.

'Yes, miss,' Annie replied, equally quietly. 'Only he's asked to take it in his room.'

'Oh, I do hope he's not sickening for something?' Miss Busby replied.

'I couldn't say, miss.' Annie shrugged. 'He's never asked for that before.'

Before she could wonder further, Lázár and Mr Ludlow entered the room, and Miss Busby saw her opportunity to make a telephone call in private. *The inspector must be told about the writer, and the implications of the memoir,* she thought. 'Do excuse me,' she said, rising from her seat, 'I ought to let Barnaby out for a moment. He's still upstairs.'

'Oh, is that the little dog who was with you this morning?' Lydia asked. 'Can I tag along for a bit of fresh air? I might even take a cigarette. It's all the rage now, and I'm told it's very good at warding off flu.'

Miss Busby fought to ensure her smile didn't waver. 'Of course. I will meet you in reception.'

'I'll come too,' Adeline said.

Miss Busby waved a dismissive hand. 'I'll only be a few minutes. Why don't you see Flora back to the lounge when she's ready? You could have a digestif. I'll join you afterwards.'

'What a lovely idea!' Flora beamed, leaving Adeline no choice in the matter.

With a reluctant look towards the deserted reception desk and telephone cubby beyond, Miss Busby went upstairs to retrieve both her dog and her jacket before returning to the hall and stepping outside with the young writer in tow.

'Thanks for letting me join you. There was rather a heavy weight of interest, inside,' Lydia explained. 'It's nice to be out for a moment.'

'I expect you'll be glad to go home,' Miss Busby said, watching Barnaby gleefully chase a squirrel up a towering chestnut tree.

'Well, yes, I thought so, but now…'

Miss Busby turned bright, enquiring eyes to the youngster.

'It's just, if there's no will,' Lydia went on, 'I think I might have found myself in rather a moral quandary.'

'Oh? In what way?' Miss Busby asked.

'Well, Olivia did hint at certain…tensions…within the family.'

'I thought Arthur, her late husband's nephew, was her only family to speak of?'

Lydia nodded. 'That's who I meant, really. It was odd to encounter him just now. She didn't speak very fondly of him.'

'Oh dear.' Miss Busby kept her gaze ahead as they walked towards the lake. She didn't ask anything further – an old trick from her teaching days. If someone had something to say, they tended to do so more readily in their own time.

'I think she felt that he'd torn through his funds, rather,' Lydia went on. 'And I sort of got the impression Olivia imagined he thought himself next in line for the hotel, and that she was a bit worried he'd tear through that, too.'

Miss Busby stopped in her tracks. 'Olivia talked to you about who would inherit Hamnett Hall?'

'Oh. No.' Lydia's cheeks reddened. 'Well. Yes, I suppose, but only in the loosest of terms. She spoke of family and friends, very briefly of course, as a sort of introduction to her circumstances. She said she was awfully fond of Clara, but found the girl rather disappointing.'

'Did she say why?'

'I'm afraid not.' Lydia stopped to take out a Player's Navy Cut cigarette and a thin, silver Flamidor lighter. 'Would you like one?' she asked Miss Busby, who politely declined. 'It was all I could think about when Clara spoke to me earlier,' she continued. 'It's awfully odd, meeting people you've only heard someone talk about – and not always kindly either. Olivia was awfully fond of a military chap, too. The Major, I assume. Although she said he had become rather dependent. And there was a fellow Hungarian working for her she said she was awfully close to when she was younger. Mr Lázár, I suppose?'

Miss Busby nodded, then asked, 'Only when she was younger?'

Lydia thought for a moment. 'It sounded like they weren't very close anymore. But this is only from bits and bobs on the telephone,' she clarified. 'It's easy to misunderstand. But she said he was a man with his own ambitions, which I took to mean he might have resented working for her, still. As if he thought he was destined for bigger things, if you catch my drift.'

'Yes, I think I do,' Miss Busby said quietly.

'And, well, it's just…' Lydia went on, lowering her voice and looking around. 'It paints things in rather a different light, knowing that she's gone. As if it was more than a memoir. Perhaps, rather, a reckoning, of sorts. Oh, but I expect I'm being dramatic. It's a writer's instinct to see plot twists around every corner. I expect I'm worrying over nothing.'

'Yes, let's hope so,' Miss Busby said, giving her a sympathetic look. 'Shall we turn back? I'd rather Barnaby didn't get any ideas about the lake.'

'Ha! Yes, of course. There's nothing quite like the smell of wet dog, is there?' Lydia laughed as they turned around, the pair walking in silence with the little dog trailing morosely behind.

Lydia stopped just shy of the front door. 'She sent me a letter. Olivia, I mean. I wonder, would you look at it? I haven't shown anyone else. As I said, I'm probably over-reacting, but that solicitor of hers has made me rather nervous.'

'Of course,' Miss Busby agreed, a mix of excitement and nerves flaring as Lydia held the door open for her. 'If it will put your mind at rest.'

Barnaby followed them up to Lydia's room, which was

every bit as handsome as Miss Busby's, and a little more spacious, to boot. The four-poster bed was draped in pale blue and gold to match the wallpaper, and two armchairs patterned with the same colours were set before the fire. Barnaby gave the carpet a thorough inspection while Lydia pulled a sheet of paper from a folder inside her suitcase, which, Miss Busby noted, featured a brass lock.

Lydia held out the handwritten sheet; several crossings out had been made on it. 'It's just the last bit, really,' she said, folding the page in two and pointing towards the end.

Written in English, but in what Miss Busby thought of as a distinctly foreign style of cursive, more loopy and upright than the style she'd taught her young charges, were the words, *What was buried must now come to light, lest a great injustice follow.* Below, was Olivia's signature.

'Ah,' she said. 'Yes. Given the situation, I can see why that would be a concern.'

Lydia took the letter back.

'I wonder,' Miss Busby said, 'might I show it to Adeline? She may be able to offer some insight.'

Lydia seemed to waver for a moment, before looking at Miss Busby nervously. 'Would you mind awfully if I said no? It's just, they were acquainted, whereas I know you never met her, so it feels less…personal, somehow. And there's a confidentiality clause with these things, you see. I've probably said far too much already, but it's such a difficult situation, with her being… gone.'

Miss Busby nodded in understanding. 'Will your editor perhaps be able to help?' she asked.

Lydia's cheeks flushed. 'Oh, well, I…I'm afraid I don't actually have one yet. We were at the very early stages, you see. It's just that the solicitor rather annoyed me, and I felt I ought to defend myself. Silly, I know,' she added. 'Perhaps I need a bit of time to think about it all.'

Miss Busby assured Lydia that she quite understood, and thanked her for her confidence. 'Shall we meet later for a drink in the lounge?' she suggested.

Lydia nodded gratefully, but Miss Busby's mind was troubled as she returned Barnaby to her room. 'What secret has been buried, and by whom? And what great injustice threatens?' she asked the little terrier, reaching into her cardigan pocket for the slice of ham she'd kept for him. He accepted with gusto, before parking himself contentedly in front of the fire. Adding another log for him, Miss Busby watched a moment as it sparked and caught. It seemed clear enough that the threat of this secret becoming public could have led to Olivia's death, but the thing that worried her now was the young writer. 'Because if this secret was dangerous enough to get Olivia killed,' she told Barnaby, 'might Lydia be next?'

He sighed and closed his eyes. Miss Busby watched his body relax into sleep, and considered.

'That's if she's telling the truth, of course,' she added quietly after some time, remembering that if there was one thing she should have learned after three previous investigations, it was never to take things at face value.

Then she remembered another young woman who just may be able to help.

CHAPTER 13

Miss Busby hurried down the stairs, pleased to see the reception desk unmanned, giving her a chance to talk in private. Making for the telephone cubby to the rear, she asked the operator for Lucy Lannister at the Oxford News. The line crackled for several moments before Lucy's cheery voice answered, 'Miss Busby! How lovely to hear from you! Alistair told me he had given you an assignment. What fun that you're working for the police. You and Adeline haven't got yourselves into trouble already, have you?'

Miss Busby smiled, imagining the young reporter's mock-stern face. 'Not yet,' she said, before dropping her voice to add, 'Lucy, it's not easy to talk here, but could you look into something for me?'

'Of course,' Lucy said, her tone switching to concern.

'A young lady named Lydia Whitfield has arrived from London. She was supposedly engaged by Olivia Fortescue – that's the lady who died – to write her memoirs.'

'Supposedly?' Lucy echoed. 'You suspect she may not be what she seems?'

Miss Busby smiled. 'I seem to have been doing that a lot lately. I don't have any specific reason to think so, but the timing is striking. I thought it best to be thorough.'

'Alistair's just the same,' Lucy said. 'I expect you've spent too much time with him!'

'Quite possibly,' Miss Busby agreed.

'I'll make some calls. We've got contacts at the London Standard,' Lucy said, before adding, 'you really aren't in trouble, are you?'

'No. But I worry that this young woman may be, if she knows too much about Olivia.'

'Should I ring Alistair?' Lucy asked.

'Would you?' Miss Busby felt a warm wave of relief envelop her at the thought of Inspector Alistair McKay knowing what was going on. It felt as if a weight was lifted from her shoulders.

'Of course. Hold the line, I've got an idea.'

Miss Busby listened to the familiar crackle, before turning her head sharply as a door opened and footsteps sounded.

'There you are, Isabelle!' Adeline strode towards her.

'*Lucy*,' she mouthed, pointing to the receiver.

'What's happened?'

Miss Busby raised her finger to her lips as Lucy picked up and said, 'Can you meet us in Quinton village later? There's a pub called the George and Dragon. Shall we say five?'

'Us?' Miss Busby queried.

'Alistair's coming. He's got some news too. Will you

be able to get away? We can get something to eat, and compare notes.'

'Yes, of course,' Miss Busby said. 'We'll see you there. Thank you, Lucy.'

'See her where?' Adeline asked, as Miss Busby replaced the receiver.

'We're going out for dinner,' she replied. 'Come on, we need to make sure our notes are in order first.'

Bemused, Adeline followed as Miss Busby headed towards the stairs, just as the door to the opposite corridor swung open and a short, sturdy woman stormed out, stopping just shy of barrelling into them.

'*Oof*,' she huffed, looking up with sharp eyes, before her expression softened. 'Sorry, m'dears, didn't see you there.'

Miss Busby took in the white apron just visible beneath the woman's grey overcoat, and hazarded, 'Mrs Burton?'

She blinked large, hazel eyes in surprise. 'Yes?'

'We've been very much enjoying your cuisine,' Miss Busby said with a smile.

'Oh, yes,' Adeline added. 'Particularly the breakfasts.'

Mrs Burton seemed taken aback, before breaking into a beaming smile of her own. 'Well now, isn't that nice to hear? Compliments have been thin on the ground since we lost our dear Mrs Fortescue.' The smile slowly faded.

'So sad,' Adeline was quick to sympathise. 'We were friends. Olivia will be greatly missed.'

Mrs Burton nodded. 'A kinder soul you couldn't meet.' She pursed her lips and gave a sharp glance back towards the corridor. 'Not like some, making us stay open and taking on new guests like nothing's happened,' she tutted, before adding, 'no disrespect to yourselves.'

'Lázár?' Adeline asked, before ploughing straight on with, 'he said it's what Olivia would have wanted.'

'Ha! What he wants, more like.' Mrs Burton drew herself up to her full height, which was more or less in line with Adeline's chest, and tutted again. 'Well, I shan't work for him, anyway. Always had delusions of grandeur, that one. More guests every day, and me on my own in the kitchen being expected to jump to it. I've just given in my notice. I can take my pick of places.' She raised her chin, before adding softly, 'I only came here for Olivia. She promised me free reign over my kitchen, and was as good as her word. You won't find another like her, mark my words.'

'But if Arthur or Clara take over,' Adeline said, 'you won't have to work for Lázár.'

Mrs Burton scoffed. 'They'd hardly be any better. Wet behind the ears, both of them. No, I'll work 'til the break, and I've said I'll cook for the funeral. It's the least I can do for her. Say goodbye, like.' Her eyes began to water, and she rubbed at them with a large hand. 'But then I shall make other arrangements. Now if you'll excuse me,' she added, 'I'll miss my bus home.'

'Well,' Adeline exclaimed as they made their way upstairs. 'That was telling! Another one who's not a fan of Lázár,' she added triumphantly.

'Or Arthur and Clara,' Miss Busby pointed out. 'Although Lázár did say she was temperamental.'

'That's just what men say when a woman doesn't take to them,' Adeline said dismissively. 'And there's all this business with the horse now, too. Clara has every reason to resent the manager. If he thought she might inherit, he may have taken pre-emptive action!'

'That was a long time ago,' Miss Busby reminded her as she opened the door to her room and they went inside. 'And Clara herself said it was an accident. They all seem so fond of Olivia,' she sighed. 'But I think you were right, we can cross Cook off our list.'

Taking a seat at the desk, she took out her pencil and did exactly that, before telling Adeline what Lydia had said, and about the letter she'd been shown. They spent quite some time discussing this new turn of events, with Miss Busby having to remind a wide-eyed Adeline that they must not indulge in wild speculation. Which, inevitably, they did anyway.

At a little before five they descended the stairs, Adeline freshly coiffed and perfumed, Miss Busby sporting her modest pearls, and Barnaby trotting jauntily behind. Clara was at reception, flicking through a ledger. She glanced up at them briefly, saying, 'Dinner's only a cold buffet I'm afraid. It's laid out in the lounge,' before turning her attention back to the book.

'Thank you, but we will be eating out,' Miss Busby replied.

Clara looked up now with interest, noting their coats and handbags. 'Off to see your friend, Mrs Fanshawe?'

'Yes,' said Adeline.

'I do hope she's feeling better,' Clara said.

'Thank you. So do we.' Adeline nodded primly, and the trio went out and climbed into the Rolls.

'Why did you say that?' Miss Busby asked as the engine growled to life.

'Lucy is a friend. And besides, should we be spotted in Quinton, we have a cover story.'

'Good point,' Miss Busby said, impressed.

Adeline turned onto the lane and motored the Rolls down into the village. The George and Dragon public house stood on the corner, warm and welcoming with its honey-coloured Cotswold stone lit by the soft glow of a gas lamp outside, and golden light spilling through the windows.

'Isn't that Richard's car?' Adeline asked, drawing up behind a black Austin Twenty.

'It is!' Miss Busby's heart lifted. 'He must have brought Lucy.'

The trio disembarked and Miss Busby opened the door to be greeted by a burst of warmth from the roaring fire in the hearth and the delicious aroma of roasting chicken. Broad wooden beams supported the low ceiling, a long bar, highly polished, took up one corner, the remainder of the room was scattered with dark oak chairs and tables.

Locals in work clothes and scuffed boots sipped pints of ale, only pausing to eye them from under flat caps. A cosy snug with cushioned benches and a long, pol-ished table sat to their left, separated by a glass partition through which Miss Busby caught sight of Inspector McKay's distinctive red hair. Lucy was sitting beside him, with Richard opposite. Richard turned and smiled, rising to his feet to greet them as Barnaby trotted straight past the inspector and went to greet Lucy, his tail wagging furiously.

'What a nice surprise!' Miss Busby said, crossing to Richard, who took her in his arms briefly and gave her a peck on the cheek.

'Lucy was concerned about you, Isabelle.' His deep green eyes reflected concern. 'I had to come along and see for myself that you were in good fettle. I hope you don't mind?'

She noted that despite a few lines of worry, he seemed to be well and looking smart in a dark blue sweater over shirt and tie. There was something deeply reassuring about his presence.

'Of course I don't mind,' she told him.

He politely turned his attention to Adeline, as Lucy rose to place a hand on Miss Busby's shoulder.

'Are you sure you're alright?' she asked. 'You didn't sound yourself on the telephone.'

'Quite sure. It's only that I was afraid of being overheard,' Miss Busby said. 'The phone cubby is in a public space, and we've already had an instance of people listening at doors.' She turned to Alistair Mckay, who was also on his feet, his usual grey suit as stern and commanding as his expression.

'Good evening, Inspector.'

'Good evening, Miss Busby.' He nodded. 'I'm very pleased to hear there's nothing amiss,' he said, his Scottish accent warm and rich, his usual stern expression softened by a smile. Miss Busby had never seen him look so calm, or indeed so pleased to see her, in the middle of an investigation. She wondered if it was the presence of Lucy by his side that made the difference.

Miss Busby returned his smile, and took a seat next to Richard.

Adeline positioned herself to the other side of him and Barnaby settled strategically under the table in easy reach of any titbits that may come his way.

A menu was neatly chalked up on a board above the inspector's head, and Adeline's eye drifted to it. There was roast chicken with buttered cabbage, roast potatoes and gravy, or vegetable soup with dumplings.

'Shall we order, now we're all here?' Richard asked.

'I'll go,' McKay offered. 'What will everyone have?'

With five orders of roast chicken placed, he returned with a tray holding sweet sherries for Miss Busby and Adeline, a stout for Richard, ale for himself, and a lemonade for Lucy. After a fortifying sip, Miss Busby told them about Lydia's arrival at Hamnett Hall, and a secret Olivia had supposedly been planning to reveal in her memoirs.

'Which must have been why she was killed,' Adeline concluded.

'But you said the young lady claimed no one else knew about the memoir.' McKay caught the discrepancy.

Miss Busby cast her mind back to be sure. 'She said she didn't think so.'

'Then it's unlikely any of them would have known about the impending threat,' McKay concluded and took a sip of ale.

Adeline's mouth opened, then closed.

'Lázár and Ludlow certainly didn't seem aware,' Miss Busby mused. 'Nor did any of the guests, given their reactions.'

'Which were?' McKay pressed, reaching into his pocket for his notebook and pencil.

'Sir Gregory was angry at first, then disbelieving,' Miss Busby said, reaching into her bag for her own notes. 'Lady Flora seemed intrigued, and offered to help, as did Clara Harrowby. Major Gresham was rather more impassive, although he did seem to enjoy goading Sir Gregory.'

'And Sir Gregory implied it was the Major who ought to be worried, if any secrets were to be revealed,' Adeline added.

'And Arthur Fortescue?' the inspector asked.

'He was quite short with Lydia at lunch. Accusatory, almost. Although he soon recovered his manners,' Miss Busby said.

'He took his lunch in his room, though,' Adeline pointed out. 'As if he were sulking over the whole matter.'

'There could have been all manner of reasons,' Miss Busby chided. The inspector made a note all the same.

'Of course this secret, whatever it may be, could have

been discovered by other means,' Adeline continued thoughtfully. 'The imminent naming of the heir, and the writing of the will may have dredged up all manner of business. The memoir could simply be directing our attention towards what has already been discovered by the culprit.'

'I did some digging regarding your memoir writer, Miss Busby,' Lucy said, adding, 'what was it that made you wonder about her?'

'Oh, she just seemed a little nervous when she first arrived. I wondered for a moment if she might be a newspaper reporter,' Miss Busby confessed.

Lucy smiled. 'Well, she's certainly a writer. I looked up the name; Lydia's from a respectable family in Southgate. Very well-educated, and beginning to make a name for herself working on memoirs for private clients.'

'Just as I thought, the girl was upset, not nervous,' Adeline said, finishing her sherry and casting a hopeful glance towards the bar.

'Regardless,' McKay broke in, 'I think the time has come to be more cautious.'

Adeline's attention was diverted back to the table.

'In light of Olivia's post mortem results, which arrived late this morning,' he continued.

An expectant silence fell over the table, before a cheery voice announced, 'Five roast chicken!' and a friendly woman with rosy cheeks and dark hair piled into a cap that was rather too small, placed plates of crisp potatoes, green cabbage and thick slices of chicken in front of

Miss Busby and Adeline. Another, younger girl did the same for the others, leaving them with a bright, 'Enjoy your meals!'

Barnaby rose to his paws with intent, as all other eyes remained fixed on the inspector.

'And what did the post mortem uncover?' Miss Busby asked, when the pair were out of earshot.

'Olivia Fortescue had high levels of cocaine in her blood, which likely brought on the heart attack,' McKay told her.

'Good Lord!' Adeline exclaimed breathlessly.

'Are you quite sure?' Miss Busby asked, eyes wide.

He nodded.

'But… what on earth would she have been doing taking such an awful substance?' Adeline asked.

'There was a significant amount of alcohol also present in her blood,' McKay said. 'A particular combination the pathologist has seen several times, although not for some years. He had a suspicion as to the cause, and telephoned Olivia's doctor for confirmation.'

'And?' Adeline pressed impatiently, the steaming roast forgotten in front of her.

'The doctor confirmed that Olivia was known to be a drinker of Vin Mariani.'

'Vin Mariani!' Miss Busby's hand rose to her pearls. 'What in heaven's name would have possessed her to drink that?'

'What is it?' Lucy asked, a long strand of dark hair falling over her shoulder. 'I've never heard of it.'

'I'm pleased you haven't!' Richard said. 'It's certainly not something anyone ought to be drinking.'

'There were many old tonics given out in Queen Victoria's day, laudanum and morphine among them,' Miss Busby explained, her mind reeling at the revelation. 'Vin Mariani is a tonic wine concocted of wine seeped with coca leaves, later versions were fortified with brandy.'

'Cocoa?' Adeline said. 'I've often had a brandy with my cocoa, and–'

'Coca,' Miss Busby repeated. 'It's a plant native to South America. Cocaine is produced from the leaves.'

Adeline's eyes widened. 'Isabelle, how on earth do you know these things?'

'Some of my favourite writers used to drink it,' Miss Busby said. 'I remember reading about it some years back in a magazine.' She turned to McKay. 'But I thought they'd stopped making it a long time ago.'

'They did,' the inspector said dourly. 'And since cocaine has been proven dangerous and made illegal, no one should be drinking it at all.'

'Then how would Olivia have had access to it?' Lucy asked. 'And why on earth would she *want* to drink it?' she added, brow furrowed in distaste.

'Vin Mariani used to be all the rage,' Richard said. 'Popular with the socialite set in London for the punch it packed. Even a small glass held a pretty powerful amount of cocaine.'

'Sir Arthur Conan Doyle was fond of it,' Miss Busby said. 'He thought it sharpened his focus. And Pope Leo was an advocate, too, for times when "prayer wasn't sufficient".'

'Good *Lord*,' Adeline repeated, then asked. 'Did he actually say that?'

'Yes, and was quoted on it,' Miss Busby said.

'It was perfectly acceptable at the time,' Richard explained. 'Doctors used to prescribe it for insomnia, and melancholy. Even influenza, if memory serves.'

'Lydia Whitfield informed me today that smoking is thought to ward off the latter,' Miss Busby recalled. 'But I recall cigarettes being referred to as coffin nails.'

'They still are, but there are any number of adverts proclaiming them to be beneficial,' Richard said. 'All sorts of people smoke now, and all sorts of people drank Vin Mariani back then. There must be dusty bottles of it still sitting in private collections here and there, and I'm sure for the right price…'

'Well, Olivia certainly wasn't short of funds,' Adeline said.

'No, and I've spoken to her doctor myself on the telephone,' McKay continued as he picked up his knife and fork. 'He was adamant she'd only ever taken it in moderation, and in fact thought she'd given it up some time ago, following his advice.'

'Obviously not,' Adeline said with a sigh.

'When I went back to the pathologist, he was equally adamant there was nothing "moderate" about the amount of cocaine found in her blood,' the inspector continued. 'At least several very large glasses of the Vin Mariani would have been needed.'

'Olivia seems to have been an astute woman,' Miss Busby considered. 'She would have known to be careful with it. Particularly if she was used to taking it.'

A thoughtful silence descended, before Adeline broke it with a dramatic, 'Someone might have laced her drink. Isabelle, we could be dealing with a *poisoner*!'

Miss Busby tutted, looking around to check that no one at the bar had overheard. 'Let's not get carried away Adeline,' she chastised. 'And it's hardly poison,' she added.

'As good as, if the dose was lethal.'

'It's a possibility,' McKay agreed. 'Vin Mariani is quite bitter, but it could have been mixed with her wine at the dinner before the ball, and then taken effect when she began dancing. Either way,' he added sternly, 'given the circumstances I feel you and Miss Busby ought to take your leave of Hamnett Hall. For your own safety.'

'Nonsense,' Adeline said, although Miss Busby noted a tremor of uncertainty in her voice. 'We are perfectly placed to look for this Vin Mariani, and dig further.'

'Can't you step in and take over, Alistair?' Lucy asked, her face drawn in concern. 'Now that you know the poor woman may have been poisoned?'

'As Miss Busby said, it's hardly poison,' McKay reminded her. 'All we know for certain is that Olivia Fortescue died of a substance she was known to use. If anything, it would be even harder to act now than previously.' He ran a quick hand through his hair. 'But that is no reason to risk your safety any further, Miss Busby and Mrs Fanshawe,' he added, looking between them. 'I have a meeting with Olivia's solicitor tomorrow morning, and will pursue matters as far as I can on my own from now on.'

'Ludlow?' Adeline asked. 'You should ask him why he had so many long chats with Olivia prior to her death. Flora told us,' she explained. 'I thought the whole thing rather fishy.'

The inspector looked sceptical, but made a note.

'Isabelle, what do you think?' Adeline continued. 'Oughtn't we stay and see this through? We've had plenty to drink since we arrived, and we are both perfectly well! If anyone intended us harm, they've had ample opportunity.'

Miss Busby looked to McKay, who gave a slight shake of his head. Richard looked resolutely down at his plate, but she noted his hand was clenched. She needed a few moments to think.

'I think we ought to eat this chicken,' she said. 'It's going cold.'

Adeline blinked in surprise, then laughed. 'Gracious, I'd almost forgotten!'

Lucy laughed too, and even the inspector smiled. Tension broken for the moment, they all focussed on the food. Miss Busby reached to give Richard's hand a reassuring squeeze, as Barnaby nudged her leg hopefully. She gave the dog a large piece of chicken as he'd been so patient.

When she'd finished her meal, Miss Busby turned to Richard and asked, 'Would a greater quantity of Vin Mariani than usual have made Olivia excitable, do you think?'

'Absolutely,' Richard agreed. 'It was taken as a mood enhancer, after all. The more you had, the more you'd feel the effects.'

'Why do you ask?' McKay looked at her, his green eyes sharp with interest.

'Both Flora and Lázár used the word '"excited" to describe Olivia's mood at the dinner,' she said. 'They put it down to the imminent revealing of the heir, but what if it was simply the effect of the Vin Mariani?'

'You mean, she may not have been excited about the revelation itself?' Adeline asked.

'It's possible,' Miss Busby mused, 'that she may have been about to reveal a perfectly ordinary, anticipated choice, and simply been carried away by the chemicals in her bloodstream.'

'Could it have influenced her decision-making, do you think?' Adeline asked Richard.

He held his hands up. 'I'm not a drinker of the stuff!' he objected good-naturedly. 'I doubt it, particularly if she'd been drinking it for a while. But it could certainly have made her feel more enthusiastic about whichever choice she'd made.'

'I think we ought to go back,' Miss Busby announced. Richard's demeanour plummeted. 'Adeline's right,' she continued. 'We are getting closer to the truth, and if anyone had wanted to hurt us they could have done so by now.'

'But it's not your responsibility, Miss Busby,' Lucy said, her eyes full of concern, before she darted an accusing look at McKay.

'May I look through your notes, Miss Busby?' McKay asked.

'Of course,' she said, passing the notebook across. Then turned to Lucy 'The truth is all our responsibilities,' she went on, giving the young woman a reassuring smile. 'And Olivia seems to have been a rather special sort of woman. I feel we owe it to her, somehow, having got to know her through her friends.'

'I thought you might want to stay,' Richard sighed. 'Which is why I brought an overnight bag. I'd like to come with you. They might think twice about taking on three of us rather than two. And I used to box, you know, when I was younger.' He sat up a little straighter and squared his jaw.

McKay looked up from the notebook to give him an appraising look, then said. 'Someone close to Olivia may know about her drinking habits, and where she kept her wine.'

'Lázár,' Miss Busby suggested. 'Or Flora. We'll ask.'

The inspector steepled his fingers and looked at Miss Busby over them for several moments, before releasing a long breath and saying, 'Very well. With a precise cause of death now, I'll be moving things along in the background, starting with her solicitor in the morning.

But as you're already established there, and they're talking to you, it could be useful for you to stay on. With Richard,' he added.

'Agreed,' he said, then all three nodded.

Lucy looked disapproving, but not surprised. 'I'll drive your car back, Daddy,' she said.

'Well, then, that's settled!' Adeline declared. 'It will be nice to have you with us, Richard.' She gave a mischievous smile. 'At least if we are poisoned, we'll be in good company. Won't we Isabelle?'

Miss Busby tutted at her friend, but her eyes shone, and she exchanged a fond look with Richard.

The inspector returned Miss Busby's notebook. She tucked it safely into her bag and they rose to leave. A cold burst of air from the door opening caused them to turn as one, and Miss Busby and Adeline looked right into the handsome face of Arthur Fortescue through the partition glass.

As recognition dawned on his features, he took in the sight of the inspector closing his own policeman's notebook, and Miss Busby and Adeline standing opposite. His eyes narrowed, a mix of what appeared to be suspicion and anger flaring, as he opened his mouth to speak before apparently changing his mind and turning smartly on his heel, leaving again almost before the door had closed behind him.

'He's fleeing!' Adeline said. 'Inspector, follow him!'

'Who?' McKay asked, looking around as he pulled on his dark overcoat.

'Arthur Fortescue,' Miss Busby said. 'And he's hardly fleeing, Adeline.'

The inspector glanced through the window at the retreating figure. 'He may be hurrying back to warn the others that you've been seen with me.'

'I told Clara we were meeting my friend,' Adeline reminded her. 'It's perfectly reasonable that she could in turn be friends with a police inspector. Besides, if they think we're involved they're less likely to murder us. Come on, let's get back.'

They said their goodbyes to Lucy and the inspector, and made their way back to Hamnett Hall in the Rolls, Barnaby settling comfortably onto Richard's lap in the back.

Lázár looked up from behind the desk in surprise as they returned, and Miss Busby introduced Sir Richard Lannister. 'I know it's late, but might he have a room?' she asked. 'We ran into him in Quinton. With the inspector,' she added quietly.

Indecision seemed to flicker in the manager's eyes for a moment. 'We have already very few staff, and more guests than expected...'

Richard gave him a sympathetic smile. 'I'll be no trouble, I promise.' He held up his small overnight bag. 'I even carry my own bag!'

Lázár gave a tight smile, then nodded. 'I will tell to Annie.'

'We'll go up to my room,' Miss Busby decided. 'Could you have Annie come there and inform us when it's ready?'

'Why not the lounge?' Adeline complained as they climbed the stairs.

'One cat has been set among the pigeons today,' Miss Busby said, slowing her step to check that Richard was managing. He waved her concerned look aside, his cane tucked under his arm, unused. 'I think it's best we keep the other cat to ourselves tonight, and face them all fresh in the morning,' she finished.

'Well, this is cosy!' Richard exclaimed as Miss Busby showed him into her own room. Annie had stoked the fire, the curtains were drawn and the lamp lit against the dark and chill. Barnaby sprang straight onto the bed, and Miss Busby perched on the edge of it beside him. Richard took a welcome seat at the desk, stretching out his leg. Adeline sank into the armchair and gazed into the flames. She gave a deep, foreboding sigh.

'Penny for your thoughts, Mrs Fanshawe?' Richard asked.

'I am quite convinced Lázár is our most likely culprit,' she said.

'But don't forget, you find Ludlow shifty,' Miss Busby said with a smile. Adeline's mind tended to run on rather faster than it should, and often found it hard to let go of first impressions, however ill-formed.

'Why Lázár?' Richard asked.

'Both Lydia and Cook have indicated the man's ambition,' Adeline explained. 'I am quite sure he feels Hamnett Hall ought to rightfully be his, given the sacrifices he made for Olivia, and the work he's done since.

And we know that if anyone were close enough to the woman to fetch her the odd drink, it would surely be him.'

'Not necessarily, it could have been any of them,' Miss Busby argued. 'They all seemed to get along with her, and could have fetched her a drink at any time. Lázár has been so open with us,' she pointed out. 'And he's kept our confidence.'

'Not that open,' Adeline countered. 'He didn't tell us about the business with the stallion.'

'I expect it's a painful memory, and it was a long time ago,' Miss Busby said. 'And certainly not something he could have predicted. He seems genuinely upset by Olivia's death; some of the others may simply have been envious of their working relationship.'

'So what about this solicitor, Ludlow?' Richard asked. 'What would he have to gain from Olivia's death? Surely, if anything, it would only lose him a client.'

'Unless he was involved in persuading her who she should choose,' Adeline countered. 'Flora told us Olivia and Ludlow talked at length recently.'

'The inspector will ask about that tomorrow,' Miss Busby reminded her.

'If she were preparing to write her will, it's only natural to talk things over,' Richard said. 'I can't see how bumping off a wealthy client could have been to his advantage in the long-run, however angry he may theoretically have been. Why kill the golden goose?' He stroked his chin for a moment. 'The same goes for our three long-term guests,' he continued, looking to Miss Busby. 'The Sir, the Major, and the Lady. They would certainly have nothing to gain by poisoning their benefactor. Which really only leaves us with Arthur and Clara as suspects, to my mind.'

Miss Busby sighed. 'That's what we thought initially. But they're both beneficiaries too, in their own ways. I fear we're going around in circles,' she sighed.

'But we know about the Vin Mariani, now,' Adeline said. 'Don't lose heart, Isabelle. We're getting close, I'm sure of it!'

A tentative knock sounded on the door as Annie arrived to inform them Richard's room was ready. Miss Busby and Adeline bade him goodnight, and both went to their beds without further discussion. The day's events had been tiring, and for once Miss Busby fell straight into a deep and restorative sleep.

CHAPTER 14

Miss Busby and Adeline, suitably refreshed, knocked on Richard's door early to take him down to breakfast. He was up and ready, dressed in navy shirt and tie, grey trousers and his silver-topped cane in hand.

'Leg's a little stiff this morning, that's all,' he said, noting Miss Busby's concerned glance.

Barnaby wagged his tail and gave a soft woof of excitement – thrilled, no doubt, to have an extra source of treats on hand.

'Should we knock for Lydia?' Miss Busby asked quietly.

Adeline glanced at her watch. 'Better not. She's very young, and you know what they're like with early mornings.'

Expecting to be the first ones in the dining room, they were surprised to see Arthur sitting at a table, arms folded, eyes fixed on the door as they entered.

'Good morning,' Miss Busby called politely.

He murmured something noncommittal and rose to his feet as he cast an eye over Richard. 'Lázár said we had another guest.'

'You would have seen him last night in Quinton, I'm sure,' Adeline said, meeting Arthur's none-too-welcoming gaze.

'I did. And the police inspector, too. Will he be joining us as well?'

'Not yet.' Adeline narrowed her eyes. 'Why? Would his presence concern you?'

Arthur gave a rather forced laugh. 'Of course not. I don't take kindly to being misled, though. Were you really friends with my aunt?' He tilted his head slightly, one eyebrow raised in challenge. 'Or is this just some sort of game to you?'

'I can assure you I do not consider death a game,' Adeline retorted, locking eyes with him.

Richard stepped forward swiftly. 'I think there may have been something of a misunderstanding,' he said calmly. 'Sir Richard Lannister.' He held out a hand, and smiled as Arthur grudgingly took it. 'My daughter, Lucy, is a good friend of both Miss Busby and Mrs Fanshawe, and she happens to be stepping out with Inspector McKay,' he explained. 'If you hadn't rushed off last night, we would have made introductions and offered you a drink. Miss Busby was so complimentary about your aunt's hotel, that I was keen to see it. I'm so sorry if we've put you out.'

'It's not me you've put out,' Arthur said, tension slowly leaving his shoulders. His dark shirt was crumpled, his eyes bloodshot with dark circles beneath, as if he hadn't slept. 'But Cook is already on a short fuse,' he continued, 'and poor Annie's rushed off her feet.'

'Then Lázár oughtn't to take any more bookings,' Adeline pointed out.

'Yes, but he's not the sort to refuse anyone,' Arthur said. Sitting back down, he ran his hands through his thick, sandy-coloured hair. 'The whole situation is absolutely impossible,' he continued. 'All this talk of some great secret, and now a police inspector lurking in the village. And none of us knows what'll happen with the place. It's a lot to take in, to be perfectly honest with you. Particularly when there's still the funeral to arrange and Olivia's body hasn't even been released yet.'

'Of course,' Miss Busby said. 'We quite understand, and we are truly sorry for your loss.'

Richard nodded, before suggesting, 'Why don't you join us for breakfast? We seem to have got off on the wrong foot, but I'm sure we can make amends.'

Arthur smiled, before shaking his head. 'Thank you, but no. I don't have much of an appetite. I only wanted a coffee.' He indicated the empty cup on the table, then looked up as the dining room door flew open and Clara Harrowby marched in. She stopped at the sight of Richard.

'It's true then.' She folded her arms across her chest. 'Annie said there was another one. Goodness, you do have a lot of friends, Mrs Fanshawe.'

'It's alright, Clara.' Arthur was on his feet once more. 'Sir Richard and I have had a chat. Why don't you come with me to the lounge? Annie could do with a hand, and I'll explain on the way. Do enjoy your breakfast,' he said to the trio. Miss Busby noted that his smile didn't quite reach his eyes.

'Well!' Adeline took up a plate. 'It's interesting that they're both up early for once. And they seem rattled.'

'We must appear terribly intrusive,' Miss Busby said. 'Especially after Lydia's arrival. I'm not sure we can blame them, really.'

'We wouldn't seem intrusive if they didn't have anything to hide,' Adeline argued, helping herself to fried bread, eggs and bacon. 'And either of them could have dosed the poor woman with Vin–'

'Shh,' Miss Busby cautioned, as the door opened and Sir Gregory strode in.

'Ah! I heard there was another Sir among us! You've caused quite the stir, sir!' He gave a genial laugh. 'Sir Gregory Penn,' he said, holding out a hand. Richard shook, and introduced himself in turn. 'Mind if I join you?' Sir Gregory asked, taking a plate. 'It'll be rather pleasant to have another chap about the place.'

Richard accepted, much to Adeline's disapproval, and she ate in seething silence as the two men discussed golf and guns, and other manly pursuits. Both of them oblivious to the daggers Adeline was throwing their way.

When Major Gresham came in, he glanced at Richard with mild curiosity, before sitting to enjoy his breakfast in his customary solitude. Annie scurried about the place, keeping things clean and tidy and topped up, and even found time to bring a small plate of sausage cut up neatly for Barnaby.

'Well,' Richard said, smiling around the table once everyone's plates were cleared, 'that was just what the doctor ordered. If you'll excuse us, Sir Gregory, the ladies have promised to show me around.'

'Of course! Come and find me later, if you like. We could play a round over at Leckhampton.'

Richard smiled noncommittally as he rose to his feet and escorted the ladies, and Barnaby, from the room.

'Can you even play golf, with your leg?' Miss Busby asked.

'To be perfectly honest, I can't even play golf without it,' he confessed.

That caused a bright smile.

'Well then, where shall we start?' Adeline asked, surveying the empty reception area. 'Should we talk to Flora?'

'She'll be having breakfast in her room,' Miss Busby said. 'We can talk to her afterwards. Let's see if Lázár's in his office.'

Richard hesitated. 'I wonder if he might prefer talking to just the two of you, as he's got to know you? I don't want to spook the fellow. I thought I might have a nose around the grounds. Take the dog.'

Barnaby's tail began to wag faster.

'You might check if Lydia's car is still out there,' Adeline said, 'as she didn't appear at breakfast. I wonder if she left for London first thing? It's the silver Talbot.'

'Righto. Divide and conquer! Come and find me in the lounge after, and we can debrief.'

Barnaby shot through the front door ahead of him.

'You didn't warn Richard about the dog's fondness for the lake,' Adeline noted as they walked across to Lázár's office.

'He'll find out soon enough,' Miss Busby said, knocking lightly.

'Come in,' Lázár called. He gestured to two chairs sitting opposite his desk. 'I thought you would come.' His eyes were careworn, his suit a little crumpled. Miss Busby thought of Arthur, and the toll matters must be taking on both of them. 'The gentleman is not with you?' Lázár asked.

'He's gone for a walk,' Miss Busby said, taking a seat.

'It is a beautiful morning for such.' Lázár looked back through the window at the early sun melting the frost on the grass.

'Indeed. Now, what's all this about Olivia drinking Vin Mariani?' Adeline asked, settling down next to Miss Busby.

Lázár's dark eyes widened. 'Vin Tonique Mariani? It is a tonic wine very popular in Hungary. Miss Olivia's father drank it to keep his mind sharp for business, and she followed in his boots when she began running the hotel.'

'But it was banned several years ago, following health concerns,' Miss Busby said.

'Was it?' Lázár's pale cheeks reddened; he looked miserable and slightly confused.

'Yes,' Adeline said. 'It contains cocaine, for goodness'

sake! I cannot believe a woman of such standing as Olivia Fortescue would even entertain the notion of drinking it.'

'But the tonic is made simply of plants,' Lázár objected. 'It is all natural.'

'Be that as it may, it is prohibited,' Adeline stated, her voice stern with disapproval. 'How did Olivia have access to it?'

'I... I do not... that is to say...' he stammered.

'It's alright,' Miss Busby assured him. 'No one will be in trouble over it. But the wine is important. We need to know how much of it Olivia had to hand.'

Lázár looked uncertainly at Adeline. 'I do not understand why it would be important. Miss Olivia had not even drunk it so much of late.'

'Her doctor was under the impression she'd given it up altogether,' Adeline said.

Lázár gave a sad smile. 'She always said doctors worry too much over all the wrong things.'

'Well they were right in this case,' Adeline pointed out.

'The coca in the wine was very bad for her heart,' Miss Busby explained.

'And her other organs, I shouldn't wonder,' Adeline added.

'But Miss Olivia drank such for many years, and there is never a problem,' Lázár said. 'She knew Queen Victoria drank Vin Tonique Mariani also, and the Empress lived to a fine age. Miss Olivia said she was in good company with her choice.'

'I understand. But if you could just tell us how much of it Olivia was in possession of?' Miss Busby suggested gently.

Lázár sighed. 'The tonic became hard to find after the death of Mr Mariani, several years ago. He failed to pass the recipe down to his family, and the wine went out of production with his passing. But there are collectors, and Miss Olivia tasked me with finding a supply. I purchased five cases after Mr Mariani's death. One case remains.'

'Did Olivia ask you to order more?' Miss Busby asked.

Lázár shook his head. 'She said soon she would not have the responsibility of running the hotel, and so the last case was more than she would need.'

'And from whom did you buy it?' Adeline demanded.

'I… forgive me, but I am not sure I should say.'

Miss Busby looked sternly at Adeline, before turning to Lázár and saying, 'Of course. We don't need the details, but the unfortunate truth is that when Olivia died there were high levels of cocaine in her blood. Enough to stop her heart.'

Lázár shook his head. 'No, this cannot be. Always she has only one glass. A small glass. As if whisky, or brandy. Never as much as to cause problems.'

'And did she drink any on the day of the ball?' Miss Busby asked.

'I only saw her drink red wine at dinner. We all drank the same. Two bottles from the same case.'

'Are you quite sure?' Miss Busby pressed.

'Yes. About the wine at dinner, at least. Miss Olivia

would drink the tonique only in her rooms. She would ask me to bring up a bottle from the cellar when needed. I did not take one up in…' he paused for thought, 'several months. The last of the previous case. A bottle would last her very many evenings. One small glass now and then was medicinal, she would say. Two glasses was drinking, and Miss Olivia did not hold with such.'

'Could someone have given her extra wine, between the dinner and the ball?' Miss Busby asked.

'I do not see how. She went straight from the dining room to the lounge, to prepare to greet the guests. It was cleared for the ball.'

'But drinks were served there?' Adeline queried.

'Yes, but Miss Olivia is most proper. She did not think it fitting to drink in front of others, unless with a meal. You may ask Annie or Jimmy, they both helped to serve, as did I. But I did not see a drop pass Miss Olivia's lips.'

'And no food either?' Miss Busby confirmed.

He shook his head. 'We had only just eaten dinner.'

'Then someone must have laced her glass with tonic at dinner,' Adeline said, turning in her seat to face Miss Busby. 'It's the only way.'

'Who would do such a thing?' Lázár asked. 'It is unthinkable. And I myself set the table for dinner. Nothing was tampered with. Besides, if tonic had been added to Miss Olivia's wine, she would have known from the taste.'

'Who sat beside her?' Adeline pressed.

Lázár thought for a moment. 'Clara to her left, and Arthur to her right.'

Miss Busby and Adeline exchanged a look.

'And who else knew Olivia drank the tonic?' Adeline asked.

Lázár considered. 'Myself, and Lady Flora I am sure; they would spend many evenings together in Miss Olivia's rooms. And Annie; she would bring away the empty bottle down when finished. Other than that, I should think no one.'

'And the last case is still kept in the cellar?' Miss Busby asked.

Lázár nodded.

'May we go and have a look?'

'Of course, if it will help.' Lázár rose to his feet. 'Please, follow me.'

CHAPTER 15

Leaving the office, they wound further down the corridor and through to the kitchen, where Cook was intently pounding a large lump of dough, sleeves rolled up, face beetroot red.

Towards the back of the kitchen was another door, leading to a narrow set of stone steps winding downwards. Lázár reached up to a small wooden shelf beside the door and pulled down a copper lantern with quatrefoil decoration. 'I am sorry, there is no electric light from here,' he explained, lighting it and holding it aloft. 'Please, mind your steps.'

'I see why Olivia preferred you to bring her the wine!' Miss Busby said, brushing a spiderweb aside as she descended.

'Jimmy and I are the only ones who come down here,' Lázár said, reaching the bottom and lifting the lantern to illuminate the last few steps. 'Cook refuses, and Miss Clara and Mr Arthur would never dirty their clothes so. The Vin Tonique Mariani is kept to the back.' He led them past low shelves holding various cases of wine and liquor, half-empty crates of assorted root vegetables and fruits, and stacks of canned goods, only to let out a breath and exclaim, 'Az anyád istenit!'

'What is it?' Adeline asked, hurrying forward.

'Please, be careful.' Lázár set the lantern down. 'There is much broken glass. The case has been opened. All the bottles, they are smashed!'

'All of them?' Miss Busby stepped forward cautiously.

Lázár bent to count the red tops of the bottles, bright against the dull grey stone. 'Eleven,' he said. 'All broken, but there should be twelve…'

Miss Busby and Adeline took in the scene.

'Why would someone smash them?' Adeline finally asked. 'It makes no sense.'

Miss Busby's brain was whirring, but she couldn't quite find first gear. 'I'm not sure; if they were doctored, it may have been to hide the fact?'

'There are easier ways,' Adeline pointed out. 'Why not just remove them?'

'Perhaps someone was afraid of being discovered.' Miss Busby glanced behind her. 'Or perhaps it was easier than trying to get the bottles out through the kitchen unnoticed.'

'But I do not understand.' Lázár looked down at the dark stains on the stones. 'Where is the twelfth bottle?'

Adeline turned to the shelves behind and began to rummage through them. 'They might have hidden it, help me Isabelle.'

Limited by the single lantern, they slowly searched the dusty shelves, even checking through the red wine cases, but there was no sign of the distinctive tonic wine bottle.

'I must clean the mess,' Lázár said with a defeated sigh.

'No! It's evidence,' Adeline warned.

'Yes,' Miss Busby agreed. 'Might you be able to lock the cellar for now?'

'I suppose I could padlock, yes.'

'I think it best. If anyone asks you to let them in, please tell us. Adeline, we need to speak to Annie,' Miss Busby said. 'If Olivia drank the twelfth bottle, the maid would have seen it in her room.'

Lázár looked at them, his face drawn with concern. 'I do not understand this,' he repeated, helplessly.

'You can be assured, Isabelle will get to the bottom of it,' Adeline told him, with what may have been an accusatory look. He seemed too upset to notice.

'I will find a lock,' he said, turning and lifting the lantern to light their way back up the stairs.

Miss Busby and Adeline were silent as they walked back through the kitchen, but once out of earshot Adeline burst into excited whispers.

'Now we have clear evidence of treachery, Isabelle. And there are only two people who accessed the cellar! And I hardly think Jimmy is responsible,' she added.

'Two people who were known to access it,' Miss Busby pointed out. 'The door wasn't locked, so anyone could have gone down there. We will talk to Jimmy though,' she said, opening the door to reception.

'Surely you don't suspect him?' Adeline's brows flew skyward.

'Of course not.' Miss Busby glanced outside to see if there was any sign of Richard or Barnaby, before making for the lounge. 'But someone may have asked him to go down there for them.'

Coming to the lounge, both women stopped dead in their tracks in the doorway.

Barnaby, mud up to his armpits, was in the middle of the room beside Richard, who stood with his arm around Annie.

'What on earth–?' Adeline breathed, hand to her chest.

The pair looked up, and Miss Busby saw Annie's tear-streaked face, her brown eyes turning red rimmed.

'Whatever's happened?' she asked, hurrying over to them.

'I... I can't find Lázár…' she sniffed, before dissolving into breathless sobs.

Miss Busby looked to Richard.

'I was looking for someone to help me clean the dog, and found her in here like this. She's frantic with worry over Lady Flora,' he explained.

'She w-won't answer her door,' Annie sniffed. 'I've knocked and called, but I c-can't hear anything from inside, and, I'm f-frightened she's…' Dissolving entirely into sobs, she buried her head in Richard's shoulder. He patted her awkwardly on the back and shot a pleading look at Miss Busby.

'I'm sure it's nothing to worry about,' Miss Busby said calmly. 'Lázár was with us in the cellar. Adeline, would you mind popping back and asking him to bring the key to Lady Flora's room?'

Adeline straightened her shoulders and bustled off with an impressive burst of speed.

'Annie, would you show us the way?' Miss Busby asked gently.

The young girl pushed a strand of dark hair behind an ear then nodded. Miss Busby, Richard, and Barnaby followed her further down the corridor to Room One, where Jimmy hovered anxiously.

'I din't know if I ought 'ter break down the door, miss,' he said, 'when Annie said she couldn't find Lázár.'

Miss Busby looked from the solid door to the skinny young man, and fought back a smile. 'He's on his way,' she said.

'I hope Lady Flora's alright.' Jimmy took his cap off and clutched it in his hands. 'She's a bit dotty, like, but in a nice way, y'know?'

'I do,' Miss Busby said solemnly

'Blimey, has 'yer dog been in the lake again?'

Miss Busby followed Jimmy's gaze to the trail of muddy pawprints behind them.

'Ah. Sorry about that,' Richard said. 'He got away from me.'

'S'alright.' Jimmy bent down to ruffle Barnaby's ears. 'I'll let it dry, then brush it off after.'

'Jimmy,' Miss Busby said, turning him away from

Annie and lowering her voice, 'when was the last time you went down to the cellar?'

'The cellar?' He shuddered. 'Oh, I hate goin' down there. Full of spiders, it is. Cook sends me sometimes. I had 'ter go down a couple of days before the ball, 'ter make sure all the drink was topped up in the bar. Lázár came to help me 'cos there was loads of bottles to bring up.'

'And did you notice any that were dropped, or broken?' she pressed, as the door at the far end of the corridor opened and muffled footsteps hurried towards them.

'No, miss,' he said, looking affronted. 'I didn't drop a single one.'

'Here's Lázár with the key now,' Richard called.

The ashen-faced manager exchanged a worried look with Miss Busby, before knocking on the door and calling, 'Lady Flora? Could you open, please?'

'I've t-tried loads of–'

He held a hand up to quiet Annie, and waited. When there was no response, he called, 'I am opening the door, madam, to see if all is well. Stand back, please,' he said quietly to the others. 'She may be in disarray.'

'Let me,' Miss Busby offered. 'If she is, I'm sure she'll prefer a lady to be present.'

Lázár nodded gratefully. Miss Busby turned the key and pushed the door open to reveal Flora lying immobile on her back on top of the bedcovers. Clad in a long, pink flannel nightgown, her mouth was open, eyes closed, arms splayed to the side.

KAREN BAUGH MENUHIN & ZOE MARKHAM

'Oh, dear Lord.' Miss Busby rushed forward.

Annie stepped in and her hand instantly flew to her mouth. The others went past her as she recoiled backwards.

'Te jó Isten,' Lázár exclaimed, the foreign words lilting and musical amidst all the confusion.

'She's alive.' Miss Busby was holding the poor woman's thin wrist. 'But her pulse is very faint.'

'Jimmy, run to telephone for the ambulance,' Lázár ordered.

'And a doctor,' Richard added as the lad sprinted down the corridor, Barnaby barking and chasing behind.

'What's happened?' Major Gresham called, having come out into the corridor. 'Why is Annie crying?' he added.

'Please, go back to your room,' Lázár shouted, hurrying to Lady Flora's side.

'It's Lady Benbow. There's something wrong,' Adeline called to the Major, fear in her voice.

'There's enough of a crowd in here,' Richard told him as he tried to work his way in. 'Wait out in the corridor, please.'

'Who are you?' the Major asked, confusion creasing his face.

'He's a friend, Major,' Miss Busby called. 'Perhaps you could look after Annie?' She added.

Lázár had taken Flora's other hand, and was calling her name.

There was no response.

Miss Busby looked around. The fire had died down to embers, and the room was cold. 'We must keep her warm.' She lifted the floral bed quilt around Flora's frail form. Adeline helped to wrap it around her.

'Should we put pillows under her head?' Lázár asked Miss Busby.

'I don't think we ought to,' she said. 'Why don't you wait outside for the ambulance, so they know where to come? You might like to talk to the others, too,' she added, as Sir Gregory's voice could now be heard from the passage.

'You will stay with her?' Lázár asked.

'Of course.'

'Then I go.' He hurried from the room and closed the door.

Adeline and Richard came to stand by the bed. All three of them looked down at the unconscious woman with concern.

'Did you notice the glass?' Richard asked, nodding to an empty wine glass on the nightstand. A faint imprint of Lady Flora's pale lipstick remained on the rim, and red liquid had settled at the bottom.

'Yes, but I didn't want to say anything in front of the others,' Miss Busby replied, just as the door flew open and Annie rushed in clutching an armful of pink blankets. 'Lázár told me to bring them. It's her favourite colour, but I didn't know how many to bring.' She stood and caught her breath, tears rimming her eyes.

Adeline took the blankets from her and shook one

out to lay gently over the quilt. 'Here, take the others back,' she said. 'And you might make some fresh coffee. I should think we'll need it after this.'

'Tea would be better,' Richard suggested. 'For the shock.'

'You could make both,' Adeline said.

'Yes, miss.' Annie took the blankets, dropped them, scooped them back up and ran out of the room. Richard closed the door behind her.

'She's very upset,' Miss Busby chided. 'You might have been a little kinder, Adeline.'

'I was being kind,' Adeline replied, affronted. 'I thought giving the poor girl something to do would take her mind off it.'

Miss Busby's expression softened; her friend's acerbic exterior often belied the warm heart beneath.

'I can hardly believe this is the same woman who was so lively and talkative yesterday lunchtime,' she said, turning her attention back to Flora and looking down at the frail figure.

'How lively?' Richard asked. 'That is, would you go so far as to say "excited"?'

'Excitable, certainly,' Miss Busby replied, then she realised what he meant. 'Of course, that's what they said of Olivia, before …' She lifted a hand to her cheek. 'And I thought it was Lydia who might be in danger.'

'Lydia!' Adeline clicked her fingers. 'That reminds me, did you see her Talbot outside, Richard?'

'I did. And I saw the girl herself, too. She was around

the back, smoking a cigarette. I'd just introduced myself when the dog took off for the lake, so I had to abandon ship. Seems a pleasant young woman, though. Very well-spoken. Although I'm not a fan of ladies smoking,' he added, a little shamefaced. 'Old-fashioned of me, I know.'

'A fad.' Adeline waved a dismissive hand. 'But that's another youngster up and about early.'

'I suppose they each have a lot on their mind,' Miss Busby said. 'Adeline, do you have a handkerchief?'

Adeline reached into the pocket of her black cardigan and drew one out.

'Use that to pick up the wine glass, Richard,' Miss Busby directed.

Richard took the handkerchief and wrapped it around the stem, holding the glass in front of him. 'What should I do with it?'

'Take it up to your room. We'll keep it for the inspector. It's evidence, and could prove the missing piece of the puzzle. A puzzle we need to solve before anyone else is hurt,' she added, with fresh determination.

'Fine,' he replied, 'and I'll be sure to lock the door.' He left with a determined step.

'Well, two ladies falling so desperately ill so unexpectedly cannot possibly be a coincidence. Someone has clearly tried to kill Flora in the same way they killed Olivia,' Adeline said.

Miss Busby nodded, her face creased heavily with concern.

'What on earth is going on, Isabelle? Why Flora?' Adeline looked down at the ashen face. 'Surely no one could suspect she would inherit.'

'No. Olivia would have needed someone much younger to take on the role. Flora couldn't possibly have been a threat to any of them,' Miss Busby said.

'Well she was clearly a threat to *someone*,' Adeline said darkly.

'We have evidence at our disposal this time, at least,' Miss Busby reasoned. 'Someone must have brought her that drink, and when we find out who, I'm sure we will have our culprit.'

'Careless of them,' Adeline said. 'Desperation, perhaps? Is our murderer getting ruffled? Or is it presumptuous of us, Isabelle. What if the glass only contained her usual bedtime tipple? We may be expecting too much from it.'

'Once we get it to the inspector, we'll find out.'

'I shouldn't think any of the others will talk to us now,' Adeline said thoughtfully. 'They'll all clam up, thinking we're in league with him.'

'Lázár knows we're in league, and he's been remarkably open with us,' Miss Busby pointed out.

Adeline's mouth creased into a moue of disapproval. 'Yes, for someone who had access to the cellar, knew of Olivia's penchant for Vin Mariani, and set the table on the night she was poisoned,' she sniffed.

'And do you really think he would have told us all that if he were guilty?'

'It could be a double bluff,' Adeline huffed. 'I said that right from the start.'

Miss Busby tried to order her thoughts. 'The smashed bottles give us proof that someone is orchestrating events,' she said, tucking the blanket tighter around Flora's chest. 'Even if we're not yet sure who.' She thought for a moment. 'Could the bottles have been smashed in an attempt to prevent further tragedy?'

'Well, it didn't work, if they were. And there are far easier ways,' Adeline said. 'Telling the police, for one.'

'Perhaps they were afraid to, or weren't sure who was responsible. Either way,' Miss Busby sighed, 'it has certainly muddied the waters.'

'Secrets and sabotage.' Adeline rose and crossed to the window, looking out over the drive. 'It's almost like a penny dreadful. A ruthless, manipulative murderer of elderly ladies, and a dank, dusty cellar filled with bottles of cocaine-infused wine. Whoever could have imagined such things would be found in the tranquility of the Cotswolds?'

'Not quite filled with bottles of it,' Miss Busby chided. Then, 'Adeline?'

'Yes?'

'Is there any sign of that ambulance?'

'No.'

'Oh, Lord.'

Adeline whirled. 'What is it?'

'I can't find a pulse.'

CHAPTER 16

Adeline rushed to Lady Flora's side, taking her other wrist. Miss Busby leaned her ear close to the frail woman's mouth, then shook her head and looked sorrowfully to Adeline.

'We must press down on her chest,' Adeline said. 'James taught me how.' Her late husband had been a highly respected surgeon. She looked down at Flora, uncertainty wavering in her eyes. 'Although, it requires a lot of pressure, and she's very delicate… I don't want to hurt her.'

'She isn't breathing, Adeline. I don't think you could hurt her, at this point.'

Adeline still didn't move.

'What would James do, if he were here?' Miss Busby asked.

Adeline took a breath. 'He would say better a broken rib than a funeral.' She squared her shoulders and leaned over, when a commotion sounded from the hallway. They both turned to the door.

'Let Doctor Woods through!' Sir Gregory's loud voice rang out over the others as hurried footsteps thudded on the thick carpet.

'Oh, thank the Lord,' Adeline exhaled, wrenching the door open and calling, 'In here, quickly!'

'Is–?'

She closed the door on Sir Gregory's anxious face as soon as the doctor was inside.

'Her pulse was very weak,' Miss Busby said, 'but now…'

He held up a hand for quiet. A mature man, dark hair greying at the temples, he was reassuringly calm with a determined set of the jaw. He placed two fingers to Flora's neck, his eyes serious and intent over half-moon spectacles. After several seconds, he bent to retrieve his doctor's bag, placing it on the dressing table and began delving inside.

'Wait outside, please,' he said with calm authority.

'But I can help,' Adeline protested. 'I know how to–'

'Send the ambulance men as soon as they arrive. And clear the corridor to allow them passage.'

'Yes, Doctor. Come on, Adeline.' Miss Busby shepherded her quickly from the room.

Questions flew around them the moment they emerged into the corridor.

'You are to go back into the lounge,' Adeline called loudly. The Major and Sir Gregory were joined by Arthur, who looked more crumpled and concerned than ever.

'You two, again?' he demanded. 'What's going on? What were you doing in there?'

'Saving Lady Flora's life,' Adeline replied. 'And I will thank you not to take that tone with me, young man.'

Arthur stepped back under her stern gaze.

'Could you please gather everyone in the lounge and keep out of the way,' Miss Busby requested with rather less assertion.

'We have been tasked with relaying instructions to the medics,' Adeline added, giving Arthur one last imperious look before she marched off down the corridor toward reception. Arthur watched her retreating figure then turned to Miss Busby. 'But what's happened to Lady Flora? Is she going to be alright?'

'Is who going to be alright?' Clara Harrowby came hurrying from the other end of the corridor, where her rooms were, Miss Busby presumed. Her high heels hampered her approach. Frustrated, she slipped them off and carried them as she almost ran towards them.

'Lady Flora,' Arthur said. 'The doctor's with her now.'

The approaching bells of the ambulance sounded before Clara could question further.

'Do excuse me.' Miss Busby hastened towards reception.

'We'd best do as the doctor says.' She heard Arthur tell the others behind her. 'Into the lounge. Give them room.'

'Room for what? And why are those two women involved again?' Clara objected. Miss Busby was sure she could feel those grey-blue eyes burning into her back as she reached the door to reception, hearing Arthur reply with a stern, 'Now, Clara. For goodness' sake,' as it closed behind her.

Adeline was already dispensing orders to two young men in brown jackets, as Lázár, Jimmy, and Annie looked on. Barnaby barked in confusion at the commotion.

'Jimmy, would you mind taking Barnaby and getting him cleaned up?' Miss Busby asked. 'It'll keep him out of everyone's way.'

He nodded as Lázár hurried down the corridor after the medics.

'Isabelle?' Richard appeared at the top of the staircase and hurried down as fast as his leg allowed. 'I heard the ambulance. How is she?'

'Why were you up there so long?' Adeline asked, peering up the stairs behind him.

'I ran into Miss Whitfield again,' he explained. 'Told her Flora wasn't well. She wanted to help, but I didn't think there was anything she could do. Too many cooks, and all that. Charming girl.' He smiled.

Adeline narrowed her eyes. 'Yes, the men certainly seem to think so.'

Richard pretended not to hear.

Miss Busby looked to the young maid. Her eyes were red and puffy, and she clutched nervously at the bottom of her apron. 'Are you alright, Annie?' she asked kindly.

'Oh, yes miss. I've made the tea and coffee, but no one came in. I didn't know what else to do...'

'They should be there now. Why don't you go along and have a cup of hot, sweet tea with them?' Miss Busby suggested.

'I… I'd rather not, miss. They'll only keep asking me questions, and I don't know any more than they do. Lady Flora's not been sleeping well since Mrs Fortescue passed away, and if she doesn't come down for breakfast I take her something up. She's never not answered the door before.'

'Is that why she took a glass of wine to bed with her?' Miss Busby asked. 'To help her sleep?'

Annie's brow creased. 'Wine? No, miss. She never takes anything other than water in her room at night. Used to have a nightcap up with Mrs Fortescue, before… but since then she's taken a small drink in the lounge before bed.'

Miss Busby gave Richard a look.

'Did she take a drink last night?' he asked.

Annie clutched her apron tighter. 'Oh, I don't know, sir. Miss Clara was doing the drinks last night. You'd best ask her.'

Richard nodded. 'Isabelle, why don't you take Annie to your room. I'll arrange for tea to be brought up.'

'Oh no, I couldn't do that.' Annie shook her head. 'I have to keep up with my work.'

'Nonsense,' Adeline said. 'You have had a terrible shock.' Taking the young girl's arm lightly, she steered her towards the stairs.

'But… Mr Lázár…' she tried to object.

'Up you go. Sir Richard will let him know where you are,' Adeline reassured her.

'Richard, would you telephone Alistair?' Miss Busby asked. 'Ask him to send a constable over for Flora's glass. It will need to be examined as soon as possible.'

'I'll do it now,' he said, 'while there's no one about.'

'Tell him not to rush over himself, not until we know what was in it,' she added quietly. 'Stress that it's only supposition at this point. We don't want him ordering us home.'

Richard's green eyes narrowed. 'Isabelle—'

'We're perfectly safe as long as we stick together,' she assured him. 'And we're getting ever closer to the truth.'

He looked ready to argue, but conceded with a nod.

'Thank you.' Miss Busby touched his arm, her eyes creasing as she smiled.

Adeline already had Annie settled in the peace and calm of Miss Busby's bedroom. The fire topped with logs, and the poor maid seated in the armchair by the fire, Adeline stood over her as Annie dabbed her eyes on the bottom of her apron. Miss Busby crossed to the drawer on the nightstand and passed the girl a clean handkerchief before taking a seat at the desk.

'I can't hardly believe it,' Annie said. 'I know Lady Flora's old, but she's been through so much you wouldn't think anything could knock her down.'

'She was missing Olivia terribly, I think,' Miss Busby said. 'Grief can put an awful strain on the heart.'

'Was it her heart, too?' Annie asked, eyes wide. 'Fancy

both of them coming down with bad hearts. Oh, I hope she doesn't go like Mrs Olivia.'

'The doctor arrived very quickly,' Miss Busby reassured her.

Annie sniffled, and nodded.

'Isabelle, you don't suppose Lady Flora tried to take her own life?' Adeline asked, head tilted to one side in thought. 'She must be feeling utterly adrift after losing Olivia, and now possibly her home. That sort of thing can push people over the edge, you know.'

Miss Busby looked at her in alarm, finding herself momentarily lost for words.

'She could have taken something in her drink,' Adeline continued. 'Although I must say she doesn't seem the type.'

Annie looked horrified. 'She'd never do nothing like that. Lady Flora goes to church every Sunday, and that'd be an awful sin.' The young maid shook her head firmly. 'No. She wouldn't even think of it. She always says there's never a problem as can't be solved. That wouldn't be her way.'

'Of course not,' Miss Busby said, darting a sharp look Adeline's way.

Adeline appeared not to notice. Perching on the end of Miss Busby's bed, she asked, 'What exactly had Lady Flora been through?'

'Beg pardon, miss?'

'She's been through so much, you said.'

'Oh. Well…' Annie looked to Miss Busby, uncertainty in her eyes.

'We didn't have as much time to get to know Flora as we'd have liked,' Miss Busby explained. 'When we spoke to her, she always talked more of Olivia than herself.'

That caused Annie to smile. 'She's like that. Always thinking of others first.' She blew her nose, before continuing, 'When that young lady said she'd come to Hamnett Hall to write about Mrs Fortescue, I thought to myself as how Lady Flora oughta get her to write about her life, too. It'd make a lovely book. A proper romance, like you see at the pictures. Only it wouldn't have a happy ending,' she added quietly. 'It'd break your heart.'

'Could you tell us about it?' Miss Busby pressed.

Annie considered for a moment. 'It's no secret, I s'pose. Everyone here knows, anyway. She told me herself soon after I started working here,' she added. 'Dead nervous, I was. Lady Flora asked all about me, to take my mind off the nerves, bless her heart. Only there wasn't much to tell,' she sniffed, 'I'm just a local girl and haven't been anywhere, so then she asked if I'd like to know about her, and I said I would, so she told me.'

'Told you what?' Miss Busby prompted.

'That she was lucky to be born to a family what was very well off, and that when she was of age, her mum was forever wanting to match her up with this Lord, or that Count, like they do. Only, Lady Flora wasn't never interested, because she wanted to marry for love, like the ladies do in books. You know,' she blushed, 'the romantic ones.'

Adeline nodded knowingly.

Miss Busby smiled.

'And these Lords and Counts that her mum thought were proper, well, Lady Flora said as they were old and fusty and there weren't a single one of them what made her heart race.'

'Often the way,' Adeline commiserated, with a sigh.

'Racing hearts can bring problems of their own,' Miss Busby cautioned.

Annie nodded. 'Yes, miss. And they did, in the end. Lady Flora turned down all the gentlemen her parents liked, and they got cross and said she'd die an old spinster if she was so fussy. Well, Lady Flora said that was fine by her, and better than being with some musty old Lord anyway. So they left her alone, and when they died she inherited the estate, her being the only child. And then lots of men came calling. Queuing right down the drive, she said!' Annie chuckled. 'All the usually fusty ones like before, but there was one younger man, too. Jake, he was called. Sir Jake Benbow. She said he was beautiful.'

'Strange word to use for a man,' Adeline remarked.

Annie nodded. 'I thought so too. But Lady Flora said as how handsome wasn't quite right. Delicate, she said he was, in his features. Anyway, he asked if he could call again, and she said as how he could, and she swore blind to me he got more and more beautiful each time he called!'

Adeline smiled.

Miss Busby sighed inwardly; although her friend could rarely resist a dashing hero, she suspected she knew how the tale would end.

'Well, Sir Jake kept on calling, and Lady Flora kept on putting off the others, and before she knew it he asked her to marry him,' Annie went on. 'And because he made her heart race like they do in the stories – she said yes!'

And he took everything she had and left her at the mercy of Olivia Fortescue's charity, Miss Busby thought.

'What happened next?' Adeline asked eagerly, as Annie stopped for breath.

'She said he swept her clean off her feet, and her life went from dull and drab to bright and beautiful. All parties and outings and laughter and…' she blushed cherry red, '…love. Just like life was meant to be, she said.'

Adeline beamed.

'Only, a year or so later,' Annie continued, 'Sir Jake's sister got sick, and he needed money for special doctors for her. Lady Flora gave him some, o'course, only it wasn't enough, because it turned out she needed to go to France where there was a doctor who could fix her. Lady Flora had to go to the bank and sign papers so Sir Jake could draw out the money for it. But the doctor wanted to be sure there was more if it were needed, what with it all being more expensive in foreign, so he had to take a loan out against the estate. And then…'

'He disappeared?' Miss Busby hazarded a guess.

Annie nodded sadly. 'When the estate was sold to pay off the debt, she was left all alone, all her family were dead and gone, and the friends she'd made with Jake all disappeared. She didn't have nowhere to go, but she'd tucked a bit of money away, and decided to come to Hamnett Hall for a few nights to think what to do. Her parents had brought her here years ago and that's how she knew it. She said she meant to stay a night or two while she worked things out, but she was in such a state when she arrived that Mrs Olivia, who she remembered from before, called Dr Woods, 'cos she couldn't stop crying. And she wouldn't take nothing for the room, neither.'

Miss Busby felt that same pang of admiration for Olivia again, thinking that she truly must have been a woman of remarkable qualities.

Outside, an engine could be heard rumbling to life, followed by the harsh peal of the emergency bells, stark in the quiet of their surroundings.

Annie sat up, startled.

'The bells are a good sign.' Miss Busby smiled. 'And how fortunate Lady Flora was to find such a kind soul as Mrs Fortescue.'

Annie nodded. 'They were made for each other, she said. Mrs Olivia had troubles of her own, and the two of them together, well, they helped one another through. Least, that's how she told it.'

'In what way?' Miss Busby asked.

'Mrs Olivia had just lost her husband, and even though she'd been in England for ages she still had an accent, and sometimes she'd get her words wrong. With her suddenly having to do all the managing, she was worried people wouldn't take her seriously.'

'It can't have been easy, taking on the running of Hamnett Hall in such circumstances,' Adeline observed.

'No, miss, it weren't,' Annie said. 'Lady Flora helped her with her English, and her manners – not that she was rude or nothing, but things are different in other countries, aren't they? And Mrs Olivia gave her a home here in return for all her help.'

'A mutually beneficial arrangement. Clever.' Adeline nodded.

'Yes, but Lady Flora said as how they became best friends over the years, and so even when Mrs Olivia didn't need help no more, she still wanted Lady Flora to stay, because she'd miss her something terrible if she wasn't there. *Best friends share everything,* Mrs Olivia told her. *And who would I share with, without you?*'

'What a beautiful way to phrase it,' Miss Busby said, with a warm look to Adeline.

Annie nodded. 'I always remember Lady Flora telling me that, because I don't have a best friend. But that's how I'll know it when I find one. We'll share everything.'

A knock sounded at the door, giving Annie the chance to pause and take a breath, and Miss Busby the opportunity to brush away a tear that threatened.

'Come in,' Adeline called, and the door opened to admit a now-clean Barnaby, along with Jimmy bearing a tray filled with tea things and a plate of scones.

CHAPTER 17

'Sir Richard asked me to bring this up, miss,' Jimmy said brightly, setting it down on the desk. 'Cook added the scones, all buttered and jammed, when she heard who it was for.' He smiled at Annie.

'How is Lady Flora?' Miss Busby asked.

'The doctor got her heart started again, miss! It must be really something, to be a doctor. One minute someone's dead, then you can bring them back to life!'

'Yes, it must be.' Miss Busby smiled. The young lad's enthusiasm was a tonic. 'And what wonderful news.'

Annie's face lit up in a bright grin, all tears and sniffles forgotten.

'Sir Richard's still down talking to the doctor and Mr Arthur. And the Major's gone with Lady Flora in the ambulance to Cheltenham Hospital. Miss Harrowby wanted to go too, but there wasn't room.'

'Clara wanted to go?' Miss Busby asked in surprise.

Jimmy nodded. 'Ever so upset, she was, when they brought her ladyship out on the stretcher. Anyway, I'll leave you to it.' He stopped to pat Annie's shoulder on the way out. 'Mr Lázár says to take 'yer time and feel better,' he told her, before making his way out and closing the door.

'I should get back now, miss. I'm so glad she's alright. I feel properly myself again!' Annie made to rise.

'Not until you've had some tea,' Adeline ordered, stirring the pot and fussing with the cups.

Miss Busby set a scone on a plate and handed it to the young maid. Not feeling very hungry herself, she gave half of hers to Barnaby, who'd no doubt had a traumatic time getting washed. It was funny how dogs adored cold, dirty water, but abhorred a bath.

The three women, and one small dog, took a moment to enjoy the treat. Outside the window the sun emerged from behind a cloud and filled the room with warm, golden light, and everything felt lighter and brighter all round.

Miss Busby took a moment to consider all that Annie had told them, before asking, 'Given how close Lady Flora was to Mrs Olivia, do you think anyone might have considered that she could be the one to inherit Hamnett Hall?'

Annie choked on her tea in surprise. 'Lady Flora? Inherit Hamnett Hall?' She coughed. 'No, miss!' Annie laughed, her brown eyes brightening. 'She'd have been the first to say she's far too old for that, and she wouldn't want it anyhow!'

'How can you be sure?' Adeline asked.

'Because she always said she didn't know how Mrs Olivia managed it all, and that she was glad she didn't have to!'

'But the wealth and security it would bring would surely offer Lady Flora great relief from her circumstances,' Miss Busby pointed out.

Annie took a fresh sip of tea, considering. 'I s'pose, but it'd offer that to just about anyone, wouldn't it? And everyone knows Mrs Olivia wanted the hotel run the same way, after she was gone. Lady Flora wouldn't be able to do that! It's ever so much work.'

Adeline took a bite of scone, and considered. 'Is there anyone who may have been jealous of Flora's close friendship with Mrs Olivia?' she asked, brushing crumbs from her blouse. Barnaby hoovered them up eagerly below.

Annie gave another light laugh. 'Miss Olivia was friends with everyone, there wasn't nothing to be jealous of.'

'And would there be any chance, do you think, that Lady Flora may have been jealous of Mrs Olivia's wealth?' Adeline pressed.

Annie's eyes widened. 'Course not, miss. They were best friends, like I said. Best friends don't get jealous.'

'Envious may be a better word for it,' Miss Busby suggested, before wiping her mouth with a napkin. 'Their circumstances were polar opposites, after all.'

Annie's brow creased in confusion.

'Lady Flora was very wealthy, then lost everything in marriage,' Miss Busby explained. 'Whereas Mrs Olivia was poor, and gained everything in marriage.'

Annie considered this for a moment. 'But Mrs Olivia lost everything first. And she worked her way back up from nothing, everyone knows that. Lady Flora always admired her for her strength of character.'

'How do you know?' Adeline pressed.

'Because she said as money can be lost, like hers, but character was for always, like Mrs Olivia's. She told me I'd do well to remember that, and I have. With strength of character, even a maid with nothing can move up in the world,' Annie said, her pale cheeks flushing slightly. 'She told me money wasn't wealth, neither.'

'How so?' Adeline asked.

'She said she was richer having Mrs Olivia as a friend than she was when she had all that money. And everyone knows how happy she is here. She wouldn't want to be anywhere else. The Major's the same,' she added.

'And Sir Gregory?' Adeline asked.

'Well, he flits about,' Annie said. 'Not like the other two. They like the simple things. Sir Gregory's more…' She stopped and thought for a moment. 'I don't rightly know how to put it…'

'More materialistic?' Miss Busby suggested.

'Erm…' Annie's brow creased.

'More concerned with money and possessions,' Adeline clarified.

'Oh, yes. Or, no, not quite… more the appearance of things, I think. I don't know if I'm saying it right.'

'I rather think you're saying it perfectly,' Miss Busby said, thinking the girl was incredibly astute.

'And what about Mr Lázár?' Adeline asked.

Both Miss Busby and Annie looked to her in surprise.

'He worked his way back up alongside Mrs Fortescue,' she expounded. 'And was clearly very close to her. Might he have been….envious….of her subsequent friendship with Lady Flora?'

Annie put her cup down on the side table, and frowned. 'Mr Lázár is staff, miss. Always was, to Mrs Olivia. It's different.'

'They weren't close, then?' Adeline was not to be deterred.

'Well, sort of, I s'pose, but it's not like friendship, not when you work for someone and have to do what they tell you.'

'But Olivia had worked for Mr Fortescue, and that ended in marriage,' Adeline pointed out. She reminded Miss Busby of Barnaby with a squirrel: relentless in pursuit. 'What would stop Mr Lázár thinking the same sort of thing could happen with Mrs Olivia?'

Annie pushed another stray strand of dark hair beneath her maid's cap. 'Well, I'd say as you'd have to ask him that, miss. Only, there's lots of us worked for her and never thought like that, so I don't see as why he would?'

'I think what Mrs Fanshawe means,' Miss Busby tried, 'is given their rather unusual history, did Mrs Olivia perhaps confide in Mr Lázár in the same way she did Lady Flora?'

'Oh! Well, why didn't you say so? She always talked

to him about things to do with the hotel,' Annie said, 'but she'd never have said about anything personal. Mrs Olivia was raised as gentry, after all. Just like Lady Flora. And Mr Lázár was raised in service, just like me. We know our places.'

'But Lady Flora talked to you about personal things,' Adeline pointed out.

Annie paused to think. 'Lady Flora's special,' she said. 'And it's different, us both being women, like.'

'Of course. Thank you, Annie,' Miss Busby said. 'You've been very helpful.'

Annie rose to her feet. 'I'll take the tray back down, shall I?'

Adeline made a grab for the remaining scone, then nodded.

'Well,' she said between bites when the door closed behind the maid, 'if Flora didn't covet Olivia's wealth, and couldn't have been seen as a threat in terms of the inheritance, we are right back to square one.'

'Not at all,' Miss Busby said. 'We now know exactly why Flora was attacked.'

Adeline blinked. 'Do we?'

'Flora and Olivia were best friends who shared everything. Just like Olivia was planning to share everything with Lydia Whitfield.'

'Yes, but Flora didn't know what Olivia was going to share with Lydia,' Adeline reminded her.

'No, but she was confident there was nothing Olivia hadn't told her, and that she'd be able to identify what she'd wanted to share, if only she knew what it was concerning.'

'You mean, Flora could have known, without knowing?' Adeline asked, brow furrowed. 'Isabelle, this is very confusing.'

'I think it's actually very simple, at heart. Both women were attacked over the same secret,' Miss Busby explained. 'And if Flora survives, as we pray she will, she may be able to tell us exactly who is so afraid of this secret being made public that they are willing to kill over it.'

CHAPTER 18

Richard knocked and entered, to find Miss Busby and Adeline in sombre mood.

'I thought the scones would've cheered you up!'

'They were lovely,' Miss Busby assured him. 'But how's Flora? Jimmy said the doctor worked something of a miracle.'

'So it seems,' he said. 'But she was still very weak. Cheltenham General's an excellent hospital, though. They helped Anthony a great deal when he first returned from the war. She'll be well looked after.'

'Could the doctor tell you what caused her collapse?' Adeline asked.

Richard shook his head. 'His sole concern was keeping her heart beating. I did talk to him about Olivia, though, once the ambulance left. He said he'd told her time and again to stop drinking that tonic wine. It was known to strain the heart, and the older you are, of course, the greater the strain. She always promised she would, but never did. The problem being, he suspects, that she never quite saw herself as old, and so greatly underestimated the danger.'

Miss Busby gave a sad smile. 'We never do see ourselves that way, do we?'

'Not until we look in the mirror,' Adeline sighed. 'That can be rather a rude awakening.'

'Not for you, Mrs Fanshawe, surely,' Richard said gallantly.

Adeline beamed at him.

'So even a small glass of the tonic, as Lázár said she favoured, may have been enough to stop Olivia's heart?' Miss Busby asked, sticking to the matter at hand.

'Difficult to say but there was more than that in her system, as we know. The doctor said the amount could have built up over time, though.'

Miss Busby reached for her notepad. 'How much time?'

'He suggested if substantial amounts were regularly consumed, then possibly up to a few weeks. It's the mix of the alcohol and the coca together, you see. It lingers in the system more than either alone would. Fascinating stuff,' he added, rising on his heels, hands behind his back as his eyes gleamed with interest.

'But there was only one bottle missing from the case,' Miss Busby reasoned. 'So Olivia couldn't have drunk an excessive amount. Especially if some of it was held back to give to Flora. Did you manage to speak to the inspector?' she added.

'What's this?' Adeline asked. 'You mean Inspector McKay?'

'I telephoned him,' Richard explained. 'Whilst everyone was preoccupied with Flora. He asked me to take the wine glass to the Post Office in Quinton. He'll arrange someone to pick it up from there. Jimmy brought me some brown paper, and tape.' He brought his hands forward to reveal a small, neat parcel. 'I thought I might walk down to the village now, perhaps take Barnaby with me.'

Miss Busby looked down at the dog. 'He's all clean. Adeline might take you in the Rolls?'

'Let's all go,' Adeline suggested. 'It will do us good to get out.'

Miss Busby agreed. It had been an upsetting morning.

As they motored down the drive, the grounds of Hamnett Hall looked idyllic in the mellow light of late autumn. They enjoyed the views in contented silence for a few moments, before Miss Busby told Richard of Flora's doomed romance and ensuing friendship with Olivia.

'One secret, one bottle of Vin Mariani, two victims,' he mused, as they turned onto the road and wound their way down into Quinton. The cottages and shops were painted a rich golden hue in the sunlight, bright and cheery and a stark contrast to the dark events they'd been discussing.

Adeline drove past the Post Office – a narrow building sandwiched between the baker and the chemist – braked hard, then reversed up the verge at speed. 'Here we are,' she announced, as Miss Busby loosened her grip on the door handle. 'Shall we get some cakes while we're here, Isabelle?' she asked, peering through the windscreen at the bakery. The window display showcased cottage loaves, soda breads and cobs on one side, and an enticing array of cakes and biscuits on the other.

'We've just had scones!'

'I know.' Adeline looked affronted. 'I was thinking for later. They might cheer everyone up.'

Richard got out, and the bell over the Post Office door tinkled merrily as he ducked inside with the parcel.

'The Chelsea buns are enormous,' Adeline said, craning her neck to see. 'I'm going to get some,' she decided.

Smiling, Miss Busby slipped from the car and took Barnaby for a short stroll down the lane. A robin sang in the hedge as they passed, and for a few blissful minutes all thoughts of Vin Mariani and dangerous secrets flew from her mind, carried aloft on birdsong, fresh country air and misted breath.

'All done,' Richard said, the first to join her. 'I left Alistair's instructions. We should have our answers soon. The woman in there was clearly dying to know what was in the parcel,' he added. 'I'm glad I wrapped the paper around it twice!'

'Thank you,' Miss Busby said. 'You're a great help, Richard. I'm so glad you're here.'

He beamed happily down at her, waving the compliment away, but she could see in his eyes what it meant to him.

Glancing further down into the valley, Miss Busby

noticed a church steeple in the distance. 'Should we walk down and say a prayer for Flora, do you think?'

'Might be a bit far for me. I didn't bring my cane. But what's to stop us saying a quiet prayer here?' he asked. 'You wouldn't find a stained-glass window more beautiful than this.'

The pair gazed out at the deep greens and russet browns of the horizon, dotted all about with the burnt yellows and bright oranges of autumn. They took a moment to savour the view, before bowing their heads.

'I've got macaroons, Isabelle!' Adeline's voice caught the light breeze and carried over to them. 'And the buns smell divine!'

Laughing softly, they turned and walked back towards the car, Barnaby scurrying after them.

'The woman serving knew Olivia well,' Adeline said as she manoeuvred the car back onto the road.

Miss Busby looked to her in surprise.

Adeline smiled. 'Cakes can serve more than one purpose,' she said, clearly enjoying her moment. 'I have been detecting!'

'And what have you discovered?' Miss Busby prompted.

'Olivia used to come here every Sunday to buy cakes for the hotel. She gave Cook Sunday afternoons off. The lady behind the counter couldn't have spoken more highly of her.'

'Did she know any of the others?' Richard called from the back.

Adeline nodded. 'She said Clara Harrowby grew ideas above her station after her parents' death, and is rarely seen in the village. She has been heard to pronounce it too provincial to be worth her time.'

'What a foolish attitude,' Richard said. 'It's a picture of pastoral perfection.'

'Very poetic,' Miss Busby teased him.

'I have been known to wax lyrical in my time,' he laughed.

'Well, it's all quite wasted on the young,' Adeline pointed out. 'And the baker's wife suggested Arthur wasn't much better,' Adeline continued. 'Although she did concede that the young man would run the odd errand for his aunt. And she spoke fondly of Major Gresham. Apparently he has a weakness for ginger snaps, and Olivia would always indulge him.'

'What about Sir Gregory?' Richard asked, as they turned and motored back up the long drive to Hamnett Hall.

Adeline *tsked*. 'She melted at the mere mention of his name. Silly woman.'

Miss Busby kept her eyes fixed straight ahead and lips firmly prim.

'He only makes the occasional appearance, now,' Adeline continued. 'Apparently he and Mr Henry Fortescue would go to the George & Dragon several evenings a week. But Sir Gregory doesn't like to drink alone, so doesn't go any more.'

'He did mention they were friends,' Miss Busby recalled, as Adeline parked unnecessarily close to Lydia's silver Talbot. Disembarking, Miss Busby caught sight of the young writer herself, dressed in a pretty, pale yellow frock and long matching cardigan, clutching a cigarette beside one of the oak trees fronting the hotel.

'Smoking again?' Adeline arched a brow as she followed Miss Busby's gaze.

Lydia waved and hurried over to them. 'None of you answered your doors, so I came down to see if your car was still here. Thought I'd wait for a bit, see if I could catch you,' she explained breathlessly.

Dropping the half-smoked cigarette to the gravel, she ground an elegant heel to extinguish it.

Adeline's eyes narrowed to slits. The writer swiftly ducked to pick it up.

'Sorry,' Lydia said with an apologetic smile. 'I wondered if I might have a word, Miss Busby?'

'Of course,' she said. Richard had gone ahead to open the doors for them and they went to file in. Lydia dropped the cigarette into a flowerpot en route, beyond Adeline's field of vision.

'Ladies,' Sir Richard said with a mock bow and a grin.

Miss Busby gave him a sideways look. 'Shall we go into the lounge?' she said. 'Adeline has bought cakes.'

'Oh, lovely!' Lydia exclaimed. 'But first perhaps we could talk in private? Upstairs?'

Adeline turned, paper bag in hand, both brows raised.

Richard offered, 'I can excuse myself, if you ladies would prefer?'

'Oh, no, that's alright,' Lydia said, smiling up at him.

'I know you're chums. In fact, I overheard Arthur telling Lázár that you're like the three musketeers!' She gave a light laugh. 'I'd be grateful for all your opinions, if you have time.'

'Of course,' Richard said, gesturing for Miss Busby to lead the way. Adeline and Barnaby brought up the rear.

'Shall we use my room?' Lydia suggested. 'There's something I'd like to show you.'

'Let me drop Barnaby back to mine,' Miss Busby said. 'He can have a sleep.'

'You'd better take the cakes, too.' Adeline handed over the bag. 'We can share them around after lunch. Put them somewhere high up!' she added, with an accusatory look at the dog.

Whilst there, Miss Busby took her notebook and pencil from the desk, before rejoining the others next door.

Adeline looked put out. 'This room is bigger than ours, Isabelle!'

'I think because ours are adjoining,' Miss Busby pointed out. 'But it's perfect for all of us to have a chat.' She smiled, taking a seat on the blue and gold cushioned bench under the window. The sun was warm and comforting on her back. Adeline took one of the armchairs upholstered in the same hues, and Lydia gestured for Richard to take the second.

'I shan't be a mo,' she said, turning to a small suitcase on the ottoman at the foot of the bed, and fiddling with the lock. 'I just need to… Ah, here we are.' She pulled a small, green, clothbound notebook from within, slightly tatty in appearance, before setting the suitcase on the floor and sitting in its place, the notebook clutched tightly in her lap.

Three pairs of eyes settled on her expectantly.

'I'm afraid I wasn't entirely honest with you,' she confessed, flicking her eyes nervously to Miss Busby.

Miss Busby tilted her head to the side in polite enquiry.

'I mean, I *was* honest,' Lydia was quick to add. 'But I… omitted…some information. Not because I had any intention to deceive,' she hurried on, 'only because I'd talked to Olivia in confidence. And even though she's no longer with us, I do still feel obliged to honour her wishes.'

'Perfectly understandable,' Richard said. 'Commendable, even.'

Lydia flashed him a grateful smile. 'I did show Miss Busby a letter that Olivia sent,' she went on. Miss Busby nodded. 'But there was something else,' she added.

Miss Busby leaned forward as Lydia held up the book, running a hand over the worn cover. 'It was such an expression of trust. I couldn't have told anyone, even you, Miss Busby, if today's events hadn't taken such a turn.'

'Lady Flora?' Miss Busby queried softly.

Lydia cast her eyes downwards and nodded. 'I went down to the lounge, after I heard the ambulance leave. I didn't want to get in the way, but I wanted to know how Lady Flora was. She seemed so sweet, it was awful to think…' She stopped, and gave her head a little shake. 'Anyway, they were all arguing in there. Arthur had overheard the maid telling the porter that Lady Flora had been given wine the night before by Miss Harrowby. And so Arthur confronted her, really quite rudely,' she added. 'She was upset because she'd been the one serving drinks in the lounge last night, and she insisted Lady Flora had only had warm milk. It all got a bit heated between them, and Lázár had to intervene. Oh,' she tutted, 'it sounds silly now I'm saying it out loud, but Arthur seemed in quite a temper, almost bullying her. I felt…uncomfortable.'

'It is quite sensible to be cautious when young men are riled,' Adeline said. 'They can be very irrational. Older men too, in fact.'

Richard cleared his throat meaningfully.

'Although there are exceptions,' Adeline conceded.

Lydia nodded. 'He was in such a bad humour, and the others all seemed so angry too; it felt as if another terrible thing could happen at any moment. Does that make sense?' she asked. 'I'm better at writing things down than saying them. You can rub bits out if the words aren't right.' She blushed, and Miss Busby noted her knuckles had turned pale around the journal.

'It makes perfect sense,' Adeline assured her. 'It's felt as though there has been a dark threat hanging over Hamnett Hall since we arrived,' she added, a little dramatically, Miss Busby thought.

Lydia looked more concerned than ever. 'Has there? I really only felt it this morning. And so I thought perhaps it's time to tell someone everything I know, but it's so hard to know *who*. I don't want to go to the police, because everything's so… *murky*, as if I'm peering into the lake and can't see the bottom. But I thought if I told you, Miss Busby, you might be able to help. You've been so kind.'

'I'll do my best, of course,' Miss Busby said, her eyes and tone soft and encouraging.

Lydia took a breath, anxiously twisting the book in her hands. 'It's about the journal,' she said.

Adeline gasped, and leaned so far forward she almost fell out of the chair. '*Olivia's* journal?' she breathed.

There was a slight pause, the room tense with expectation, before Lydia nodded. 'Her most recent one,' she confirmed. 'Olivia never kept them once each book was filled. She told me she burned them in the fire, in a sort of a ritual – as if her thoughts were being freed.'

'How extraordinary,' Miss Busby remarked.

'Yes, she seemed such a unique sort of soul. But it's not really a journal in the traditional sense,' Lydia went on. 'Her entries are very short. Just notes, really. Prompts. She said all she'd been able to think about lately was the memoir, and that's why she sent me this one. She thought it would help me get a feel for things. Sort of an amuse-bouche, before we met and tucked into the main course. But there was something that leapt off the page when I looked through it. It's a bit…delicate,' she finished.

CHAPTER 19

Adeline waved a hand. 'When you get to our age, Miss Whitfield, you'll find there's very little left that will shock you.'

'Absolutely,' Richard agreed. 'Just come out with it. Like ripping off a sticking plaster!'

His warm smile was contagious.

'Right! Yes, I will.' She cleared her throat. 'I think Arthur Fortescue may be illegitimate.'

Richard blinked.

Adeline's mouth fell open.

Miss Busby was the first to recover. 'And what makes you think that?' she asked, her voice deceptively calm as her mind raced ahead.

'Well, I think *Olivia* thought it,' she clarified. 'It's probably easier if I just read it to you?'

'Couldn't we have a look at–'

'That would be fine,' Miss Busby said, stopping Adeline in her tracks. The poor writer looked tortured enough at sharing the information, there was no use trying to take the book from her.

Nodding, Lydia flicked to a page towards the back. Many of the pages were empty, Miss Busby saw, or contained only one or two words, but she recognised the same flowing handwriting she'd seen on the letter Lydia had previously shown her.

'There aren't any dates,' Lydia said. 'Although the pages are numbered. It's one of the longer entries, just here.' She pointed to the top of the page, then took a breath and read, '*I still wonder why Henry's brother, Lionel, took so long to abandon all pretence and move away. They were never happy in their marriage.*'

'Sad, but hardly unusual,' Adeline commented, sounding somewhat disappointed.

'Yes,' Lydia said, 'but underneath she's added: *Arthur doesn't favour him in the least, neither in looks nor temperament.*'

Adeline blinked. 'Well, again, it happens.'

Miss Busby threw her a sharp look, before encouraging Lydia with a gentle, 'Do go on.'

'*I fear the rumour may be true, for in both he favours... another.*'

Adeline's brow creased. 'Who?'

'She doesn't say,' Lydia said, holding up the book so Adeline could see the blank lines beneath.

'Is there nothing more about it at all?' Richard asked.

Lydia turned several pages, and read, '*All that money, yet Lionel never knew how to be happy. The other has none, but seeks happiness in the wealth of others. Arthur follows in his footsteps.* That's all there is,' she said, looking up from the page.

'*The Other,*' Adeline echoed, eyes alight with the intrigue of it all. 'Who could it be? Sir Gregory was a friend of the family, he may have heard this rumour. We ought to ask him,' she suggested eagerly.

'If a rumour is all it is, it won't be enough to settle anything,' Miss Busby remarked.

'That's exactly what I thought,' Lydia agreed glumly. 'It's not the sort of thing you *could* take to the police, really. But after what happened today… it worries me.'

'Of course,' Adeline said, completely ignoring Richard. 'Because if the boy is illegitimate, he can have no claim, either legal or moral, to Hamnett Hall. Now *there* is a secret worth killing over.'

Lydia dropped her head into her hands, the book falling into her lap.

'Are you alright, Miss Whitfield?' Richard asked.

'Yes,' Lydia replied through her fingers, before composing herself and looking up. 'I'm so sorry. It's just that's exactly what I thought, too. I was hoping you'd tell me I was being silly.'

'I am afraid you are not,' Adeline said.

Lydia sighed. 'And the *really* awful thing,' she said, 'is that at lunch yesterday, if you recall, Lady Flora offered to help me with the memoir on Olivia's behalf, suggesting she could tell the same story. And now…'

'She is gravely ill,' Adeline finished. 'Isabelle, it's

exactly as you thought. They were attacked over the same secret.'

Lydia looked between the two women, eyes wide.

Miss Busby nodded, although there was something niggling at the back of her mind.

'Flora was silenced to prevent Arthur's illegitimacy coming to light,' Adeline concluded.

'I'm not quite sure she was,' Miss Busby said, brow furrowed. 'If Flora knew, she could have said something before now.'

'But she had no reason to,' Adeline objected. 'Not until Miss Whitfield arrived and ruffled feathers.'

Lydia gave a soft moan.

'A secret is only dangerous when it rises to the surface,' Adeline went on. She looked to Lydia. 'Did Olivia write anything more concerning Arthur?'

'Only the odd implication that he was hapless with money. Nothing more concerning his parentage.' Lydia closed the journal and clutched it to her chest. 'And I suppose it *was* only a rumour, after all.'

'Rumour can be enough,' Miss Busby said. 'In fact, it can do far more harm than truth. Oh, truth!' she repeated, picking up her notebook and flicking back through the pages. 'Olivia told you people were *owed the truth of it,*' she recalled. The young writer nodded. 'I doubt she would have used the word to refer to a rumour.'

'Unless the rumour had somehow been confirmed in the meantime,' Lydia suggested.

All eyes turned to her.

'How?' Adeline asked. 'A full confession from the cad in question?'

'I don't know. Truly,' she added, her face flushing slightly. 'But I can't stop wondering about it.'

Miss Busby looked down at her notes again, to the wording of Olivia's letter. 'Arthur inheriting Hamnett Hall could have been the *injustice* Olivia feared,' she said. 'It fits.'

'Does Arthur know, I wonder…' Miss Busby considered. 'It would explain his increasing frustration with us. Is he concerned enough to act dangerously rashly with Flora's wine, perhaps. With his parents' inheritance dwindling, and no apparent gumption of his own to make a living, what would he do without Hamnett Hall?'

'Flora may have simply been a warning,' Richard suggested, standing in front of the fire, hands clasped behind his back in his customary thinking pose. 'An attempt to frighten us off.'

'Nonsense,' Adeline huffed. 'She would have been dead if we hadn't fetched the key and intervened.' She shook her head. 'No, we are dealing with a cold-blooded killer. If he wanted us out of the way, he would have poisoned us, not Flora.'

'Poison?' Lydia gasped. 'Is that how it was done? How *horrible*. When the others were arguing I thought it was just that Lady Flora had been given too much wine. I wondered if it might have interfered with some medication, or an underlying condition. I never imagined… *poison*.' She shuddered. 'Are you certain?'

'Nothing is certain,' Miss Busby sighed. 'We're relying heavily on supposition. Our good friend Enid would despair of us thus far. But… I believe so. And we don't drink in the lounge in the evenings, Adeline,' she added. 'We would have made more challenging targets. Flora may have offered the opportunity for killing two birds with one stone,' she considered. 'Silence and warning both.'

'And will you heed the warning, do you think?' Lydia asked, her face a mask of concern. 'It seems awfully dangerous, if the…' she struggled with the word, '…killer, is still in the hotel. I'm… well, I'm rather afraid,' she confessed.

'You ought to go home,' Richard said, looking down at her with concern. 'Back to London, where you'll be safe. You can leave the journal with us. Isabelle will see matters through,' he assured her.

'Yes,' Miss Busby agreed. 'There's no need for you to stay.'

'But why would *you* all stay?' Lydia asked, concern turning to confusion in her eyes.

'Because we are allied with the authorities,' Adeline said importantly.

'Ah. I did wonder if you might be,' Lydia said shyly. 'I wasn't sure, but you do have that sort of air about you.'

'Well, we do our bit.' Adeline puffed her chest out.

Lydia took a deep breath. 'Then I would like to stay

too,' she said. 'To help, if I can. I feel responsible for all of this, after all.'

'Don't be silly.' Miss Busby's tone was gentle. 'Olivia engaged your services of her own accord; you are not in any way to blame.'

'Even so, I'm involved, and I feel… an obligation of sorts. She not only trusted me with her journal, but with the task of telling her story.' She took a deep breath, smoothing the short blond bob back behind her ears. 'I should like to see things through,' she continued, her voice wavering between nerves and determination.

'Well said!' Adeline gave the young woman a rare look of approval. 'So, Isabelle. Tactics?'

Miss Busby eyed Lydia with concern. 'Are you quite sure?' she asked.

'Never more so!' The writer's pretty face shone with a determined smile.

'Well then,' Miss Busby went on with a nod, 'we will need to find out more about Arthur's background. But,' she cautioned, 'we'll have to be discreet. We mustn't provoke any further attacks.' She thought for a moment. 'I'll start by talking to Sir Gregory,' she said, rising to her feet.

'No, Isabelle.' Alarm rang in Richard's voice. 'Let me do it. I'll ask him for that round of golf he mentioned. Talk to him man to man.'

'You said you can't play golf,' Miss Busby reminded him.

'*I* will talk to him,' Adeline said, rising from the chair

and drawing herself up to her full height. 'I'll take him for that drive in the Rolls he wanted.'

'I'd rather you didn't isolate yourself in that manner, Adeline,' Miss Busby cautioned.

'Um, I'm afraid I'm not going to offer, if that's alright,' Lydia said quietly. 'I found him rather offensive even before things started to feel dangerous.'

Miss Busby laughed, and Richard, and eventually even Adeline followed suit.

'We must stick together,' Miss Busby said, recovering her composure. 'Perhaps tackle things with no less than two of us at a time, for safety. Adeline,' she said, 'Gregory likes you, and I suspect he'll talk to you much more openly than Richard.' She shot him an apologetic look. 'But you are not going alone. I'll come with you, and we'll talk to him together.'

'Good idea,' Adeline agreed, before Richard could object. 'And Arthur tolerates you far more than me, so you may take point on that one, but I will be with you.'

'And what can I do?' Lydia asked.

'Keep that journal safe,' Miss Busby said. 'You have done plenty already.'

Lydia rose and locked the book back in her suitcase.

'And don't drink any wine,' Adeline added, for good measure.

'Well, what about me?' Richard flung his arms wide. 'Am I to sit and do nothing?'

'You can walk Barnaby,' Miss Busby said. 'But keep him on his leash, so he doesn't need another bath.'

'Might I come for a walk too?' Lydia asked, adding, 'I think I might scare myself half to death if I just sit here alone.'

'Of course!' Richard said, offering an arm. She took it gratefully.

'I'll give you his leash,' Miss Busby said. They walked together to her room. Barnaby was thrilled to have the young writer for company, and glued himself to her feet immediately. Glancing down at his watch, Richard said, 'Time's running on. Shall we meet you in the dining room for lunch afterwards?'

Miss Busby nodded.

'Just let me freshen up first,' Adeline said, striding through to her own room.

Lydia wished Miss Busby luck, before leaving with Barnaby, telling the little dog how handsome he was. Miss Busby took Richard's hand for a moment before he followed.

'I will be careful,' she promised. 'As long as you do the same.'

'Of course,' he said, bending to kiss her hand. 'I shall see you at lunch.'

As soon as he'd gone, the weight of the secret surrounding the Fortescue family felt heavier and more dangerous than ever. Miss Busby shivered; the fire had begun to die down, but that wasn't the reason. As she sat on the bed and waited for Adeline, she felt truly afraid for the first time since arriving at the hotel. The delicate balance of power, wealth, and social standing threatened to shift within the walls of Hamnett Hall, and she knew that the truth of Arthur's birth could threaten more than just his inheritance. *Lives will be ruined*, she thought. *If Olivia was right, more than one person may have been willing to kill over such a secret.*

'Isabelle, do these shoes make my ankles look unsightly?' Adeline strode through from her connecting room in a cloud of Shalimar, her skirt and blouse swapped for a dress in swirling patterns of red and cream. Her high heels, complete with thin, intricate ankle straps gave her even more impact, as she stood tall and elegant in the doorway. Ever confident, nothing seemed to frighten her. Miss Busby took courage from her indomitable spirit.

'Of course not,' she said. 'You look lovely.'

CHAPTER 20

Finding the lounge empty when they entered, Miss Busby and Adeline went to the dining room, where Annie was busy setting the tables for lunch.

'Where is everyone?' Adeline asked.

'Lázár's in his office, miss,' Annie said, 'and Mr Arthur and Miss Clara was in the lounge, last I saw.'

'Well they're not there now,' Adeline said.

'I s'pect they'll be along for their lunch any moment. Everything's a bit behind today,' she added. Her eyes were still red rimmed but she looked happier than before.

'Of course,' Miss Busby said. 'But do you know where we might find Sir Gregory?'

'Yes, miss. He's in the conservatory.' She pointed to the glass door at the far end of the room. 'Said he needed a bit of sun after all that happened this morning, only it's too cold for him outside.'

Smiling, Annie went back to the tables, and Miss Busby and Adeline made for the conservatory beyond. Lush, green plants, including orchids, lined the low-bricked walls, the large windows filling the room with midday sun. Sir Gregory was the only occupant. Seated in a wicker chair facing the grounds, newspaper in hand, a small glass of what appeared to be sherry on the table beside him.

He turned as they entered.

'Ah, hello! I don't usually get company in here. No bar, you see,' he added with a faux grimace. 'Although I like to bring a little tipple in now and then.'

'It's a beautiful spot,' Miss Busby said, taking in the picturesque view of the grounds beyond.

Sir Gregory nodded. 'Gets awfully hot in summer, and it's absolutely perishing in winter. Perfect in the autumn and spring, though!' He rose to his feet with a smile. His pale suit was crisp, a red rose today gracing his lapel, and his brown eyes shone as he took in the sight of Adeline in her frock and heels, lips brightly painted.

'Mrs Fanshawe, you are a vision,' he declared. 'I should be delighted if you'd join me.' He pulled out the chair opposite his own. Adeline obliged.

Miss Busby waited expectantly, before tutting and fetching her own chair across.

'You have quite divided opinion this morning!' Sir Gregory said, sitting opposite them both.

'Me?' Adeline asked.

'Both of you! Now,' he mused, 'which is it? Arthur has warned us you have been planted by a Scottish police inspector to investigate us all, whilst young Annie insists you are the very souls of compassion.' He looked between them.

'Can't both be true?' Miss Busby asked in response.

He looked to her in surprise before letting out a short bark of a laugh. 'Well, I suppose it's possible! One doesn't often associate compassion with police inspectors, though. They always seem so severe.'

'The Scottish ones in particular,' Adeline agreed.

Sir Gregory's face lit up with delight. 'Ha! Indeed! *Biting and scratching is Scots folk's wooing. Fair words won't make the pot boil.* An old Scottish proverb,' he explained. 'I've lived up there for years. The locals can be awfully plain spoken, although I do admire them for it.'

'May we talk to you about Arthur's parents?' Miss Busby asked before Adeline expounded on the inspector's temperament.

'What on earth for?' Sir Gregory said, leaning back in his chair and tilting his head in surprise. 'Ah!' His eyes widened. 'Am I being interviewed? Should I call my lawyer?' He barked another laugh.

Adeline gave a delicate laugh of her own in response. 'Of course not. But we understand you were a close friend of the family?'

'Of Henry and Olivia, yes. Never had much to do with the older brother, Lionel, if I could help it. Gloomy kind of fellow. The sort to hide the good whiskey when one called round, and was never short fo money.'

'What about his wife?' Miss Busby asked.

'Muriel?' He gave a shudder. 'Ghastly woman. Severe as a schoolmistress.'

Miss Busby bristled.

'The reason Lionel was always so glum, I expect,' he continued. 'Muriel probably set the poor chap lines every time he didn't come up to snuff.' He laughed at his own joke.

Miss Busby fought back a sharp retort.

Adeline took over once more, plumping for the direct approach. 'And had you ever heard any talk of the woman indulging in an illicit relationship?'

Sir Gregory blinked, his mouth dropping open, before he pushed his chair back from the table, threw his head back and laughed at the very idea. It was some time before he was able to speak. 'Muriel Fortescue? Good Lord, no!'

Miss Busby found herself caught off guard; hilarity hadn't been the response she was expecting.

Sir Gregory beamed and shook his head. 'Mrs Fanshawe, you are a tonic. I haven't laughed like that since before poor Olivia died.'

Adeline frowned.

Miss Busby noted how the laughter relaxed his features, making them less severe, more handsome; coupled with the crisp, light suit, he looked rather dashing in the sunlight, and Adeline's prior grievances with the man seemed to be melting away.

Sir Gregory recovered himself enough to ask, 'What on earth could possibly have given you that idea?'

'We have been made aware of a rumour,' Miss Busby said.

'By whom?'

'I'm afraid I'm not at liberty to say. The concern raised, however, was that Arthur Fortescue may not be legitimate.'

Sir Gregory was neither quick nor flippant in response this time. 'That's a rather more venomous suggestion,' he said. His tone was still light but there was no trace of levity in his eyes. 'Whoever made it ought to be cautioned against spreading fanciful tales.' He steepled his fingers, and considered. 'This has something to do with Lady Flora, I suppose? It's the sort of addled nonsense she would come out with, after a glass or two.'

'May we remind you Lady Flora is extremely unwell,' Miss Busby said sharply.

'There's no need,' Sir Gregory said. 'I wish her a speedy recovery, but her current condition doesn't preclude the fact she is terminally prone to flights of fancy and a seasoned embroiderer of the truth.'

Miss Busby leaned across the wicker table, her eyes flashing a challenge. 'She seemed perfectly sensible to me.'

Sir Gregory scoffed. 'I have known her rather longer than you have, my dear.'

Miss Busby's eyes narrowed dangerously at the patronising endearment.

'Details of her supposedly young and dashing husband change on a daily basis, for one,' he went on, oblivious.

Adeline, noting Miss Busby's expression, diffused the situation by saying, 'I'm sure you'll understand, Sir Gregory, that we cannot reveal our sources.' She puffed her chest out importantly. 'I *can*, however, say it was nothing to do with Lady Flora.'

Sir Gregory considered Adeline for a moment, and his expression relaxed once more. 'Just like in the detective stories, eh? Well, take it from me: Muriel Fortescue would never have entertained anything even remotely illicit. She was fond of the moral high ground and would never have released her hold on it long enough to break her marriage vows. Nor, I might add, could I imagine any chap would ever have indulged the notion! Objectionable woman. Utterly unattractive inside and out. Lord only knows what Lionel saw in her.'

'The marriage wasn't a happy one, by all accounts,' Adeline continued.

Sir Gregory shrugged. 'I shouldn't think it was. And between her insufferable righteousness and his dull avarice it's no wonder Arthur turned out the way he did.'

'We quite understand,' Adeline said. 'I do hope you don't mind us asking. We must leave no stone unturned, after all.'

Sir Gregory waved a hand. 'Do what you must. I only wish Olivia could hear you ask. Her sister-in-law was so prim and proper she would have found the notion an absolute hoot!' He picked up his glass and tilted it towards Adeline before draining the contents. 'It is rather a serious accusation, however,' he added, setting the glass down. 'You ought to be careful. If Arthur catches wind of it there's no knowing what he'll do. He's tightly wound as it is.'

'Well, if there's no truth to the rumour we needn't trouble him with it, I'm sure,' Adeline replied.

'*I* certainly shan't,' Sir Gregory agreed. 'I wouldn't rush to put my head into that lion's mouth! And I'm glad you don't plan on doing so either.' He looked to Adeline. 'One should never risk such a charming head, after all.'

Adeline's cheeks flushed pink.

Miss Busby tutted a little louder than she'd intended, attracting Sir Gregory's attention. 'All differences of opinion aside, Miss Busby,' he said softly, 'I truly would hate to see you fall foul of any old ghosts that may be lurking, imagined or otherwise.'

Miss Busby felt a shiver travel along her spine as he folded his newspaper and rose to his feet.

'Now, if you'll excuse me, Annie said it's tomato soup for lunch. I shall my change my shirt, so as not to tempt fate. If there's anything more you'd like to ask, Mrs Fanshawe, perhaps you might do so over a drink this evening?'

'I shall bear that in mind.' Adeline smiled as he bowed before turning and leaving the room. His loud tones could be heard a moment later, announcing, 'Just through there, Sir Richard! And I haven't forgotten about that round of golf, you know!'

Barnaby came trotting into the conservatory, with Richard close behind.

'How did you get on?' he asked.

'Close the door,' Adeline commanded, before hastily recounting all that Sir Gregory had told them.

'It's interesting that he didn't suspect for a moment the idea may have come from Olivia herself,' Richard mused.

Something clicked inside Miss Busby's brain.

'He didn't think the idea of the memoir had come from Olivia either,' she said, casting her mind back to his initial reaction to the news of it. 'He said *someone must have put her up to it.*'

'The same person who put the question of Arthur's parentage into her mind?' Richard wondered. 'Although he could be lying, of course. He does seem prone to putting a certain spin on things.'

'Only, I think, if it benefits him directly,' Miss Busy considered.

'Well, he seemed entirely sincere to me,' Adeline said.

Miss Busby suppressed the urge to point out she hadn't been *quite* so sure of this previously, when he'd made such a fuss of Lydia. 'He was certainly very charming,' she said carefully. 'And charm can be a very effective persuasion.'

Adeline *harrumphed*. 'I am quite old enough and sensible enough to know the difference, Isabelle,' she insisted. 'There was no hint of defensiveness or anger in either his eyes or his tone when I raised the question of a dalliance.'

'And when he pressed us to reveal the name of the accuser?' Miss Busby asked.

Adeline sniffed. 'It's only natural to want to know who may be spreading dangerous lies about.'

'He did seem to find the notion genuinely amusing,' Miss Busby conceded.

'Yet he warned you off asking Arthur,' Richard observed. 'Or anyone else, if his talk of old ghosts is to be taken seriously.'

'He was concerned for us,' Adeline objected. 'Lydia says Arthur has quite the temper, and it would appear Sir Gregory concurs.' She looked between Richard and Miss Busby, exasperation taking hold. 'Now, look here,' she said firmly, 'for all his faults, Sir Gregory could simply have refused to answer the question. I believe his candour in this instance speaks of his character, however flighty he may appear when pretty young ladies are present,' she concluded, a slight flush to her cheeks.

Miss Busby nodded, raising a hand to Adeline's arm and patting it softly. 'You're quite right, of course.'

'The timing of it all has to be key,' Richard suggested. 'If there is genuine doubt over Arthur's parentage, surely the issue would have been raised long before now?'

'It may have been,' Miss Busby said. 'Things like that can lurk beneath the waters for decades. It might only have risen to the surface following Olivia's death.'

'Or someone may have slipped the notion under the surface as soon as Olivia's intention to choose an heir was floated on the waters,' Adeline countered.

Miss Busby sighed. 'Either way, the waters are all so very *murky*, as Lydia put it.' She massaged her temples and took a moment to think, before continuing, 'If someone did maliciously put the idea into Olivia's head, then the question becomes not *Is Arthur illegitimate*, but *Why would someone want Olivia to believe he was.*'

'So he wouldn't inherit Hamnett Hall,' Adeline replied swiftly.

'Yes, but if Olivia hadn't been killed, that wouldn't be at issue,' Miss Busby said. 'It has to all be connected.'

'Perhaps someone is trying to ruin the family name, or garner revenge for some sort of age-old slight,' Richard suggested. 'It may not be connected to controlling the estate at all. There could be several motives at play.'

'I do hope not,' Miss Busby sighed. 'Two perpetrators with opposing agendas would surely be impossible to unravel.'

'It would make sense, though,' Adeline remarked. 'If Flora were attacked over her possible revelation of Arthur's parentage, why would someone have gone out of their way to put the idea into Olivia's head in the first place?' Adeline gave a little puff of exasperation. 'Every time we take a step forward, Isabelle, we are pushed two steps back.'

Barnaby, having settled contentedly in a patch of sun, spotted a fly whirring softly at the window pane. With a scrabble of claws on tiles he flew into action, his short back legs turning into springs as he leapt after it, jaws snapping. They watched his endeavours quietly for a minute or two, before a successful leap and snap finally silenced the insect.

He never gives up, Miss Busby thought to herself. *The idea of it never so much as enters his little head*. She took a breath. 'If someone *did* put ideas into Olivia's head,' she said, 'it must have been someone close to her, for it to stick. And by all accounts, all those close to her are gathered here.'

'Then the answer must be here, too,' Richard replied. 'Only we can't *see* it. Is it always like this, when you're investigating?'

'Yes,' Miss Busby and Adeline replied in unison, bringing a short laugh and lightening the mood.

'What did you do with Lydia?' Miss Busby asked, registering the young writer's absence.

'I suggested she take her own table for lunch. Thought she'd be safer keeping separate from us, at least in public.'

'Good idea.' Miss Busby smiled up at him in approval.

'As is lunch,' Adeline said, rising and making for the door. 'Food for thought, Isabelle!'

'I should think we have quite enough of that already,' Miss Busby murmured, but followed along all the same.

CHAPTER 21

Sir Gregory, now sporting a dark navy shirt, had joined Lydia at her table. The young writer looked uncomfortable as he chatted and flattered in his customary manner.

'She may need rescuing,' Miss Busby whispered to Adeline, who instantly launched into action.

Pulling up a chair from the next table, she squeezed herself in next to Lydia, saying, 'Do you mind,' without any hint of a question mark. Annie was serving Arthur and Clara at a table on the other side of the room. As soon as she'd set their bowls down, Adeline caught her eye and the young maid hurried over to relocate cutlery and crockery for her with a smile, before taking her order.

Miss Busby and Richard settled at the table to the other side of them, Barnaby sitting hopefully at his mistress's feet. As Sir Gregory turned to engage Richard in conversation, Miss Busby's attention was drawn to Arthur. The young man was stirring his soup, his expression dark, frame tense. Opposite him, Clara had yet to pick up her spoon. She rested her chin on her right hand, index finger hovering at the corner of her mouth as if she were about to chew a nail.

Sensing Miss Busby's gaze, Clara caught her eye briefly before taking a napkin from the table, folding it methodically and placing it in her lap.

Miss Busby's head turned as the dining room door opened to admit Lázár and the lawyer, Mr Ludlow. As Ludlow strode through to the table furthest from them at the back, Lázár stopped beside Miss Busby and gave a polite bow. His tie, a smart black with diagonal silver stripes, was a little askew, as though he had tied it in a rush.

'My apologies for the lunch delayed,' he said. 'Such a morning. But how are you now both?' he asked. 'Recovered from shock, I hope?'

'We're fine,' Miss Busby assured him. 'Is there any news of Lady Flora?'

He shook his head. 'Nothing, I am sorry.'

'They say no news is good news,' Richard remarked.

'I do hope that is so,' Lázár replied with a smile.

'What's he doing here?' Adeline asked, looking to Ludlow with suspicion.

Miss Busby recalled that he had been due to speak with the inspector that morning.

'Mr Ludlow is Lady Flora's solicitor also. And so I informed him of the sad situation. Although of course we pray his services will not be needed.'

'Flora left a will?' Miss Busby asked, looking up with

interest. Knowing her financial circumstances, it hadn't occurred to her Flora would have anything to leave.

Lázár nodded. 'Yes, indeed.'

'But what does she have to leave to anyone?' Adeline asked. 'She said her husband left her destitute.'

Sir Gregory scoffed. Miss Busby gave him a hard stare.

'I believe there is one single item Lady Flora wished to bequeath. A trinket, of sentimental value only, was to be left to Miss Olivia,' Lázár explained.

Lydia drew a hand to her mouth.

Sir Gregory, Miss Busby noticed, gave a very ungentlemanly roll of his eyes.

'Oh, Lord, but that is heartbreaking,' Adeline cried.

Clara's head snapped up, then she rose and hurried over.

'What's happened?' she asked. 'Is it Lady Flora? Has she…?'

'What's this?' Arthur called from his seat. 'Lázár? Is there news?'

Lázár rushed over to him, calling, 'No, no. I am sorry. I was speaking only of Lady Flora's wishes, should–'

'What wishes?' Arthur demanded, brow creasing heavily beneath his sandy-coloured fringe.

Clara looked across to him with irritation. 'Flora's locket. She always said she wanted Olivia to have it. Don't you *listen*?'

Arthur blinked in surprise. 'Not when women prattle on about necklaces, no. And I should imagine they'd have thanked me not to. Private matters of this nature oughtn't be discussed with all and sundry.' He looked first to Clara, then Ludlow, with a scowl. 'I really can't comprehend why my aunt's business is continually paraded in front of strangers, as if it were some form of macabre street theatre.' Standing abruptly, he knocked the table with his leg. Both bowls fell to the floor. 'It really isn't on,' he shouted, watching broken crockery and rich, red soup spread across the tiles, before turning and stalking from the room.

Annie rushed in to see what had happened, then dashed off to fetch a mop and bucket as Lázár crouched to pick up pieces of broken crockery. Richard gallantly rose to assist, and Sir Gregory, not to be outdone, followed suit. Barnaby trotted over to investigate the spillage, huffing his displeasure at finding no meat involved. Amidst the ensuing fuss, Clara silently slipped a scrap of paper into Miss Busby's hand, before hurrying out into the corridor.

Miss Busby glanced across to see Lydia and Adeline watching Sir Gregory's efforts to help, looks of disbelief on both their faces. 'There,' he was calling to Lázár. 'There's a piece there. And another. Over there.'

He doesn't want to crease his trousers, Miss Busby thought. Richard, in contrast, was leaning to pick up each piece he saw, with no thought for his bad leg. Miss Busby felt a rush of warmth for him.

Annie began cleaning with the mop and Richard returned to their table.

Miss Busby stood up. 'You need to wash your hands,

Richard. I'll walk with you. I'm not feeling very hungry after all.'

'Are you alright?' Adeline asked, looking back to her with concern.

Miss Busby nodded. 'Stay and enjoy your lunch. And keep an eye on the others,' she added quietly, as Sir Gregory proceeded to tell Annie the most efficient way to mop up a spill.

'What is it?' Richard asked, as the dining room door swung shut behind them.

'From Clara,' Miss Busby whispered, before showing him the note.

'Room 4,' Richard read.

'She must want to talk in private.' Miss Busby slipped the note into the pocket of her cardigan. 'It'll be this way. Past Flora's room.' She set off with purpose.

Clara opened the door the moment Miss Busby knocked, looking nervously down the corridor before shepherding them inside.

'I hope you don't mind me bringing Sir Richard,' Miss Busby said, making rare use of his title in the hopes it would inspire confidence.

Clara shook her head. 'No. I thought you would. Arthur said you were all nosing about together.'

Miss Busby bristled.

'*Nosing about* is a bit strong,' Richard objected.

Clara ignored him. Twisting her hands together in front of her, she looked at the door as if it were about to spring open. 'I thought you'd bring the other one, too.'

'Mrs Fanshawe is otherwise engaged,' Miss Busby said, rather put out by the girl's tone.

'Oh. Well, sit down then. Please,' Clara added, turning from the door to point them to a two-seater sofa upholstered in red velvet beneath the window. The room was spacious, with bright paintings hung on the walls, books stacked neatly on a tall shelf unit, and a gramophone and several records lying on a large desk beside the wall. A fire burned in the corner, although the window was cracked open to let in the fresh November air. Clara pulled a plush footstool from beside a wingback chair by the fire across, and sat opposite them.

She took a breath.

'I feel awful about what I've done,' she began. 'I suppose they've all told you.'

Miss Busby felt her heart start to race. 'Let us imagine, for a moment, they haven't,' she said carefully.

Clara lowered her eyes to the carpet, scrunching her stockinged toes into the deep pile. 'I'll bet they have,' she said, a spoiled, sulky tone to her voice. 'But it's all true,' she continued in a whine. 'I was *horrible* to Olivia for years, but I should give anything to take it all back.' She looked up at both of them, seeming perfectly in earnest. 'And I told her as much. She was a saint about it, of course,' she went on, rapid-fire. 'Olivia would forgive anyone anything. But that makes it worse,' she complained. 'I was beastly to her and I shan't ever forgive myself.'

Tears threatened at the corners of Clara's large, grey-blue eyes, and Miss Busby felt her fear soften into sympathy. 'If

Olivia forgave you, I'm sure she'd hate to see you getting upset over it now,' she told the young girl kindly.

Clara blinked up at her, owl-like. 'I suppose she would. But I *deserve* to be upset. I was an absolute horror.'

'What on earth did you do that was so awful?' Richard asked, his tone light and smile warm, as if he could hardly believe her capable.

Clara didn't hesitate. 'I was a thoroughly deplorable spoiled brat,' she insisted. 'After my parents died, I blamed it all on Olivia. I thought that if she hadn't expected Daddy to look after that horrible horse, they would have still been alive. *I* wouldn't have been orphaned. I thought she'd ruined my whole life and I hated her for it for years.'

Miss Busby thought she saw something dark flash in Clara's eyes, before the tears gathered weight and began to fall.

'She hadn't, of course,' Clara continued, brushing them aside with her fingers. 'It was an accident. These things happen. But I didn't understand that at the time.'

'Of course you didn't,' Richard said. 'You were only a child.'

'Yes,' Clara sniffed. 'But I took forever to grow up. I was an ungrateful fiend for years. A decade, even.'

Richard looked to Miss Busby for assistance.

'You were grieving,' she said. 'Grief makes us do all manner of strange things, even as adults. Suffering such a devastating loss so young, it's no wonder you lost your way. All that matters is that you found it again.'

Clara looked at her intently. 'You are very like Olivia.'

Miss Busby felt her cheeks redden. 'Am I? It's kind of you to say.'

'You are both very kind. And I'm a horror.' She held up a hand to forestall any objection. 'Olivia saved me from the orphanage. You hear terrible things about those places. Drudgery, and misery. She gave me a wonderful home, and beautiful things. In return, I caused her no end of trouble. She sent me to the best schools, where I would behave so poorly they refused to keep me. She introduced me to the right sort of people, to whom I was so awful that the only sort who would tolerate me afterward were the wrong sort. And as I got older I'd be silly with drink and get myself into scrapes from which Olivia would constantly have to extricate me. I was a weight around her neck for so long I don't know how she bore it.'

'I've never had children of my own,' Miss Busby said gently, 'but I've taught many of them over the years and believe, in the main, that's precisely what their mothers do.'

Richard nodded. 'Fathers, too! Lucy was an angel, but if you'd seen my son at fourteen years of age…' He shuddered.

'Oh, fourteen-year-old boys are always vile,' Clara said. 'In fact, most of them are vile for an awful lot longer. But Olivia wasn't my mother. She didn't *have* to do anything. She could have taken me to the orphanage and washed her hands of me.' Clara hiccoughed a sob. 'It took me so long to see it. How unselfish she was. How *fortunate* I was. It wasn't until the day I was brought home in a police car that I began to understand.'

CHAPTER 22

Miss Busby's eyes widened. 'Gracious,' she said. 'When was this?'

Clara stood and crossed to a tall chest of drawers, pulling a handkerchief from within. She dabbed delicately at her eyes and nose. 'Several months ago. I was being stupid at a club in Cheltenham. They got cross and telephoned for the police. A constable had to bring me home. I should have been mortified but I found it all quite exciting at the time. Olivia sat me down and said I needed some direction. She said that a lot. I never usually took any notice, but this time...'

'There was something different?' Miss Busby guessed.

Clara nodded. She perched back down on the stool, legs folded under her, hands clasped in her lap. 'Olivia said it was high time Hamnett Hall had another pair of hands readying themselves in the wings. To ensure its continued success. And she said they ought to be young hands, filled with all sorts of fresh ideas. Then she asked if I'd like to learn how the place was run. She was always trying to come up with ideas to get me straightened out. Usually it was secretarial courses or other silly ideas. Things that would keep me out of the way. This time, though, it felt like she was trusting me with something much more important.' Clara looked down at the floor. 'It shocked me. After the way I'd behaved, that she would trust me in that way.'

Richard nodded. 'As Olivia knew it would, I'm sure.'

Miss Busby agreed. 'She was clearly a very clever woman.'

'Yes, and I was such a dolt,' Clara sighed. 'I wasted so many of the chances she gave me. When she offered me this one, I finally saw her for who she really was: a kind soul who truly cared about me. Not just a condescending Lady Bountiful who indulged me out of guilt. I'd been so sure that was what it was, before,' she said, gazing up and out of the window as she considered. 'Even though if anyone ought to have felt guilt it was Lázár. But it changed everything when she talked to me about the hotel. And she began straight away. Took me up to her rooms and showed me the schedule for the very next day. The deliveries due, the bookings expected. And everything followed on from there.'

'And you enjoyed it?' Richard asked.

'God, no!' Clara laughed. 'I hated it!'

'Oh.' Richard's face crumpled.

'It was deathly boring, in itself,' Clara explained. 'But the fact that she was keen to teach me made it…special, somehow. It's hard to put into words. Even though I hated it, I sort of loved it at the same time.'

'Because of the closeness it brought?' Miss Busby asked.

Clara nodded. 'I hadn't felt anything like that since Mummy died. Even though Olivia had given me so much, it never felt *personal*. This was different. I grew to adore spending time with her. It wouldn't have mattered what the topic was. Actually, no, it did matter,' she corrected. 'It mattered because Hamnett Hall had a huge piece of her heart, and so somehow I did too. And it finally made me want to give a piece of mine in return.'

Miss Busby sat in silence for a moment, before saying, 'What a wonderful way to look at it, Miss Harrowby. I'm sure Olivia was very proud of you. But if you don't mind me asking, why are you telling us this?'

A shadow fell across her features. 'I don't really know. I wrote my room number after they took Flora away; I was going to put it under your door. I'm sorry I was rude about you, then. It was the shock. Then I thought I should just knock and talk to you. Then I didn't know what to do. Everything feels so strange. It's been in my pocket ever since.'

Richard nodded. 'There is certainly a great deal of tension in the air.'

Clara rose to her feet again and pushed the stool back towards the chair. She leaned back against the edge of the desk for a moment, deep in thought. 'When Olivia talked about a pair of hands in the wings, I wondered if she meant for me to run the place, after she'd gone. I never presumed. Certainly not after the way I behaved.

But as she showed me the ropes it felt like the only logical explanation. Unless it was just something to keep me focused,' she mused. 'That's the trouble. I just don't *know*. Olivia was very subtle about the whole thing. She certainly didn't broadcast what we were doing. I sometimes wondered if she were afraid of what others might think.'

'By others, do you mean Arthur?' Miss Busby pressed.

Clara pushed a long tress of blonde hair behind her ear, pulling at the lobe absentmindedly as she considered. 'Not just him,' she said. 'But I think his nose would've been put out of joint. He saw me doing more about the place; they all did. I expect they thought I was finally earning my keep. Being the servants' girl, anything else would have been unthinkable.'

Miss Busby laid a subtle, restraining hand on Richard's arm. She suspected he'd want to jump in with something kind, but she thought it best not to interrupt. The girl seemed to be working her way up to something.

There was a long pause, and then, 'I think that's why Olivia said the reveal of her heir would be a surprise,' Clara concluded, looking up. Her eyes were determined now, jaw set. 'I think she meant it to be me.'

'I see.' Miss Busby nodded. 'And do you have any proof, at all, that this may have been the case?'

'No. It was just a feeling. I'm quite glad there's nothing. I think that might be what's keeping me safe.' She hung her head. 'That's awful of me, isn't it? If Olivia wanted me to run the place then I ought to fight for it. Like she would have done.'

'Then why don't you?' Richard asked gently.

'Because Arthur's so *angry* all the time, and Lázár just stands about looking officious and telephoning Ludlow every time something awful happens. And I've got no one now.' Her voice wavered. 'I'm as dependent on Olivia as Flora was, and you saw what happened to her.' She closed her eyes. 'If only we had the will. I was so sure it would be in her safe. It was the first place I looked.'

'You have the code?' Miss Busby asked, surprised.

'Yes, she gave it to me when she first started teaching me about the place. All the spare keys are kept in there, and some petty cash for emergencies. Lázár's had access to it for years, of course, but I–'

'Sorry,' Richard said, holding his hand up. 'This is Olivia's personal safe, in her rooms?'

'Yes.'

'Why would Lázár have the code?'

'In case anything happened, I suppose.' Clara shrugged. 'Before Olivia felt able to trust me.' Her cheeks flushed. 'It should never have taken so long.'

Miss Busby rose to her feet and crossed to take the young woman's hand. 'You got there in the end, Miss Harrowby,' she said. 'And that is all that matters.'

Richard nodded agreement. 'And you mustn't worry,' he added. 'Miss Busby and I are in close contact with the authorities. They'll soon get to the bottom of things.'

Miss Busby smiled and nodded, before asking, 'Is there anything else you can think of, anything at all, that seemed unusual prior to Olivia's death?'

Clara furrowed her brow. 'Well,' she said slowly, 'I don't know if I'm only thinking this because of how awful he's been since, but Arthur was being nicer to her than ever. A few times I saw him sitting and chatting to her. Usually he just hared up and down to his parents' house in London and only made use of the bar while he was here. But he even helped out in the lounge, before the ball. Unpacked some of the boxes from the cellar with Jimmy. I remember, because Jimmy said how Arthur's jacket had got dusty and he had to go and change it. But he wasn't cross, he was laughing. That wasn't like Arthur at all. Perhaps we were both different,' she sighed. 'I suppose that's one comfort. That Olivia found us both a little kinder, in the end.'

'Indeed,' Miss Busby said, and they both stood as the conversation came to an end.

Miss Busby's brain was going nineteen to the dozen as they left Clara's room, picturing all the different threads and how they might be connected.

'Well,' Richard said once out in the corridor. 'What now?'

'Let's collect Adeline and Barnaby.'

The dining room was quiet. Sir Gregory had left, leaving Adeline and Lydia talking over coffee. Lázár was deep in discussion with Ludlow, but he looked up as they entered and hurried over.

'Are you feeling better?' he asked. 'Mrs Fanshawe said you were unwell.'

'Yes, thank you. I just needed a moment of quiet.'

'I am glad to hear.' Lázár smiled. 'Would you like some lunch, after all? Perhaps some wine?'

'No!' Richard said sharply. All eyes turned to him in surprise. 'Thank you,' he added, clearing his throat. 'Sorry. Didn't mean to shout.'

'We came for Barnaby,' Miss Busby said. 'He's due a walk.'

The little terrier tore his eyes from the table and wagged his tail at the word.

Miss Busby gave Adeline a pointed look.

She pushed her cup and saucer aside. 'A brisk walk after lunch is just the ticket. I'll come with you,' she announced.

Lázár gave another of his customary bows before returning to Ludlow.

'Shall we see you in the lounge anon, Miss Whitfield?' Richard asked politely.

Lydia nodded and smiled, before returning to her coffee.

They followed Barnaby through the front doors and crunched across the gravel. Miss Busby called him to heel, turning to walk pointedly in the opposite direction to the lake, as Richard recounted Clara's tale to Adeline.

'There, you see!' Adeline said. 'Why would Olivia give the code to her manager? Keys and petty cash should be held in the office safe, surely?'

'Hamnett Hall was Olivia's home as well as her business,' Miss Busby said. 'It makes sense for there to be some crossover between the two.'

'I'm not so sure about the manager, now,' Richard admitted. 'Assuming Olivia kept the draft of her will in the safe, Lázár could have looked at it at any time. When Olivia said she would be announcing her heir, and implied it would be a surprise, curiosity may have got the better of him. Had he looked and seen Clara's name on the document, all those years of servitude, hardship, and separation from his home country may have risen to the fore and formed into anger and resentment.'

'There are quite a few *coulds, woulds,* and *mays* to your theory,' Miss Busby pointed out dryly.

'But it fits,' Adeline said excitedly. 'Lázár knew about the Vin Mariani and was perfectly placed to access Olivia's supply.'

'And he set the table for dinner that night,' Richard added. 'It would have been easy for him to give Olivia a dose concealed in the red wine they all drank.'

'But he said she would have tasted the difference,' Miss Busby recalled, as Barnaby flushed a pigeon from a shrub and the air filled with frantic flapping.

'Perhaps, depending on the grape. If he'd been clever and chosen a petit verdot, or a mourvèdre, the flavour may have been strong enough to mask it. And the inspector did say there was a considerable amount of alcohol present in her blood.'

Miss Busby decided to ignore yet another *may*, and indulge him. 'And do you suppose, then, that Lázár also attacked Flora?'

Richard stopped beside a circular rose bed to consider. Orange and red hips stood out brightly among the bare stems. 'He certainly would have been well placed to do so. He even offered you wine, just now,' he added.

Adeline gave a little gasp.

'Don't be silly,' Miss Busby chided. 'It's the middle of the day, and there are witnesses.'

'He is as thick as thieves with that solicitor again,' Adeline said. 'What if Lázár is trying to persuade Ludlow to mock up some sort of fake document that will indicate the hotel ought to be left to him?'

'That's almost as absurd an idea as Lázár poisoning me in the dining room,' Miss Busby said firmly, turning back towards the hotel. Barnaby had done what he needed to do, and the wind was getting up. She shivered in her light cardigan. Richard noticed, and took off his jacket to place over her shoulders.

She smiled her thanks.

'Why is it absurd?' Adeline asked, sounding hurt.

'It would look far too suspicious at this point, for one. As things stand, Arthur will likely inherit. Ludlow will know it would be almost impossible, under the circumstances, to elevate a staff member above family.'

'But that's exactly what Clara thinks Olivia was about to do!' Adeline objected.

'Clara wasn't staff. Olivia had seen to it she was well educated, and mixed with the right set. And she was training her. The girl was a work in progress. All of which would explain why she'd wanted to announce it so soon, as I'm sure she saw it, before her death. So that everyone had a chance to come to terms with her decision.'

They walked in silence for a moment, before Richard said, 'Arthur won't be an issue if the rumour surrounding his birth comes to light.'

Miss Busby stopped.

Richard and Adeline looked to her.

'Which means, what? You think Lázár attacked Flora to protect *Arthur's* inheritance?' she asked, brow furrowed.

'Arthur was in Lázár's office the day we first talked to him!' Adeline remembered. 'The three men may have joined forces to prevent a young woman they deem unsuitable inheriting the hotel.'

'How do you know they deem her unsuitable?' Miss Busby asked, head tilted, eyes bright with inquiry.

'Clara herself said her behaviour had been abhorrent until recently,' Richard said. 'And why else would Olivia have kept it a secret? She must have been concerned about how the others would react.'

'But Flora told us Olivia seemed excited about the revelation,' Miss Busby reminded them.

'Very possibly due to the coca, if you recall?' Adeline said.

'But she hadn't been drinking it prior to that evening,' Miss Busby pointed out.

'According to Lázár,' Adeline countered with a raised brow. 'We only have his word for so much of it. And he has been perfectly placed to manipulate and conceal matters behind the scenes.'

Miss Busby sighed. Supposition surrounded them. 'When we have the findings from Flora's glass, we'll be better placed to move forward,' she said. She called Barnaby, who trotted across from where he'd been checking for mice under the laurel.

'McKay always says to consider motive, means, and opportunity,' Adeline muttered, determined, as they approached the front doors. 'And Lázár can be argued to possess all three.'

'So can Arthur,' Miss Busby countered. 'And we now have the young man's temper thrown into the mix. Not to mention the fact he may have been involved with drinks brought up from the cellar that night.'

'Drinks in the lounge,' Richard specified. 'Olivia didn't drink anything there that night.'

Adeline beamed at him.

Miss Busby thought for a moment. 'You don't suppose Olivia may have been playing the two of them off against one another?' she suggested. 'It's odd that they both started to help out around the place at the same time.'

'Was that a *may*, I heard?' Richard asked, a single teasing brow raised.

'At least it was only one,' Miss Busby riposted.

'The lady in the baker's said Arthur would often run errands for Olivia,' Adeline said. 'I expect Clara didn't notice, if she was running around all the time being awful.'

Richard held the door open for them both.

'Well, if there's one thing we can be sure of it's that *someone* is working to control Olivia's legacy,' Miss Busby said quietly before stepping through.

'And to eliminate any potential threats to their machinations en route,' Richard added. 'Which we shall have to hope doesn't include us.'

CHAPTER 23

Miss Busby and Richard, not having had lunch, were sitting by the fire in Miss Busby's room enjoying a Chelsea bun when a frantic knock sounded at the door.

Exchanging concerned looks, Richard rose to open it and revealed a beaming Annie, cap askew, hands clasped to her chest as she announced, 'Lady Flora's awake!'

Miss Busby peered around the door, her blue eyes wide. 'Oh! But how is she?' she pressed. 'Is she recovered?'

Annie nodded happily. 'Yes, miss! They say as she can come home in a couple of days! Isn't that just the best thing you ever heard?'

Miss Busby rose from the chair, all the fatigue and concern of the long day lifting from her shoulders in an instant.

'It most certainly is,' she declared, a bright smile lifting her features, as Richard echoed her sentiment.

Adeline, who'd been having a lie-down in her own room, bustled through, somewhat crumpled and bleary-eyed, to see what all the fuss was about.

'Wonderful!' she exclaimed, when Annie told her the news. 'Did she say anything about the wine?' she asked keenly.

Annie looked confused for a moment, before remembering. 'Oh, no miss, the Major said as how she doesn't remember anything from before it happened. It's all like a thick fog, the day before, she told him. He's just come back in a taxi. He's down in the lounge now, miss. They all are. Everyone's ever so happy. I've to get back to the kitchen and try to find some biscuits or something for them all, but I thought as you'd want to know straight away.'

'Yes, of course, thank you, Annie! What a relief!' Miss Busby took the young maid's hands for a moment, and smiled.

'Take the cakes,' Adeline said.

The others turned to her in confusion.

'I bought cakes in the village this morning,' she explained to Annie, looking around the room for the bag. Spotting it on the desk, she handed it to the maid. 'Take these down for everyone to share. There are plenty.'

'Oo, thank you miss!' Annie said, bobbing a quick curtsey.

'We'll come down with you.' Miss Busby reached for her cardigan from the back of the chair. Richard took a hurried, final bite of his bun and nodded agreement, as Adeline hastened to get her shoes and run a brush through her hair.

For the first time since arriving at the hotel, they were greeted with smiles on entering the lounge. The atmosphere was genial, with Major Gresham the centre of attention at his usual chair, and Clara, Arthur, Lázár, Lydia, and Sir Gregory clustered around him.

The trio joined the throng, Barnaby making straight for Lydia, who bent happily to fuss him.

'Annie has told us the news,' Miss Busby said, looking to Major Gresham. 'How wonderful!'

The Major nodded, a rare smile on his face. Miss Busby realised it was the first time she'd seen him look anything other than grave. It took years off him.

'Flora should be home by the end of the week,' he said happily. 'And they think there's no harm done.'

'Do they have any idea what caused it?' Sir Richard asked. 'She looked so awful, poor thing. I must confess, I'm afraid I didn't hold out much hope.'

'Nor I,' the Major admitted, shaking his head. 'Matron had a decent pow-wow with her when she came round, woman to woman, that sort of thing. She thinks it likely a combination of lack of sleep, the loss of Olivia, and concern over the situation with her home caused an immense attack of nerves. As if it all caught up with poor Flora at once.'

'And she doesn't remember?' Miss Busby pressed.

'Not a thing. The whole day seems to have turned foggy in her mind, poor soul. They'll keep an eye on her for a couple of days, then, assuming all is well, she'll be back with us. Where she belongs,' he added, firmly.

'They may want to perform some tests,' Miss Busby said, trying to keep her tone light.

The Major shrugged. 'She was sitting up in bed drinking a cup of tea when I left her. Best test there is, I should say. Especially at our age.'

Clara nodded. 'Olivia always said there wasn't much a cup of tea couldn't fix.'

'We ought to keep a closer eye on her when she's back,' Arthur said. 'Make sure she's eating properly, that sort of thing. Aunt Olivia used to do that.'

'I would be pleased to take extra notice of Lady Flora,' Lázár offered with a bow.

Annie came in, pushing a trolley laden with the buns, macaroons, and assorted biscuits, along with pots of tea and coffee.

Lázár pulled over extra chairs for the newcomers, and the group tucked in companionably, the relief in the air palpable. Even Sir Gregory looked pleased that Flora was recovering.

'We ought to celebrate, don't you think?' he asked the group at large. 'Lord only knows we've been a gloomy bunch of late.'

The Major frowned. 'I should think that a bit crass, given Olivia's passing.'

Sir Gregory shook his head. 'Not at all. Olivia would be the first one to suggest a do in honour of Flora's recovery.'

'She'd have the grace to wait for the woman in question to be present,' the Major chided.

Sir Gregory huffed. 'Alright, why not two celebrations, then? What do you think, Arthur?' He looked eagerly to the young man. 'She was your aunt, after all.'

Arthur ran a hand through his sandy hair. 'It *is* Guy Fawkes Day,' he said. 'Should I go and buy some fireworks?'

The Major turned disapproving eyes his way.

'Perhaps a bonfire?' Richard suggested. Miss Busby knew fireworks could still upset those who'd fought in the Great War, and suspected he was thinking of his son Anthony as much as the Major. She smiled, giving him a nod of approval.

'Should we?' Arthur asked, looking to Lázár in turn.

'I can have Jimmy find some wood,' he said. 'Always there is plenty.'

'Don't we need a guy to burn?' Clara asked.

'If you please, miss,' Annie suggested nervously, 'the little 'uns in the village will have made one. I s'pect for a few pennies they'd be happy to give it up, and make another.'

'I'll drive down,' Arthur decided. 'See what I can do.'

'Potatoes!' Adeline exclaimed.

Eyes turned to her in confusion.

'We could wrap them in tin foil and cook them on the bonfire. Jemima does it for the boys,' she added. 'And perhaps some toffee apples? If you think it appropriate,' she added, noting the Major's expression.

Arthur nodded before striding from the room.

'I'll fetch my gramophone,' Clara said. 'If I put it in the conservatory we'll be able to hear it outside. Olivia *did* love a party, Major,' she said gently.

He sighed but conceded with a nod, before asking

Annie if he could have a cup of tea, muttering that coffee played havoc with his insides. She was quick to oblige.

Decision made, Lázár set off to find Jimmy, and Clara went to fetch her music.

Miss Busby, Adeline, and Richard moved closer to the fire, taking the now-empty seats, and chatted genially to Lydia and the Major, with Sir Gregory interjecting every now and then. Soon the Major's eyes began to droop; the rush to the hospital, the worry, and the relief all taking their toll. Miss Busby was quick to take the cup from his hands before it spilled. Sir Gregory took advantage of the break in the chatter to begin regaling Richard with details of his Scottish estate, leaving Adeline, Miss Busby, and Lydia to talk quietly of the day's events.

'*Why* can't Flora remember anything?' Adeline puzzled. 'If it truly was worry, and fatigue, why is it just that one evening that eludes her?'

'Could it be her age?' Lydia ventured. 'I've an aunt who's nearly eighty and she often forgets things from the day before. Mind you,' she considered, 'she can tell you what happened fifty years ago like that.' She clicked her fingers.

'It's possible,' Miss Busby considered. 'I'd like to talk to her, but if the hotel's closing in two days I don't imagine we'll get the chance.'

'We could visit her in the hospital,' Adeline suggested.

'Might that be a bit much for her, do you think?' Lydia suggested in concerned tone. 'If she's still finding her feet, I mean.'

'I'm not sure,' Miss Busby said. 'She *did* look awful. And she's been through so much.' She thought for a moment. 'We ought to let Alistair know, and then he can do what he thinks best,' she decided. 'I'll telephone him now, while everyone's busy.'

'I'll walk that way with you,' Adeline said. 'I'll need to put on something warmer if we're having a bonfire this evening.'

'I'll come too,' Lydia added. 'My cigarettes are upstairs.'

Adeline gave a soft sniff of disapproval.

'I feel a bit silly, now that Lady Flora's on the mend,' Lydia continued, not noticing. 'Everyone seems so much nicer, don't they? Even Mr Ludlow was quite pleasant when he heard!'

'Ludlow? Where is he?' Adeline asked, glancing around suspiciously, as if he might be lurking nearby.

'He left just before you came in,' Lydia explained. 'Once he knew Flora was well, he said he ought to get back to the office.'

Rising to her feet, Miss Busby wasn't quite so sure the young writer should feel silly at all. There were still so many questions left unanswered. But with the darkness seeming to lift from the hotel at last, she decided not to press the point. It was nice to see smiles about the place, after all. Arthur and Clara finally seemed like the youngsters they truly were, excited over music and a bonfire, smiles on their faces rather than the weight of the world on their shoulders. *It brings rather a different perspective to it all*, she thought.

Richard, left at the mercy of Sir Gregory's exuberant tales and the Major's gentle snores, gave a small sigh as they left the room.

Barnaby sat at Miss Busby's feet in the phone cubby, Lydia chatting merrily to Adeline as they climbed the stairs above. She asked to be connected to Inspector McKay at Oxford Police Station. The line crackled for so long she was beginning to wonder if she'd have to hang up and try again, when a warm Scottish brogue came on the line.

'Good afternoon, Miss Busby, is all well?'

'Very well, thank you Inspector,' she assured him, as she passed on the news.

'Well,' his voice lifted in surprise, 'I'm glad to hear it, of course, but it wasn't the news I was expecting.'

'How so?' Miss Busby queried.

'If someone were successful in the first attack, it seems unlikely they'd fail in the second,' he reasoned, echoing a thought that had been lurking in the back of Miss Busby's own mind.

'It does seem strange,' she admitted, 'particularly with Flora appearing so much more frail than Olivia.'

'Aye, but appearances can be deceptive,' he said. 'Someone may have thought less was needed in her case, and underestimated. But there's no use speculating until we have the results from the wine glass.'

'You have the glass?' Miss Busby checked.

'It was collected from Quinton and taken for testing, but it's unlikely to be looked at until tomorrow afternoon at the earliest,' he added, regret and annoyance mingled in his tone. 'We just don't have the manpower.'

'Well, I don't suppose it's all that urgent now,' Miss Busby considered. 'Given Flora's recovery.'

'Hmm. I'm not so sure.' The inspector sounded his usual, sceptical self. Which made Miss Busby feel somewhat better about her own misgivings. 'I'll push it through as quickly as I can from my end,' he confirmed.

'Ludlow seemed pleased, apparently,' Miss Busby said, switching tack. 'Did you have a productive talk with him this morning?'

'Aye, he was very professional and no-nonsense. Keen to help as much as he could, but quite reserved in the main.'

'Adeline doesn't like him,' Miss Busby said, eyes momentarily lighting with mischief.

The inspector was silent for a moment, before saying, 'Odd. Opposites usually attract.' Miss Busby's lips twitched. 'He said there's no love lost between Clara Harrowby and Arthur Fortescue,' he went on, 'and thinks either one of them would be a disaster for the hotel. His money was on Lázár to inherit.'

'Was it?' Miss Busby's brows rose. 'Adeline doesn't like him, either. She will be quite beside herself.'

The inspector gave a warm chuckle, which made Miss Busby smile.

'Ludlow said the manager is the only one there with an ounce of sense,' he explained.

'Interesting,' she said, thinking it perhaps made sense of why the pair seemed so close. The solicitor must have expected the hotel manager to become his new employer. Well, the atmosphere here is very different this afternoon. Jolly, almost. There's talk of a bonfire party tonight. Adeline has requested toffee apples.'

The inspector barked a full-fledged laugh. 'My mother lost a tooth in one once, tell her to be careful! I may visit Lady Flora in hospital tomorrow, if I've time. And I'll be in touch as soon as I have news from the lab. Take care, Miss Busby,' he said sternly.

'I always do, Inspector.'

CHAPTER 24

It was a little after 7 o'clock when the festivities began. Music played on Clara's gramophone in the conservatory, where chairs and tables had been cleared to form an impromptu dance floor. Adeline and Sir Gregory were making good use of it, laughing as they tried to keep up with a lively ragtime tune. The doors stood open to the lawn beyond, leading to the impressive bonfire Jimmy had built at short notice. Flames leapt and licked eagerly at the crudely made guy perched atop it. Small, tin-foil parcels sat at the base of the fire, and Clara, Annie, Lydia, and Jimmy were attacking toffee apples beside it; the Major, Richard, and Lázár stood a little way back, brandy glasses in hand as they watched the flames.

Miss Busby had taken a moment to telephone Enid back at Spring Meadows, bringing her friend up to date with all the news, and enquiring after Pud, who was in Cook's bad books after managing to swipe an entire chicken off the kitchen countertop and escape outside with it. Enid said she hadn't laughed so much at the sight of him wrestling it into the garden for years. She had also cautioned Miss Busby to remain vigilant – seeming in agreement with the inspector that something still wasn't right. 'Nothing has changed, really Isabelle,' she'd cautioned. 'Other than the murderer making a mistake. Look for whoever is the most concerned,' she'd advised. But as Miss Busby regarded the scene before her, it seemed as if none of them had a care in the world.

Richard turned at her approach, smiling widely. 'How's Pud?'

'In disgrace,' she replied. 'Arthur's done rather a good job,' she said, taking in the scene.

'Yes, not quite so useless, after all eh?' Richard said. 'He's gone to get plates and what-have-you. Cook's gone home, but he said he can manage potatoes with butter and cheese.'

'Has he been drinking?' she asked quietly.

'A few brandies, I think. Clara's had a couple too. And Adeline,' he added, with a wry look back to the conservatory. 'I asked Lázár about the wine served at dinner the night Olivia died but he said it was merely one of the better house wines.'

'So it would not have covered the taste of an extra dose of Vin Mariani,' she replied.

'No, but, where are my manners? Would you like to dance?' he asked, grinning as the Charleston started up.

'I'd need several brandies before even attempting it,' Miss Busby laughed, but they watched Adeline and Sir Gregory, and when Arthur returned to the group, they all enjoyed a simple meal accompanied by a generous helping of laughter and merriment, and Miss Busby found herself thinking that no wine, coca-infused or otherwise, could offer such a tonic.

Breakfast the following morning was a much quieter affair, although the atmosphere in the hotel was still relaxed, with its occupants remaining much more at ease with one another. Clara sat with Major Gresham, the pair having chatted around the bonfire and even attempted a good-natured waltz in the conservatory the night before. Arthur sat alone reading the paper and drinking coffee, but had a nod and a smile for everyone. Sir Gregory had attached himself to Adeline once more, buoyed, no doubt, by the laughter and dances they'd shared. Adeline, although rather more cautious in the cold light of day, was more tolerant of him. Lydia came to sit with them, safe in the knowledge his attention was now focused elsewhere.

With no immediate concern for Flora, they lingered over eggs, mushrooms, grilled tomatoes and black pudding, with toast and tea. Barnaby did exceptionally well in the form of treats slipped under the table, and even the early morning sun put on a bright face as it shone to warm the room.

Just as cleared plates were being pushed aside, Lázár came into the dining room, his expression hard to read. Spotting Miss Busby, he crossed to her table and bent to quietly ask if she would mind accompanying him to reception. 'With Mrs Fanshawe and Sir Richard, if it is convenient,' he added.

The three exchanged looks, before rising to follow him.

'What's this now?' Sir Gregory asked, looking rather put out.

'A phone call for Miss Busby and her friends,' Lázár said. 'Please, excuse us.'

Miss Busby looked over her shoulder as they followed him out; it was hard to tell who looked more annoyed, Sir Gregory at losing Adeline, or Lydia at gaining Sir Gregory.

Barnaby looked from his mistress, to Lydia's empty plate, then hurried along after them.

'Is it Inspector McKay?' Miss Busby asked as they reached the desk.

'No, it is Mr Ludlow,' Lázár said, looking over his shoulder in a nervous manner.

'What?' Adeline asked. 'Why? What does he want with us?'

'I could not say.' He looked to Miss Busby, adding, 'He asked most for you, but mentioned your friends also, so I thought it best.' He gestured, rather helplessly, at the phone. 'I will be in my office, if you need me.'

As he hurried off, Adeline eyed the handset warily.

Miss Busby looked to Richard, who shrugged.

Sighing, she picked it up and said, 'Hello? This is Miss Busby.'

Adeline lunged forward to listen in as Ludlow's voice sounded from the other end.

'Good morning Miss Busby. I have just spoken with

Inspector McKay. He asked me to forewarn you of the news.'

'What news?' Adeline hissed loudly, making Miss Busby jump.

'Sorry, Mr Ludlow, there seems to have been a crossed line,' she said, taking a pointed step away from her friend. 'What news?'

'I received a letter this morning, postmarked the morning of Mrs Fortescue's death.'

Miss Busby felt her heart begin to race.

'It is from Mrs Fortescue herself, and contains a draft of her last will and testament.'

'Goodness me!' Miss Busby exclaimed.

Adeline's eyes were like saucers, whilst Richard's brow creased in concern.

'Included is an accompanying note containing significant information regarding the inheritance of Hamnett Hall.'

There was a pause. 'If you don't mind my asking, Mr Ludlow, I'm not quite sure what this has to do with me?' she said.

'I telephoned Inspector McKay as soon as I read the note. He informed me you are here at his request, and as such, he would like you to be present when I read the will at Hamnett Hall. He is expected at The Abbot's Kitchen in Oxford on another matter.'

'Oh,' Miss Busby said. 'And when will that be?'

'At 11 o'clock this morning,' he said. 'Would you kindly ask Lázár to gather the others in the lounge?' And he rang off.

Miss Busby looked to the clock on the wall. It had just gone 10.

'For goodness' sake, Isabelle!' Adeline exclaimed. 'What is going on?'

'Shall I fetch Lázár?' Richard offered into the surprised silence that followed Miss Busby's succinct explanation.

'Well,' Adeline exclaimed as he strode off with purpose. 'Our first time being recognised as on official police business, Isabelle!' She puffed out her not inconsiderable chest. 'It's about time we were properly recognised for our powers of observation!'

'Hmm,' Miss Busby said, not seeming quite so sure. 'Although I shouldn't think they'll take kindly to us being present.'

'Hard cheese,' Adeline declared, her eyes bright with intrigue. 'We are finally about to discover the great surprise for which Olivia may have died, Isabelle! Although I shall be sorry to leave Hamnett Hall, it's all been rather exciting, hasn't it?'

Miss Busby opened her mouth, then closed it.

'And how clever of Olivia,' Adeline added. 'She must have known how the vultures would circle, looking for the will. She can't have trusted any of them, and little wonder.'

'Perhaps. But how on earth could the letter have taken six days to reach Ludlow?' Miss Busby wondered.

'A hapless postman, I expect. Like your young Dennis,' Adeline added, rather unnecessarily cruelly, Miss Busby thought. Although, since the very pretty young Rowena had moved in next door to Lavender Cottage, her own post had certainly begun to take a lower priority.

Lázár returned with Richard, his expression solemn. 'I shall gather the others, right away,' he said. 'Please, excuse me.'

'Wait,' Miss Busby called.

He turned.

'Did Olivia ordinarily send her own mail, or would you do it for her?' Miss Busby asked.

'I would take it,' Lázár answered. 'To Quinton Post Office, early in the morning. It would travel much faster that way.'

'And do you remember her giving you a letter to post on the day she died?' Miss Busby asked.

'I remember most certainly that she did not,' he replied. 'There was no post to take that day, after such a flurry of invites and acceptances for the Halloween Ball. And I was most relieved, as the rain that morning was relentless.'

'Thank you,' Miss Busby said, nodding, as he hurried off towards the dining room.

'There, you see?' Adeline breathed. 'She didn't trust *him* either! Come on, let's go through and wait with the others!'

'I wonder if we'd do better to wait for the man himself,' Richard suggested. 'The natives might turn rather unfriendly if we presume to join them for such a personal matter.'

'Not if we get ourselves settled in the lounge first,' Adeline said. 'Quickly!'

'If Olivia didn't trust Lázár, or any of the others, who *did* she trust?' Richard asked Miss Busby quietly as they followed along in her wake.

'I imagine we're soon to find out,' she replied, calling Barnaby to heel behind them.

Miss Busby, Adeline, and Richard took what they felt to be discreet seats in the lounge at one of the round tables. Richard had picked up a newspaper from the bar on the way in, and Adeline feigned interest in the view through the window. Barnaby settled at Miss Busby's feet, and she bent to rub his ears as the others slowly filed in.

Major Gresham looked anxious, whilst Sir Gregory appeared unusually stern. Clara's cheeks were flushed with what could have been nerves or excitement; she gave Miss Busby a tight smile on her way past, making her suspect the latter. Arthur's expression, warm and friendly so soon before, was now dour.

'Do you think it'll be Clara?' Richard asked softly.

'It would fit,' Miss Busby said. 'Although I can't see the others taking it well.'

'They were all getting along yesterday,' he said. 'They might surprise us.'

Lydia peered around the door, spotting them with a wave and hurrying over. 'I didn't know what to do,' she said, 'or where you'd gone. Do you think it will be alright to stay?'

Richard rose to pull out a chair for her. 'I'm sure it will,' he said quietly. 'They all seem rather too preoccupied to notice.'

Lydia smiled gratefully. 'I do hope Flora will be mentioned,' she said. 'The certainty would help her recovery, don't you think?'

Miss Busby smiled and nodded at the young writer. *So considerate*, she thought.

Lázár was the last in, solemnly shepherding Annie, Jimmy, and Cook ahead of him. Annie waved to Miss Busby, and Barnaby, nose twitching, ears aloft, trotted over to sit with Jimmy as low murmurs of chatter filled the room.

Clara's voice rose above the others. 'It's no wonder we couldn't find the will! Olivia was always so organised, it makes perfect sense she would have posted it. I don't know why we didn't think of it before.'

'Because it wouldn't take that long for a letter to get to Cheltenham,' Arthur called back from his armchair beside the fire. 'And it doesn't make sense at all. Ludlow came to dinner that night, why didn't she just give him the will then?'

'It's more proper if it's posted,' Clara said.

'No it isn't,' Arthur objected. 'What difference does that make? Especially when it takes *six* days.'

'Well, it's more official,' Clara insisted.

'Mr Ludlow mentioned there were not enough stamps on the letter he received,' Lázár interjected. 'And this was the reason of the delay.'

'There, you see?' Arthur said, frustration evident his tone. 'Aunt Olivia was organised, and she was hardly likely to have been so remiss.'

'She was hardly likely to have considered publishing a memoir, either,' Sir Gregory added, 'but none of you baulked at that.'

'What do you mean?' Arthur asked, as the Major grumbled, 'Not this again,' and the entire group began to bicker.

'Perhaps Olivia anticipated her wishes would cause discord,' Adeline suggested loudly. 'With the document already signed, sealed, and en route to its destination when she broke the news, there could be no argument.'

All eyes turned to their table.

Miss Busby sighed.

CHAPTER 25

'This is family business,' Arthur said, his old self returning with a vengeance.

'Then kindly do not shout it across a public lounge,' Adeline retorted.

'It's hardly public!' Arthur objected, before Clara cut in with, 'Olivia never worried about arguments. No one could change her mind once it was made up!'

'I'm not so sure,' Sir Gregory said. 'I suspect someone here grew rather adept at influencing Olivia of late.'

'What are you implying?' Clara shot back, hands on hips as she turned to face him.

'Sir Gregory thinks Olivia didn't know her own mind,' Major Gresham accused.

'Of course she did,' Clara said, before all four of them started to shout over one another.

'Oh, Lord,' Miss Busby murmured as all trace of the previous day's pleasantries evaporated.

Lázár called for calm but couldn't make himself heard.

He held up his hands, tried clapping, and grew more and more wretched with each failed attempt.

'I should think that's quite enough!'

The participants turned in surprise to see the cook, Mrs Burton, short of stature but powerful of voice, on her feet, her hazel eyes stern. 'A fine credit to Olivia you all are, fighting like children in the playground.'

Mouths dropped in surprise.

'There's not one of you fit to take over from her, if you ask me,' she continued, directing a venomous look towards Lázár, her face a stark red against the whiteness of her apron and cap. 'And I've no interest in seeing you acting like this when the good woman's not even buried…' Her voice broke at the last, and she turned and bustled from the room, almost bowling Mr Ludlow over as he entered.

Raising his eyebrows at those gathered, Ludlow strode towards the fireplace to face them. Reaching into the top pocket of his brown suit, he removed a pair of gold rimmed spectacles and perched them on the end of his nose. His expression was sombre as, without a word, he reached into his worn leather briefcase and removed three sheets of paper. Two of them were typewritten, the other featuring Olivia's now-familiar loopy handwriting.

Looking rather disapprovingly at his silent audience for several moments, he then announced, 'I have today received a letter from Olivia, sent on the day of her death, formally expressing her intentions for the estate.'

Major Gresham shifted forward in his chair. Sir Gregory did the opposite, leaning back on the sofa and looking around with a wry smile on his face. As if to give the impression, Miss Busby thought, that he remained unaffected by the whole business.

Ludlow straightened the pages, beginning, 'It reads as follows: *Ludlow, I have drafted and enclosed my wishes, as advised. Hamnett Hall's future is to be protected and my values to live on as my legacy within its walls. To that end, I wish it to pass to one who understands what it means to come from nothing. Overcoming adversity shapes a person in a way those born to entitlement cannot comprehend. Merit, above all, must be considered. Yours, etcetera,*

Olivia Fortescue.'

He looked up.

Miss Busby cast a glance to Clara; the young woman's eyes were bright, lips curling up ever so slightly into the hint of a smile. Arthur, in contrast, was staring stonily at Ludlow. Lázár, standing to the rear of the group, kept his head lowered and eyes to the floor, hands held stiffly behind his back.

Clearing his throat, Ludlow turned to the next paper and continued, 'The enclosed reads: *Ludlow, please draft the following into the correct legal parlance: In the event of my death, I, Mrs Olivia Fortescue, leave all my personal possessions and property to Miss Clara Harrowby.'*

Clara gasped, raising her hands to her mouth.

Arthur's head, in stark contrast, fell into his hands.

'*Note that with regard to Hamnett Hall,*' Ludlow continued, '*certain conditions must be met. The hotel must be preserved in my memory and continue to be run to my methods. Clara must agree to these conditions. Should she decline, I have no choice but to leave Hamnett Hall to Arthur Fortescue in her stead.'*

A murmur filled the room. Arthur's head shot up. 'What conditions?' he asked Ludlow.

An expectant hush fell.

'Unfortunately,' Ludlow replied, 'the conditions are not specified here.'

'Well then!' Arthur scoffed, looking to Clara, 'How could anyone be expected to agree to them, or otherwise? This is a farce,' he complained.

'I don't think so,' Clara said. 'I think it's perfectly clear what Olivia wanted. *The hotel must be preserved in my memory and continue to be run to my methods.'*

'What methods?' Arthur queried, exasperated. 'Do you have to live in her rooms? Let her friends stay on gratis until they expire? Retain the same staff? Fetch cakes every Sunday afternoon, and drink that god-awful tonic wine she always thought we didn't know about?'

Adeline bolted upright. Lydia blinked in surprise. The smile on Clara's face, Miss Busby thought, widened slightly.

'I don't see why not,' she said. 'Although Olivia gave the tonic up some time ago. When she started showing me the ropes, actually. *I* was her tonic, she said.'

Sir Gregory barked a laugh. 'Tonic? You were more of a constant headache for the woman, dear girl.'

Clara's eyes flashed dangerously in his direction. 'Really? That's rich, coming from you.'

'What's that supposed to mean?' he snapped.

'Don't pretend you don't know—'

'That's enough!' Arthur said, rising to his feet. 'This is utterly farcical. I'm surprised you gathered us here for this, Ludlow. The letter you read is not legally binding. It brings us no closer to any conclusion.'

Ludlow removed his spectacles. 'I take the view that it offers the best opportunity to carry out Olivia's wishes,' he said. 'Her intent is clearly expressed; as such, it would be a difficult document to dispute, legally or otherwise.'

'I don't see why,' Arthur complained. 'It hasn't even been witnessed!'

'Well, it's all we have,' Clara snapped. 'So, we might as well just get on with it.'

'Yes, of course *you'd* say that,' Arthur retorted. 'It falls in your favour. Sir Gregory's right, you caused my aunt nothing but pain, and you stand there expecting to—'

'It's not *quite* all we have,' Ludlow interjected quietly, his words cutting the others off more effectively than any raised voice. 'Although I'd hoped it would be all we'd need.' He paused. All eyes turned to the third piece of paper, the handwritten one, Miss Busby noted, that he drew to the front. 'Olivia included an addendum, entitled *Should Conflict Arise.*'

'Well?' Arthur asked impatiently. 'It has. So what does it say?'

Ludlow read, '*With reference to Arthur's likely objection, it is with regret that I must acknowledge the rumours surrounding his parentage.*'

Arthur's face turned as grey as his suit, as his face went from disbelief to anger in the space of a heartbeat.

Miss Busby and Lydia exchanged a knowing look.

'What rumours?' Arthur spluttered. 'This is preposterous! Let me see that.' Rising, he crossed to Ludlow and tore the paper from his hand.

'Now, there's no call for that sort of behaviour!' Major Gresham admonished.

Richard made to stand, but Miss Busby laid a restraining hand on his arm. 'Ludlow can manage,' she whispered.

Arthur scanned the page, scoffed, and in one swift movement crumpled it and tossed it straight into the fire.

'No!' Clara shouted, lunging forward. Ludlow threw out an arm to hold her back. Flames were already licking at the paper.

'My secretary has mimeographs of the documents,' he told her. 'Your aunt goes on to suggest that Arthur's true father is, in fact, Sir Gregory Penn.'

Arthur froze, his whole body fraught with tension. 'I have never heard such nonsense,' he hissed, his other fist clenched, knuckles dangerously white.

Sir Gregory added his own objection. 'Nor I. Or indeed anything quite so malicious,' he said, no humour or charm in his tone this time. He turned in his seat, looking around at the others. Jimmy and Annie stood at the back of the room, mouths hanging open, whilst Arthur now looked as if he were about to be sick. Adeline had gone pale, and Miss Busby, Richard, and Lydia were wide-eyed. Major Gresham's eyes had taken on a hungry look, and Clara stepped closer to Ludlow, as if afraid.

'Someone had been feeding Olivia poisonous lies, Ludlow,' Sir Gregory continued. 'This is calculated defamation. I'll have my own solicitor on them when I find out who is responsible,' he concluded.

'As will I,' Arthur added. His face was now ashen and his shoulders were shaking.

Sir Gregory rose and stood beside him. Arthur flinched away in horror. 'I suspect this is nothing more than the fanciful, idiotic, notions of those with declining faculties and nothing better to do,' Sir Gregory accused, his eyes locking with the Major's.

Miss Busby winced in anticipation of an explosion, but the Major only smiled and said, 'So that's what you truly thought of Olivia, is it?'

Clara's high, shaky tone cut across the bickering. 'What does all this *mean,* Ludlow?' she asked.

He looked towards the flames, then back to the others.

'Olivia went on to say in her letter that she wanted no mention of this rumour made in the final will. She thought that if it became public knowledge, then it would bring shame upon him and the hotel,' he explained.

'Ha! So it means nothing!' Arthur shouted. 'Why even mention it, then? It would be laughed out of court.' He shook his head. 'She has only done it to belittle me, and elevate Clara higher, like she always did! And when I find out who's been lying...' He cast dark eyes around the room, lingering dangerously on Miss Busby before turning on his heel. Before he reached the door, he turned to shout, 'I shall be telephoning my solicitor without delay!'

'I shall contact my man, too,' Sir Gregory said. Looking straight at Miss Busby, he added, 'Although I do have some idea where to begin looking.'

'I should be very careful where you lay your accusations,' Richard said, his voice ominously low.

'Yes, come off it, Gregory,' the Major added brightly. 'I always knew you must have some hold over poor Olivia. It makes perfect sense, now. Blackmailed her into letting you stay, did you?'

Sir Gregory stood perfectly still for a moment. The room seemed to hold its breath, before he offered a scornful laugh. 'To your addled brain, Gresham, of course it would make sense. To the rest of us, as the boy says, this whole business is nonsense.' And he, too, strode from the room.

'Like Father like son,' Adeline declared darkly, as the door swung shut behind him.

Ludlow tucked the remaining papers back into his suitcase. 'I believe that concludes our meeting. I also believe Olivia's intentions, although not legally binding, are clearly expressed. As such, it is my professional advice that we proceed with her wishes as given. Morals, after all, should be just as binding.' He locked eyes with Clara, who nodded.

'Jimmy, Annie, there is much work to do before we close,' Lázár called, his voice shakier than they'd yet heard it. 'I will walk you to your car,' he added to Ludlow, who followed him from the room.

Major Gresham rose slowly. Clara offered an arm.

'I can manage, thank you,' he said dismissively, before looking up at her as if for the first time. 'Well, will you do it?' he said. 'Will you run the place as she would have wanted?'

'I... I suppose... I mean... I'm sorry,' she replied, 'it's all rather overwhelming.'

He held her gaze for several moments. 'Well, we shall see, I'm sure,' he concluded, before making his own exit in turn.

Richard stood. 'May I fetch you something from the bar, Miss Harrowby?' he asked. 'I expect your nerves are completely frayed.'

Adeline opened her mouth. Miss Busby kicked her gently under the table.

'Oh, no, thank you,' Clara said, looking at them as if noticing them for the first time.

'You were right about Olivia,' Miss Busby said softly.

Clara nodded. 'Yes. I ought to feel...well, I'm not sure what I ought to feel, really.'

'Vindicated,' Richard said. 'You see, she trusted you after all.'

'Yes, but...the way Arthur reacted. His temper...'

'That young man has revealed himself to be a bully. They must always be faced down!' Adeline insisted.

Clara nodded, but Miss Busby wondered... She had seen a different side to Arthur the night before, and his shocked reaction had seemed nothing if not genuine. Clara certainly seemed nervous, though, and perhaps, she thought, not without cause.

'If you'll excuse me, I think I need to…' Clara waved a vague hand.

'Of course,' Miss Busby said. 'Oh, and Clara?'

The girl turned.

'Congratulations,' Miss Busby told her.

Smiling, she nodded, before taking her leave.

CHAPTER 26

'Well!' Adeline exhaled. 'What a chaotic affair. I cannot for the life of me imagine why Olivia would have been excited for such an extraordinary bun fight.'

'Yes,' Richard agreed. 'No wonder Alistair wanted you to observe, Isabelle,' he said. 'Ludlow must have told him what was in the documents. I expect he knew there'd be fireworks!'

'Oh, was that your phone call?' Lydia asked.

'Yes,' Miss Busby said. 'We didn't have time to tell you about it.'

'Oh, of course, that's fine. But what exactly did–'

'You'll be going home now, I should imagine?' Adeline went on. 'With Arthur out of the picture, you needn't worry about any injustice. And the news Olivia wanted to reveal in her memoir is surely out, albeit perhaps not in the way she would have wanted. But the end result will be the same. It all comes out in the wash.'

'We ought to pack up too, I suppose,' Richard said.

'With Flora on the mend, and Olivia's wishes expressed.' He smiled down at Miss Busby.

'Perhaps not until after lunch, though,' Adeline added thoughtfully. 'It will be interesting to observe them all. Do you suppose Gregory really *is* the boy's father?'

'It would make sense of his hostile response to your arrival, Lydia,' Miss Busby said, looking to the young lady. 'If he were afraid of the truth coming out. Not to mention his dismissal of the Major and suggestions as to the unreliability of Flora's mental state. If the two were both considered unreliable, any rumour they may have indicated would have been easy to dismiss.'

'But why would Sir Gregory be worried?' Lydia asked. 'It's not as if he'd lose his inheritance.'

Adeline *tsked*. 'You must consider reputation, Miss Whitfield. A value the young so often forget! Should word get out concerning Sir Gregory's dalliance with the boy's mother, his honour would hang in tatters.'

'Well, if it is true, he certainly sounded adept at hiding any concern when you first mentioned the rumour,' Richard pointed out. 'Using humour and charm to disarm the offensive without a moment's thought.'

'Would that quick charm have been enough to seduce Arthur's mother, I wonder,' Miss Busby said.

'He had no desire to do so,' Adeline snapped. 'He said she was wholly unattractive.'

'We'd have to find a photograph, to be sure, and I think that would not be easy,' Miss Busby suggested. 'But he did seem to find the notion genuinely amusing,' she conceded. 'It's hard to reconcile that reaction with the one we have just witnessed.'

'Arthur certainly does have a temper,' Richard added thoughtfully. 'And he knew about the wine, too.'

Adeline nodded. 'I noticed that. And Clara. It must have been common knowledge.'

'Wine?' Lydia asked, brow furrowed. 'Flora's wine, do you mean?'

'Vin Mariani,' Richard explained. 'Olivia drank it as a tonic.'

Lydia frowned, then, 'I'm sure I've read that name somewhere… of course!' she exclaimed, 'Olivia mentioned it in her journal.'

'Did she?' Miss Busby, Richard, and Adeline said in rapid unison.

Lydia nodded, looking at their expressions with surprise. 'I think so, yes. Gosh, is it important? I'm sorry, I didn't realise…'

'What did she say?' Miss Busby pressed, a hint of urgency in her tone.

'I just remember the name really,' Lydia confessed. 'It wasn't much more than that, I shouldn't think. Her entries were so sporadic, and brief.'

Barnaby gave a soft whine at Miss Busby's feet.

'Someone wants a walk,' Richard said. 'Shall we, Mrs Fanshawe?' He shot Miss Busby a knowing look.

'But–?' Adeline spluttered.

'We could work up an appetite for lunch,' he added.

'Good idea,' Miss Busby said. 'I'd like to complete my

notes, while everything's still fresh in my mind. And I wonder, Lydia, if you'd mind showing me that journal entry?'

'Of course,' Lydia said. 'I ought to come up and start packing my things anyway. I suppose our adventure here has come to an end, after all!'

'But–!' Adeline, desperate not to miss out, tried again.

It's such a lovely day, we could walk him to the village. Perhaps we can telephone Alistair from the Post Office, bring him up to date with the news.'

Visibly mollified at the prospect of talking to the inspector, Adeline left with Richard and Barnaby, although she insisted they took the car.

Miss Busby and Lydia climbed the stairs, Lydia chattered amiably about how she'd rather miss the place, as Miss Busby's mind scrambled to gain purchase and make sense of all they'd heard. Several things, she felt, didn't add up.

Why, she wondered, *would Olivia consider publishing in a public memoir something she didn't want mentioned in a private legal document? If she truly feared it would bring shame upon the hotel she loved, it surely couldn't have been the secret she meant to reveal.*

She stopped halfway up the stairs to catch her breath, thinking, *And if Olivia truly believed Arthur to be illegitimate, would she really want him to inherit the estate if Clara turned it down?*

Waving a hand to Lydia to show she was perfectly well, she recommenced her steps, thinking back to

Olivia's letter, and a particular phrase that had jarred: 'Overcoming adversity shapes a person in a way those born to entitlement cannot comprehend.'

But Olivia was *born to entitlement,* she thought, entering the upstairs corridor. *Circumstances may have cruelly taken everything from her, but that, surely, was a rather different matter.*

Making for Lydia's room, her last thought was of Adeline's assessment of the whole business as a chaotic affair. *Why indeed,* Miss Busby wondered, *would Olivia have been excited for the revelation when she appeared to know it would have turned into a colossal scrap?* Her foresight in posting the letter appeared to be telling, and yet—

'Here we are!' Lydia called cheerfully. 'Sorry about the mess!' Sweeping a pile of clothes from the armchair beside the fire, she bade Miss Busby sit and catch her breath, while she unlocked her suitcase and retrieved the journal. Handing it over, she smiled. 'It can't do any harm, now that everything is resolved.'

'Thank you.' Miss Busby took it reverently, opening it and flicking through the pages. As Lydia had said, and shown them previously, many pages were blank or contained only a line or two of the extravagant hand.

'It's towards the back, I think,' Lydia said and perched on the bed to face her.

Miss Busby flicked through the pages. A Bible verse, one of the longer entries, caught her eye at the top of one page:

Proverbs 13:4: *The soul of the sluggard craves and gets nothing, while the soul of the diligent is richly supplied.*

The rest of the page was blank save for the letters *GP*.

'Sluggard…' Miss Busby pondered softly.

'Hmm?' Lydia asked, head tilted.

'Sir Gregory Penn,' Miss Busby said, showing her the entry, and the initials.

'Oh! I'd thought that a reminder to telephone her doctor!'

It was Miss Busby's turn to tilt her head in enquiry.

'General Practitioner,' Lydia explained. 'Mama always refers to ours as her *GP*. I never thought… but it makes sense, now!'

'She knew Sir Gregory well enough to be fully acquainted with his nature,' Miss Busby mused.

Lydia nodded. 'It looks like she didn't want him getting his hands on the place. I suppose if Arthur did inherit, that would be a possibility?' she added.

'Hmm.' Miss Busby wasn't quite so sure. It simply added to the list of questions already fizzing in her head. *If Olivia thought Sir Gregory a sluggard, why had she let him stay?*

'Here's where she mentions Vin Mariani,' Lydia said, flicking to the last entry and passing the book back to Miss Busby.

Vin Mariani. Fortifies and Refreshes Body & Brain.
'Drink to The General Joy of The Whole Table.'

'Macbeth,' Miss Busby noted, recognising the quote. Lydia nodded.

She read on.

But they say I oughtn't.

'Have we no wine here?'

That's from *Coriolanus,'* Lydia said, noting Miss Busby's confusion. 'We did it at school. Deathly boring, I always thought.'

'With *They* being Dr Woods,' Miss Busby surmised. 'He warned her several times to stop.' She read on:

I say they are wrong.

And I am not the only one.

I shall drink to Joy.

'Good for her. I don't see the harm in a little wine.' Lydia shrugged.

'Yes, normally I'd agree.' Miss Busby flicked back through the pages again. One entry stated: *They all depend on me*, but didn't elaborate further. The opposite page posed the question, *Which of them can I depend upon?* Others listed dates, and figures, one seemingly the amount Olivia thought Arthur to have lost. *A fortune*, was written beneath it, *An unbearable waste,* several lines beneath that, and at the very bottom of the page, one single word: *Wastrel.* There were seemingly disjointed fragments of Bible verse scattered throughout. Most of the notes, Miss Busby realised, were so obscure as to be unintelligible.

'I wonder what she'd thought you'd gain from reading these entries?' Miss Busby said, running her hands over the last page again. The pen here, and throughout, had been used with a heavy hand, pushing through the pages to leave the letters raised on the underside.

'Sort of how her mind worked, I think,' Lydia said, taking the journal back. 'You can see that she was a religious sort, and well-read. And how her mind jumped about. It's actually super useful and made me even more intrigued and excited to work with her.'

'Did it really?' Miss Busby asked, not quite understanding.

'Oh, yes! Some people have everything all listed in chronological order, and it's the most boring thing you can imagine, just drafting it all up. Anyone could do it. But with something like this,' she ran a hand over the journal's cloth cover, 'it's like a puzzle! You sort of have to draw the information out, and it's infinitely more interesting!'

Miss Busby smiled. 'Yes, I suppose it must be,' she conceded. 'Although I think I should much prefer a more straightforward task.'

Lydia laughed, her eyes bright and pretty, her delicate features relaxed. The youngster was rather a tonic, Miss Busby thought.

'You're not dashing off right away, are you?' she asked.

Lydia looked unsure. 'I don't really know what would be the done thing. I wondered if Miss Harrowby might like to keep Olivia's journal. Some of it may mean more to her, and I feel I can hand it over to the right person, now, with everything resolved. Perhaps I'll ask her at lunch, do you think? I ought to ask if she'd like Olivia's payment back, too,' she added.

Miss Busby nodded. 'I shall see you in the dining room later,' she said, rising to her feet with a smile.

Making her way back to her own room, mind awash, her thoughts were interrupted as she slipped on something just inside the doorway and almost lost her footing. Regaining her composure, Miss Busby looked down to see a folded piece of paper had been pushed under the door. Bending to open it, she read: *Don't believe all you hear. There are lies within lies. Justice demands more for Olivia than this.*

CHAPTER 27

Busby sat at the desk and reached into the drawer for her notebook. She carefully read back over all they'd discovered so far, before noting the morning's events and the questions dancing in her mind. Tucking the note neatly inside the pages, she gazed up at the grey sky through the mullioned window and considered.

Lies within lies. She was inclined to agree. Things didn't quite add up as neatly as the will might suggest, and whoever left the note had succinctly implied the same attempt to mislead and manipulate that they'd suspected for some time. But to Adeline, Richard, and Lydia, the presence of the will seemed to have closed the case.

Initial suspicion of foul play at Hamnett Hall had sprung from the will being missing, she conceded. Now it had been found, it was natural that suspicion would dissipate as the new order settled.

But is it the order Olivia truly wanted? she wondered. And it seemed she wasn't the only one.

A knock at the door startled her from her thoughts.

'Come to check your fire, miss,' an unusually despondent Annie called.

Miss Busby thanked her, and the young maid set to with the poker, agitating the embers. Her eyes were a little puffy, her shoulders hunched, and her spark noticeably absent.

'Is everything alright?' Miss Busby asked.

'Yes, miss,' Annie said, sniffing as she placed fresh kindling on the glowing cinders.

Miss Busby tilted her head and considered. 'Are you worried about your position?' she asked.

Annie gave a small shrug, followed by an even smaller nod.

'Well, I shouldn't think you need be,' she went on kindly. 'Olivia stated she wanted the hotel run to her methods, which I would certainly take to include retaining the current staff.'

'If Miss Clara takes it on,' Annie qualified, reaching for a fresh log as the kindling caught. 'She didn't say nothing about Mr Arthur having to do the same if he took over.

'It was implied, I think,' Miss Busby said, trying to comfort the girl, although she realised she had a point. 'I'm sure Ludlow will clarify and formalise everything. And I'm almost certain Clara will accept. She was telling us only yesterday how close she'd begun to feel to Olivia. I don't imagine she'd want to let her down.'

Annie looked to her with sorrowful eyes. 'Not to speak ill of anyone miss, but you don't know Miss Clara like we do. She was always going off to have fun with her friends at night. I can't see as she'd want to give that up to sit and do the accounts at the end of the day, or get up early to sign for this and that and talk to the guests and whatnot.'

'What sort of fun?' Miss Busby asked. The fire was beginning to catch. Checking her hair in the mirror above the mantel, she reached for the door.

'I couldn't say exactly, miss,' Annie muttered, following her from the room. 'But it's the sort as makes you ever so unwell in your room sometimes. It's me as has to clear it up.' Her cheeks flushed. 'Not that I mind. I know it's my job. But my mum says leopards don't change their spots, and Jimmy says Miss Clara hasn't got any spots but he doesn't think she'll want to give up being a sociable light.'

It took Miss Busby a moment. A *socialite*. Sir Gregory had termed Clara the same. 'I think Miss Clara was already in the process of trying to change *some* of her spots,' she said, keen to give the girl the benefit of the doubt.

'Yes, miss. Only,' Annie dropped her voice to a whisper, looking both ways down the corridor before adding, 'if she doesn't change all of them, who's going to tell her off?'

Miss Busby blinked. Another good point. 'What about Arthur?' she asked, trying to find a positive. 'Might he make a better job of things?'

Annie considered, rubbing at a smudge of ash on

her white apron. 'I don't know, miss. He's not here very often, and nobody seems to think much of him.'

'Well,' Miss Busby said, trying to fill her tone with purpose as she turned to lock the door behind them. 'Whoever ends up running Hamnett Hall will need reliable, experienced staff. I'm sure they'll be glad to keep you.'

Annie attempted a smile. 'Thank you, miss. It's just, oh Mum'd clip my ear for sounding ungrateful saying it…'

'I promise *I* won't.' Miss Busby's blue eyes shone with a mischievous smile.

Annie giggled, then sniffed, 'Mrs Olivia said as she'd see us right, the staff and all. At least, I think that's what she meant. As if it might be something… more.' Annie's cheeks flamed.

'Go on,' Miss Busby prompted.

'Well, she was excited about it all, that night she had the dinner with everyone. When I was clearing the plates she took my hand and said, *You're not to worry, Annie. You and Jimmy are family too. Hard work may be its own reward, but there's nothing saying I can't add something extra!* And she gave me such a smile, miss! Like she couldn't have been happier.'

There was that word again, Miss Busby thought: *excited.* And then she remembered something she should have asked long before.

'Annie, do you remember taking empty bottles from Olivia's room when you cleaned? Green bottles, with red tops?'

'Her special wine?'

Miss Busby's heart picked up speed. 'Yes. A tonic wine.'

Annie nodded. 'Lots of times. She used to be ever so fond of it.'

'And can you remember when you last saw a bottle there?' she pressed.

Annie scratched her head. 'Not rightly, miss, no. She had one in here for ages, but I ain't seen it anywhere. Might have been thrown away, I suppose. I do remember Mrs Olivia always said she had it on good authority it was just what was needed when you felt a bit under the weather, though.'

'Did she say whose authority?' Miss Busby asked, recalling the journal entry she'd just seen. *I say they are wrong. And I am not the only one.*

Annie shook her head. 'But she told me once that Queen Victoria drank it, and I should think that's good authority, isn't it?'

'Mm, yes, I'm sure.' Miss Busby nodded, wondering if in fact it might not have been someone a little closer to home. 'So Olivia *had* been feeling unwell recently?' Miss Busby asked.

Annie's brow creased, then her eyes widened. 'Oh! I thought under the weather meant as if you were under a cloud. A bit down in the dumps. Did I get it wrong?' Her face began to crumple.

'Not at all. It can mean exactly that,' Miss Busby said, before the girl could get upset again.

Annie raised a hand to her chest and exhaled in relief. 'Oh, good! Are you coming downstairs then, miss?'

Miss Busby turned and was about to say yes when out of the corner of her eye she noticed one of the double doors at the other end of the corridor stood open.

Someone must be up in Olivia's rooms and they forgot to close it, she thought. 'I've forgotten my cardigan,' she said instead. 'You go on down, I won't be long.'

'But miss, you're wearing it!' Annie said brightly, pointing to the lavender woollen Miss Busby was sporting.

'Yes,' she said, thinking on her feet, 'but this is my *indoor* cardigan.'

Making as if to unlock the door, she waited until Annie had turned the corner before hurrying to the other end of the corridor and ducking through the open door.

'Hello?' she called up the stairs. Hearing muffled footsteps but receiving no response, she began to climb. Just as she reached Olivia's door, Clara appeared, looking every bit as glum as the young maid had.

'Oh, it's you,' Clara said.

'Yes,' Miss Busby said, gesturing rather vaguely and adding, 'I saw the door was open…'

'Come in,' Clara offered, waving her through. 'I'm in the bedroom.'

The rose-pink bedcovers were disturbed and strewn with papers featuring Olivia's elegant, looping hand. Clara retook her spot amongst them, folding long legs elegantly beneath her as she sighed and took stock.

'You must think us a rotten bunch, like weeds gathered around a rose.'

'Not at all,' Miss Busby said politely.

'Well, you ought to. We leeched the goodness from Olivia and gave nothing in return.' She stared mournfully at the scattered ledgers, seeming to have fallen into the exact same dour humour as the day before.

'Oh, I expect we all feel a bit like that at times, and all families have their quirks,' Miss Busby said diplomatically. Clara, she had come to realise, possessed something of a flair for the dramatic. 'I myself have a nephew who I find neither use nor ornament, but my sister is incredibly fond of him.'

Clara blinked in surprise, then laughed. 'I've just been looking through the accounts,' she said, picking a page seemingly at random. 'I had so little time with her, in the end…' She sighed. 'There's so much to try and grasp. I'm afraid I'm finding it all a bit overwhelming.'

'That's perfectly natural,' Miss Busby said. 'But you're young, and bright, and you'll soon get the hang of it. May I?' she asked, picking up one of the papers.

Clara nodded. Miss Busby scanned the notes and the figures written beside them. The sevens were crossed in the continental style, the ones elegantly written with a sweeping leading stroke, making the figures look almost like art on the page.

'I'm not so sure,' Clara said, picking up two further sheets and putting them straight back down again. 'I wasted so much time when I could have been learning.

Not just the hotel,' she added, 'but school, and college. I was never any use at maths and this is all making my head spin.'

'It's probably all much more simple than it looks,' Miss Busby offered. 'Most things are.' She lifted her chin, catching the same faint hint of lavender she'd noticed the day they'd arrived. It gave the room a calm and tranquil air. 'There's such a lovely scent in here,' she noted.

'Is there?' Clara asked distractedly. 'I hadn't noticed.'

'Is it Yardley's?' Miss Busby asked, taking a step towards the dressing table where the pretty porcelain dish stood.

'What? Oh, I don't know,' Clara said, brow furrowing. 'Probably. Old ladies always smell of lavender, don't they?'

Miss Busby stepped back as if stung. She was rather fond of it.

'Look, you're a clever sort,' Clara continued, oblivious. 'What do you think of Olivia's will? I mean, why do you think she gave me the option to decline?' she specified.

Miss Busby turned back to her. 'Well, she wanted to be sure you were happy about it, I expect. *Will* you be happy, do you think?' she added, noting the girl's face had turned rather pale.

'I don't know,' Clara said, a mixture of frustration and a hint of annoyance in her voice. 'I just thought I'd have so much more time.'

'But you'll have Lázár to help you. He must know as much about the place as Olivia did, more even, in some respects,' Miss Busby said. 'And Ludlow will advise you too, I'm sure. Assuming you'll keep them both on?' she pressed gently.

'That's the thing, you see. I'm not entirely sure,' Clara confessed. 'Olivia would want me too, I know, but I'm quite sure neither of them *like* me. And so I don't know that I'd trust them to help me. I sort of get the impression they might enjoy seeing me fail.' She looked down, running her thumb over the hem of her black dress.

'I'm sure that's not the case,' Miss Busby said. 'They'll want to see Olivia's wishes carried out as much as you do. Ludlow seemed quite adamant. And I suspect Lázár could run the place with his eyes closed until such a time as you feel you're ready.'

'That's *another* thing,' Clara whined. 'Why didn't she just leave it to him? He'd do a better job.'

'Because she wanted you to do it,' Miss Busby said firmly.

Clara sighed. She picked up another sheet of paper at random and began to fold it into a neat triangle as she considered. 'You said she'd want me to be happy,' she repeated.

Miss Busby nodded.

'What if the thought of running the hotel doesn't make me happy? What if it frightens me?'

'Why would it frighten you?'

'Because I might make a terrible mess of it all and fail miserably.'

'Failure's nothing to be afraid of,' Miss Busby told her. 'As long as you try your best.'

'You were a teacher, weren't you?' Clara narrowed her eyes. 'They always say that, but they never mean it.' She rose to her feet, turning her back on the papers. 'It's not just that, though. I'm afraid Arthur will never stop being cross about me taking what he feels ought to be his. What if he does something awful to get his own back? Or what if Lázár gets so annoyed when I make a mistake that he leaves, and then I make a hundred more? Ludlow will be so stern and disapproving about it all that he'll start looking for some sort of legal loophole to save the place.'

Miss Busby offered a kind smile. 'I suspect you may be overthinking things,' she suggested.

'I hope so,' Clara said glumly, leading the way from the room. 'Because I keep thinking I'm awfully vulnerable and might be in danger. The absolute last thing I want is to be right,' she concluded, ushering Miss Busby through the door to the staircase.

She thought of Arthur's temper as they descended. 'Might you talk to Arthur?' she suggested. 'I expect it was the shock of it. He may have calmed down by now.'

'I won't risk it yet,' Clara said, pulling the double doors closed behind them. He'll most likely be out in the stables, anyway. That's where he goes when he's in a mood. I hate it there,' she added softly.

'Of course,' Miss Busby said, thinking of the girl's parents.

Telling her she needed a breath of fresh air, Miss Busby said her goodbyes and walked out to the front of the hotel, casting a glance down the drive for any sign of her friends, and her dog, returning. Seeing no one, she walked around to the rear and made her way to the old stable block beyond the lawn.

CHAPTER 28

It was a fair distance off, and gave her time to think over all that Clara had said. She thought, too, of the wording of Olivia's letter: *all my personal possessions and property* to go to Clara. Only Hamnett Hall would pass to Arthur if Clara declined. Whilst surely the most valuable asset, it came with a heavy weight of responsibility attached. If Clara were to refuse, Miss Busby suspected the hotel had generated enough income for the Fortescues over the years that she would still inherit enough to enjoy a carefree existence for the rest of her days. Would a young lady so fond of having fun with her friends pass up such an opportunity? Had Olivia set her a test to see if she was truly committed?

Arthur had no such luxury. Hamnett Hall was his only option, and a second-hand one at that. Did Olivia think he'd rise to the challenge if Clara baulked at it? It would be a risk, surely. He could be annoyed enough at the initial slight to refuse just to spite her.

Can you spite a dead woman? Miss Busby wondered,

as she approached the hotel's small stable block. She shivered in the chill. The sun was cloud covered, and last night's frost still glittered in sheltered spots, with the ground hard underfoot.

The smell of hay was warm and pleasant as she looked over the open top half of the stable door. She saw four stalls, three of which were vacant, clean and brushed out. The fourth held a large Welsh cob with a black coat and four white fetlocks. The horse turned to see who it was, and Miss Busby saw its bright, white blaze.

'Hello,' she called softly. 'Aren't you pretty?'

'And she knows it.' Arthur's gruff voice made Miss Busby jump, as he emerged from the tack room with a curry comb.

'Is she yours?' Miss Busby asked.

'Aunt Olivia's. Clara's now, I suppose. The other horses go to the livery for the winter break, but Meggie always stays.'

'What a lovely name,' Miss Busby said, adding, 'May I come in?'

He nodded. 'Come to say goodbye? I would say it's been a pleasure, but under the circumstances…' He sighed, moving into the stall and clucking softly to the mare before patting her rump and beginning to work the comb through her coat.

'I wanted to see how you were,' Miss Busby said. 'The news must have been a terrible shock.'

He scoffed. 'I'd hardly call it news, it's a vicious lie. My mother would never have done such a thing, and certainly not with someone like Sir Gregory. The age difference, alone.' He shook his head, distaste souring his handsome features. 'And he never cared for her, either. There was none of the fawning nonsense he displays when someone catches his eye. It's lunacy to even think it.'

'And you'd never before heard any suggestion…?' Miss Busby asked, as gently as she could.

'Didn't you hear what I said? Of course not!' Arthur snapped, holding the comb aloft, anger flashing in his eyes.

Miss Busby took a step back.

The young man's other hand rose to his face, fingers pinching the bridge of his nose in frustration. 'I'm sorry,' he said quietly. 'I just can't understand why no one else can see it.'

'See what?' Miss Busby prompted.

'That someone had obviously fed Aunt Olivia the most ludicrous lie.'

Lies within lies, Miss Busby thought. 'Do you have any idea who might do such a thing? And why?' she asked.

'Someone who doesn't like me, which could be any of them,' he said, using the comb to gesture back towards the hotel. 'You're the only one who's come to see if I'm alright,' he added. 'None of them care a jot about me. As for why: to make sure I didn't get the hotel, I suppose. None of them think me capable.'

'Olivia must have done,' Miss Busby pointed out, 'to include you.'

'As second choice,' he said. 'Clara always came first. Aunt Olivia saw herself as a champion of the underdog. Forgot her aristocratic roots, if you ask me. Or felt guilty about them. She adored a sob story. Hence Hamnett Hall becoming a haven for the homeless.'

Miss Busby gave a small smile. 'If Clara refuses the inheritance, will you keep it as such?'

He rested his arms on the horse's back for a moment, considering. 'Flora and Gresham could stay on, but I'd give Sir Gregory his marching orders. He can afford to pay his own way.'

Miss Busby thought for a moment. *If Arthur was the lesser choice, surely the terms of his inheritance should have been tighter than Clara's, rather than non-existent.* 'Do you think it odd that Olivia put no conditions on the inheritance in your case?' she asked.

He shrugged. 'Not really. I'm her last resort, after all. There's nothing she could threaten me with. Except leaving it all to Lázár, maybe,' he said, with a humourless laugh.

'Hmm.' Miss Busby crossed to a straw bale, swept it clean of loose strands with her hand, and perched on the centre of it. *It wasn't an entirely unreasonable suggestion,* she thought. 'What will you do now?' she asked.

Arthur shrugged. 'What can I do? The rumour will spread of course, they always do, and with my name in question I'll have nothing if Clara takes Hamnett Hall. The irony,' he exclaimed drily. 'I expect my aunt would have far more sympathy for me in that state.'

'What did your solicitor suggest?' Miss Busby asked.

Arthur's pale cheeks flushed. 'I didn't bother. I mean, Ludlow made it quite plain there's no point…it'd just be throwing good money after bad.'

Money he likely didn't have, Miss Busby realised.

Arthur turned his attention back to the curry comb, and Meggie's coat began to gleam beneath it. For a few moments the puffing sound of the horse's breath and the rhythmic scratch of the comb were all that could be heard, until Arthur sighed and said, 'I did try to do right by my aunt, you know. I ran errands for her when I was here, and came running as soon as she summoned me for that infernal dinner. I actually did far more about the place than Clara ever did, but she never cared for me half as much.'

'And you're quite sure it couldn't have been because the rumour was brewing even then?'

He nodded. 'Aunt Olivia wasn't the shy sort. If she'd suspected then, she'd have let me know. She was always telling me where I was going wrong, I don't see how that would have been any different.'

'But it would hardly have been your fault,' Miss Busby pointed out.

He stopped for a moment. 'No, I suppose it wouldn't. It would've been Sir Gregory's.'

'And she let him stay,' Miss Busby said, mind whirring.

'Yes. You see?' Exasperation crept into Arthur's tone. 'It's a total nonsense. Someone must have fed the idea to her recently. Although I thought she'd have more sense than to bite.'

Switching tack, Miss Busby asked, 'Would you have liked to inherit the hotel? Under Olivia's conditions?'

Patting the horse, he set the comb on the side of the stall and crossed to sit next to Miss Busby, resting his elbows on his knees and his chin in his hands.

'I'd have preferred it without the conditions,' he admitted. 'But, yes, I should have enjoyed getting to grips with the place. I might have sold the house in London, and gotten away from the city altogether.' He fell silent for a moment, then added, 'Hamnett Hall is my *right*. Henry Fortescue was my uncle.' His tone grew cold, his eyes steel. 'And if it hadn't been for my family, Aunt Olivia would have been nothing more than Olivia Kovacs, chambermaid. Perhaps she ought to have remembered that.'

He rubbed at the light, sandy stubble on his chin, then tried to smooth his hair back. It refused to comply. Reaching into the inside pocket of his hacking jacket, he pulled out a silver hip flask. Proffering it politely to Miss Busby first, who declined, he took a sip.

'I don't understand why she even got into this will business in the first place. She'd never even been unwell,' he said.

'Several people mentioned her having the odd dizzy spell, and feeling under the weather,' Miss Busby told him.

'That'll be that god-awful wine she drank,' Arthur said dismissively. 'It'd make anyone dizzy. But Ludlow had been telling her for years she ought to sort out her affairs, and she'd always waved him off before.'

What *did* make her think of it now, Miss Busby wondered. Had the person who'd whispered a venomous rumour in her ear been the same one to persuade her to put pen to paper on a legal document? *But she hadn't quite done so, not entirely, in the end...*

'Mind you, I wasn't here all the time,' Arthur went on, replacing the flask. 'Just the odd weekend. Always the last to know, I suppose. Anyway, nothing I can do about it.' He shrugged. 'Thought I'd take Meggie out for a quick ride. I don't know when she'll next get one,' he added, looking morosely at the cobb.

'At least you still have your house,' Miss Busby said. 'Perhaps you could take her?'

Arthur shook his head. 'No room. And livery fees in the city would make your eyes water. Lázár will take care of her. I'll remind him. It wasn't my fault, you know,' he continued, turning to her earnestly. 'The money.'

She tilted her head in polite enquiry.

'I lost my father's shares,' he clarified. 'I took on a broker when I returned from the war. A chap who told me he'd managed Father's finances for decades. He said he could grow them into a decent nest egg for my future family.' He sighed. 'In the first two months he just about lost the lot. And when I went through all of Father's things properly, his name was barely mentioned. He'd just been a minor assistant of some sort. I'd fallen for a con.'

Miss Busby gave a little 'Oh' of surprise, and sympathy.

'I suppose it *was* my fault, really,' he went on. 'Bad judgement and all that. But in my defence, I didn't come back in the best of states.' His eyes took on a faraway look.

'I didn't know you'd served,' Miss Busby said softly.

He shrugged. '*War is an ugly thing,*' he quoted. 'I don't talk about it.'

'Not even to the Major…?' Miss Busby suggested.

Arthur scoffed. 'Medals and bluster. I served under one just like him.' His eyes grew dark again. Dangerous.

'Richard's son, Anthony, came home with shell shock,' Miss Busby said. 'He was unwell for a long time. I simply can't imagine…' She reached a hand to his arm.

Arthur flinched, and she drew it back.

'He's getting much better now, though,' she went on. 'He's grown rather fond of my neighbour, a gregarious young lady who recently moved to the village and seems to be… taking his mind off things.'

Arthur's eyes softened and he turned to her with a raised brow. 'You don't sound entirely enamoured?'

Miss Busby smiled. 'I'm glad he's feeling brighter. But she's perhaps not the *most* suitable young woman, long-term.'

'They never are. Clara and I once stepped out, you know.'

Miss Busby's own eyebrows shot up.

'A few years back now,' he went on. 'It was a terrible idea, of course, but she'd been awfully keen. Always wanting to go to this or that club in London. Wanting me to introduce her to people, that sort of thing. She got into a terrible sulk when I said I didn't think we clicked.'

'That must have made things…difficult,' Miss Busby said, wondering what else they hadn't known about.

'You could say that,' he replied with a wry laugh. 'I don't think it endeared me to Aunt Olivia much, either. Although she'd never have seen me as good enough for the girl anyway. She ought to have been glad I broke it off.'

'I wonder,' Miss Busby said, trying to find the most delicate way to phrase it, 'if she knew you all that well at all? If any of them did, in fact.'

His brows rose with interest. 'How do you mean?'

'Well, not one of them mentioned you'd served, and there seems to be the overall impression that when it came to the shares…'

'…I'd squandered them?' He came to her aid. 'Yes, well, I suppose I did, really. I wasn't of a mind to trust anyone after the broker's efforts, so I tried to manage what was left of the shares myself. Trouble is, it's so complicated. And everyone lies to you about the worth of everything. I ended up losing what remained, and…' he waved a hand '…here I am. As for the others, my life is my own and I prefer to keep to myself. I can't stop them making assumptions, if they've nothing better to do.'

'And you never thought to ask your aunt for help?'

He shook his head. 'I knew she didn't think much of me. Didn't want to lower that opinion even further.'

What a shame, Miss Busby thought, suspecting it would have changed his aunt's opinion of him entirely.

'I would have liked a second chance, though,' he admitted. 'I think with Lázár's help I could have made a decent job of running this place.'

'You may still get the chance,' Miss Busby reminded him. She wished she'd seen more of this reflective side to the young man sooner. The temper and the darkness was still there, just beneath the surface perhaps, but there was softness and light too.

Arthur rose to his feet, brushing dust from the back of his riding breeches. 'I doubt it. Clara would be a fool to turn the place down.' He fixed earnest grey eyes on Miss Busby. 'But I'll manage. I'm glad you came to find me, Miss Busby.' He offered a hand, which she gracefully accepted, standing in turn. 'I don't normally rattle on this much,' he said. 'Felt a bit desperate earlier, to be truthful. It isn't nice thinking people are making up such appalling lies about one, when I've done nothing to deserve it. Doesn't bring out the best in a chap, I'm afraid.'

Miss Busby nodded in understanding. 'I'm glad, too,' she said. 'I do hope you can find some comfort, and peace. I'm sure brighter days will come.'

He nodded, smiling, although his eyes remained sombre. 'I ought to get out quickly with Meggie, before lunch,' he said. 'Unless you'd like me to walk you back to the hotel first?'

Miss Busby insisted she'd be fine and took her leave as he ducked back into the tack room. She heard the purr of the Rolls in the distance, and arrived back at the front of the hotel as Adeline parked at a jaunty angle behind Lydia's silver Talbot. Barnaby trotted excitedly over to her, tail aloft.

CHAPTER 29

'He's had a capital time,' Richard called, crossing to her with a smile. 'Saw off a fox sleeping in a thicket by the river and set it off running. Never seen the little fellow look prouder!'

Adeline smoothed her deep-green dress as she alighted. 'We have walked about a hundred miles,' she huffed. 'Has anyone said what's for lunch?'

'It was about a mile, and my knee held up well,' Richard said quietly, as they followed Adeline inside. 'I couldn't get hold of Alistair, so I left a message with Lucy. It might be best not to leave until we've spoken to him.'

'Good idea,' Miss Busby said.

Adeline made straight for the dining room.

Miss Busby called, 'I need to wash my hands. And change my cardigan,' she added. 'I've been in the stables.'

'What on earth were you doing there?' Adeline asked, turning in surprise.

'Walk with me, and I'll explain,' she said.

Adeline gave a longing look down the corridor, before

swinging the door shut and joining Miss Busby and Richard as they climbed the stairs.

Miss Busby recounted, in hushed tones, Clara's fears and what Annie had said about Olivia and the wine. Once they were safely instilled in the privacy of her room, she added all that Arthur had told her, and the extra entries from Olivia's journal that she'd seen.

'Perhaps Olivia wasn't so clever, after all,' Richard suggested, as Miss Busby paused to recover her breath. Barnaby hopped up onto the bed beside her, and curled up with his side resting against her hip, as was his wont. 'She refused to stop drinking that infernal tonic wine,' Richard continued. 'And her nephew wasn't useless at all, he was damaged. So many young men came back from the war broken. She ought to have been kinder to him.'

Miss Busby couldn't help but agree. Although she, too, had thought Arthur rather acerbic to start with.

'How odd that Arthur and Clara stepped out,' Adeline remarked. 'They seemed at each other's throats when we first arrived.'

'Resentment, I should say.' Richard suggested. 'The girl won't have taken kindly to being told no.'

'The whole morning has only thrown up more questions,' Miss Busby said, selecting a mauve cardigan from the wardrobe. 'Before the will was found we were sure someone was manipulating events behind the scenes. Now that it's been found, and read, I'm afraid I'm even surer.'

'Is that a word, Isabelle?' Adeline asked.

'Yes. And I don't appear to be the only one in the hotel

who thinks as much.' She took her notebook from the drawer and showed the pair the note.

'Ah,' Adeline said.

'Indeed,' Richard added.

'This whole business with the wine has to be key,' Miss Busby said. 'It must be connected to someone influencing Olivia's decisions.'

'But we know she drank the stuff of her own accord. And, to my mind at least, the will reads rather reasonably, under the circumstances,' Richard pointed out.

'I'm not so sure.' Miss Busby crossed into the adjoining bathroom, calling back, 'think of all the people Olivia invited to the dinner.'

Adeline counted them off on her fingers.

'Why so many,' Miss Busby said, emerging, 'when only Arthur and Clara were mentioned in the will?'

'Because it concerns them all,' Adeline said. 'They are each connected to the hotel.'

'And Olivia did reference them all, albeit in umbrella terms,' Richard added. 'That's what I took her *run to my method* comment to mean.'

'Perhaps,' Miss Busby conceded. 'If you discount Annie's mention of a reward. But neither choice would have been a surprise, as such. As promised by Olivia. They were both the only logical candidates.'

'But we know she didn't think much of Arthur, and Clara's behaviour leaves much to be desired. Logical choice or no, some would have been surprised at the outcome,' Richard reasoned.

'Then the only issue would have been in choosing between them,' Miss Busby said. 'Yet both were provided with the opportunity to inherit.'

'Well then, perhaps the surprise will come in seeing what Clara will do?' Richard suggested. 'Ditto Arthur, although I suppose he wasn't given any alternative.'

Miss Busby nodded. 'Exactly. If he doesn't wish to run the hotel to her specifications, there can be no possible consequences. He could sell the place and spend the money on wine, women, and song if he so desired. Does that sound like something Olivia would have countenanced?'

'Not at all,' Adeline admitted, cottoning on. 'So Olivia would have to be entirely sure Clara would accept.'

'Which makes sense, given their relationship towards the end,' Richard said.

'But why would Olivia leave even the remotest possibility that Arthur could destroy everything she'd worked for?' Miss Busby objected.

'Mentioning Arthur may have just been a courtesy,' Richard said.

'And she would have known Clara wouldn't want to lose out to him,' Adeline added. 'The idea of him getting the place could simply have been included to chivvy her on.'

'But it hasn't,' Miss Busby reasoned. 'If anything, it seems to be doing the opposite.'

'Was Olivia trying to be fair in giving both of them a chance?' Richard wondered.

'Or did someone take advantage of Arthur's resentment at how Olivia treated him, and Clara's lack of experience, to sway her final decision?' Miss Busby asked.

There was a moment's confused silence.

'Isabelle, you are not making sense,' Adeline complained.

'I'm trying,' she retorted. 'But I can't quite see how all the pieces fit, yet. We have our whisperer of rumours, our smasher of bottles, a delayed letter of immense significance, two victims, and a mysterious note. One person surely can't be responsible for all of them.'

'You suspect others have formed an alliance?' Richard asked.

Miss Busby nodded. 'Finding a shared agenda regarding Olivia's fortune.'

'But who?' Adeline cried, becoming increasingly frustrated. 'Flora, the Major, and Gregory Penn are all in the same boat. If Clara accepts, they may be expected to continue as they are. If the hotel passes to Arthur, nothing is certain.'

'I'm not sure Sir Gregory would want to stay,' Richard said, 'after such an accusation. And we know Arthur would likely boot him out.'

'Let's go down to lunch. We can keep a close eye on them all,' Miss Busby said. Barnaby's head shot up at the word *lunch*. She patted him with a smile, but something was still gnawing at her brain; she just couldn't quite put her finger on it.

Lázár, Ludlow, Major Gresham, and Clara were all seated together in the dining room, talking in hushed tones. Sir Gregory sat alone at a separate table, with Arthur not appearing to have returned from his ride.

Lázár looked up and hurried over to them as they walked in, Barnaby trotting ahead with his nose twitching in anticipation.

'Cook has not returned, I am afraid, but Annie has made sandwiches for all.' The manager gestured to a mountain of rough-cut sandwiches at the back of the room. 'Please, help yourselves, and accept my apologies for a service so poor.' he added, head bowed.

'Of course,' Miss Busby said kindly, as Adeline asked, 'What kind of sandwiches?'

Lázár took her to the available selection, and Miss Busby followed with Richard. She could see Major Gresham questioning Clara intently, then Ludlow in turn. Ensuring his accommodation was secure, she supposed, although something in his expression troubled her. It appeared harsh, almost cruel in its insistence. He'd been the first to question Clara after the will was read, she recalled. And the one to accompany Flora to hospital. And there was no love lost between him and Sir Gregory, now clearly ostracised by the group.

Could the Major be the ringleader behind the manipulation? Miss Busby wondered. He'd said he'd never lost a battle, citing meticulous planning as a factor. The sort of planning that would surely be needed to fox both the authorities and Olivia's closest friends.

Richard passed her a plate, drawing her from her thoughts.

Adeline, fully loaded, turned to pick a table.

Miss Busby cleared her throat and nodded towards Sir Gregory when Adeline caught her eye.

Richard turned to her and raised an eyebrow.

'I think Sir Gregory may have sent the note,' Miss Busby told him softly. 'I thought perhaps Arthur, to begin with, but since we spoke I'm not so sure…'

'Sir Gregory's parting remark to you earlier was hardly complimentary,' Richard reminded her.

'No, but they are the two with the most to lose. And it didn't read like Arthur,' she added, feeling as if she had got to know the young man better in the space of several minutes in the stables than in the entirety of the time they'd been at the hotel.

She took two salmon sandwiches, and one egg and cress, before nodding to Sir Gregory and taking a seat opposite him.

Barnaby settled hopefully beside her chair.

Sir Gregory eyed them laconically. 'Well?' he asked, his manner relaxed but his tone tinged with accusation. 'Have you discovered any new rumours I ought to be aware of?'

'No,' Miss Busby replied swiftly, before Adeline or Richard could object, 'but I have given some thought to your notion that Olivia was influenced in her decision-making.'

'About time,' Sir Gregory huffed. 'And did you come to any conclusion as to who may be responsible?'

'I wondered if it might have been you,' she said.

'Ha!' Sir Gregory barked his now-familiar laugh of disbelief. 'You think it likely I would dishonour my name in order to ostracise myself in this manner?' He gesticulated to the others seated away from him, shaking his head. 'Could do better, Miss Busby,' he said drily. 'That's the sort of thing schoolteachers write on their pupils' work, isn't it?'

'Funnily enough,' Miss Busby replied calmly, 'it's the sort of thing Olivia wrote about you in her journal.'

The smug smile on Sir Gregory's face evaporated.

'You are mentioned in rather unflattering terms, I'm afraid,' she continued. It was possibly stretching the truth a little, but his initials did sit on the same page as the word 'Sluggard', after all.

Sir Gregory's brow furrowed, before his eyes narrowed in suspicion. 'Olivia didn't keep a journal,' he said. 'She never had the time. The appointments diary and the accounts were the only things she wrote in the evenings, which I believe is when women with nothing better to do indulge themselves in such self-important frivolity.'

Adeline glared at him. 'Women, is it? I take it you wouldn't refer to Samuel Pepys, then, as *frivolous*?'

'Not at all. As a member of parliament, and the navy board, he had something relevant to write, and most of his notes were aide memoires.'

'Whereas a member of the foreign aristocracy ousted from her own country who rebuilt a successful life for herself here, *didn't* have anything relevant to write?' Adeline challenged, her eyes flashing dangerously.

Sir Gregory sighed. 'As I have already said, Olivia, thanks to her successful life, simply didn't have the time.'

'It would appear she did,' Adeline countered, 'as we have seen the journal for ourselves.' The satisfaction was as evident in her tone as in the smile she directed at him.

Miss Busby saw a flicker of uncertainty in his expression, but it was fleeting.

'Were you truly acquainted with Olivia, Mrs Fanshawe?' he asked, leaning back in his chair to consider her. 'She never mentioned you, and I have to say I've never encountered so many dangerous falsehoods springing up within Hamnett Hall prior to your arrival.'

Adeline pulled back and gave a sharp intake of breath. 'How *dare* you—'

'Where exactly did you find this mysterious journal?' he asked, leaning forward and crossing his arms over his chest. 'Did you rummage through Olivia's rooms like the others?' His eyes flicked once more to Gresham's table.

'I should think you might do better to ask what was said about you in this journal, Sir Gregory,' Richard suggested.

He laughed. 'I never was one for fiction, Sir Richard. I have better things to do with my time.' He eyed Miss Busby. 'I'm afraid in looking to me as the influencer you are barking up entirely the wrong tree. Were I in any way capable of influencing Olivia,' he said, lowering his voice, 'I should have made her Lady Penn as soon as was appropriate after Henry's demise.'

There was a moment's silence.

'Ah. I see,' said Miss Busby.

Sir Gregory pursed his lips. 'Yes. Well. Again, better late than never.'

Miss Busby, in gentler tone despite the slight, asked, 'You loved her, then?'

'Of course I did,' he replied quietly. 'I loved her for years. But despite the nonsense you have heard today, I would never have interfered in a marriage. And Henry Fortescue was my friend. When he died, I thought I could honour him by taking care of Olivia, as well as indulging my own feelings. I'd have been utterly mad to let the opportunity pass,' he went on. 'So I told Olivia my feelings, and asked her the question.'

'And?' Adeline prompted.

'I'd have thought that was evident. She turned me down. Said she would never marry again. And that was that. I had to be content with friendship.' Looking back to Miss Busby, he added, 'So, I suggest you look elsewhere. And rather more carefully.' Rising to his feet and dropping his napkin on his plate, he cast one last look at the others. 'Some people see shadows where none exist, Miss Busby, and others see right through them as if they weren't there.'

And with that, he turned and left the room.

CHAPTER 30

'Well!' Adeline complained. 'The man's manners are a disgrace to his title.'

'Or possibly a reflection of his title being disgraced,' Miss Busby countered.

'I'm surprised you let him speak to you like that, Isabelle,' Richard chided quietly.

'As am I!' Adeline agreed.

'I think he was telling the truth,' Miss Busby said. 'He seems frustrated that we don't see what he sees.'

'Well then why doesn't he *tell* us what he sees, rather than faffing about with riddles!' Adeline huffed.

'I'm not sure,' Miss Busby admitted with a sigh. 'But I did wonder from the start whether he may have proposed. It makes sense. And I expect it's the primary cause of the resentment between him and the Major,' she added quietly.

Adeline considered for a moment, before suggesting, 'What if, upon having his affections spurned, Gregory decided to take his revenge?'

'After so long?'

'It *is* a dish best served cold,' Adeline argued.

'Hm. But if that were the case, why would he tell us about the proposal?' Miss Busby asked.

'Because… Oh! I am not an expert in the psyche of spurned men, Isabelle!' Adeline objected.

Richard gave a low chuckle. 'Olivia must have wounded both their pride in turning them down,' he said to Adeline. 'And rather than taking it out on the woman they both loved, I suspect they preferred to take it out on each other. But you're right, Isabelle,' he said, placing a hand on Miss Busby's. 'His admission of his failure speaks to genuine feeling, and, I should think, honesty.'

Miss Busby nodded. 'And I am quite sure now that he sent the note,' she added.

'I'm not,' Adeline objected. 'Why on earth would he send it and then jump down your throat the minute you act upon it?'

'Because I acted upon it incorrectly,' she answered patiently.

Further objections from Adeline were silenced as Arthur, pink cheeked from his ride in the cold autumn afternoon, strode into the dining room. Nodding politely to Miss Busby, he went straight to Clara's table. All eyes followed him.

'Don't forget to take care of Meggie, will you, Lázár?' he said. 'I'm going back to London tomorrow and I'd hate to think of her being forgotten.'

Lázár's brow furrowed. 'Of course. But…are you sure…?' He looked to Ludlow, and then Clara.

'Quite sure. I'll come back for Aunt Olivia's funeral, of course,' Arthur went on. 'Even though she thought so little of my mother, I'd like to show her more respect than she has shown me.' His expression was relaxed, proud, even. 'If there's anything you need from me before I leave, I'll be in my rooms, packing.'

Nodding, and offering Clara a tight smile, he turned to leave.

'Wait!' she called, springing to her feet. Her cheeks flushed as all eyes now turned to her. 'We ought to talk, Arthur. I'll walk with you.'

Surprise crossed his refined features, but he gave a small shrug, and a nod, and the young pair left the dining room together.

'They certainly would have made a handsome couple,' Adeline said softly into the ensuing silence.

Miss Busby's reply was cut off as Annie raced into the room from the kitchen, face aglow, calling loudly for Lázár. 'The hospital's on the telephone! Lady Flora is to be sent home!'

Exclamations of surprise and delight rang out at the news. Lázár was the first to his feet, rushing to take the call and make arrangements. Major Gresham followed close on his heels, calling that he ought to be the one to meet her.

'Well, there's some good news, at least,' Richard said, as Ludlow rose and followed Gresham in turn.

'What's your take on all this?' Adeline called bluntly to the solicitor, eyeing the retreating figure with her usual suspicion.

He turned slowly to face her. 'I beg your pardon?'

'You must have known Olivia well; were you surprised by the decision revealed in her letter?' Adeline asked, undaunted by the icy response.

'My discussions with my clients are strictly confidential,' he said. 'Unless you are in possession of a police badge?'

Miss Busby hid a smile as Adeline's hackles rose.

'I thought not.' He turned pointedly to Miss Busby. 'I'm due back at the office. Inspector McKay can reach me there if I'm needed.'

'Thank you,' Miss Busby said.

He left with the briefest of nods.

'There is a veritable *plague* of rudeness amongst the men of this hotel,' Adeline muttered.

'No one enjoys accusations flying their way,' Richard said. 'I shouldn't take it personally,' he added kindly.

'It was a simple question, not an accusation!' Adeline remonstrated. 'And perfectly reasonable, to boot. The man is thick as thieves with Lázár all the time, and *he* doesn't have a badge,' she grumbled.

'It's a matter of tone, I think,' Miss Busby said. 'But I wonder if we oughtn't to be thinking more about Major Gresham?'

The question immediately distracted Adeline. 'What, why?' she asked, then stopped when Lydia walked in.

'There you are!' she called brightly. 'There's ever such a commotion in reception.'

'Lady Flora is coming home,' Miss Busby explained, to Lydia's delight.

'I'll show you where the sandwiches are,' Adeline offered, picking up her now-empty plate.

Miss Busby noted Lydia had brought the journal down with her.

'I was going to give it to Clara,' she explained, as she sat down and eyed her luncheon meat sandwich uncertainly.

'Cook didn't come back,' Adeline offered by way of explanation, two of the same sandwiches now gracing her own plate.

Lydia took a bite. She grimaced.

Barnaby trotted to her side, his small brown eyes alight.

'May I?' Lydia asked Miss Busby, who nodded.

The little terrier, proud as punch with an entire sandwich of his own, hurried off to lie down and enjoy it in a patch of sunlight.

'You just missed Clara,' Richard said, nodding to the book.

'Yes, I saw her outside. She was deep in discussion with Arthur and I didn't like to interrupt. I'm sure I'll catch her later.'

Adeline began recounting all the young woman had missed so far, between bites, coming full circle as she asked Miss Busby, 'Now, what's all this about the Major?'

'Well, he sounded very keen to be the one to meet Flora, and he was also the one who accompanied her to the hospital initially.'

'Oh, it's rather sweet!' Lydia said. 'They must be terribly close.'

'Perhaps, although I didn't quite get that impression when we first arrived,' Miss Busby pointed out.

'The place was in rather a state, Isabelle,' Adeline reminded her.

'Yes,' Miss Busby agreed. 'It's just, unlike Sir Gregory, and even Arthur, the Major has no way to support himself without Olivia's generosity. Which makes me wonder if he may have had more reason than the others to engineer matters to suit his own ends.'

'Flora has no way to support herself, either,' Richard reminded her.

'No,' Miss Busby agreed. 'But if we think Flora was poisoned, that rather lets her off the hook.'

'But surely she can't have been poisoned after all?' Lydia's face creased into confusion. 'Not if she's quite well now.'

'Hm,' Miss Busby murmured. 'Well, we shall find out for certain soon. Ludlow said the inspector was expected at The Abbot's Kitchen this morning.'

'Whose kitchen?' Lydia asked, clearly confused.

'It's a chemistry lab in Oxford,' Richard explained. 'Connected to the University. You think he may have taken the glass there for testing?' he asked Miss Busby.

She nodded. 'I expect it would be quicker than waiting

for it to filter through police channels, if the wait for the post mortem was anything to go by.'

'But I thought everything was all settled now,' Lydia said.

'Oh, it is, I should think,' Miss Busby assured her. 'It's just nice to tie the ends together.'

'Shall I telephone Lucy?' Richard asked, glancing down at his watch. 'The pair are inseparable at the moment. I expect she'll know how he got on.'

'Let's wait until Flora's back,' Miss Busby suggested. 'She may have remembered something. Oh, here's Lázár now. What news?' she called, as the manager came in closely followed by Annie, who was still beaming.

'Mr Arthur and Miss Clara have gone to fetch her, miss,' Annie said excitedly. Lázár smiled down at her. It is most nice to see the two young ones united in this, at least.'

'It certainly is,' Miss Busby agreed. 'Did Major Gresham accompany them?'

'To his consternation, no. But Miss Clara thought Lady Flora may need room to rest on the back seat. I do hope you will stay?' he enquired politely. 'I am sure she would be most pleased to see you.'

Adeline nodded eagerly. 'Of course. We shall look forward to it.'

'I'm going to go and make Lady Flora's room all nice for her,' Annie said proudly. 'Pick the last roses from the garden, and everything!'

Lázár cleared his throat meaningfully.

'Once I've tidied the lunch things,' she added, rather more glumly.

'Well, it won't take them long to fetch her from Cheltenham. I must go and freshen up,' Adeline said, rising to her feet. 'Are you coming, Isabelle?'

'I think I should like to sit for a while,' she said. 'Gather my thoughts.'

'And I think I ought to take Barnaby for a constitutional,' Richard said, looking over to where the little dog was lying in the sun, not a crumb to be seen. 'Have him walk off that luncheon meat!'

'I will serve drinks in the lounge upon Lady Flora's return,' Lázár said.

'Will she be well enough, do you think?' Lydia asked.

'The matron tells me on the phone that she is quite recovered and most full of beans,' he explained. 'I hope to see you all later.'

As he hurried off to prepare the lounge, and Annie disappeared into the kitchen with the dirty plates, Miss Busby and Lydia were left alone. The silence felt both companionable and comfortable, only occasionally broken by Annie apologetically flying in and out with plates and the carpet sweeper.

'You know,' Lydia said after a while, looking at Miss Busby appraisingly, 'I ought to leave you my card in case you and Mrs Fanshawe ever want my help writing about your investigations.'

Miss Busby laughed. 'Oh, I doubt anyone would want to read about our bumbling about.'

'I wouldn't be so sure,' Lydia said thoughtfully. 'Will you promise to telephone me if you ever decide to do it?'

Miss Busby nodded, smiling, as she could think of little less likely.

'Perfect! You know, I think I might pop out for a walk, too, until the others get back.'

'Shall I keep the journal for you?' Miss Busby asked. 'You won't want to walk about clutching it.'

'Oh,' said Lydia, as Miss Busby reached down for her handbag, and swept the book inside with a smile. 'Yes, thanks.'

'If you see Richard, will you remind him to keep Barnaby away from the lake!' Miss Busby asked, before wishing her a pleasant constitutional.

With everyone now gone, Miss Busby walked through to the conservatory and took a chair in a warm patch of sunlight. Tucking her bag at her feet, she closed her eyes for a moment and considered all that had happened since the solicitor arrived with Olivia's letter.

Richard woke her with a gentle hand on the shoulder half an hour later.

'Oh!' She looked around, momentarily confused. 'Did I fall asleep? How embarrassing! I wasn't snoring, was I?'

Richard smiled. 'You looked very peaceful. It's been such a busy day I almost left you to your rest, but I thought you'd want to see Flora.'

Miss Busby rose rather stiffly to her feet. 'Of course! How is she?'

'She looks remarkably well,' Richard said, leading her

from the room. 'You'd hardly think she was at death's door a couple of days ago.'

'Not so much at it, as halfway through it,' Miss Busby said.

'Everyone's in the lounge, come on.' Richard held the dining room door for her, and they followed the sound of merry chatter to find Flora sitting by the fire, surrounded by happy faces. Adeline had managed to gain pride of place by her side, to Major Gresham's clear annoyance, and even Sir Gregory, Miss Busby noted, stood over the frail figure somewhat protectively. Barnaby had installed himself in Flora's lap, and her fingers were idly running through his long white fur. He gave a little *wuff* of recognition as he spotted his mistress crossing the room.

CHAPTER 31

'Miss Busby!' Flora said, her wan face creasing into a bright smile. She wore a long dress in her usual black, with a wide lace collar and the same bright yellow cardigan Miss Busby had seen her in before. The yellow against the white lace brought daisies to mind, and Miss Busby returned the elderly woman's smile. 'I'm afraid I can't remember a thing about it,' Flora continued, 'but I have it on good authority that you and Mrs Fanshawe are responsible for my continued presence among the living.' She bowed her head almost reverently. Barnaby looked up and aimed a lick at her nose. She laughed in delight.

'Barnaby, get down,' Miss Busby chided, afraid he would be too much for her.

'Barnaby, stay put!' Flora countered. 'He is doing my soul the world of good. Such a lovely welcome from you all!' She beamed at the room in general.

'It's Annie who's responsible, really,' Miss Busby said, moving closer. 'She was so concerned when you didn't answer your door, and chivvied us all into action. Do you really remember nothing at all from the evening before?' she pressed.

'Not a thing, although I'm assured this is quite normal. Old age is a strange adventure,' she sighed, then looked over her shoulder to where the young maid stood. 'And yes, Annie is my guardian angel!' A blush blossomed on the maid's cheeks. 'I am going to talk to Ludlow and change my will. I have found the perfect person to take care of my locket when I'm gone.'

Annie looked as if she didn't know what to do with herself, giving a smile, then a sob. Jimmy, standing beside her, patted her shoulder awkwardly. 'You're alright,' he said, 'Lady Benbow 'ent going anywhere yet.'

Flora laughed. 'Quite right!'

'It is wonderful to have you home,' Clara said. 'Are you sure we can't bring you a sweet sherry to mark the occasion?'

'Quite sure,' Flora replied, brushing a stray wisp of fine white hair back from her forehead. 'I should like a cup of tea, though. Hospital is a constant disappointment,' she announced. 'They never warm the pot.'

'I'll make it, miss.' Annie looked relieved to have something to do. 'Shall I bring it to your room for you?'

'That would be perfect,' Flora said with a contented sigh.

Clara held up a hand. 'Actually, would you mind staying a moment longer, both of you?' she asked, looking to Annie as well. 'Arthur and I have been talking, and there's something we'd like to tell you all.'

An immediate hush fell over the room.

'Is this about Olivia's will?' Flora asked into the silence. 'They told me in the car,' she explained to the others. 'I'm so pleased it has been found! Go on, then, dear!' she said, waving a frail hand in Clara's direction.

Clara took a breath, before beginning, 'I don't feel I'm ready to take over Hamnett Hall. I know it's what Olivia wanted, and I feel awful thinking I'm letting her down,' she added, as several intakes of breath had been audible. 'But she'd only been teaching me for a few months, and I think I'd let her down much more by taking the place on and making a total pig's ear of it.' She paused, glancing at Arthur, who nodded. 'So, we've talked, and we've decided that Arthur is going to step up and make the commitment I wish I could.'

Miss Busby looked to Annie, who appeared shocked by the revelation, then to Lázár, who looked almost relieved. Major Gresham's stony expression was impossible to read, but Sir Gregory looked as if the rug had been pulled from under him.

No one said a word.

Arthur cleared his throat and took a step closer to Clara. 'We realised there's no point arguing over it all,' he said. 'And that, really, we both have rights to the place, as well as responsibilities to Aunt Olivia.'

'Yes, and I believe Arthur has more right than me, really,' Clara conceded gracefully. 'And the thing is, he's better with responsibility, he's a bit older, and a man, of course. It's so much *easier* for men, isn't it?' she asked the room in general.

'Poppycock!' Flora exclaimed.

Clara blinked in surprise.

'Olivia ran this place perfectly well as a lady, and there's absolutely no reason you cannot do the same,' she declared.

'Now, Lady Flora, Clara has…' Arthur trailed off helplessly as the elderly woman fixed him with a steely gaze.

Clara laughed. 'Olivia was much cleverer, and stronger, than I am, Lady Flora,' she said. 'I can be full of the best intentions but the slightest thing will frighten me off, and that wouldn't do. I should never forgive myself if I made a hash of it all.'

'And what makes you think Arthur will fare any better?' Flora asked, peering intently at both youngsters in turn.

'Because he's fought in the war, and I go to pieces if I even have an argument.' Clara's reasoning was succinct, and, Miss Busby thought, rather sensible.

She knew he served, Miss Busby realised. *And yet she'd never thought to mention it…*

'If Olivia hadn't known you could do it, she wouldn't have left the place to you.' Flora was not to be deterred. 'I told you that in the car, and I stand by it.'

'I know, *bless* you,' Clara said. 'But Arthur and I had talked all the way to the hospital, and we really do both think it best.'

'So you are simply going to walk away from your home and have no further involvement in the place?' Sir Gregory asked.

'Not quite. I do want to honour Olivia's wishes, so I'm going to have Ludlow draw up a contract.'

Arthur nodded. 'I've already telephoned him. He'll join us for afternoon tea later, so we can arrange everything legally.'

'Arthur's going to run the place exactly as Olivia wanted me to,' Clara explained. 'With the same staff, if you're happy,' she added, looking to Lázár, Annie, and Jimmy, who all nodded.

'And with the same principles,' Arthur said. 'Meaning that you, Lady Flora, are of course welcome to stay as long as you like. And you, Major,' he added.

It was as if a great weight was suddenly lifted from the man's shoulders, as all the tension left his face. He looked years younger in an instant. 'Awfully decent of you,' he said, his voice rather thick. 'Ah, both of you,' he added.

'What about Sir Gregory?' Adeline asked, never one to shy away. All eyes flew to him.

'Yes,' he said, 'what about me?' He wore a smile intended, Miss Busby was sure, to indicate nonchalance, but the strain was evident in the clenched fists held tight by his side.

'Do you want to stay?' Arthur asked, his tone a little chilly.

'Not if I am not wanted here,' Sir Gregory replied carefully.

'We want to do what *Olivia* wanted,' Clara said, giving Arthur's elbow a slight nudge.

'Yes.' He sighed. 'And she wouldn't have wanted you thrown out on the street.'

'He can just go back to his own home, for goodness' sake!' Major Gresham objected.

Sir Gregory ignored the interruption, keeping his eyes fixed on Arthur.

'I believe my aunt would want you to stay,' Arthur said, his expression stern. 'But I won't have these lies about my mother hanging over the place. To that end, Sir Gregory, if you are prepared to sign a statement in front of Ludlow, stating fully and succinctly that you had no involvement with her, then you will be welcome to stay at Hamnett Hall whenever you choose.'

Adeline's eyes had grown wide.

'Nothing would give me greater pleasure than signing such a document, except perhaps plastering copies anywhere and everywhere anyone might see!' Sir Gregory replied.

'What's this?' Flora piped up, looking between Arthur and Sir Gregory with confusion.

Miss Busby realised that no one had yet told her. 'Would that perhaps best be explained over a cup of tea, in the comfort of your own room?' she suggested, concerned the shock might have an effect.

'I have no idea,' Flora replied, 'not knowing what the matter concerns.'

'All you need to know, Lady Flora, is that Hamnett Hall remains your home,' Arthur said kindly.

'It's awfully decent of you, Clara, to hand over the reins like this,' Sir Gregory observed. 'Will your place at the Hall also be guaranteed?'

'Yes,' she replied. 'But it's time for me to move on. And Olivia did make other provision for me.'

Miss Busby wondered, again, how much money Olivia would have put away. She suspected Clara would still be a rich young woman.

'And I'll be selling the house in London,' Arthur added. 'And I'll gift Clara the money in good faith. Hamnett Hall will be my home now, and the centre of my life.'

'Well, this is all quite the turnaround from this morning,' Sir Gregory commented.

Miss Busby had been thinking the very same.

'Yes. Well. I stand by what I said, but I'm not proud of my temper,' Arthur admitted. 'When Clara made the suggestion, I realised there's a much better manner in which to deal with things.'

'Ludlow will draw everything up and make sure it's all above board,' Clara concluded. 'And we hope you'll all join us for tea at four? I've sent Jimmy off to Quinton for some treats, as Cook's abandoned ship. I thought we could eat in the conservatory for a change.'

Nods and murmurs followed.

The Major offered to walk Flora to her room, Barnaby close on her heels, as Annie scurried off to arrange afternoon tea.

'What's all this about Gregory?' Miss Busby heard her ask him en route.

Sir Gregory didn't seem to hear, he was crossing towards Arthur, and she was surprised to see him offer a hand to the young man, which was accepted, shaken, and returned.

Sensing her gaze, Sir Gregory looked up. His eyebrows rose a little in question. Miss Busby gave a subtle shake of her head.

No, she thought, *I am no further on in finding the deceiver, but does it even matter, now?* Things, after all, seemed to have turned out amicably enough.

'Penny for them,' Richard said softly, making her jump.

Lázár had crossed to Arthur now, and they, too, shook hands.

'Everyone seems rather pleased,' she said.

'Yes, a happy ending, for once! Just shows you, I suppose.'

'Shows me what?' Miss Busby asked.

'That there aren't *always* shadows,' he said. 'Sometimes it's just perhaps that there's not enough light.'

Miss Busby puzzled over his choice of words as Adeline joined them.

'Well, they certainly made amends swiftly,' she said, one eyebrow arched.

'That's the young for you,' Richard said. 'It gives one heart, I think, that they don't tend to hold a grudge.'

'Hm.' Miss Busby wasn't so sure. Many of her young charges in the classroom had held really quite impressive grudges over the years. Often over the smallest things. They were *very* young, though. 'I suppose in this instance no one has actually *lost* anything,' she mused. 'Except each of them their home, although Arthur has a replacement, and Clara has funds enough to go wherever she chooses.'

The young woman herself walked towards them, smiling.

'I wanted to thank you, Miss Busby, for listening to me whinge on so. On not one but two occasions!'

'Not at all. I'm very impressed with how the two of you have handled things.'

Clara smiled. 'Thank you! I hope Olivia would be, too. Now, if you'll excuse me, I ought to start packing. I hope to leave in the morning.'

'Where will you go?' Adeline asked.

'London,' Clara said. 'I have friends I can stay with until the money comes through.'

'How lovely,' Miss Busby said, as Clara nodded excitedly and took her leave.

'We ought to get packed up too,' Richard said. 'So we're ready to leave after tea. There's no need for us to stay any longer, I suppose.'

'Yes, if it's not too late we should collect Pud from Spring Meadows, before he takes root.' Miss Busby wondered what Enid would make of their adventures.

Lydia, who'd been watching proceedings with quiet interest, walked back to the staircase with them, when Miss Busby paused. 'I ought to telephone Inspector McKay,' she said. 'I'll be up in a moment.'

With reception empty, and the inspector at his desk at the station for once, she was able to tell him about the reaction to the reading of the will, and the decision Clara had made.

He was silent for a moment, the line crackling faintly as he digested the news. 'So the two of them turned out not to be such great rivals after all.'

'Yes, it was quite the turnaround,' Miss Busby agreed.

'Hmm.'

She waited, half hoping, she realised, that he'd spot something she'd overlooked.

'Well,' he said, 'it seems to have all worked itself out.'

Miss Busby's heart sank a little. *But it should lift*, she thought. *What on earth is the matter with me?*

'There's certainly not enough evidence for me to pursue matters any further,' the inspector continued.

'Nothing of concern in Flora's glass?' Miss Busby asked. 'No coca?'

'I'm afraid the residue that was left didn't provide enough of a sample, according to the lads at The Abbot's Kitchen.'

'Oh.' The wind dropped further from Miss Busby's sails. 'What about blood tests run on Flora at the hospital?' she rallied.

The inspector sighed down the phone. 'Not comprehensive enough to say. They tested for blood type, in case she needed a transfusion, and for diabetes, in case that was the cause of her collapse.'

'That's all?'

'Aye. She's O-positive. And not diabetic.'

'Oh,' Miss Busby repeated.

'Indeed.' He cleared his throat. 'Still, all's well that ends well, I suppose.'

'Yes. One of my favourite plays, incidentally,' she added, feeling she hadn't contributed much to the conversation.

'I don't see anything in them,' he grumbled. 'But Lucy persists in dragging me to the theatre in the hope I'll change my mind.'

Miss Busby smiled. The two of them were certainly getting along well at the moment.

'I did speak to the Matron,' he said, returning to the matter at hand. 'She expects Flora to regain her memory over the next few weeks. Perhaps you could ask her to telephone me, if she remembers anything of concern?'

'Of course.'

'When are you leaving?' he asked.

'Later today. Clara has asked us to stay to afternoon tea.'

'Lucy and I are having dinner at the Duck and Pheasant in Cheltenham, after a matinee at The Everyman Theatre. I'm just about to leave,' he added. 'Why don't you and Richard join us this evening? And Mrs Fanshawe,' he added, after a slight pause.

'That's kind, but we'll all be glad to get home, I think. And if we're having tea-time treats shortly…' She let the thought hang, worrying that the waistband of her skirt was getting a little snugger after several days of indulgence. 'You know,' she went on, 'I still can't help but wonder about the missing bottle of Vin Mariani.'

'I shouldn't let it concern you. I checked with the pathologist again and he's adamant there was more than a single bottle's worth of coca in Olivia's blood.'

'But with all the others smashed…'

'It's odd, certainly, but the woman clearly had little concern for dangerous substances. And with no evidence of foul play, there's nothing more we can do.'

'I see. Well, Richard thinks it a happy ending…' *But why don't I?* she wondered. However conveniently things seemed to have concluded, the nagging suspicion remained that someone had manipulated events. And if they'd got away with it once, what was to stop them doing so again in the future?'

'I expect he's right. Good afternoon, Miss Busby.'

'Good afternoon, Inspector. I'll be sure to tell Flora what you said.'

As she hung up the receiver, it suddenly occurred to Miss Busby that the only person who hadn't seemed entirely pleased with the way things had ended, was Lady Flora Benbow.

CHAPTER 32

Jimmy loaded Miss Busby, Richard, and Adeline's cases into the Rolls in readiness for their later departure. Barnaby darted excitedly about his ankles threatening to trip him up.

'It's good you're all staying for tea,' he said, merrily squashing Richard's smaller bag alongside Adeline's large case. 'There's a treacle sponge *and* a Swiss roll. And something called gunpowder tea!' he went on, looking up at Miss Busby and beaming.

'That can be rather bitter,' Adeline said, watching disapprovingly as the young man leant all his weight on the boot in an attempt to close it.

'Only if it's steeped for too long,' Miss Busby said. 'Otherwise it's delicious. Citrussy, and a little smoky.'

'Tell Annie to use water off the boil,' Adeline cautioned. 'And to set out some honey, in case people want it sweetened.'

'I will, miss,' Jimmy said. 'She's that pleased we're all keeping our jobs she doesn't even mind all the extra faffin' about!' He bent to ruffle Barnaby's ears. 'I reckon even Cook might come back, once she's had a bit o' time to calm down. Mr Arthur ain't that bad, really. Shall I walk the dog for you, miss?' he added, as Barnaby spun on the spot, chasing his tail. 'I'll miss him when you've gone! He's lovely, ain't he?'

'He can be,' Miss Busby said with a wry smile.

'You'd do better to run and tell Annie about that tea,' Adeline sniffed. 'We shall walk him.'

'But thank you for the offer, and indeed for all of your help,' Richard added kindly, delving into his pocket and bringing out a ten-shilling note.

'Blimey, you're welcome, sir!' Jimmy beamed and pocketed it eagerly, before hurrying off back into the hotel.

Miss Busby, Richard, Adeline, and Barnaby took one last quick turn of the grounds. The temperature was beginning to drop and they were keen to return to the cosy warmth of the hotel.

In the conservatory, four tables had been pulled together and places neatly laid, filling the room with a soft orange hue. Although electric lights hung from the wall, they remained unlit as candles had been set all around the room. Beyond the tall windows trees and shrubs were cast dark and backlit by the setting sun

'How beautiful it looks,' Miss Busby remarked.

Clara Harrowby stood over the gramophone in the corner of the room, setting a classical record playing quietly. She turned and smiled.

'The golden hour,' she said, looking out over the grounds. 'It was always Olivia's favourite time of day.'

Barnaby jumped up onto the low windowsill and settled himself in the long rays of the dying sun.

Arthur had entered the room with Lady Benbow on his arm. Miss Busby turned to see her look from the horizon to the young woman, before softly quoting, '*Lost, between sunrise and sunset, one golden hour, set with sixty diamond minutes.*'

'Horace Mann.' Ludlow, too, had entered quietly behind.

Flora turned to give him a look of approval. His dress was casual, the work day apparently over for him, with no tie, jacket, or briefcase. It made him look less stern, more approachable. 'Yes, well done!' she said.

'Mann spoke of the importance of truth,' Ludlow explained. 'An issue rather pertinent to my profession.'

'And to the human condition as a whole,' Flora concurred with a grave nod. '*If any man seeks for greatness, let him forget greatness, and ask for truth.*'

'*And he will find both,*' Ludlow concluded.

Their gazes drifted back to the scenery outside, and as Clara bowed her head, Arthur followed suit. A form of prayer for Olivia Fortescue, Miss Busby felt, as she too lowered her gaze. The gentle sound of violins filled the room for several moments, before Lázár and Annie arrived with trolleys filled with sweet treats and the sharp, citrus scent of the delicate tea. All was dutifully set on the table as Arthur signalled for everyone to take their seats. Sir Gregory came hot on the heels of the trolleys, with Major Gresham not far behind.

As Annie and Lázár turned to leave the room, Arthur called, 'Won't you stay? Oh, but perhaps fetch Jimmy, first?'

Miss Busby saw Annie's eyes widen in surprise.

'Can we?' she asked, turning to Lázár eagerly.

The manager smiled and nodded to Arthur. 'Jimmy is in the scullery,' he informed her, before she rushed off.

Flora laughed. 'A lovely touch,' she said, flashing Arthur a look of approval.

'They've had to work hard, with all of us here. And Cook abandoning us didn't help.'

'Do you think she may come back, now matters are settled?' Miss Busby asked.

'Well, I'll certainly ask her. Her roast dinners are rather legendary. Perhaps once she's had time to recover, do you think?' Arthur said, looking to Lázár as he pulled extra chairs to the table.

Lázár nodded. 'I believe she may relent when she sees all is being done as Olivia wished.'

'Sorry, am I interrupting?' Lydia said, popping her head through the door.

'Of course not.' Clara smiled up at her and pointed to the chair opposite Miss Busby. 'Do come and sit down.'

Miss Busby nodded a greeting, before reaching for a madeleine lightly dusted with icing sugar and placing it on the pretty plate set before her. Burgundy, pink, and yellow roses decorated the edges of the delicate white china, and Clara reached over to pour steaming tea from the matching pot into the equally pretty cup and saucer at her side.

As she inhaled the smoky scent, Miss Busby caught the scent of something floral and familiar. Lavender? She glanced up. Lydia was the source, *how nice that the younger set do enjoy the old-fashioned aromas after all.* Annie hurried in with Jimmy in tow and extra plates in hand, all abustle. With some good-natured shuffling everyone was seated, and with all cups and plates filled Arthur stood and proposed a toast, 'To Aunt Olivia, and Hamnett Hall.'

Teacups were duly raised in salute. Miss Busby noticed Jimmy wince at the taste of the tea, and hid a smile behind her napkin. Opposite her, Lydia took up her own napkin and folded it into a neat triangle before placing it in her lap and reaching for a slice of sponge.

As polite conversation started up around the table, a spark ignited in Miss Busby's brain. She tried to focus as the chatter around her gathered pace.

'Well, Miss Whitfield, with all that has happened, might you write about Olivia and Hamnett Hall after all, do you think?' Flora asked.

Lydia laughed. 'I should like to, it's such a beautiful place. I can see why Mrs Fortescue loved it so. Perhaps Mr Fortescue would like to engage my services?'

Arthur gave a rather endearing blush, before shaking his head. 'I shouldn't think anyone would want to read about me blundering about learning the ropes. Perhaps come back for a visit in a year or so, see how we're doing then.'

'It's a date!' Lydia said.

Arthur grinned. Then blushed, frowned, and grinned again.

What a difference in them all, Miss Busby thought, as the tension of the last few days finally left the hotel.

'Actually, I might be travelling a little further afield,' Lydia said, glancing down coyly.

'Oh?' Adeline asked, a cream eclair halfway to her lips.

'I've been thinking of going to America for ages, and as my contract here has effectively been cancelled, perhaps now is the time,' Lydia explained.

'Oh, how exciting,' Adeline remarked. 'I have never been. I am not over fond of boats.'

'I went once,' Sir Gregory said. 'New York. Found it rather overrated.'

'Had to pay for things there, did you?' Major Gresham asked, one eyebrow raised.

Flora tried, and failed, to stifle a giggle.

'My late husband studied medicine at Columbia University for a year. He always spoke very fondly of the country,' Adeline said, with a narrowed gaze in Sir Gregory's direction.

Sir Gregory smiled. 'Clever sort, was he? Lots of wealthy women over there, of course,' he added to Lydia. 'I expect you could pen no end of memoirs, and make your fortune!'

Lydia smiled rather tightly in turn.

The spark in Miss Busby's brain grew first to a bright flame, then jumped to a burgeoning inferno. As Sir Gregory began quizzing Lydia on which port she'd sail to, and Flora asked Adeline which branch of medicine her husband had worked in, her mind raced to connect the dots. She was faintly aware of Major Gresham giving Arthur several suggestions on how to make the hotel rooms more appealing, and saw Jimmy surreptitiously reaching for a third custard tart, but her lack of focus or participation was noticed by Richard, who leaned close to ask her if she was alright.

'Yes,' she replied softly. 'Quite alright.' Then, lowering her voice further, she added, 'I think I know who killed Olivia Fortescue.'

Before Richard could ask who, Miss Busby rose to her feet, drawing the immediate attention of the others.

'Miss Whitfield, you have given me a wonderful idea.' Turning her attention to Arthur, she asked, 'Would you mind if my dear friend Lucy Lannister was to join us? You saw her briefly in the George and Dragon with us, if you recall, and she is in the locality this evening.'

Arthur blinked in surprise. 'Oh, well, no, not at all.'

'She works as a journalist for the *Oxford News*,' Miss Busby went on. 'As you're all gathered for what might be the last time, perhaps it would be nice if she collected some of your stories of Olivia for a special obituary and dedication?'

'But I could write that for you!' Lydia offered. 'I already feel as if I knew Olivia! And I wouldn't charge,' she added.

'Of course, and nor would Lucy, but I thought she could perhaps include a review of the hotel, and the new management.' Miss Busby smiled warmly at Arthur. 'It might give Hamnett Hall a boost after the sadness of a death on the premises.'

Arthur looked unsure, running a contemplative hand through his sandy hair. 'It's a kind offer, but I'm not sure we're quite ready for publicity,' he said. 'Prospective guests might be put off by my being new to all this.'

'Yes, and our personal circumstances oughtn't to be newspaper fodder,' Clara added.

'Absolutely. Lucy would focus purely on the hotel and Arthur's enthusiasm. It's a lovely notion, to run the place in Olivia's memory. What do you think, Lázár?' Miss Busby asked, fixing her gaze intently upon him.

The manager tilted his head for a moment, considering. 'I think,' he answered, 'that some kind words from Miss Lannister may indeed help disperse the cloud that has hung over us since the Halloween Ball.'

'But I shouldn't imagine the cloud has been seen by anyone outside of these walls,' Clara complained. 'Why draw attention to it?'

'A death on the premises will always be talked of,' Lázár explained. 'Great pains would normally be taken in a hotel to keep such matters silent, but Miss Olivia was well loved and news spread quickly of what happened. Some people pay great heed to such details.'

'Well, it's as you wish, of course. It was just a thought,' Miss Busby said, making as if to sit back down.

'We could discuss the idea, at least,' Arthur said, causing her to remain upright. 'And it probably *is* the last time we'll all be together like this.'

'Yes,' Flora added. 'I think it would be nice to mark the occasion. And a fitting tribute to Olivia.'

'Let me nip out to make a quick telephone call,' Miss Busby said. 'I'll ask her to come and talk to you all, and if you decide after doing so you don't want anything published, I know she won't take the least offence.'

Murmurs of approval filled the room, but Adeline's expression creased into confusion as Miss Busby asked Lázár if he wouldn't mind accompanying her, saying she sometimes struggled with the telephone in the cubby.

'Of course. You may use the one in my office.' Lázár rose and accompanied her from the room. 'Something is wrong?' he asked softly as they made their way back through the dining room and down the corridor to reception.

'I'm afraid so, and we must act swiftly,' Miss Busby said. As they reached the office, she told him to ask the operator to connect to The Everyman Theatre and request Inspector McKay come to the phone as a matter of great urgency. While they waited, she took a sheet of paper and a pen from the desk and penned a hurried list of items.

'Would you mind running to fetch these for me?' she asked, as the line crackled and they waited for Inspector McKay to answer.

Brow creased, Lázár read the list and nodded before hurrying from the room.

'McKay,' the deep Scottish voice announced into the silence of the room.

'Inspector, thank goodness.' Miss Busby clutched the receiver. 'I know who killed Olivia Fortescue. How soon can you come?'

There was the briefest of pauses, then, 'Are you in danger?'

'No,' Miss Busby assured him.

'I can be there in ten minutes. Possibly five, if Lucy drives,' he added.

Miss Busby smiled, the tension easing slightly. 'The sooner the better. If you both come straight to the manager's office, I'll explain everything.'

Lázár arrived first, setting the strange combination of items Miss Busby had requested on the desk. She reached for one of them, the tattered green notebook, and began to examine it intently.

Tyres could soon be heard outside on the gravel, swiftly followed by footsteps hurrying down the corridor. Inspector McKay, looking somehow taller and even more handsome in his casual sports jacket, rested a hand lightly on Lucy's back as Miss Busby went to the door to meet them.

'What's happened?' McKay asked, his green eyes sharp with concern.

'Are you alright?' Lucy said, looking her over intently as if she may have been damaged in some way. 'Where's Daddy?' she added, looking from the manager to Miss Busby.

'He's in the conservatory with all the others. And I'm quite well, thank you, if rather annoyed that I've been so short-sighted. Inspector, if you wouldn't mind,' she added, gesturing towards the desk, 'I need your opinion on something…'

CHAPTER 33

Miss Busby ushered Lucy through to the conservatory and made introductions. Sir Gregory's eyes lit up; Lucy always looked effortlessly lovely—her skin smooth, her lips and eyes delicately made up, her dark hair catching the light with a soft gleam. For their evening out, she'd chosen a charming yellow dress, complemented by a cream shawl draped with graceful ease over her shoulders. It was a refined ensemble that showed her at her best.

Arthur seemed equally taken with the young reporter as he hurried to offer his seat, and Lady Flora was quick to exclaim that yellow was her favourite colour, and asked where the dress came from.

Lydia, Miss Busby noted, remained circumspect, offering only a tight smile. Was it a case of not appreciating competition, she wondered? And Arthur, having previously seemed charmed by her, was now distracted. But perhaps there were other factors at play?

'Thank you so much for inviting me,' Lucy said. 'Miss

Busby has told me all about Olivia and she sounds so wonderful, it would be my pleasure to write a dedication to her.' She had been brought up to date with proceedings, and knew the part she was to play. Lázár had furnished her with a small notebook and pencil, and she settled in quickly and chatted easily with the others about Olivia's life, to the clear bemusement of both Adeline and Richard. The ruse was necessary, however, to give Inspector McKay and Lázár time to set everything up in the lounge.

It wasn't long until the manager popped his head through the door and locked eyes with Miss Busby. She gave him a small nod.

'If you would all please to excuse,' he announced, 'Inspector McKay requires your presence in the lounge.'

A surprised silence ensued, before Arthur found his voice.

'What? Why is he here? Who let him in?'

Lázár shifted uncomfortably, but didn't reply.

'Right. I'll deal with this,' Arthur said, rising to his feet.

'I'll come too,' Clara added, quick to follow.

Sir Gregory was next, before all the others rose and followed in turn, with Lázár and Barnaby bringing up the rear.

Upon reaching the lounge they discovered one of the round tables had been pulled to the centre of the room, with several items placed on its top and chairs arranged in a circle around it.

Murmurs of curiosity resounded as everyone approached the table. Barnaby made directly for the fire at the far end of the room, yawning as he stretched out in front of it, entirely unconcerned by the tension already forming. McKay had been standing in silence beside the door, and it wasn't until he closed it with a ring of finality that all eyes turned to him.

'What's this about?' Arthur challenged. 'This is my hotel now. You can't just waltz in here and make demands.'

'Sit down, please, sir,' McKay said, politely but firmly. 'And I'd like the rest of you to take a seat too.' He waved a hand at the circle of chairs, his face set and serious.

'Don't tell us what to do. Tell us what's going on,' Clara said. Her eyes were wide and her voice trembled slightly.

'I have to say I quite agree,' Adeline added. 'What *is* going on here?'

Miss Busby steeled herself. There'd been no opportunity to talk to Adeline or Richard once she'd realised who had killed Olivia. She'd had to think on her feet and act fast, and would simply have to make amends later. For now, she took a deep breath and crossed to stand beside the table. Every eye in the room turned to her as she announced, 'I believe I now know the truth behind the death of Olivia Fortescue.'

A murmur of confusion ensued, over which Clara complained, 'Oh for goodness' *sake*. Olivia had a heart attack.'

'That's right,' Arthur added. 'I demand to know what's happening!' He looked to the inspector, who nodded towards Miss Busby.

'Miss Busby is about to explain,' he said, his Scot's accent rumbling over the words.

'With the greatest respect, Inspector,' Major Gresham said, 'why are we to listen to a civilian, when you are the police?'

'Yes!' Clara nodded. 'Why!'

'Because I am telling you to,' he replied sternly. 'Miss Busby came to Hamnett Hall at my request, and you will hear her out.'

'Now, look here,' Arthur said, his tone heavy with affront, 'I won't have—'

'I believe I know who killed your aunt,' Miss Busby cut across his anger.

The room resounded with gasps. Annie squealed from the back, both hands flying to her cheeks. Jimmy's mouth hung open. Flora paled, and the Major drew closer to her, murmuring softly. Sir Gregory's eyes darted around the room, as Lázár looked determinedly down at his feet.

Miss Busby felt the stab of nerves as the weight of tense expectation fell on her shoulders. Thinking back to her time in the classroom, when her young charges had looked at her expectantly on a daily basis, she took a slow, calming breath, readying herself for the inevitable confrontation.

'Olivia's own heart killed her,' Clara shouted in exasperation. 'Why must you make us re-live this over and over? It's done with!'

'Because Olivia's heart was placed under deliberate, debilitating attack,' Miss Busby replied, resolute. Turning to the items on the table before further objections could arise, she took up the green, clothbound notebook and held it aloft.

'This is Olivia's journal, given to Miss Lydia Whitfield as background for the memoir she'd been asked to write. It is a forgery.'

All eyes darted from Miss Busby to the tatty book, then the young writer.

'Oh!' Lydia exclaimed. 'But you were supposed to give me that back! I was going to leave it with Clara, but … whatever do you mean?' she stammered.

'I mean the entries within it were not written by Olivia Fortescue.' She held the book face forwards, and flicked through the pages.

'Ha!' Sir Gregory shouted, startling the others. 'I said right from the start that Olivia never kept a journal!' He looked straight at Miss Busby, a smug smile of satisfaction twisting his mouth.

'But that's Olivia's handwriting,' Clara said, peering at it. 'Look!'

'May I see?' Flora asked, reaching out a hand. 'I'm afraid my eyes aren't what they were.'

'Just a moment, please.' McKay stepped forward and took the book from Miss Busby's hands. She was surprised to see he'd donned a pair of white gloves. 'This is evidence,' he added solemnly, before crossing to where Lady Flora could see the written words.

'It is very like her writing!' she said. 'Olivia had the most beautiful hand. I was always so envious.'

'Yes,' Major Gresham concurred, peering over her shoulder. 'And a hand like that wouldn't be easy to forge.'

Miss Busby nodded. 'Which is why our culprit was forced to trace the letters.' Gesturing to the inspector, he returned the notebook. She took it and held a page poised carefully to the light. 'There is a heavy imprint on each page, which doesn't transfer through to the one behind. From that we can surmise that each page was created with some sort of backing behind it. Olivia's unique, rather exotic style of handwriting was copied onto tracing paper, then traced painstakingly onto each page in pencil before being overwritten with ink. The pencil marks were then erased.'

Voices rose in shock and confusion in equal measure.

Miss Busby put the book down and turned to a separate piece of paper on the table, holding it up in turn. 'This is an invoice written by Olivia. There are plenty of examples. See how her writing flows lightly, leaving barely any imprint?'

Clara rose to examine the invoice closely. 'But what if she just leaned on the paper in a different manner when she wrote her journal?' she asked. 'It seems the most preposterous notion otherwise.'

'Yes, and that's been the problem,' Miss Busby said, shaking her head with a small sigh. 'It all seems rather preposterous, until taken as a whole. I wasn't sure myself until I took several minutes to observe the pages in detail in Lázár's office. But there's something else which caught my attention when we spoke earlier in Olivia's rooms,' she told Clara. The others were all listening in rapt attention. 'When I looked at some of Olivia's accounts, I noticed she always crossed her ones and sevens in that noticeably continental style. Whereas the figures written in her journal,' she added, flicking through the hand-numbered pages once more, 'are written in more of an English fashion.'

Clara's brow furrowed. 'Well, doesn't that show that the journal wasn't traced after all, then?'

'I think, rather, it shows that someone added them at a later point, thinking they could get away with numbers as they're less distinctive. Also adding things like references to rather more obscure Shakespeare plays, and turns of phrase that are quintessentially English in nature.'

'But, why in God's name would anyone have gone to so much trouble?' Arthur asked.

'To get their claws on Hamnett Hall, of course,' Sir Gregory replied.

'What are you inferring? Arthur shot to his feet leading to a flurry of alarm and more raised voices.

Inspector McKay stepped forward, crossing his arms over his broad chest, asserting his presence and calming the situation without having to say a word.

'How did you come to be in possession of this journal, Lydia?' Miss Busby asked, ignoring the outburst.

'Well, I told you,' Lydia said, looking hurt. 'Olivia gave it to me when she engaged my services.'

'But you also told me you hadn't met in person,' Miss Busby reminded her.

Lydia's cheeks reddened as all eyes turned to focus on her. 'Well, no, but we corresponded. I told you that, too,' she added, her voice rising.

'Ah. So the journal was posted to you?'

Lydia nodded, before her expression hardened. 'I don't understand why you're turning on me like this, Miss Busby. I've done nothing but try to help, and now I'm being viewed with suspicion!' She looked around, her eyes wide, as if searching for aid.

'Yes, steady on,' Sir Gregory piped up. 'I have been on the receiving end of your accusations too before now. It's not pleasant,' he admonished. Turning to Lydia, he added, 'You mustn't upset yourself, dear girl.'

Adeline's *tsk* was clearly audible even over the excitement.

Miss Busby ignored both, and continued, 'Lázár, you dealt with the post for Olivia, do you remember her asking you to send a parcel to London?'

The manager looked up, surprised. 'I… cannot say that I do.'

Lydia gave an exasperated cry. 'Well of course she would have posted it herself! She didn't want anyone else to know about the memoir!'

'Yes. Of course.' Miss Busby turned her attention to Clara. 'Clara, where did you say you went to school?'

Clara blinked in surprise. 'I told you, I went to several over the years,' she replied with a shrug.

'Most recently?' Miss Busby pressed.

The woman gave an exasperated sigh. 'Devenham Ladies College. Although what difference it makes I can't possibly imagine.'

Miss Busby gave a small nod of acknowledgement before turning back to Lydia. The young writer cast a quick, anxious look towards the door. Inspector McKay, noting this, took a step back, effectively blocking any possible exit.

'You attended the same school, Lydia, didn't you?' Miss Busby continued.

'That's no concern of yours,' she protested.

'You and Clara were friends. Are friends, in fact.'

A stunned silence fell at Miss Busby's words, broken only by a sharp cry from Clara, who then covered her face with her hands as the others turned to her in shock.

Arthur looked from one young woman to the other. 'Is this true?'

Lydia's expression grew hard, whilst Clara's shoulders began to wrack with silent sobs. Neither answered the question.

Miss Busby felt the warmth of relief fill her. Everything had come together so quickly in her mind that in her rush to set up the confrontation she'd worried at the last moment that she could have made a mistake. But their reactions showed the clear truth of it. Not wanting to lose momentum, she reached next for the powder puff sitting in the pretty porcelain dish on the table. Shaking it gently before her, a faint cloud of talc drifted into the air, diverting attention from the disparate reaction of the two young women.

'Yardley's!' Flora exclaimed, as the scent of lavender filled the room. 'Olivia's favourite.'

'Indeed, yes, it was Olivia's favourite talc. But it does not only contain Yardley's finest powder,' Miss Busby said. 'The talc has been laced with cocaine.'

This brought the most severe reaction yet. Gasps and shouts of disbelief and anger from all but the two young women. Lydia simply stared stonily ahead, whilst Clara's head remained hung, her hands covering her eyes.

Arthur was the first to speak. 'Cocaine?' he echoed, incredulous. 'I don't understand.'

Miss Busby looked to McKay, who cleared his throat and added, 'I confirmed this myself upon arrival. The drug has a uniquely bitter taste, courtesy of the plant from which it is extracted.'

'Tasting is the only way to be sure,' Miss Busby continued. 'Cocaine powder looks identical to any other, and possesses no scent of its own. Talcum powder is the perfect hiding place for it.'

'So is wine,' Lydia said darkly. 'The stuff Olivia drank was full of it.'

'Not full enough to contain a fatal dose,' Miss Busby responded calmly.

'The rest of the talcum powder present in Olivia's rooms will be sent to the lab to verify matters beyond any doubt,' Inspector McKay added.

'Are you saying someone *poisoned* Olivia with cocaine?' Major Gresham asked, his voice tightened by shock.

CHAPTER 34

Miss Busby nodded gravely. 'I'm afraid so. Someone had laced her powder and it slowly built up to dangerous levels in her blood. Each day Olivia put on talc she unknowingly exposed herself to the drug. This led to her dizzy spells and the increased excitement many of you noticed in her recent demeanour. On the night of the Halloween Ball, Olivia was given a large dose of that same cocaine. This, coupled with the small doses which had been slowly and steadily absorbed through her skin, was enough to send her heart into fatal arrhythmia.'

The shock and disgust in the room was palpable. Annie had now joined Clara in sobbing, and Flora made a heart-rending, mewling noise of distress. 'But…why?' she exclaimed breathlessly. 'Why would anyone do such a despicable thing?'

'Perhaps Miss Lydia Whitfield could explain?' Miss Busby replaced the powder puff on the table.

Lydia's expression remained stony as she replied, 'I can assure you none of this has anything to do with me.

I was hired to write the woman's memoirs, and had no idea of the cloak and dagger nonsense that awaited me. I should have left the day I arrived, but instead I stayed in good faith to try and help.'

'In trying to help, you certainly painted a very specific picture of Olivia,' Miss Busby said. 'For me, at least. One tailored perfectly to my suspicions. And if you hadn't made a small error at tea just now you may well have gotten away with the whole business.'

Lydia's icy demeanour wavered for a moment. 'What are you talking about?'

Miss Busby reached for the linen napkin on the table, folding it into a neat triangle in front of her. 'I noticed you folded your napkin in the exact same manner as Clara, and remembered from my own school days how precisely we were taught our table manners.'

Lydia laughed. 'That's *it*? Two people folding their napkins neatly?'

'Yes, and Clara also folded a paper in the same way. Those actions were enough,' she explained, 'to bring everything else together.' She turned to look at Clara. Tears were flowing freely down the young woman's face. 'The two of you worked together to kill Olivia Fortescue and divide the spoils between you.'

'The monsters!' Major Gresham shouted, his face twisted with disgust.

'Oh! But how *could* you?' Flora cried plaintively. 'How could you hurt such a kind and generous woman? After all she did for you, Clara...' She clutched her chest in distress; Annie sprang from her seat to rush to her side.

'Don't take on so, Lady Flora, please,' she implored. 'I couldn't bear it if we lost you, too.'

'We very nearly did,' Miss Busby said, holding no truck with Clara's tears as she faced her. 'Didn't we, Clara? Was it you or Lydia who laced Flora's wine with the same cocaine powder? Or did you give her a glass of Vin Mariani?'

Major Gresham rose unsteadily to his feet, making as if to lunge for one or both of the young women, when the sound of alarm bells rang from outside and tyres sounded on the gravel.

Arthur stumbled in shock, his face ashen as he looked to Clara. 'I always thought you were a bad egg,' he croaked. 'Lazy and entitled, never showing my aunt the respect she deserved. Not that I was much better. But I didn't know…couldn't have known…you were *evil*,' he said, his voice so quiet yet somehow so much more threatening than a shout could ever have been.

'I'm not!' Clara wailed. '*She* is!' She pointed an accusatory finger at Lydia, shouting, 'It was all her idea! She *made* me do it! And she's done it before, too! I made an awful, horrible mistake, but I was so frightened of her. She came here to make sure I did everything she'd told me to—'

'Shut up, you idiot,' Lydia hissed, her face contorted with rage. 'Shut your stupid big mouth before you get us both *hanged*.'

Inspector McKay opened the door, calling, 'In here,' before two uniformed policemen ran into the room.

'Clara Harrowby and Lydia Whitfield,' he announced, 'I am arresting you for the murder of Olivia Fortescue, and the attempted murder of Lady Flora Benbow.' His next words were drowned out by screamed insults from Lydia, and frantic barking from Barnaby as the two policemen set about handcuffing and subduing the enraged young woman. Clara, in contrast, sat sobbing and wouldn't move. It took McKay's firm hand on her elbow to lift her and steer her from the room.

The silence that fell once both women were removed from the lounge, and the bells of the police car faded into the distance, was strange and eerie.

Lady Flora was still breathless. Major Gresham and Annie were by her side, ready to help. Barnaby trotted over and jumped lightly into her lap, licking her hand.

'Should I telephone for the doctor, miss?' Jimmy asked Miss Busby. His skin was pale, his usual grin replaced by a frown of shock.

'Good idea,' Miss Busby said. 'Just in case,' she added with a gentle smile, crossing to pat Flora's hand.

'I can't believe it,' Sir Gregory finally breathed. 'It's all so... I just can't...'

'Nor I,' Adeline added. 'Isabelle, how on earth did you deduce what that despicable pair had done?' *And why didn't you tell me?* The additional question shone clear and accusatory in her eyes.

'It was the napkin, as I said. It was such a practiced

369

and familiar movement. And I'm truly sorry to have had to spring it all on you like that, but there wasn't time for it to be any other way. Once Lydia was on her way to America, we'd have lost her for good. And Clara was about to leave for London. I needed them both here, to be sure of it all.'

'You weren't *sure?*' Sir Gregory asked, pulling out a chair for Miss Busby, who sat with a grateful smile.

'Well, not entirely. The napkin told me they knew each other, and from there it wasn't hard to piece together all the other odd little bits and pieces. The discrepancies in Olivia's journal, and so forth. There's no actual proof, you see. It wasn't as if Inspector McKay could just waltz in and arrest them. I had to make them *show* what they did.'

'Well, you certainly did that,' the Major said. 'That awful young woman's temper spoke volumes.'

'As did Clara's tears,' Sir Gregory added.

'Crocodile tears,' Arthur said softly.

'I had to do it.' Miss Busby looked to Flora with concern. 'It was the only way.'

'Oh, don't worry about me. I'm...quite alright,' she assured her, trying to catch her breath. 'I have resolved not to die of shock. I shouldn't like to give that awful pair...the satisfaction,' she managed.

'That's the spirit,' Sir Gregory remarked. 'But how on earth did you get from napkins to cocaine powder?' he asked Miss Busby.

'Yes,' Richard said softly. 'I wondered the same.'

'And me,' Lucy admitted. They had all drawn together close to the table, as if closing ranks.

'It was the scent of lavender,' Miss Busby told them. 'I caught it when Lydia came into the conservatory. It made me think of things you'd said, Adeline…' she looked to her friend, and smiled, 'about socialites using coca, do you remember?'

Adeline nodded.

'And you, too, Annie, when you mentioned that Clara was often unwell after being out with her friends. It all just came together. Two young women, friends pretending to be strangers. One often in trouble with the police, one from London where, if I recall, almost any vice can be freely indulged. Lydia must have taken a little of the cocaine laced talc herself this afternoon, in celebration of her victory, no doubt.'

'More than a little, I should think,' Richard said. 'It would explain her anger and agitation. I suspect under normal circumstances she'd have been far more reserved and controlled.'

Miss Busby nodded. 'Yes, as she had been all along. I think that's why they kept the talc – to use it. Stupid of them, yet Lydia was such a clever girl, spinning her carefully constructed fiction. Poison can take many forms, after all.'

'Such as her poisonous lies about Olivia suspecting me of adultery?' Sir Gregory asked.

'It was an insult,' Arthur said. 'I didn't believe any of that was true.'

Miss Busby shook her head. 'I don't imagine it was. I'm sorry I didn't see it before,' she added. 'If Olivia had truly suspected you were illegitimate, Arthur, she would never have considered you as an heir to the hall, or made provision for Sir Gregory, either. It simply wouldn't have made sense.'

'We couldn't see the wood for the trees,' Richard mused sadly.

'There were rather a lot of them,' Adeline pointed out. 'Many of them twisted and diseased,' she added darkly.

'But the tracing of the journal, the talcum powder, cocaine… It's all so…intricate.' Arthur went on. 'I could never have imagined Clara had the intelligence.'

'I don't think she did,' Miss Busby conceded. 'From each of their reactions, I wonder if it wasn't all down to Lydia.'

'But without Clara, Lydia would never have been able to do it,' Richard said, understanding dawning.

'But, *why*,' Arthur asked. 'What was the point of it all? Clara most likely only had to wait. I always thought Aunt Olivia would leave the place to her anyway.'

'I suspect, for one reason or another, Lydia couldn't wait,' Miss Busby said. 'There may be more to her desire to rush off to America than we yet know.'

'Yes, I think the same,' Lucy said, looking up excitedly. 'Clara said she'd done it before. Would you excuse me for a moment? I'd like to make a quick phone call.'

She looked to Lázár, who nodded.

'And Clara would have been tempted by the notion of enjoying Olivia's fortune with none of the accompanying responsibility,' Flora said softly. 'The girl has enjoyed that luxury for over a decade, after all.'

'Both young ladies would have got exactly what they desired,' Lázár said sorrowfully. A thin sheen of sweat coated his forehead, and his eyes were red-rimmed and watery. 'Poor Miss Olivia lost her life to the greed of a girl she only wanted ever to help.'

'It's despicable,' Major Gresham hissed. 'Utterly despicable. The pair of them must hang.'

Flora winced. 'I don't see how more death will ease matters,' she objected.

'Justice,' Sir Gregory said, nodding to Major Gresham. 'Justice demands it.'

Miss Busby looked up.

'Yes,' Sir Gregory said, nodding. 'I sent you the note. I knew there was more to all this. But even I couldn't ever have imagined...'

'Well, they're both caught now, aren't they, Miss?' Annie ventured nervously. 'They won't ever be able to hurt anyone again.'

'Yeah, that Inspector McKay got them bang to rights!' Jimmy added.

'Thanks to you, Isabelle,' Richard said, his eyes warm with pride and affection. 'Alistair certainly knew what he was doing, dispatching you here.'

'And Adeline,' Miss Busby said quickly. 'I could never have solved it on my own.'

Adeline tutted, but puffed her chest out a little as the frown slowly lifted from her forehead.

'You have a true task before you now, young man,' Major Gresham said to Arthur. 'To honour Olivia in your running of Hamnett Hall, and make up for the mistake she made in trusting that awful girl. And I for one will be glad to help in any way I can.'

'As will I,' Sir Gregory added.

Miss Busby noted, with happy surprise, that his expression was genuine and humble, with no hint of his usual arrogance.

'I, too, will do all I can,' Lázár added quietly.

Arthur nodded at each of them. 'Thank you, all of you. I let Aunt Olivia down too. I shan't make the mistake again. Not after this…'

'There, you see?' Flora said, reaching for Major Gresham's hand and taking it lightly. 'Matters *can* be set right, in a fashion, after all. And justice, Sir Gregory,' she added, using his title for the first time, 'may take many forms.'

Miss Busby smiled, thinking that however clever Lydia may have been, Lady Flora Benbow was perhaps the wisest of them all.

EPILOGUE

November 17th, 1923

'Inspector McKay, good afternoon! Please come in, before all the warm air escapes.'

Miss Busby ushered the tall Scot quickly through the front door and into the cosy sitting room of Lavender Cottage. Adeline turned from her seat on the chintz sofa to give him an appraising look. His red hair had been nearly trimmed, he sported a smart, double-breasted navy-blue suit, and, rather unusually, a wide smile.

'I'm just warming the pot for afternoon tea,' Miss Busby said. 'Will you join us?'

'Aye, that would be nice,' he agreed, crossing to the fireplace to bend and stroke Barnaby's ears. The small terrier had enjoyed a long walk around Little Minton Lake with his mistress and Adeline, and was drying off beside the crackling log fire.

'No cat?' McKay asked, looking around the room.

'He's upstairs on my bed,' Miss Busby said. 'Sulking.'

McKay raised a quizzical brow.

'He misses Enid. She's coming for supper this evening with Mr Waterhouse. Pud will deign to grace us with his presence then, no doubt. Do sit down.' Miss Busby gestured to the sofa.

McKay duly sat beside Adeline, who asked, 'What news of the young partners in crime?'

'Yes, do tell,' Miss Busby called from the small kitchen, over the chink of crockery and the whistle of the kettle.

The inspector sank back against the softness of the cushions and stretched his legs out comfortably. 'Miss Clara Harrowby, at the advice of her solicitor, has been very co-operative whilst detained, and has made a full and frank confession to the murder of Mrs Olivia Fortescue.'

'Which solicitor?' Adeline asked. 'Not Ludlow, surely?'

McKay shook his head. 'Ludlow refused to have anything to do with her. One of her friends from London stepped in. Bit of a devoted beau.'

'Devoted to a *murderer*?' Adeline's eyebrows shot skywards in horror.

'Clara is a young, blonde, and rather pretty murderer,' Miss Busby pointed out, entering the room with tea tray in hand. 'You know how men are.'

'Not all men,' McKay said as he leapt up to take the tray from her and place it on the low coffee table in front of the sofa.

She gave him a grateful smile before returning to fetch plates, along with the Victoria sponge she'd baked that morning.

Adeline *tsked*. 'Blockheaded men, perhaps,' she muttered.

'Aye, well, either way he advised Clara Harrowby that the only chance of avoiding the noose was to tell us everything.'

'And will it suffice, do you think?' Miss Busby asked, cutting generous slices of cake and handing out plates and napkins.

'Probably,' MacKay sighed. 'No one wants to see a young lady hang, after all.'

'And if Arthur Fortescue had doctored his aunt's talcum powder with cocaine?' Miss Busby asked. 'Would the gallery not bay for the noose in his case, for the very same crime?'

The inspector looked a little uncomfortable as he pondered the question. Adeline forked a large piece of cake, then chewed thoughtfully, before answering for him. 'You are perfectly right, Isabelle. Women's Rights ought to be an all-or-nothing affair. If Clara was intelligent enough to plan something so despicable, and brazen enough to see it through, she ought to pay the price.'

Miss Busby turned her favourite armchair to face the sofa and cut a small piece of cake with her fork.

'Actually, Clara still maintains the entire thing was Lydia Whitfield's idea,' McKay told them. 'Although she accepts responsibility for acting under her instruction.'

'Has Lydia made a confession as well?' Miss Busby asked.

He shook his head. 'She insists she had nothing to do with it, and was in fact duped by Clara and made a scapegoat.'

'I suppose it's each of their words against the other,' Miss Busby said with a concerned look.

'Not quite.' The inspector smiled. 'As it turns out, Olivia Fortescue wasn't the first dowager to engage Lydia Whitfield's services and meet an unexpected end.'

Adeline gave a sharp intake of breath, as Miss Busby placed her teacup down with a clatter.

'Wasn't she?' she asked breathlessly.

'Clara knew it, Isabelle!' Adeline said excitedly. 'Don't you remember? That last afternoon, she shouted that Lydia had *done it before!*'

McKay nodded. 'Your suspicion that there was something off about the girl from the start was spot on, Miss Busby,' he said. 'When I picked Lucy up to take her to dinner last night, she told me she'd had a telephone call from a chap at the *London Standard*. He'd been away for a couple of weeks and so hadn't got either of the messages Lucy left, but he recognised Lydia Whitfield's name and went back through the records. Several months ago, Miss Whitfield was mentioned as the only attendee of the funeral of Lady Maslow.'

'Who?' Adeline asked, brow creased.

'An eccentric but extremely wealthy woman who lived as a recluse,' the inspector explained. 'I went straight back to the office, of course, and made several calls of my own—'

'Leaving poor Lucy without dinner?' Adeline shot him a look of disapproval.

'Well, yes, but this was more important. And besides, I made amends soon after.'

'And these telephone calls?' Miss Busby prompted, keen to get to the bottom of the matter.

'Yes, of course. It transpired that the police looked into Lydia Whitfield's presence at the time, and discovered she'd taken a large retainer to begin work on Lady Maslow's memoir, which was never completed. And, there was no cash found in the house at all, which was unusual as the Lady was thought to have kept a great deal.'

'Good Lord,' Adeline breathed.

'Aye.' Inspector McKay nodded solemnly.

'Why on earth wasn't the awful girl arrested there and then?' Adeline demanded, entirely forgetting, Miss Busby noted, that she'd been Lydia's staunchest defender from the outset.

'No evidence of wrongdoing was found. Lady Maslow was in her eighties, and died of a heart attack.'

'And her wealth?' Miss Busby asked.

'What was left in the bank along with her stocks and shares, was left to the RSPCA. On the proviso they find foster homes for her two cats, Ginger and Marmalade.'

Miss Busby liked the woman immediately. 'So she possibly did die of natural causes, but Lydia took whatever cash she could find,' she mused.

'It's possible,' he agreed. 'And she had the extremely generous retainer paid to her for no work whatsoever.'

'A trial run!' Adeline exclaimed. 'A chance to perfect her methods, perhaps?'

'Was a post mortem performed?' Miss Busby asked.

The inspector shook his head. 'Lady Maslow was several years older than Olivia Fortescue, and both the doctor and police were satisfied it was natural causes. Her body will, however, be exhumed now, so an examination can take place.'

Miss Busby shuddered, and her voice fell to a whisper as she asked, 'How many others might this have happened to?'

'We're looking into that now, although we don't think there will be others. If Lady Maslow was the trial run,' he said, with a nod to Adeline, 'then Olivia Fortescue was most likely the single main event.'

'What a vile, greedy monster of a girl,' Adeline snapped.

McKay sighed. 'Indeed. But Clara Harrowby has signed a statement recognising Lydia Whitfield as the mastermind behind the scheme, and if we find evidence from the exhumation, then she will face the noose.'

'How ever did Clara become entangled in it all?' Miss Busby asked.

'She confessed to having complained to Lydia, who was a close friend from school, on several occasions when they'd met in London. She told her how Olivia Fortescue was, and that she'd feared she'd never be free of her influence, even after she died.'

'Suspecting certain conditions would have been placed on any future inheritance?' Miss Busby guessed.

He nodded. 'Yes and Clara admits to searching for the will. She'd been through Mrs Fortescue's safe before the pair put Lydia's plan into action.'

Miss Busby leant forward in her chair. With all the talk of hangings and exhumation, she'd quite forgotten the will.

'Upon finding the draft of Mrs Fortesecue's *actual* will and testament,' he went on, 'she flew into a blind rage at the contents, and flung the document into the fire in a fit of temper.'

'What *were* the contents?' Adeline asked, the remnants of her cake long forgotten as the tale twisted to its conclusion.

'The hotel, and Olivia Fortescue's fortune, were to be left to Arthur Fortescue in their entirety.'

'Ah. So Olivia did trust the young man, after all,' Miss Busby mused.

'Blood does tend to be thicker than water,' the inspector pointed out. 'But Olivia did express the wish that Arthur continue to provide for several people, Clara Harrowby included.'

'Only a wish?' Miss Busby asked.

'Aye. Her own wish, left at his disposal. He was under no direct obligation.'

'Clara told us Olivia always wanted to save everyone,' Miss Busby remembered. 'And Arthur certainly doesn't seem as terrible as some of them liked to make out. I expect she thought it would be the making of him, and show him in his true light.' Miss Busby considered a moment, mind whirring. 'And perhaps the making of Clara, too. She would likely still be catered for, but would also have the one thing that had been missing for so many years – the impetus to strike out on her own.'

'Well, it certainly showed *her* in her true light,' Adeline said.

'Yes,' Miss Busby sighed. 'And Clara, not at all liking what she saw, created a new will. She placed the same conditions on Arthur that she'd feared Olivia would have placed on her.'

The inspector nodded. 'And posting the forged article to Ludlow.'

'A task she was clearly unused to,' Miss Busby mused. 'Hence the incorrect postage was applied.'

'Indeed,' McKay nodded. 'She couldn't leave it to Lázár, as Olivia Fortescue would have done. Nor did she want to ask for help at the Post Office, lest any questions arose.'

'And this was all at Lydia Whitfield's suggestion?' Miss Busby pressed.

'According to Clara Harrowby. Whilst she admits to feeling aggrieved at the thought of being left to Arthur's mercy, Lydia's need was more pressing. Her family, despite being of good standing, is in debt to a very serious degree.'

'She wanted the money to pay the debts off?' Adeline asked, brushing crumbs from her cardigan.

'No, she planned to go to America to begin a new

life out of the creditors reach. We found notes of dates and prices in her belongings, along with her passport.'

'What about her family?' Miss Busby asked.

'They were responsible for running up the debts in the first place, and as such Lydia had no desire to help them.'

'Well,' Miss Busby breathed. 'You have certainly got to the bottom of it all.'

He smiled. The afternoon was drawing on, the light in the room fading. 'Thanks to your attention to detail,' he said. 'The pair of them would no doubt have got away with it otherwise.'

'And Lucy's diligence, of course,' Miss Busby added.

He smiled, his eyes warmly reflecting the dancing firelight. 'Aye,' he agreed.

'But what about the Vin Mariani?' Adeline asked. 'How was it administered to Olivia?'

McKay took a last bite of Victoria sponge. 'Olivia had stopped drinking it, as advised by her doctor. Clara went to join Olivia as she was dressing for the ball, and offered to finish the old bottle of Vin Mariani with her. *One last drink, just for fun!* she said. Clara prepared it, and added more cocaine. Naturally she said Lydia had ordered her to do this.'

'So that was how it was given to her?' Miss Busby said.

'It was,' McKay confirmed. 'When Lydia arrived and saw the full case of twelve bottles in the cellar, they argued over what to do with it. They were worried the contents would be tested and that would reveal there wasn't enough cocaine in the brew to account for the amount Olivia had consumed. In the process an arm was flung wide in anger and one of the bottles fell to the cellar floor and broke.'

'They were both down in the cellar?' Adeline asked, nostrils flared in distaste.

'On one occasion only, after Lydia became concerned that you were more than just a guest, Miss Busby,' he explained. 'As that first bottle landed, they decided to smash the others and be done with it. When only one remained, Clara said Lydia panicked and thought it best to hold one back in case of need.'

'And what did they do with it?' Adeline pressed.

'Gave some to Lady Flora and poured away the rest,' the inspector said, watching them both as their eyes widened. '

'Dear Lord,' Miss Busby exclaimed.

Adeline blinked. 'Yes, but what about the old bottle Clara had used to pour a last drink for poor Olivia the night she died? What did she do with *that*?'

'She confessed she took it into Cheltenham on November 3rd, and dropped it into the first dustbin she came across,' he replied.

Of course, Miss Busby thought, as it came flooding back to her. The strange bulge she'd seen in the young woman's overcoat that morning. 'Were you able to recover it?' she asked.

'No. The binmen had already collected. But it's no matter. We have all we need. Neither of them will be able to hurt anyone again.'

Miss Busby rose to her feet in turn and began to collect the tea things.

'But…I'm a little confused with where all these bottles went,' Adeline said, brow furrowed as she fought to make sense of it all.

'I thought it was clear. Annie and Lázár knew she drank the tonic, so did the doctor. There was an old bottle left over from one of the previous cases of Vin Mariani that Lázár had found for her – that was the one still in Olivia's room. Clara gave the last of it to Olivia the night of the ball having added more cocaine and then disposed of it–' the inspector's patient explanation was cut off.

'We know that!' Adeline made a noise of increasing frustration, 'what did she do with *the twelfth* bottle? The one used to dose poor Flora?'

'Same thing. Once it was emptied, she wiped the fingerprints and into a random bin it went,' he said.

'So simple,' Miss Busby said.

'Hardly!' Adeline objected. 'My head's spinning with it all!'

'Did Clara say why poor Lady Flora was attacked?' Miss Busby asked, turning on the electric lamp to dispel the gathering dusk.

'Done to ensure she was out of the way and couldn't object when the false will was read,' he said. 'Also they didn't know what Olivia may have confided to Lady Flora and didn't want to take the chance of her saying something. The poor lady is older and more frail than

Olivia Fortescue was. One large glass was enough to bring on an attack and it almost killed her.'

'And if it hadn't, I suppose they'd simply have tried again,' Miss Busby reasoned.

He nodded. 'Clara Harrowby had been adding more and more cocaine powder to Olivia Fortescue's talcum powder in the weeks leading to her death, building up enough of a dose so that a final addition to a glass of her tonic wine would do the rest.'

'And, as we've said, banking on her well-known liking for it being enough to explain away any concerns that could arise afterward,' Miss Busby agreed.

'Well,' Adeline breathed, as Miss Busby drew the curtains. 'They certainly thought of everything.'

'Almost everything,' the inspector said, nodding to Miss Busby.

She felt her cheeks flush.

'Well, I'd best be getting back.' He stood to brush down his trousers. 'Thank you for the tea and cake. And for all your help, of course.'

'Not at all.' Miss Busby went to the door with him, her mind still busy with the elaborate deception that had almost come to fruition. *If Lydia hadn't touched the talc before afternoon tea, and if she hadn't noticed the scent of lavender, or the folded napkin...*

'Oh, one more thing,' he said, hand on the door handle. 'Are you free on Saturday evening?'

'Hmm?' Miss Busby, pulled from her thoughts, looked up. 'Oh, yes, I should think so.'

'Good. Because Lucy and I would like to invite you to Lannister House for a small celebration.'

'Celebration?' Adeline appeared in the hallway, making Miss Busby jump.

'You too, of course, Mrs Fanshawe,' he continued, a wry smile crossing his handsome features. 'To announce the engagement of Lucy and I, to be precise.'

Before caffeine reigned supreme, there was Vin Mariani—a tonic so refined it came dressed in a wine bottle and carried the air of medical authority.

Created in 1863 by the French chemist Angelo Mariani, the formula was simple and irresistible: Bordeaux wine infused with the coca leaf—the very plant from which cocaine is derived. It contained, in each glass, a modest dose of that curious stimulant. Not enough to cause scandal, but just enough to make the weary feel splendidly revived.

And splendid they did feel. Queen Victoria herself was said to be fond of the tonic, as was Pope Leo XIII, who not only drank it but awarded Mariani a papal medal and appeared—smiling beatifically—on a promotional poster. Thomas Edison credited it with fuelling his tireless inventiveness, while Sir Arthur Conan Doyle, creator of Sherlock Holmes, is rumoured to have had a bottle or two nearby when writing. Other famous enthusiasts included Jules Verne, Ulysses S. Grant, and even Sarah

Bernhardt, who may have liked it more for the glamour than the pharmacology.

Vin Mariani promised to cure fatigue, soothe the nerves, enliven the mind, and fortify the soul—and for a time, it rather did. It was not so much a medicine as a civilised indulgence; one took it with the same trust one gave to warm baths, decent whisky, or a friend who didn't ask too many questions. It even inspired the creation of Coca-Cola, originally formulated in the U.S. as a similar coca-based tonic.

Alas, as the 20th century progressed, the winds of public opinion shifted. Cocaine's darker nature emerged from under the lace doilies, and tonics like Vin Mariani were swept aside by legislation and prudence. By the 1920s, it was fading into memory—still whispered of fondly, but no longer served.

Today, it remains one of those fascinating artefacts of the age: a miracle in a bottle, endorsed by popes and queens, and lost to time.

I do hope you have enjoyed this book and if you'd like to leave a review, I will be eternally grateful!

Would you like to take a look at the **Heathcliff Lennox website**? As a member of the Readers Club, you'll receive the **FREE** audio short story, including the ebook itself, 'Heathcliff Lennox – France 1918' and access to the 'World of Lennox' page, where you can view portraits of Lennox, Swift, Greggs, Foggy, Tubbs, Persi and Tommy Jenkins. There are also 'inspirations' for the books, plus occasional newsletters with updates and free giveaways.

You can find the Heathcliff Lennox Readers Club, and more, at karenmenuhin.com

You can also follow me on Amazon for immediate updates on new releases, plus special deals, sales and free giveaways.

* * *

Here's the full Heathcliff Lennox series list. All the ebooks are on Amazon. Print books can be found on Amazon and online through your favourite book stores.

Book 1: Murder at Melrose Court
Book 2: The Black Cat Murders
Book 3: The Curse of Braeburn Castle
Book 4: Death in Damascus
Book 5: The Monks Hood Murders
Book 6: The Tomb of the Chatelaine

There are Audio versions of the Heathcliff Lennox series read by Sam Dewhurst-Phillips, who is superb. He 'acts' all the voices – it's just as if listening to a radio play.

The audio versions of Miss Busby Investigates are narrated by the amazing Corrie James and extremely popular.

These can be found on Amazon, Audible and Apple Books.

Here's the list so far of the Miss Busby series.

1920s, Cozy crime, Traditional Detectives, Downton Abbey – I love them! Along with my family, my dog and my cat.

At 60 I decided to write, I don't know why but suddenly the stories came pouring out, along with the characters. Eccentric Uncles, stalwart butlers, idiosyncratic servants, machinating Countesses, and the hapless Major Heathcliff Lennox. A whole world built itself upon the page and I just followed along.

Now, some years later I have reached number 1 in the USA and sold over a million books. It's been a huge surprise, and goes to show that it's never too late to try something new.

I grew up in the military, often on RAF bases but preferring to be in the countryside when we could. I adore whodunnits, art and history of any description.

I have two amazing sons – Jonathan and Sam Baugh, and his wife, Wendy, and five grandchildren, Charlie, Joshua, Isabella-Rose, Scarlett and Hugo.

My wonderful husband is Krov Menuhin, a retired film maker, US special forces veteran and eldest son of the violinist, Yehudi Menuhin. We live in the Cotswolds.

For more information you can
contact me via my email address,
karenmenuhinauthor@littledogpublishing.com

Karen Baugh Menuhin is a member of The Crime Writers Association, The Author's Guild, The Alliance of Independent Authors and The Society of Authors.

* * *

ABOUT CO-AUTHOR ZOE MARKHAM

I'm an ex-teacher living in West Oxfordshire with my teenage son and our Jack Russell terrier. I'm fortunate enough to edit fiction for a living, and have had three Young Adult novels published. Miss Busby is my first foray into both adult fiction and the 1920s!

Printed in Dunstable, United Kingdom